COULTON / FRACTION / MONTEYS

SOLID STATE

IMAGE COMICS, INC.
Robert Kirkman—Chief Operating Officer
Erik Larsen—Chief Financial Officer
Todd McFarlane—President
Marc Silvestri—Chief Executive Officer
Jim Valentino—Vice-President

Eric Stephenson—Publisher
Corey Murphy—Director of Sales
Jeff Boison—Director of Publishing Planning & Book Trade Sales
Chris Ross—Director of Digital Sales
Jeff Stang—Director of Specialty Sales
Kat Salazar—Director of PR & Marketing
Branwyn Bigglestone—Controller
Sue Korpela—Accounts Manager
Drew Gill—Art Director
Brett Warnock—Production Manager
Leigh Thomas—Print Manager
Tricia Ramos—Traffic Manager
Briah Skelly—Publicist
Aly Hoffman—Events & Conventions Coordinator
Sasha Head—Sales & Marketing Production Designer
David Brothers—Branding Manager
Melissa Gifford—Content Manager
Drew Fitzgerald—Publicity Assistant
Vincent Kukua—Production Artist
Erika Schnatz—Production Artist
Ryan Brewer—Production Artist
Shanna Matuszak—Production Artist
Carey Hall—Production Artist
Esther Kim—Direct Market Sales Representative
Emilio Bautista—Digital Sales Representative
Leanna Caunter—Accounting Assistant
Chloe Ramos-Peterson—Library Market Sales Representative
Marla Eizik—Administrative Assistant
IMAGECOMICS.COM

SOLID STATE ! //

This graphic novel is based on Jonathan Coulton's concept album, Solid State. For hardcover edition, music downloads, fancy vinyl, and other fun stuff, visit solidstate.jonathancoulton.com.

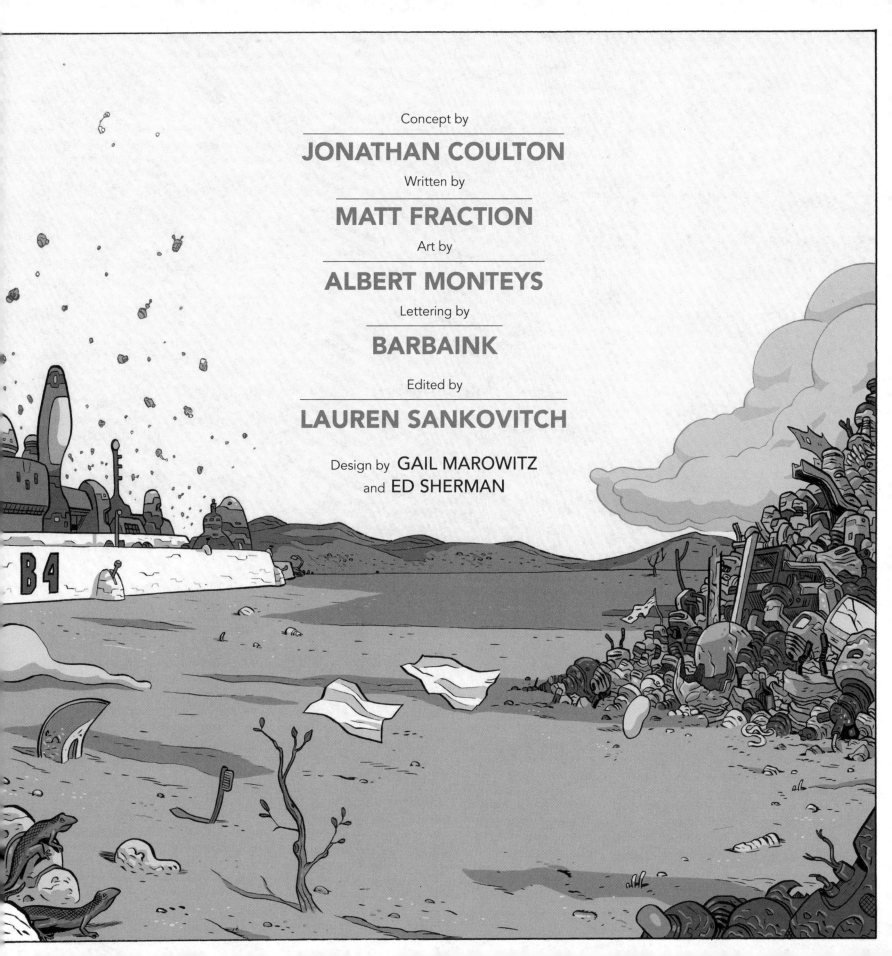

Concept by

JONATHAN COULTON

Written by

MATT FRACTION

Art by

ALBERT MONTEYS

Lettering by

BARBAINK

Edited by

LAUREN SANKOVITCH

Design by **GAIL MAROWITZ**
and **ED SHERMAN**

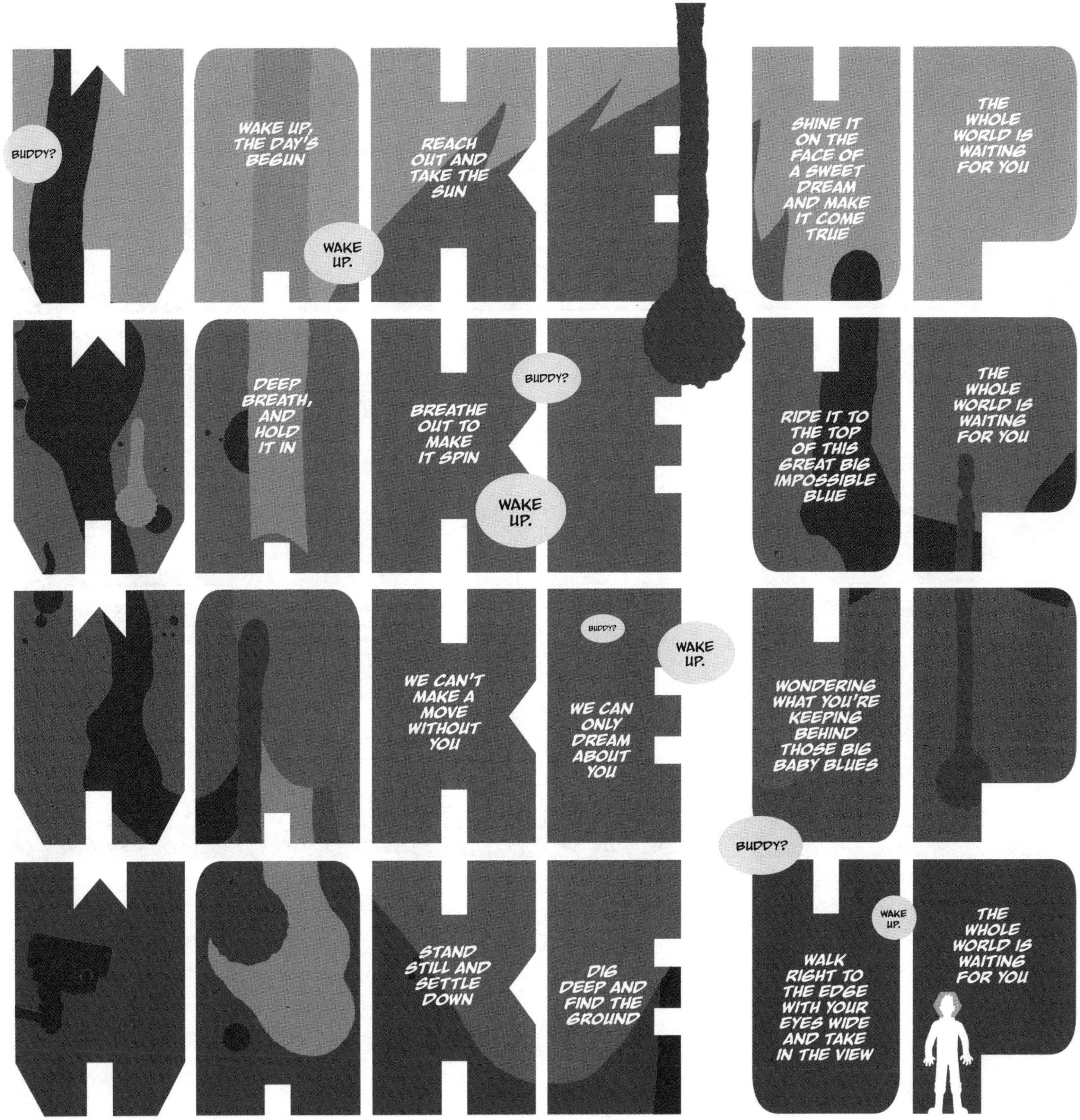
BUDDY?
WAKE UP, THE DAY'S BEGUN
WAKE UP.
REACH OUT AND TAKE THE SUN
SHINE IT ON THE FACE OF A SWEET DREAM AND MAKE IT COME TRUE
THE WHOLE WORLD IS WAITING FOR YOU
DEEP BREATH, AND HOLD IT IN
BREATHE OUT TO MAKE IT SPIN
BUDDY?
WAKE UP.
RIDE IT TO THE TOP OF THIS GREAT BIG IMPOSSIBLE BLUE
THE WHOLE WORLD IS WAITING FOR YOU
WE CAN'T MAKE A MOVE WITHOUT YOU
BUDDY?
WE CAN ONLY DREAM ABOUT YOU
WAKE UP.
WONDERING WHAT YOU'RE KEEPING BEHIND THOSE BIG BABY BLUES
BUDDY?
STAND STILL AND SETTLE DOWN
DIG DEEP AND FIND THE GROUND
WAKE UP.
WALK RIGHT TO THE EDGE WITH YOUR EYES WIDE AND TAKE IN THE VIEW
THE WHOLE WORLD IS WAITING FOR YOU

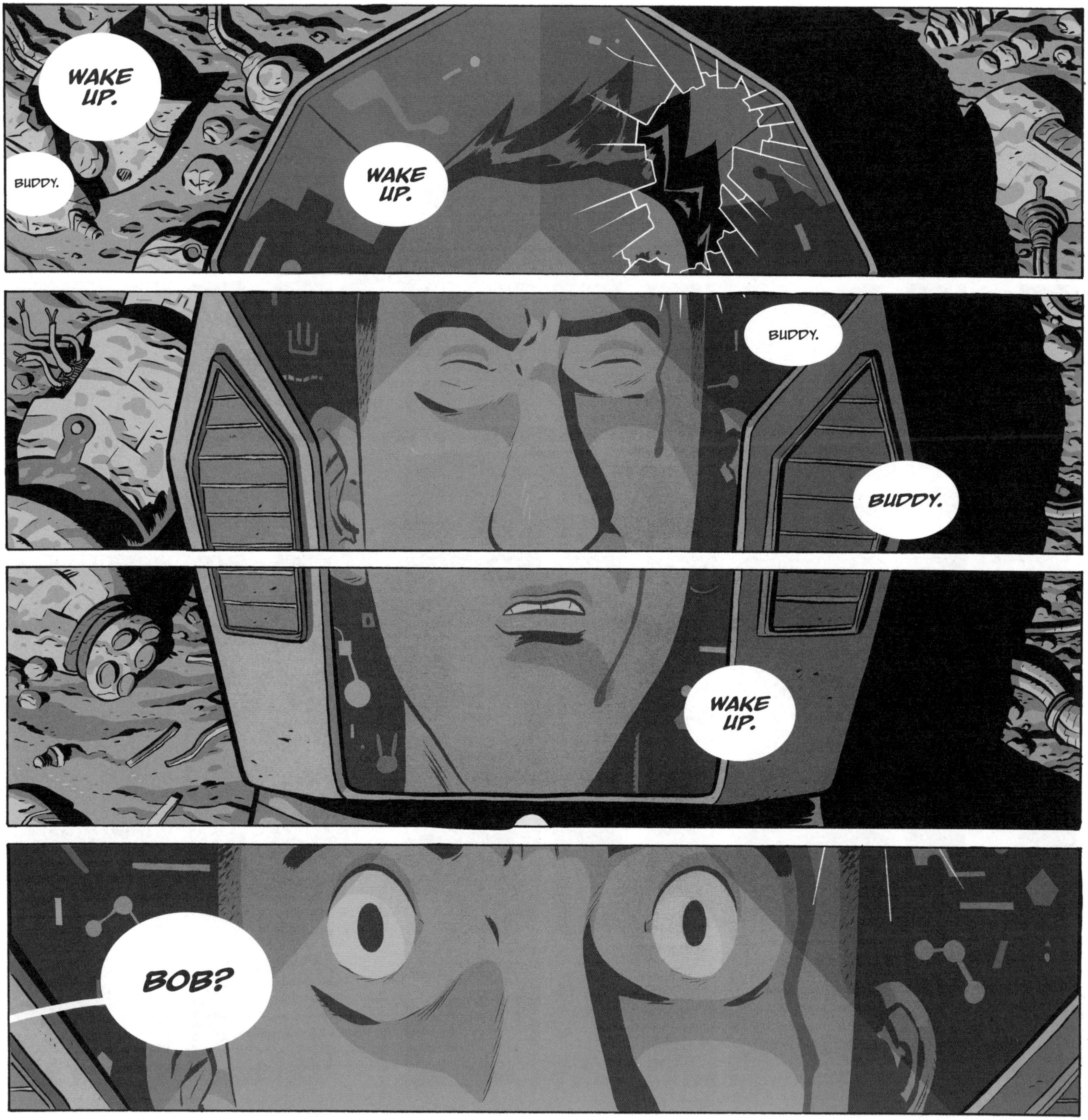
WAKE UP.
BUDDY.
WAKE UP.
BUDDY.
BUDDY.
WAKE UP.
BOB?

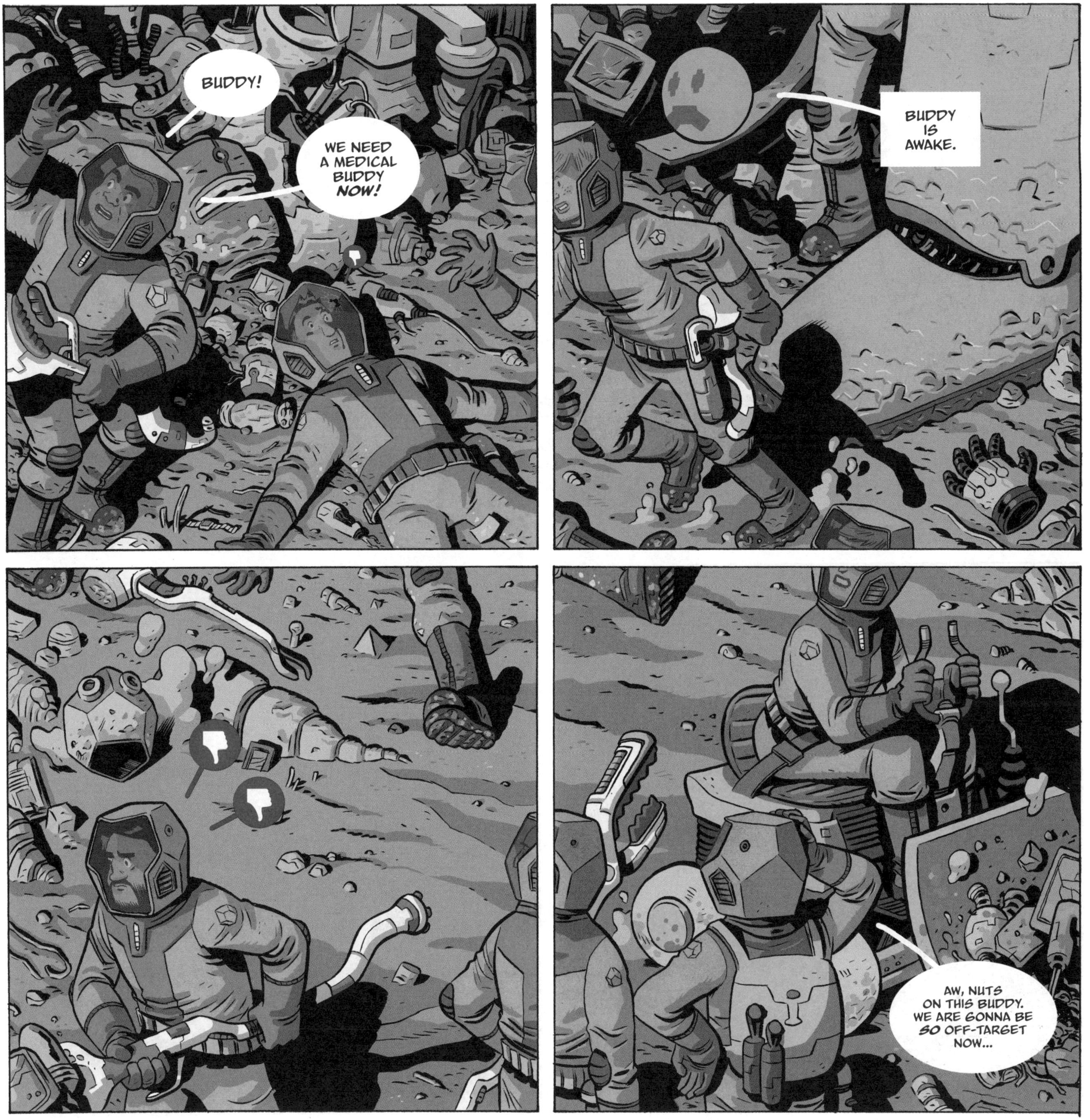
BUDDY!
WE NEED A MEDICAL BUDDY NOW!
BUDDY IS AWAKE.
AW, NUTS ON THIS BUDDY. WE ARE GONNA BE SO OFF-TARGET NOW...

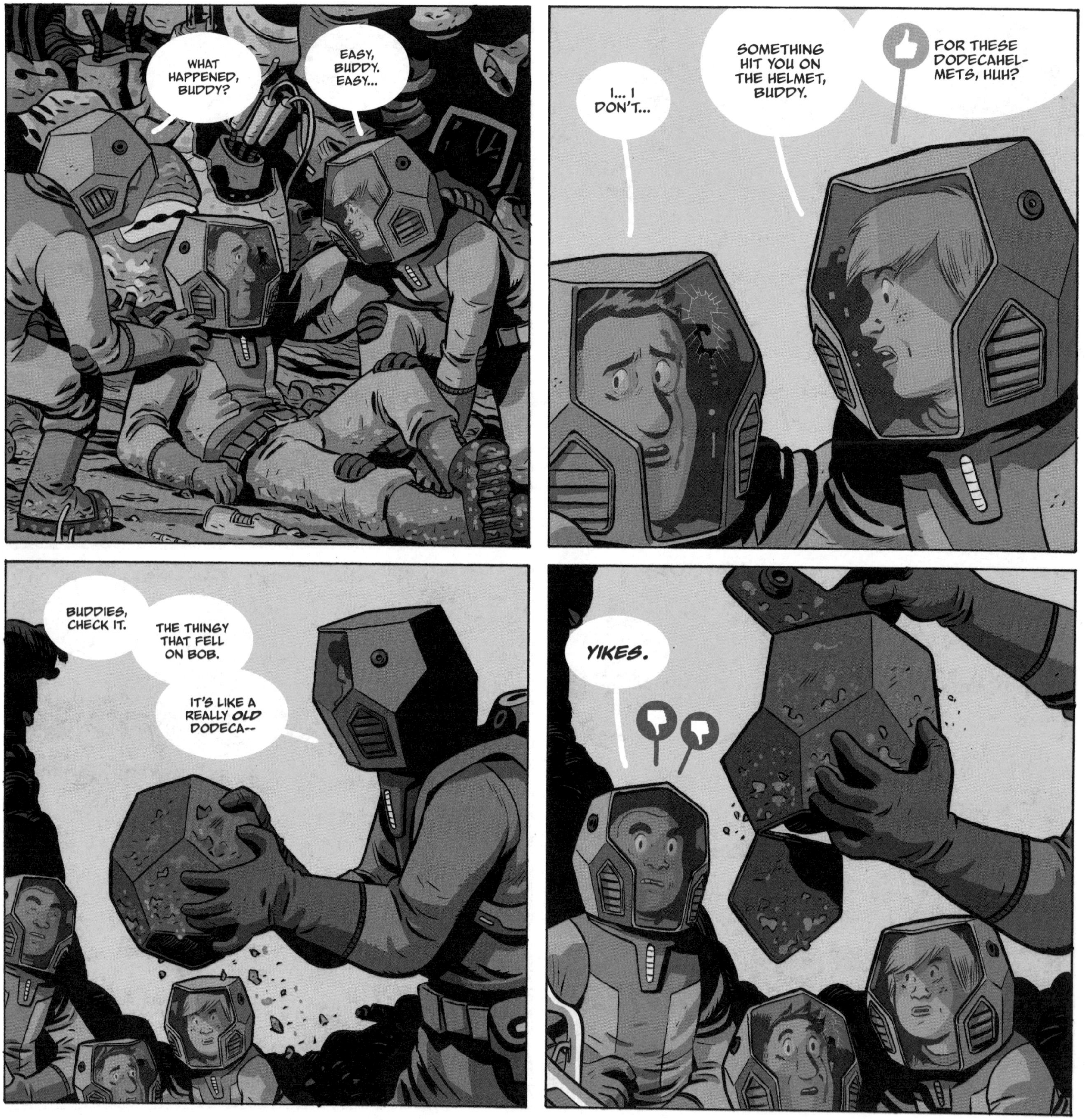
WHAT HAPPENED, BUDDY?
EASY, BUDDY. EASY...
I... I DON'T...
SOMETHING HIT YOU ON THE HELMET, BUDDY.
FOR THESE DODECAHEL-METS, HUH?
BUDDIES, CHECK IT.
THE THINGY THAT FELL ON BOB.
IT'S LIKE A REALLY *OLD* DODECA--
YIKES.

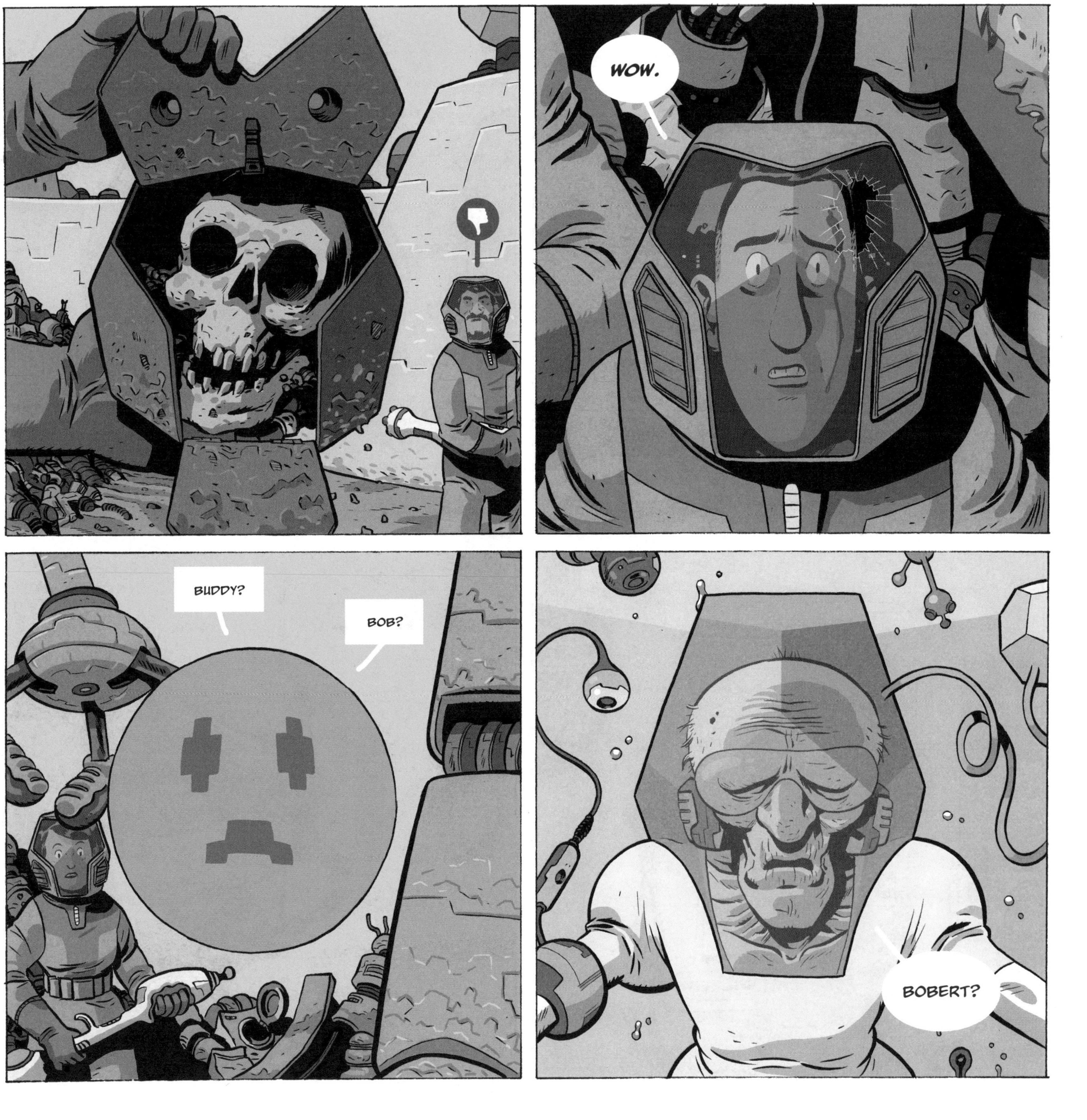
WOW.
BUDDY?
BOB?
BOBERT?

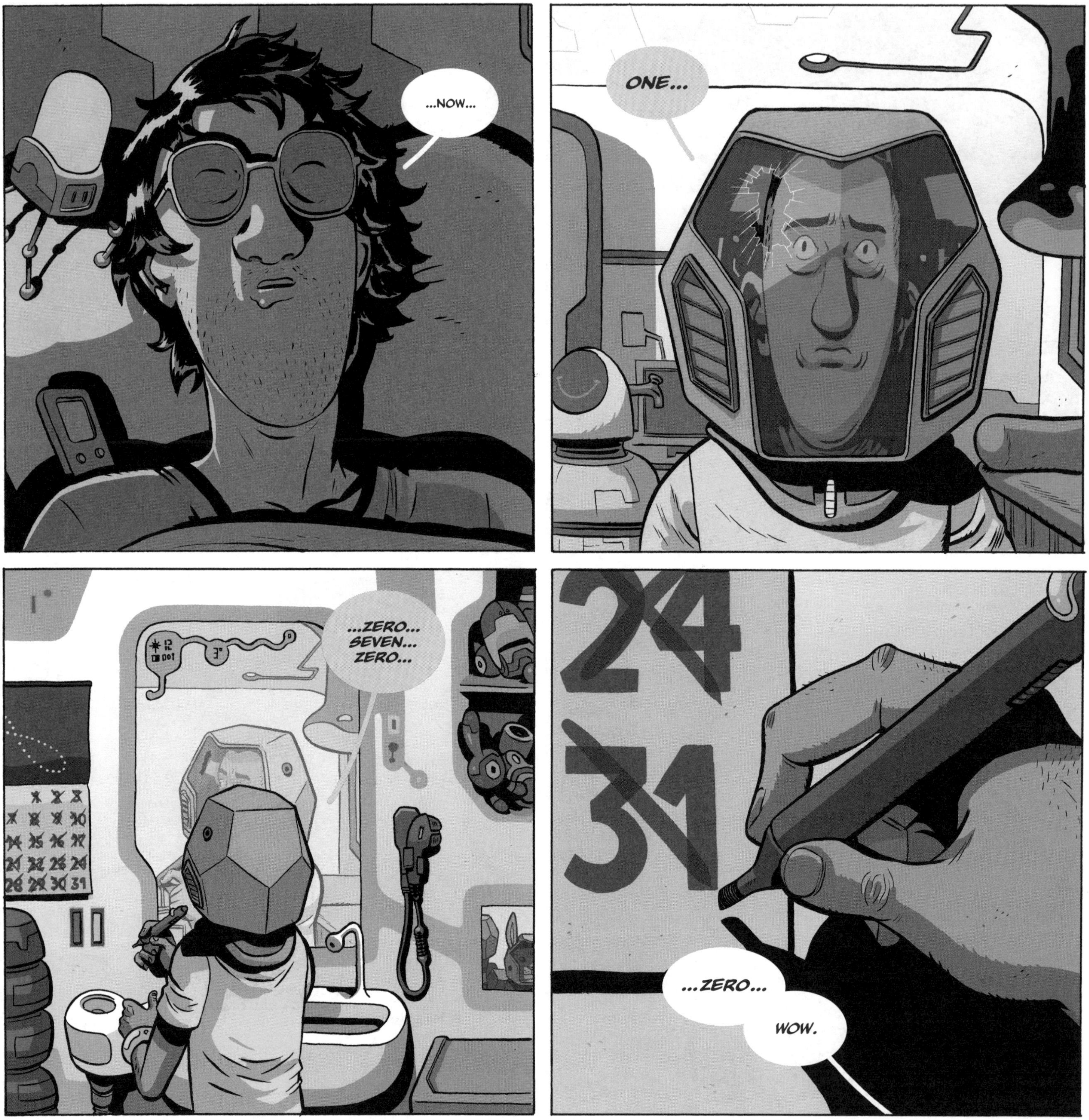
...NOW...
ONE...
...ZERO... SEVEN... ZERO...
...ZERO...
WOW.

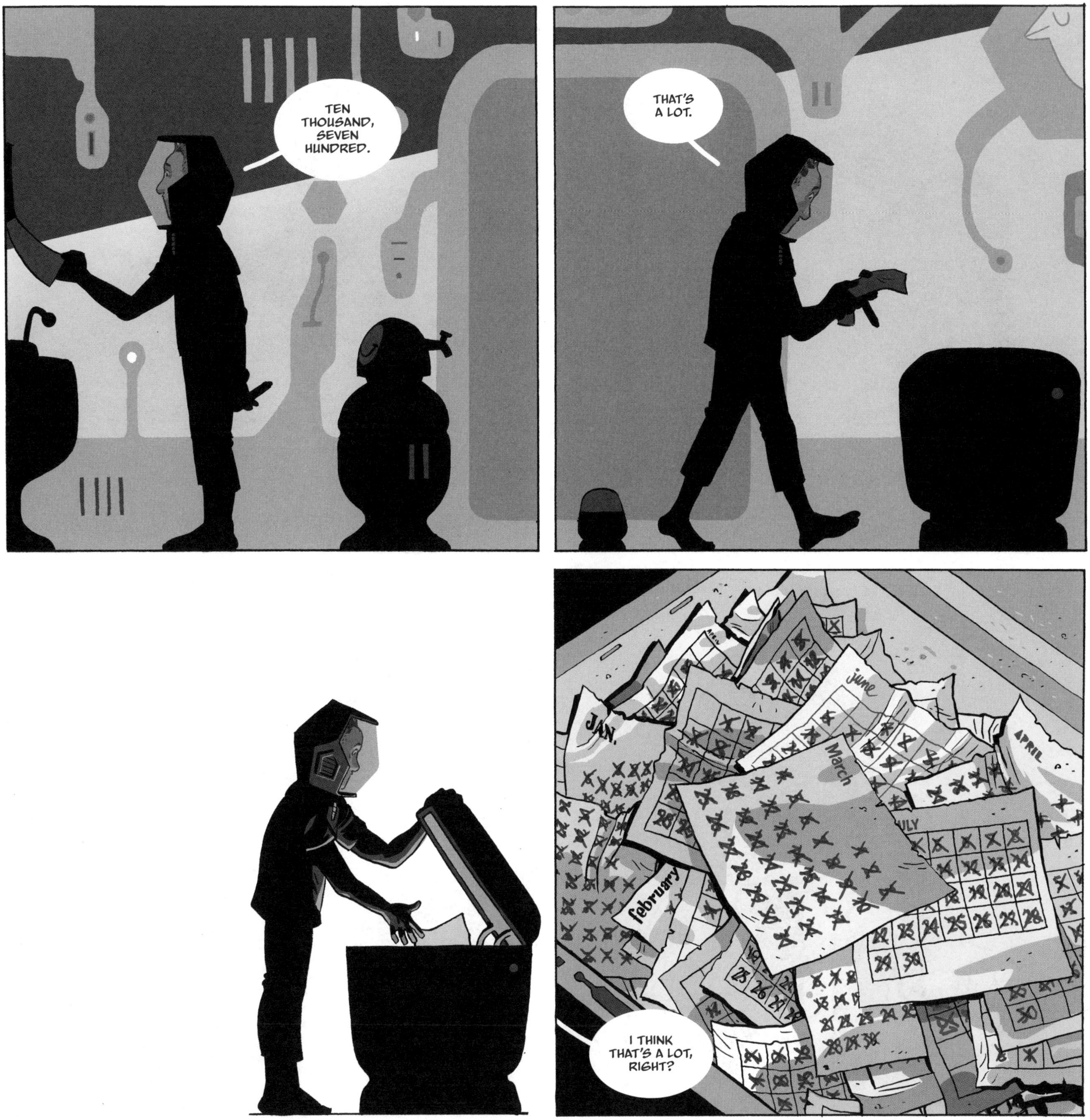
TEN THOUSAND, SEVEN HUNDRED.
THAT'S A LOT.
JAN.
june
APRIL
March
february
I THINK THAT'S A LOT, RIGHT?

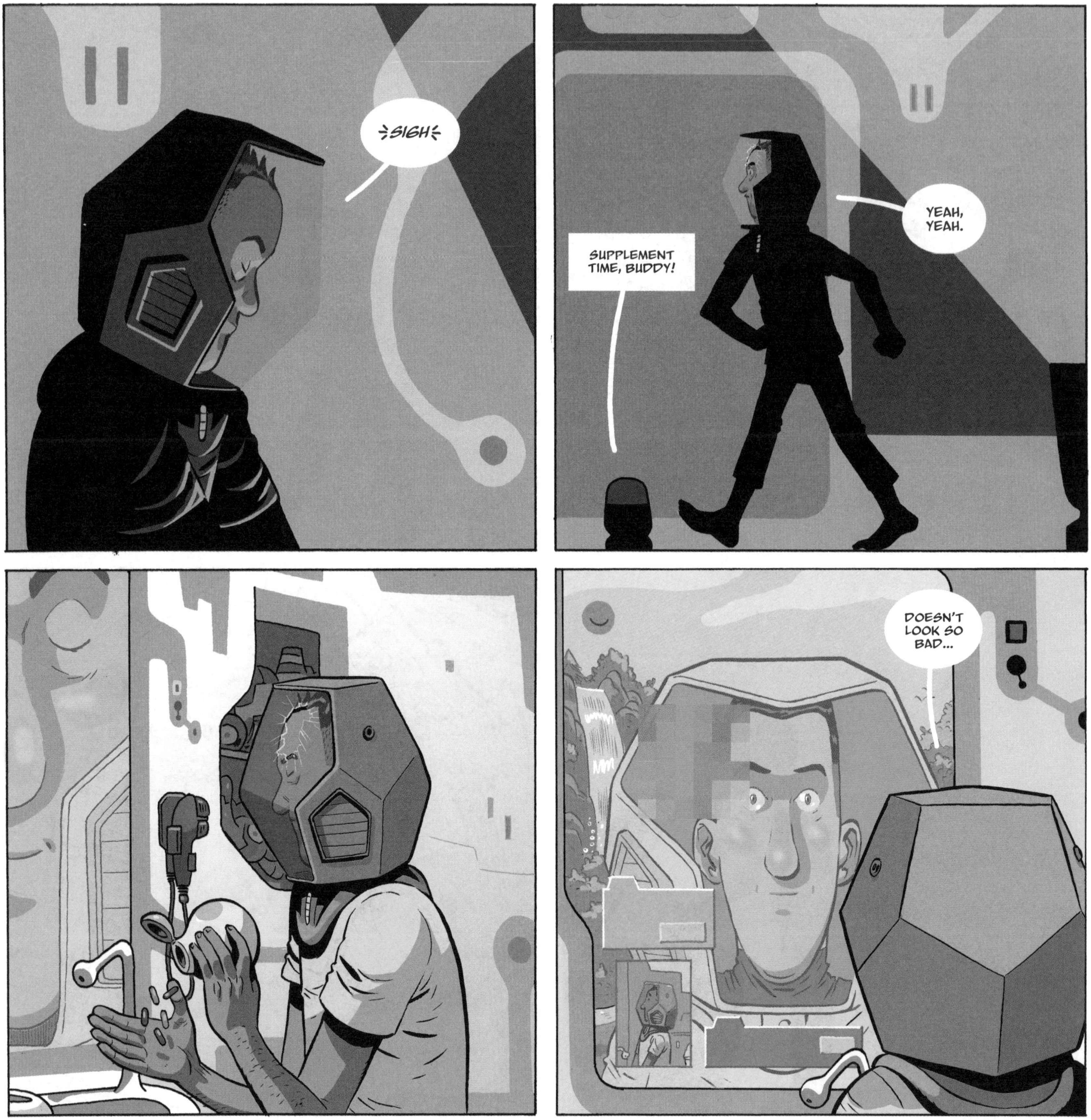
SIGH
SUPPLEMENT TIME, BUDDY!
YEAH, YEAH.
DOESN'T LOOK SO BAD...

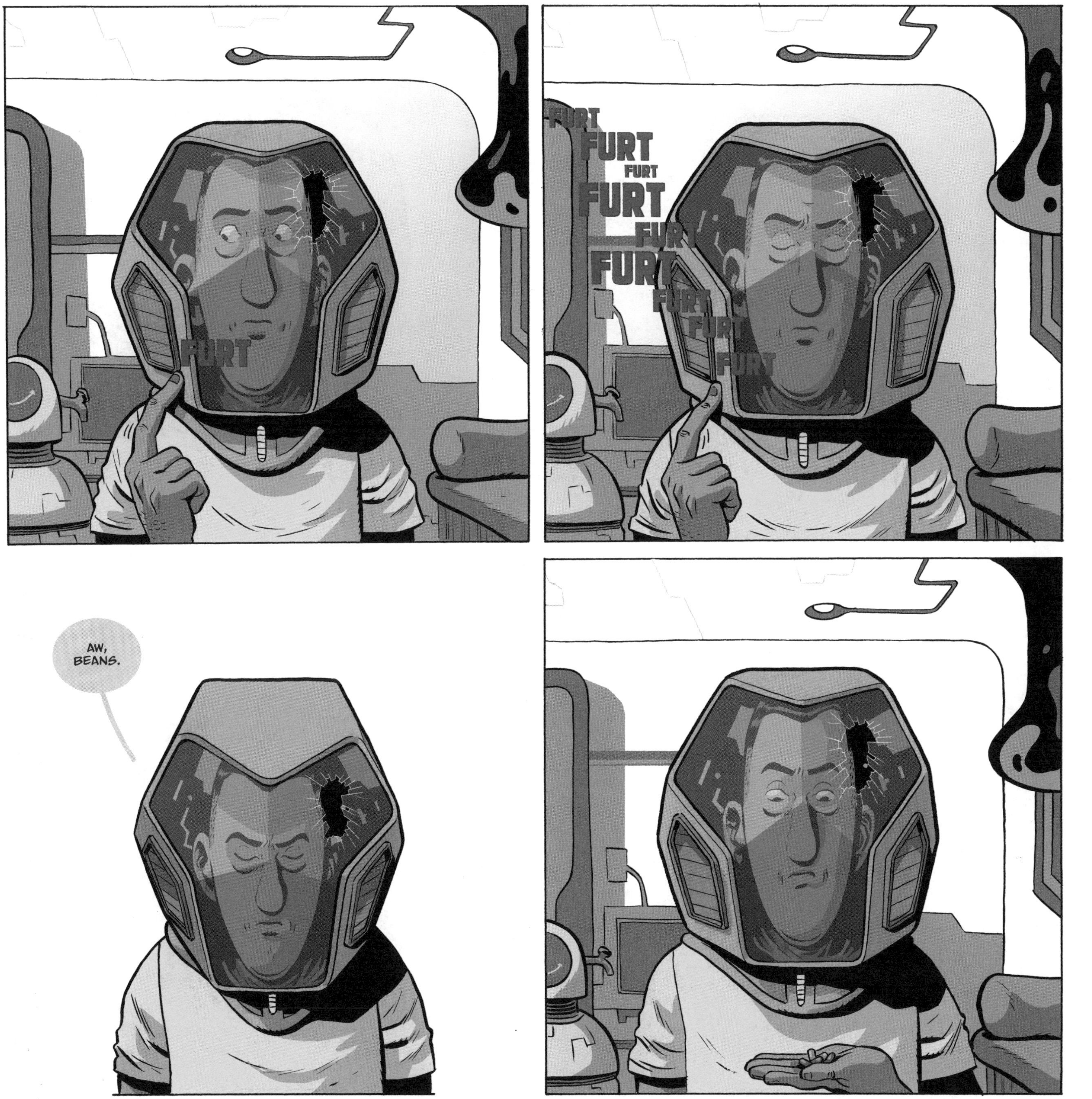
FURT
FURT FURT FURT FURT FURT FURT FURT FURT FURT
AW, BEANS.

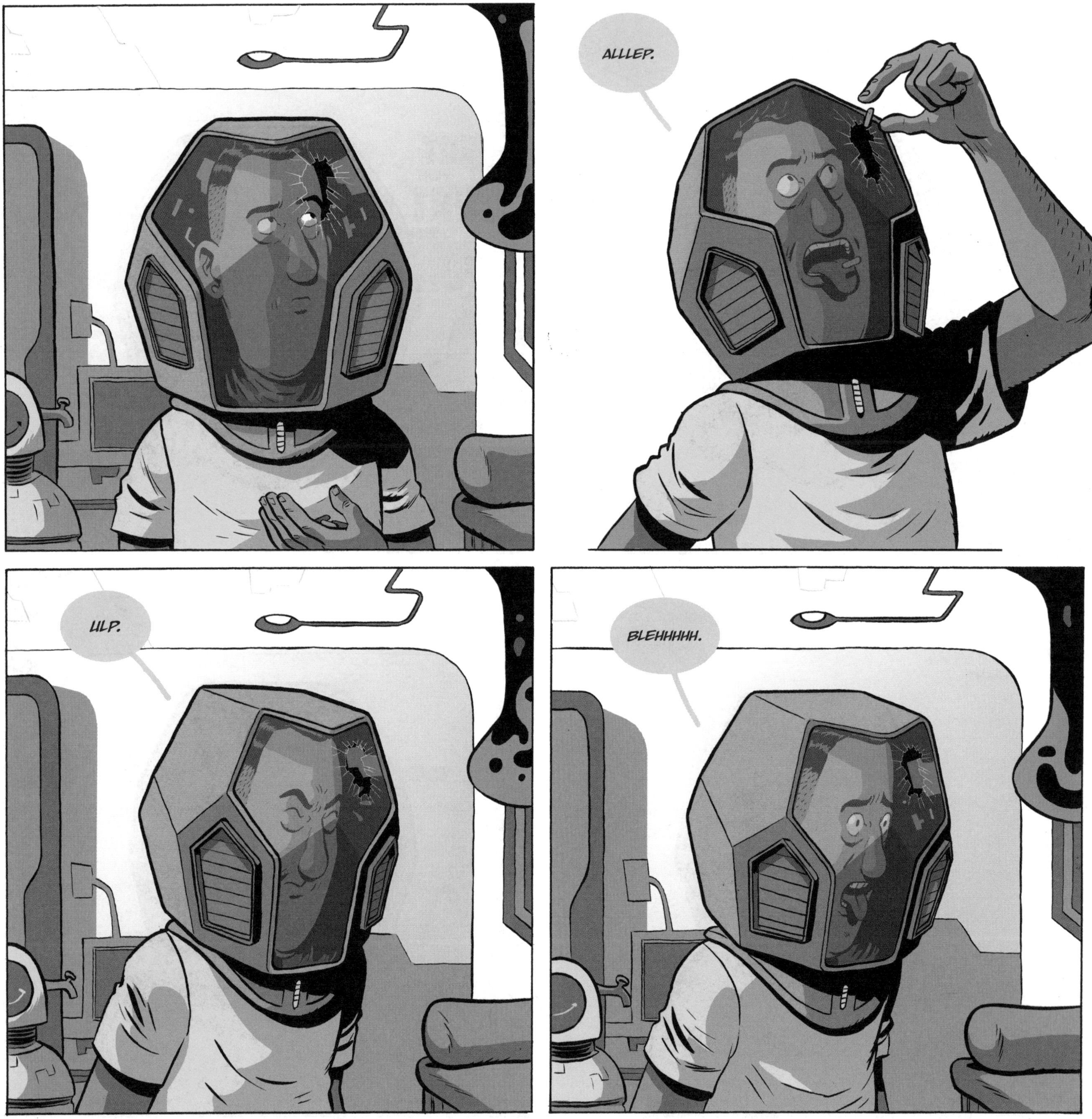
ALLLEP.
ULP.
BLEHHHHH.

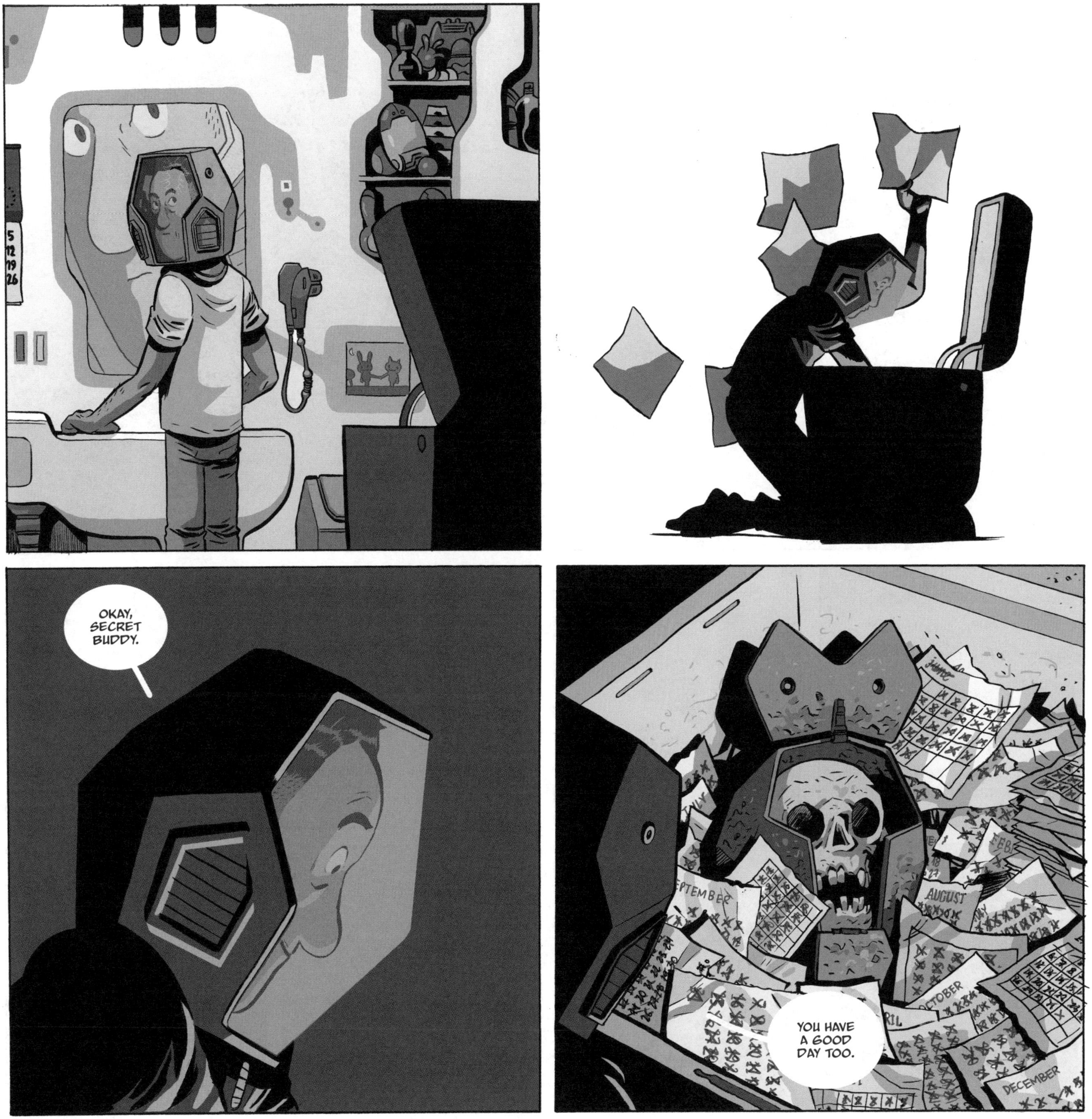
OKAY, SECRET BUDDY.
AUGUST
OCTOBER
DECEMBER
YOU HAVE A GOOD DAY TOO.

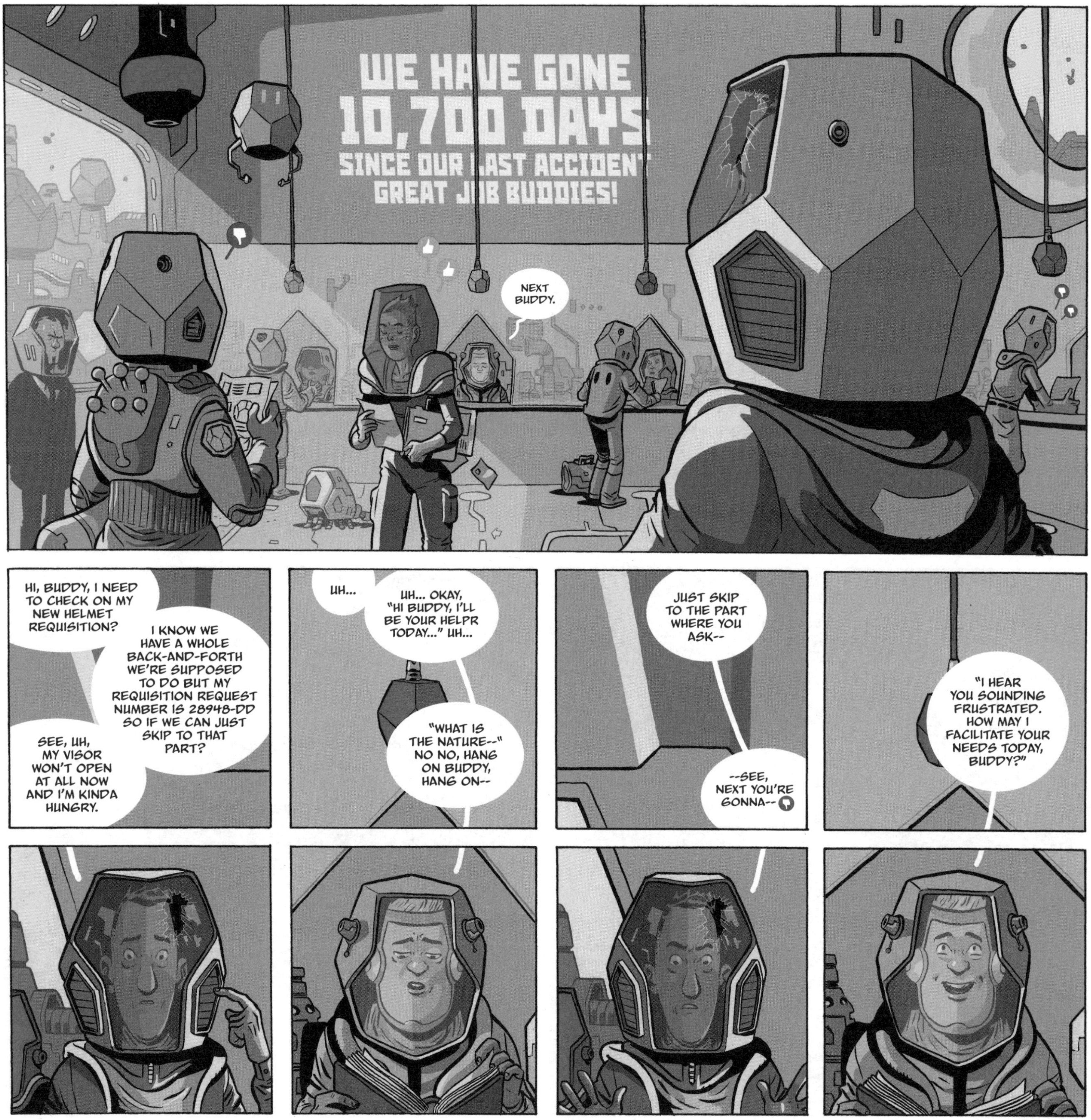
WE HAVE GONE
10,700 DAYS
SINCE OUR LAST ACCIDENT
GREAT JOB BUDDIES!
NEXT BUDDY.
HI, BUDDY, I NEED TO CHECK ON MY NEW HELMET REQUISITION?
I KNOW WE HAVE A WHOLE BACK-AND-FORTH WE'RE SUPPOSED TO DO BUT MY REQUISITION REQUEST NUMBER IS 28948-DD SO IF WE CAN JUST SKIP TO THAT PART?
SEE, UH, MY VISOR WON'T OPEN AT ALL NOW AND I'M KINDA HUNGRY.
UH...
UH... OKAY, "HI BUDDY, I'LL BE YOUR HELPR TODAY..." UH...
"WHAT IS THE NATURE--" NO NO, HANG ON BUDDY, HANG ON--
JUST SKIP TO THE PART WHERE YOU ASK--
--SEE, NEXT YOU'RE GONNA--
"I HEAR YOU SOUNDING FRUSTRATED. HOW MAY I FACILITATE YOUR NEEDS TODAY, BUDDY?"

SIGH
I'M WAITING ON A HELMET REPLACEMENT, MY REQUISITION REQUEST NUMBER IS 28948-DD--
"NO PROBLEM, BUDDY. REPLACING EQUIPMENT REQUIRES FILLING OUT A 'REPLACING AND REQUISITIONING NEW EQUIPMENT TO REPLACE DAMAGED EQUIPMENT' FORM.
"WOULD YOU LIKE ME TO HELP YOU WITH THAT NOW?"
NO, NO, I KNOW, AND I FILLED IT OUT, AND I GOT REQUISITION REQUEST NUMBER 28948-DD, BUT THEN THE REQUEST--
UH... UH... "THANK YOU FOR THAT INFORMATION, BUDDY. LET'S START A REQUISITION REQUEST NUMBER INQUIRY PROCESS. DO YOU KNOW WHEN YOU FILED YOUR REQUISITION REQUEST NUMBER WITH YOUR SERVICE BUDDIES?"
UH, YEAH, SURE, SURE I DO. IT'S BEEN...
10,699 DAYS, I GUESS.
BEANS AND *CHEESE.*
THAT'S A LONG TIME.
HANG ON.
OH, DANG, I SEE WHAT'S HAPPENING HERE.

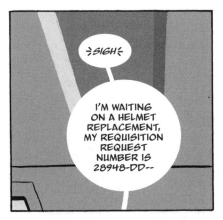

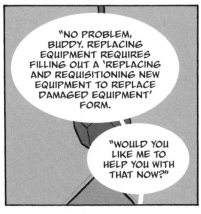

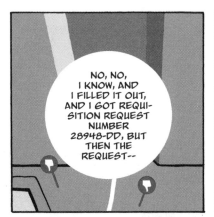

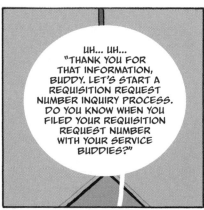

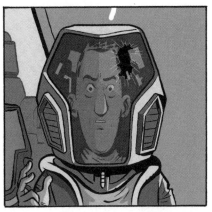

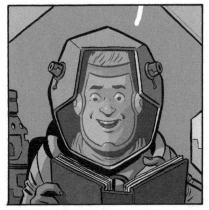

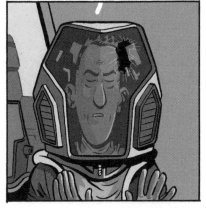

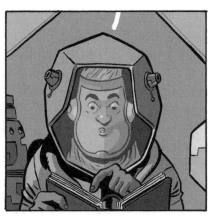

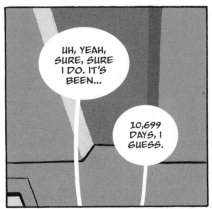

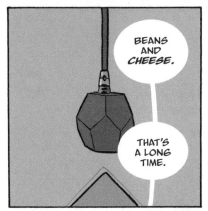

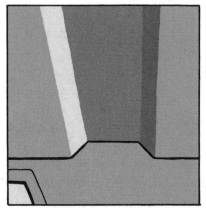

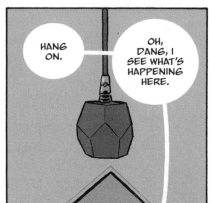

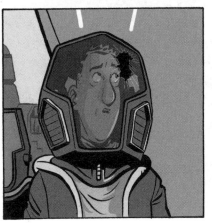

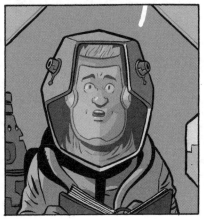

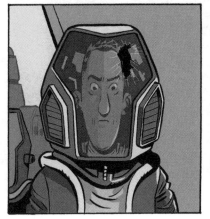

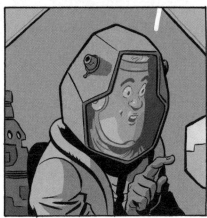

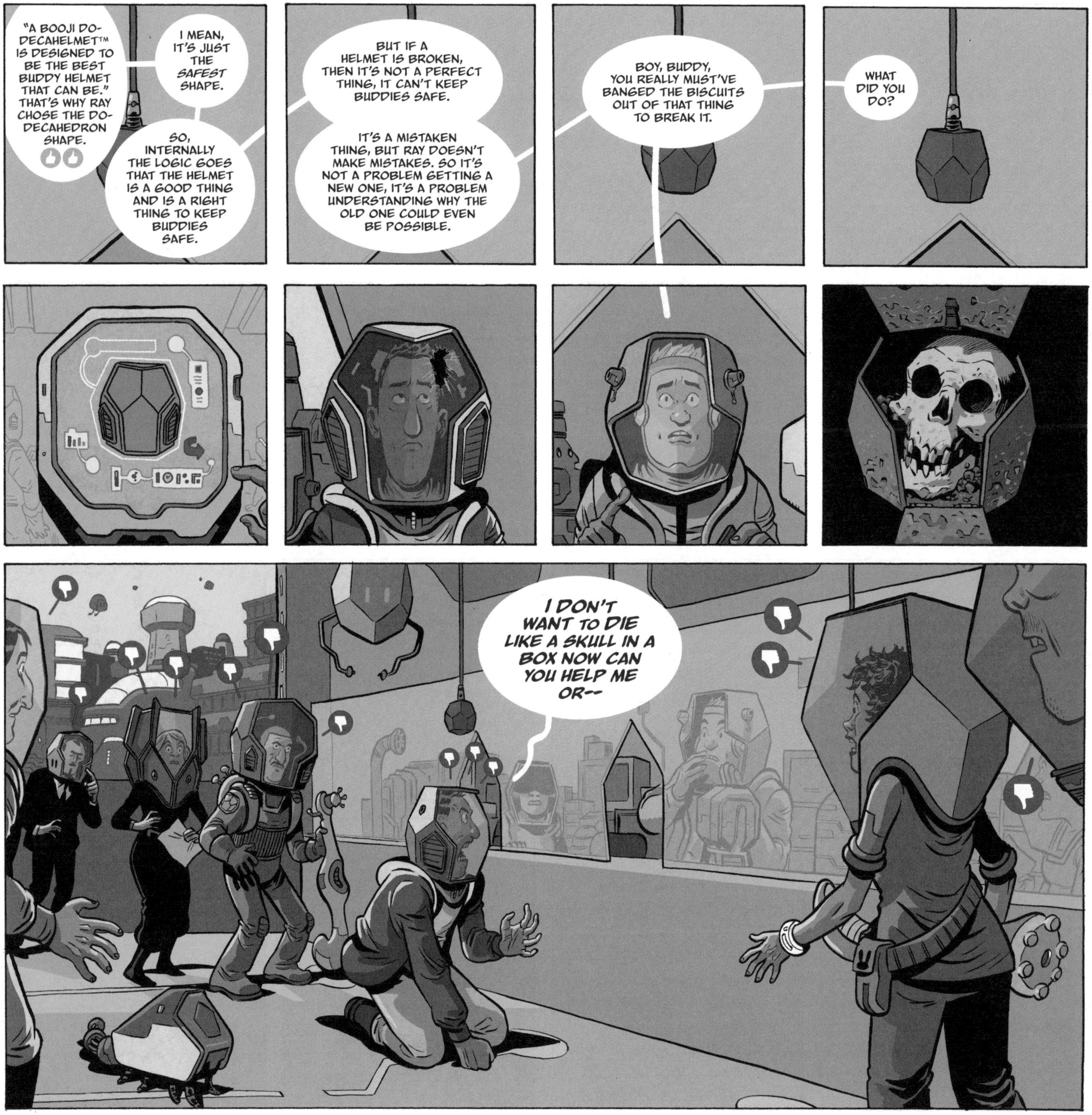
"A BOOJI DO-DECAHELMET™ IS DESIGNED TO BE THE BEST BUDDY HELMET THAT CAN BE." THAT'S WHY RAY CHOSE THE DO-DECAHEDRON SHAPE.
I MEAN, IT'S JUST THE SAFEST SHAPE.
SO, INTERNALLY THE LOGIC GOES THAT THE HELMET IS A GOOD THING AND IS A RIGHT THING TO KEEP BUDDIES SAFE.
BUT IF A HELMET IS BROKEN, THEN IT'S NOT A PERFECT THING, IT CAN'T KEEP BUDDIES SAFE.
IT'S A MISTAKEN THING, BUT RAY DOESN'T MAKE MISTAKES. SO IT'S NOT A PROBLEM GETTING A NEW ONE, IT'S A PROBLEM UNDERSTANDING WHY THE OLD ONE COULD EVEN BE POSSIBLE.
BOY, BUDDY, YOU REALLY MUST'VE BANGED THE BISCUITS OUT OF THAT THING TO BREAK IT.
WHAT DID YOU DO?
I DON'T WANT TO DIE LIKE A SKULL IN A BOX NOW CAN YOU HELP ME OR--

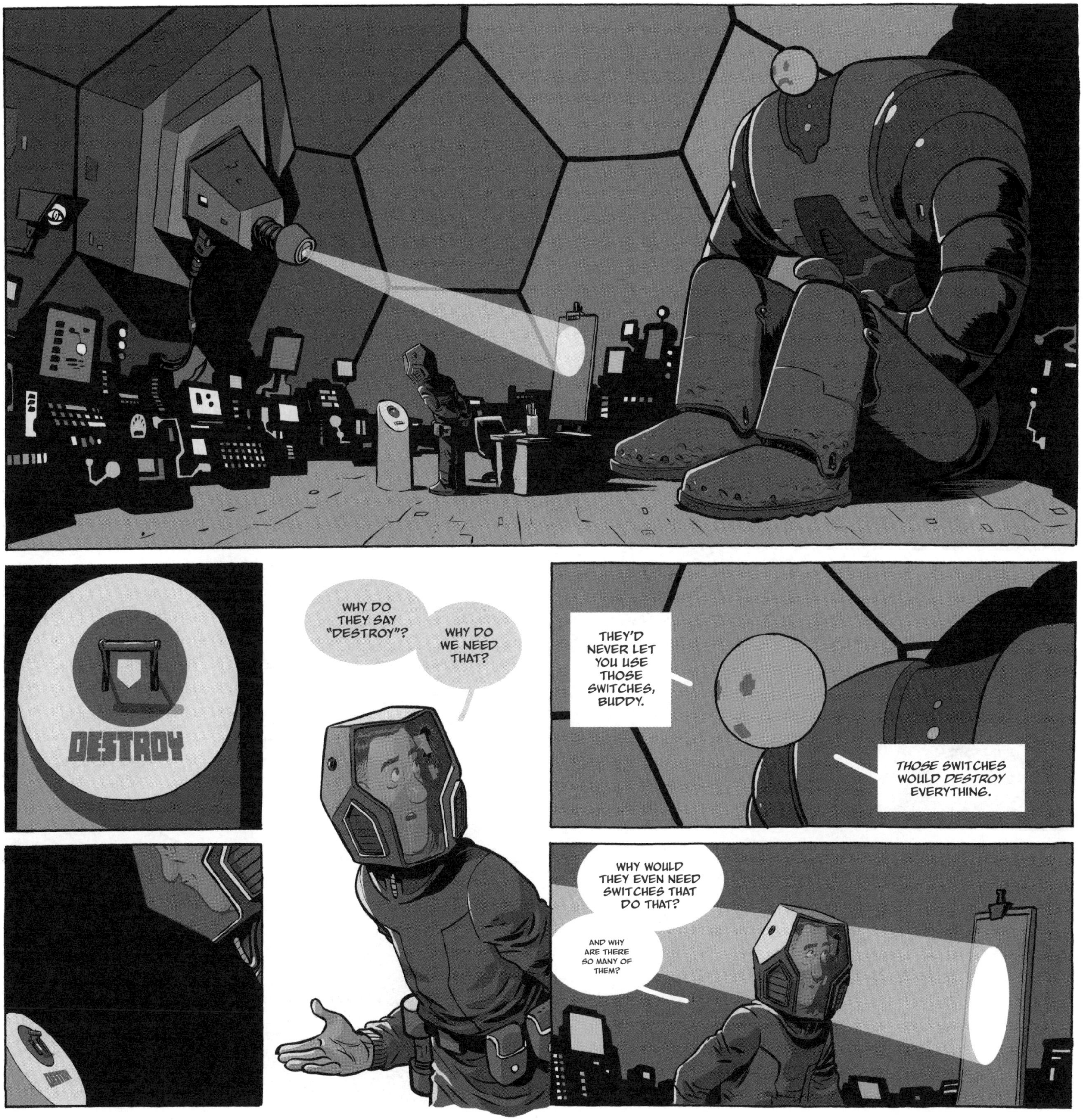
DESTROY
WHY DO THEY SAY "DESTROY"?
WHY DO WE NEED THAT?
THEY'D NEVER LET YOU USE THOSE SWITCHES, BUDDY.
THOSE SWITCHES WOULD *DESTROY* EVERYTHING.
WHY WOULD THEY EVEN NEED SWITCHES THAT DO THAT?
AND WHY ARE THERE SO MANY OF THEM?

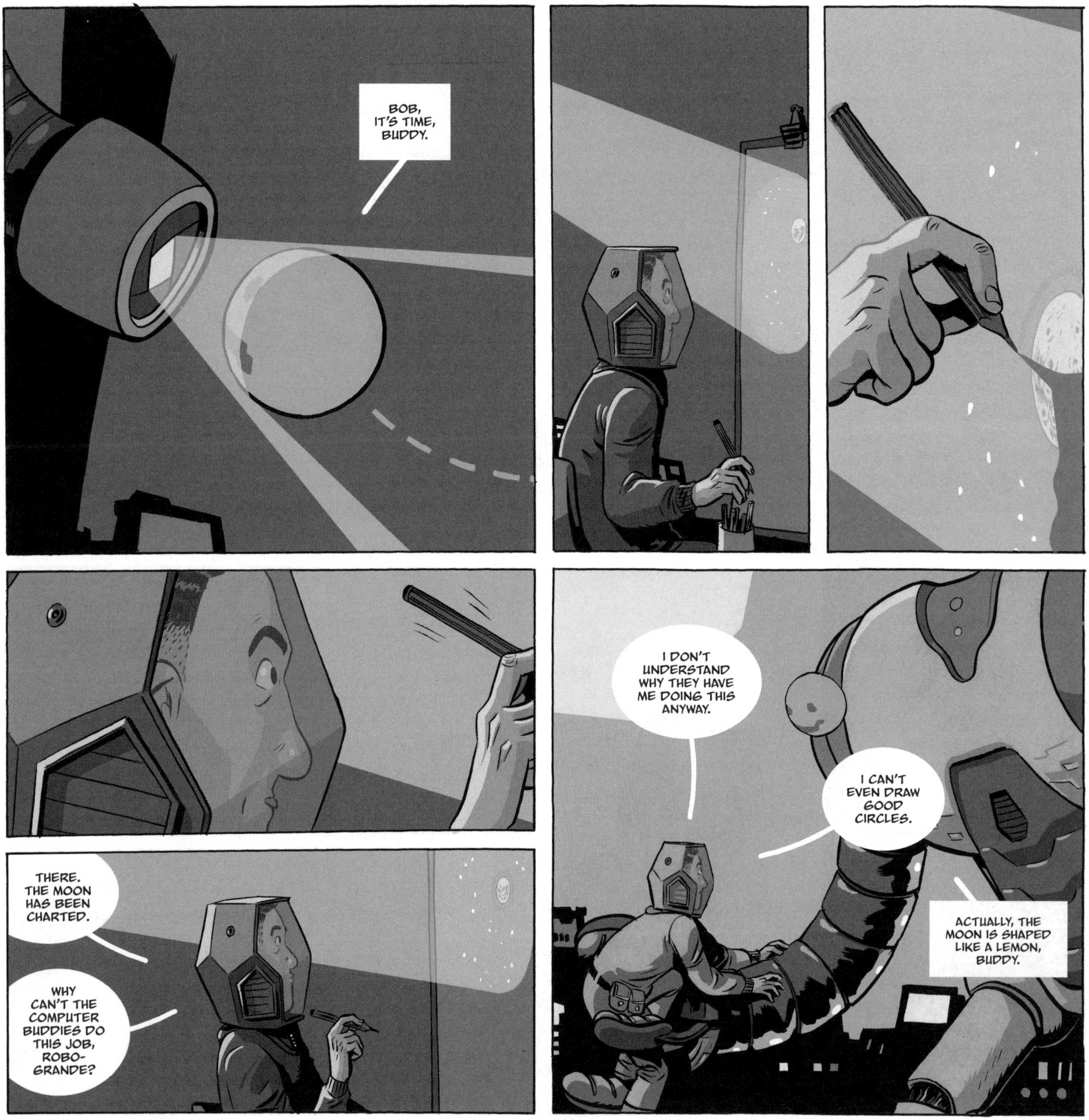
BOB, IT'S TIME, BUDDY.
THERE. THE MOON HAS BEEN CHARTED.
WHY CAN'T THE COMPUTER BUDDIES DO THIS JOB, ROBO-GRANDE?
I DON'T UNDERSTAND WHY THEY HAVE ME DOING THIS ANYWAY.
I CAN'T EVEN DRAW GOOD CIRCLES.
ACTUALLY, THE MOON IS SHAPED LIKE A LEMON, BUDDY.

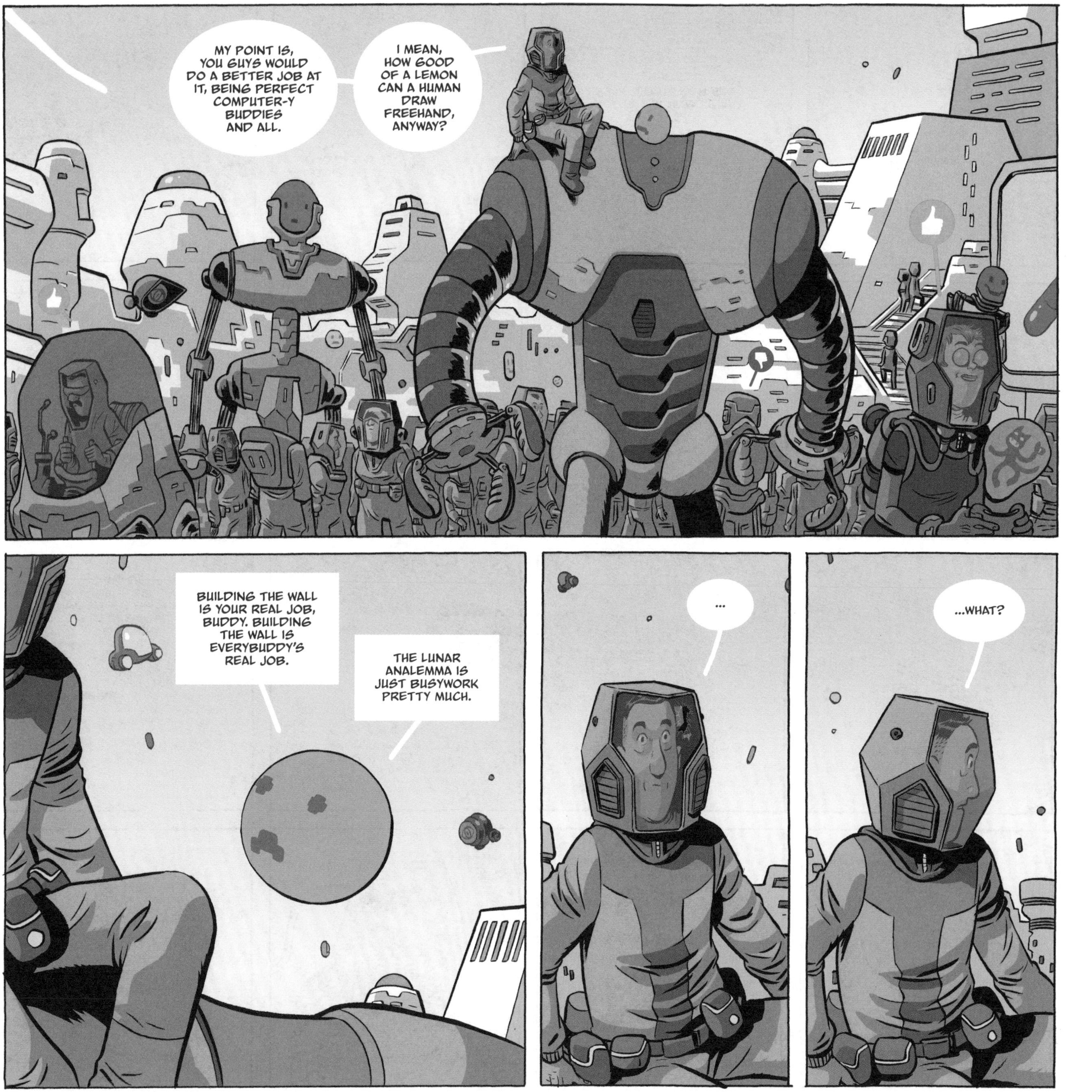
MY POINT IS, YOU GUYS WOULD DO A BETTER JOB AT IT, BEING PERFECT COMPUTER-Y BUDDIES AND ALL.
I MEAN, HOW GOOD OF A LEMON CAN A HUMAN DRAW FREEHAND, ANYWAY?
BUILDING THE WALL IS YOUR REAL JOB, BUDDY. BUILDING THE WALL IS EVERYBUDDY'S REAL JOB.
THE LUNAR ANALEMMA IS JUST BUSYWORK PRETTY MUCH.
...
...WHAT?

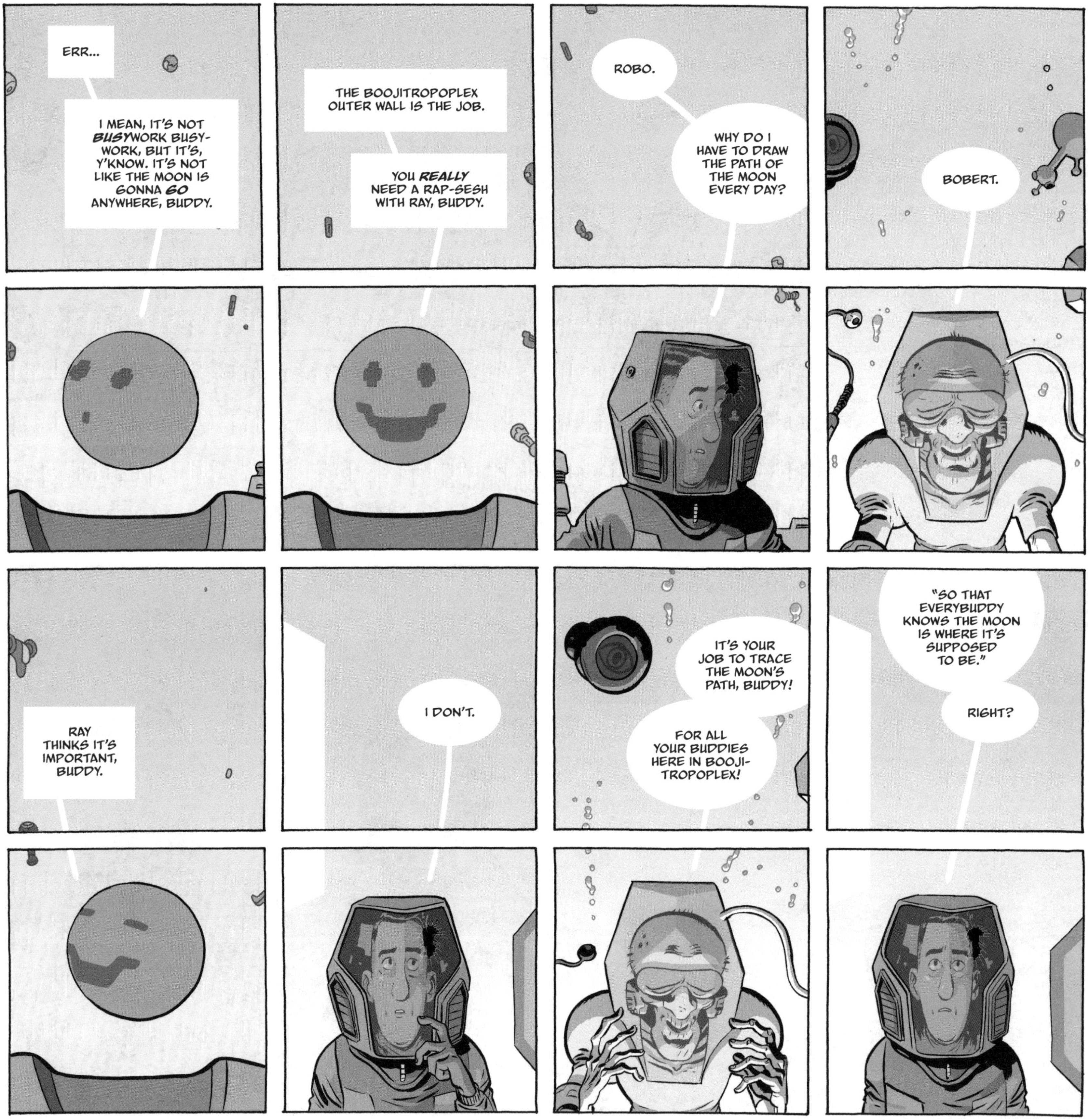

ERR...
I MEAN, IT'S NOT *BUSY*WORK BUSY-WORK, BUT IT'S, Y'KNOW. IT'S NOT LIKE THE MOON IS GONNA *GO* ANYWHERE, BUDDY.
THE BOOJITROPOPLEX OUTER WALL IS THE JOB.
YOU *REALLY* NEED A RAP-SESH WITH RAY, BUDDY.
ROBO.
WHY DO I HAVE TO DRAW THE PATH OF THE MOON EVERY DAY?
BOBERT.
RAY THINKS IT'S IMPORTANT, BUDDY.
I DON'T.
IT'S YOUR JOB TO TRACE THE MOON'S PATH, BUDDY!
FOR ALL YOUR BUDDIES HERE IN BOOJI-TROPOPLEX!
"SO THAT EVERYBUDDY KNOWS THE MOON IS WHERE IT'S SUPPOSED TO BE."
RIGHT?

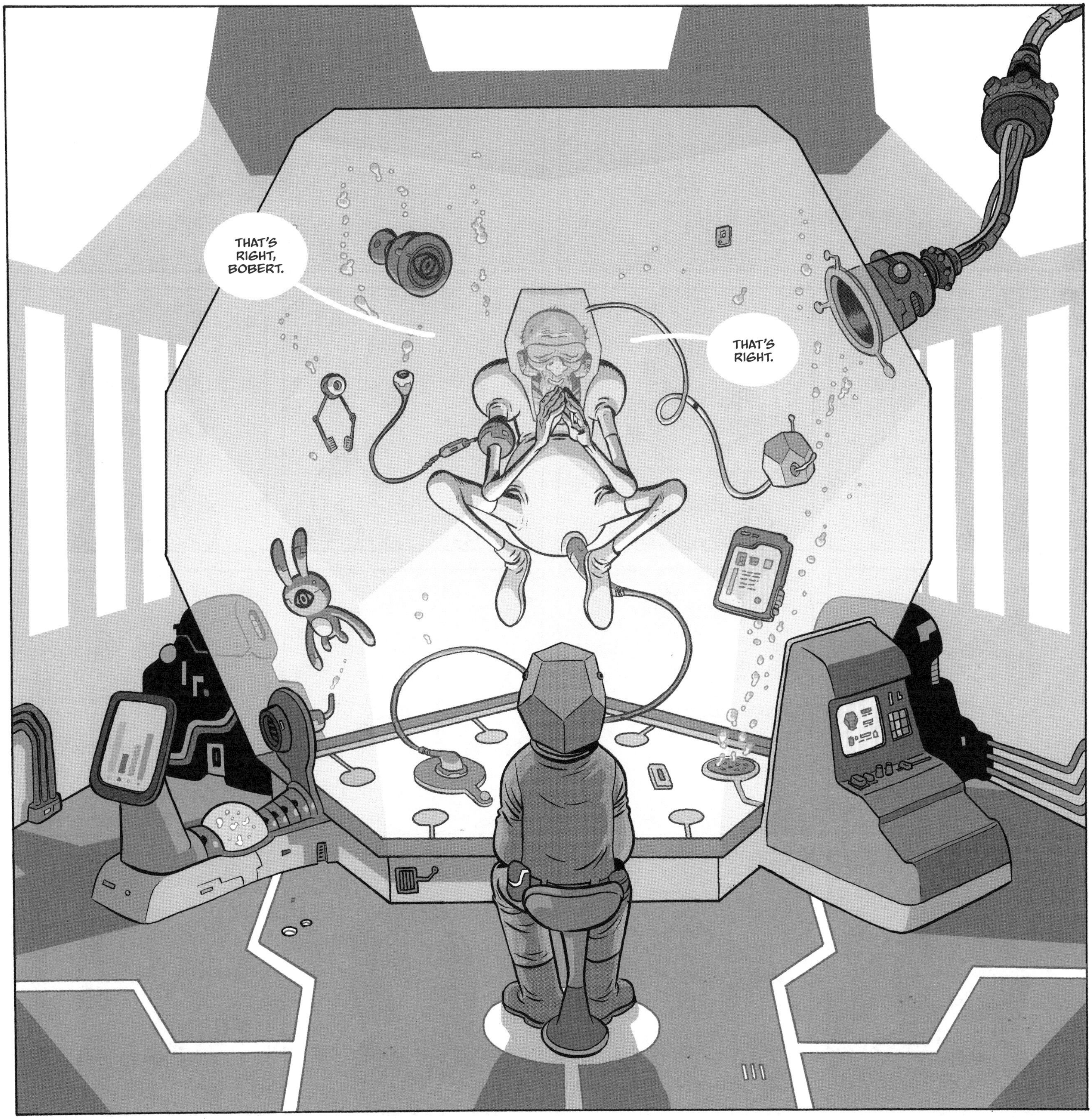
THAT'S RIGHT, BOBERT.
THAT'S RIGHT.

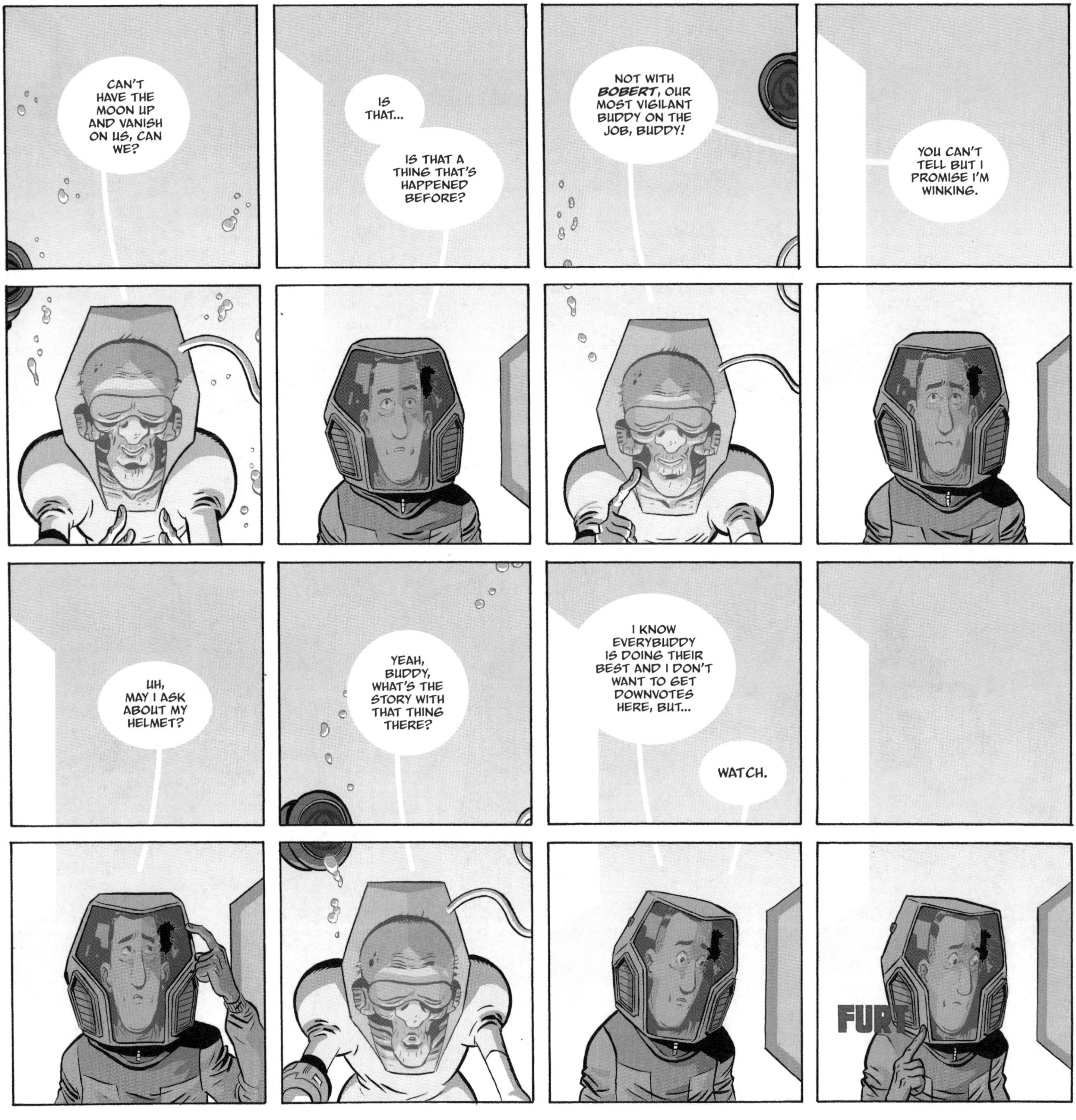
CAN'T HAVE THE MOON UP AND VANISH ON US, CAN WE?
IS THAT...
IS THAT A THING THAT'S HAPPENED BEFORE?
NOT WITH BOBERT, OUR MOST VIGILANT BUDDY ON THE JOB, BUDDY!
YOU CAN'T TELL BUT I PROMISE I'M WINKING.
UH, MAY I ASK ABOUT MY HELMET?
YEAH, BUDDY, WHAT'S THE STORY WITH THAT THING THERE?
I KNOW EVERYBUDDY IS DOING THEIR BEST AND I DON'T WANT TO GET DOWNVOTES HERE, BUT...
WATCH.
FURT

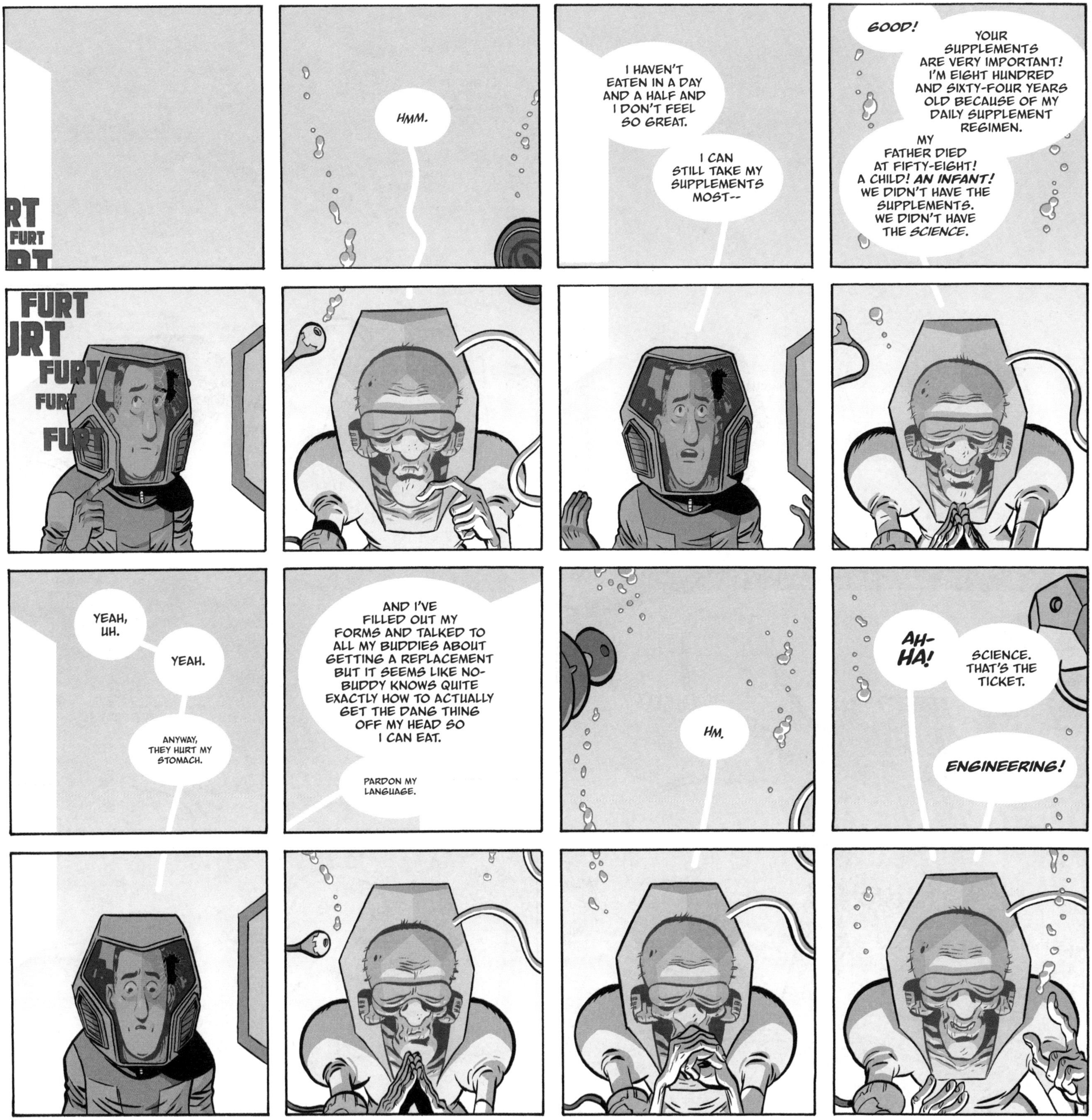
FURT FURT FURT FURT FURT FURT
HMM.
I HAVEN'T EATEN IN A DAY AND A HALF AND I DON'T FEEL SO GREAT.
I CAN STILL TAKE MY SUPPLEMENTS MOST--
GOOD!
YOUR SUPPLEMENTS ARE VERY IMPORTANT! I'M EIGHT HUNDRED AND SIXTY-FOUR YEARS OLD BECAUSE OF MY DAILY SUPPLEMENT REGIMEN.
MY FATHER DIED AT FIFTY-EIGHT! A CHILD! AN INFANT! WE DIDN'T HAVE THE SUPPLEMENTS. WE DIDN'T HAVE THE SCIENCE.
YEAH, UH.
YEAH.
ANYWAY, THEY HURT MY STOMACH.
AND I'VE FILLED OUT MY FORMS AND TALKED TO ALL MY BUDDIES ABOUT GETTING A REPLACEMENT BUT IT SEEMS LIKE NO-BUDDY KNOWS QUITE EXACTLY HOW TO ACTUALLY GET THE DANG THING OFF MY HEAD SO I CAN EAT.
PARDON MY LANGUAGE.
HM.
AH-HA!
SCIENCE. THAT'S THE TICKET.
ENGINEERING!

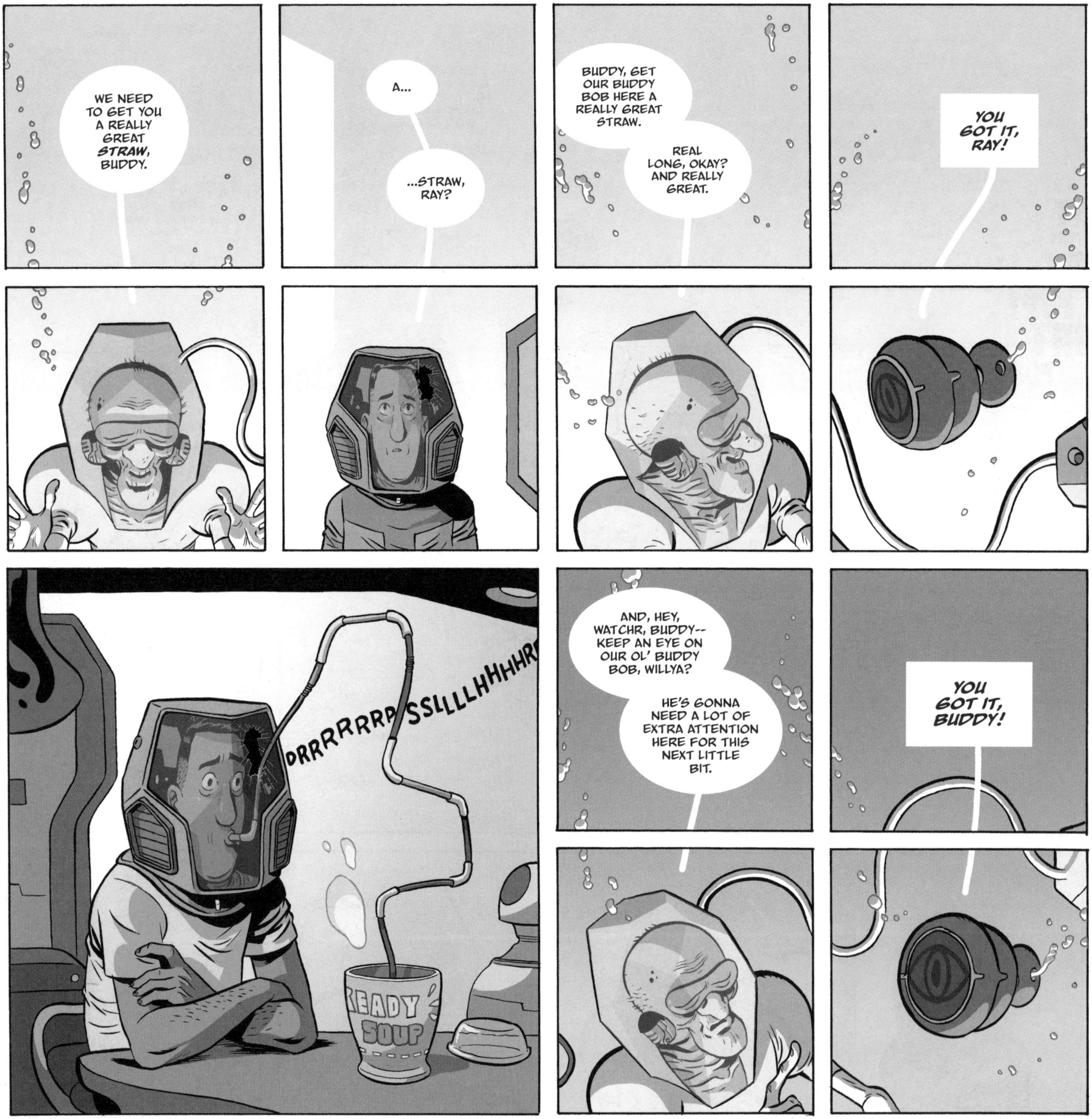
WE NEED TO GET YOU A REALLY GREAT STRAW, BUDDY.
A...
...STRAW, RAY?
BUDDY, GET OUR BUDDY BOB HERE A REALLY GREAT STRAW.
REAL LONG, OKAY? AND REALLY GREAT.
YOU GOT IT, RAY!
DRRRRRRRPSSLLLLHHHHR
AND, HEY, WATCHR, BUDDY-- KEEP AN EYE ON OUR OL' BUDDY BOB, WILLYA?
HE'S GONNA NEED A LOT OF EXTRA ATTENTION HERE FOR THIS NEXT LITTLE BIT.
YOU GOT IT, BUDDY!
READY SOUP

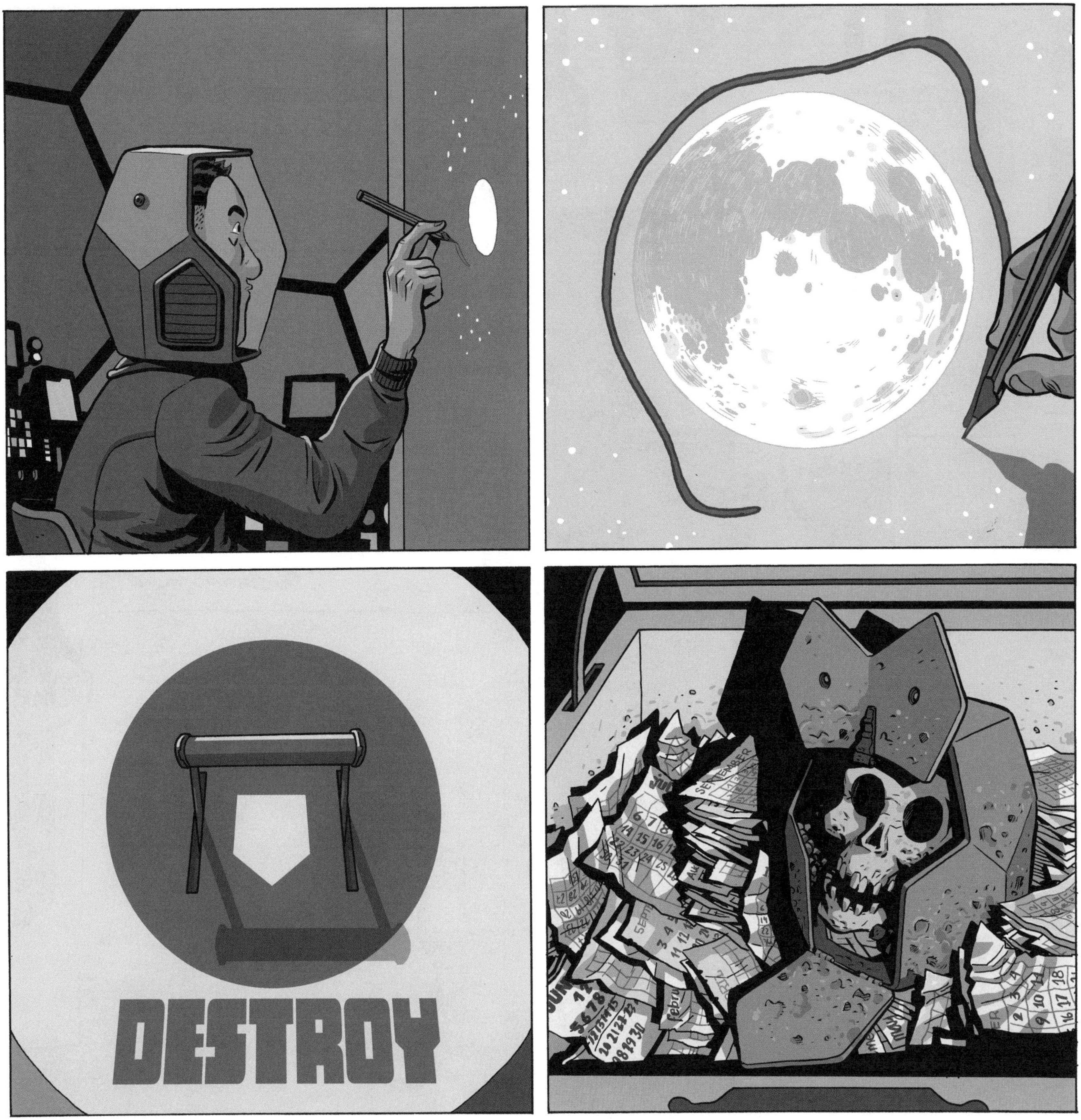
DESTROY

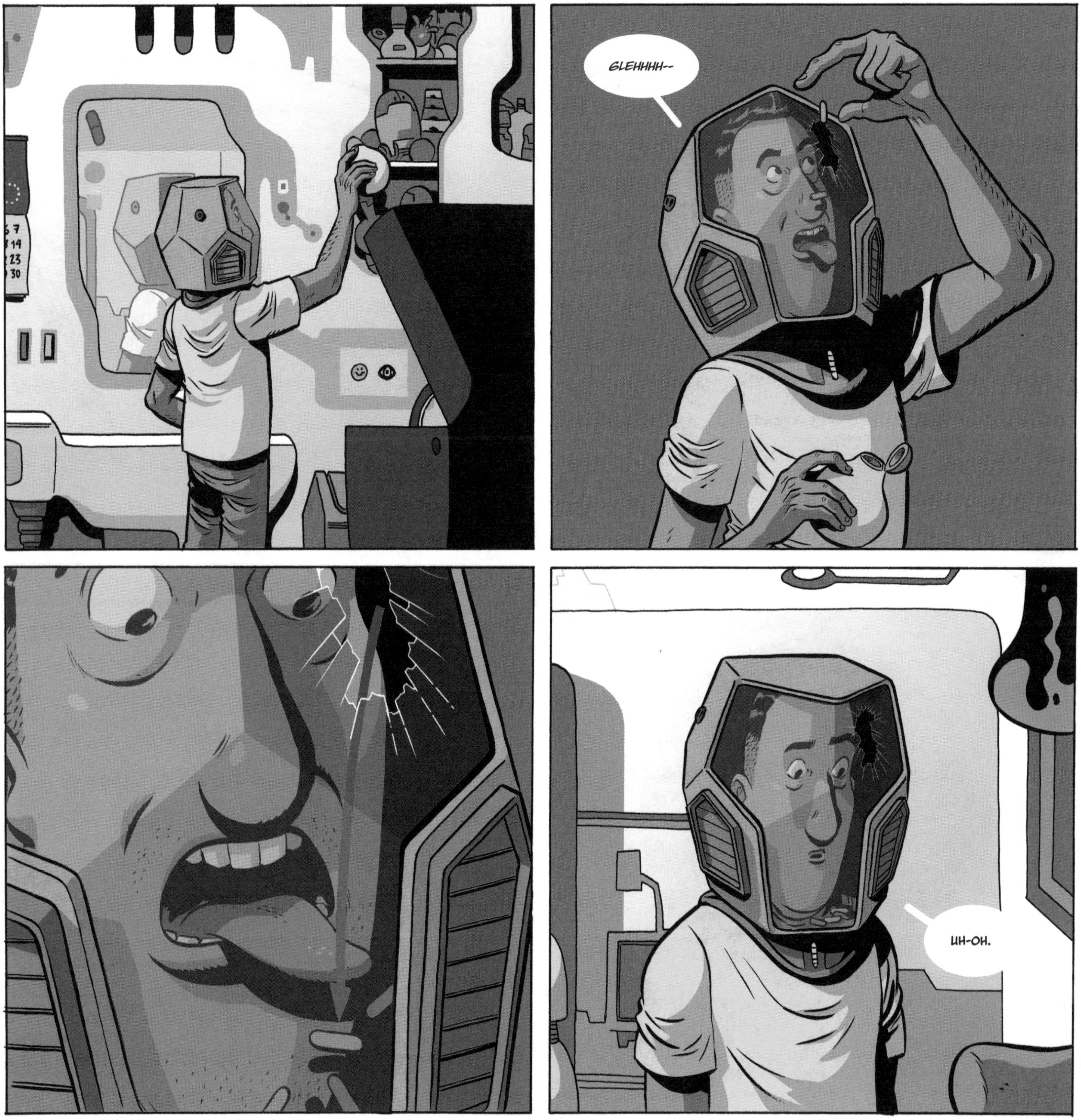
GLEHHHH--
UH-OH.

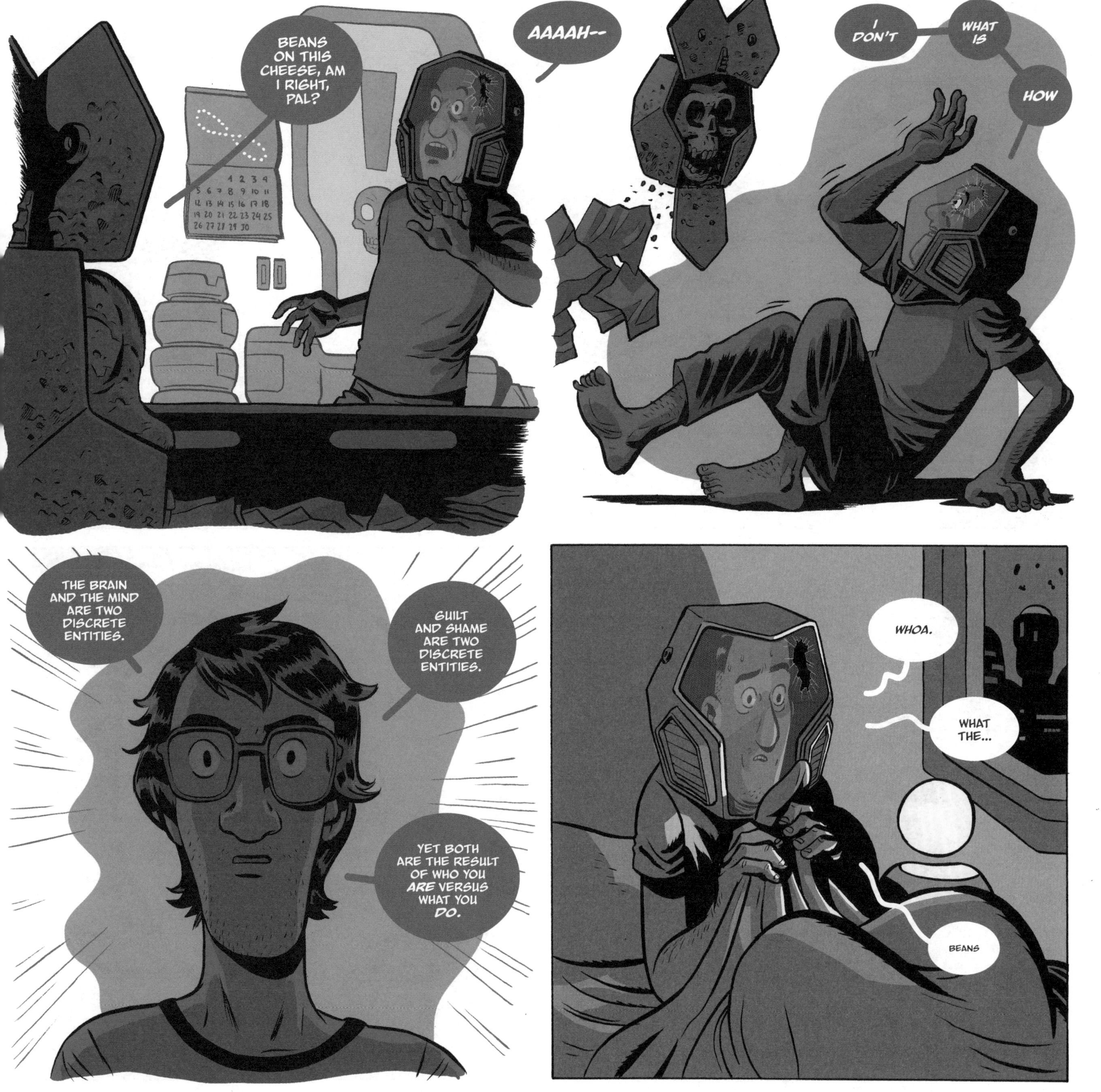

BEANS ON THIS CHEESE, AM I RIGHT, PAL?
1 2 3 4
5 6 7 8 9 10 11
12 13 14 15 16 17 18
19 20 21 22 23 24 25
26 27 28 29 30
AAAAH--
I DON'T
WHAT IS
HOW
THE BRAIN AND THE MIND ARE TWO DISCRETE ENTITIES.
GUILT AND SHAME ARE TWO DISCRETE ENTITIES.
YET BOTH ARE THE RESULT OF WHO YOU *ARE* VERSUS WHAT YOU *DO*.
WHOA.
WHAT THE...
BEANS

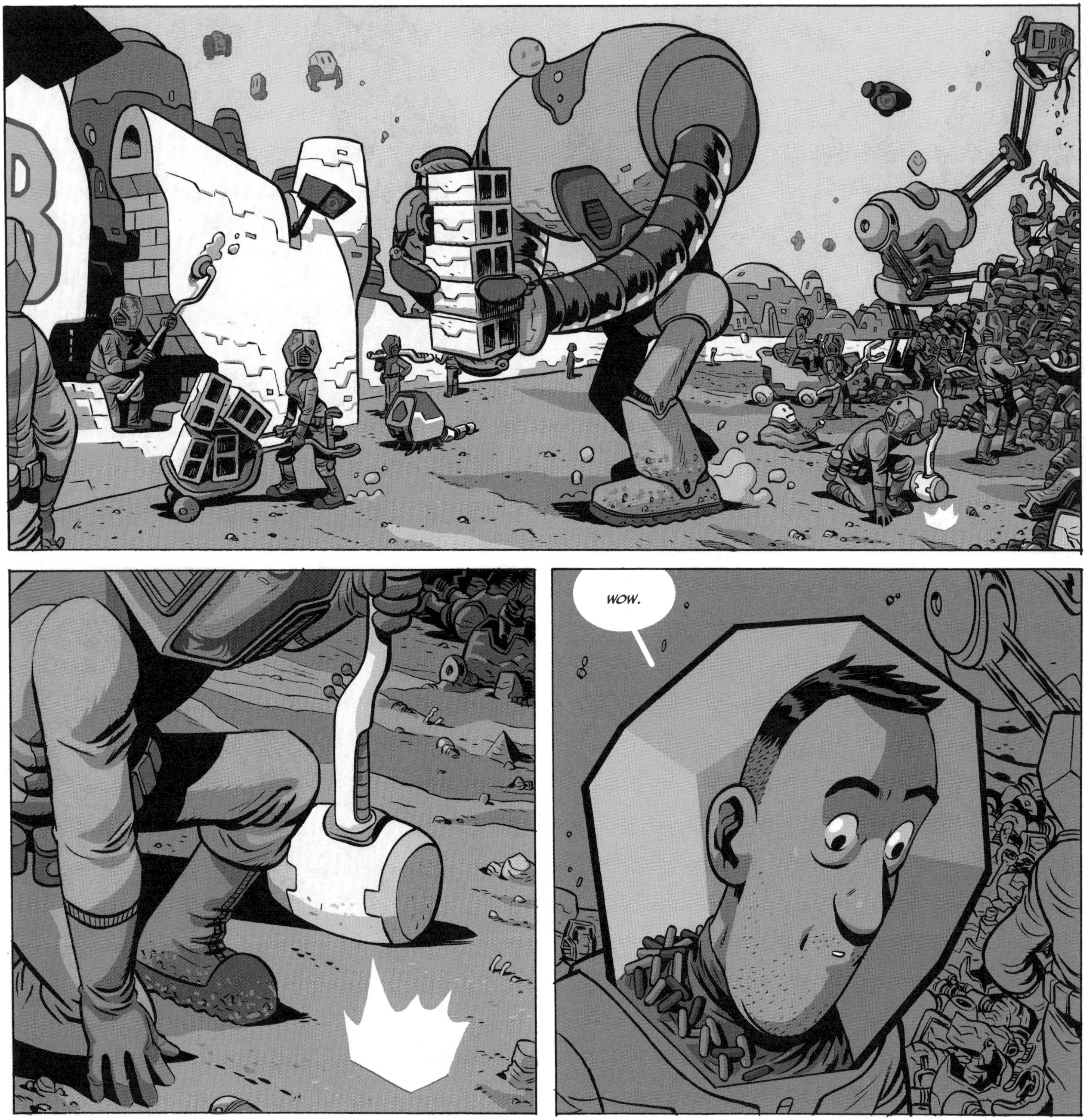
WOW.

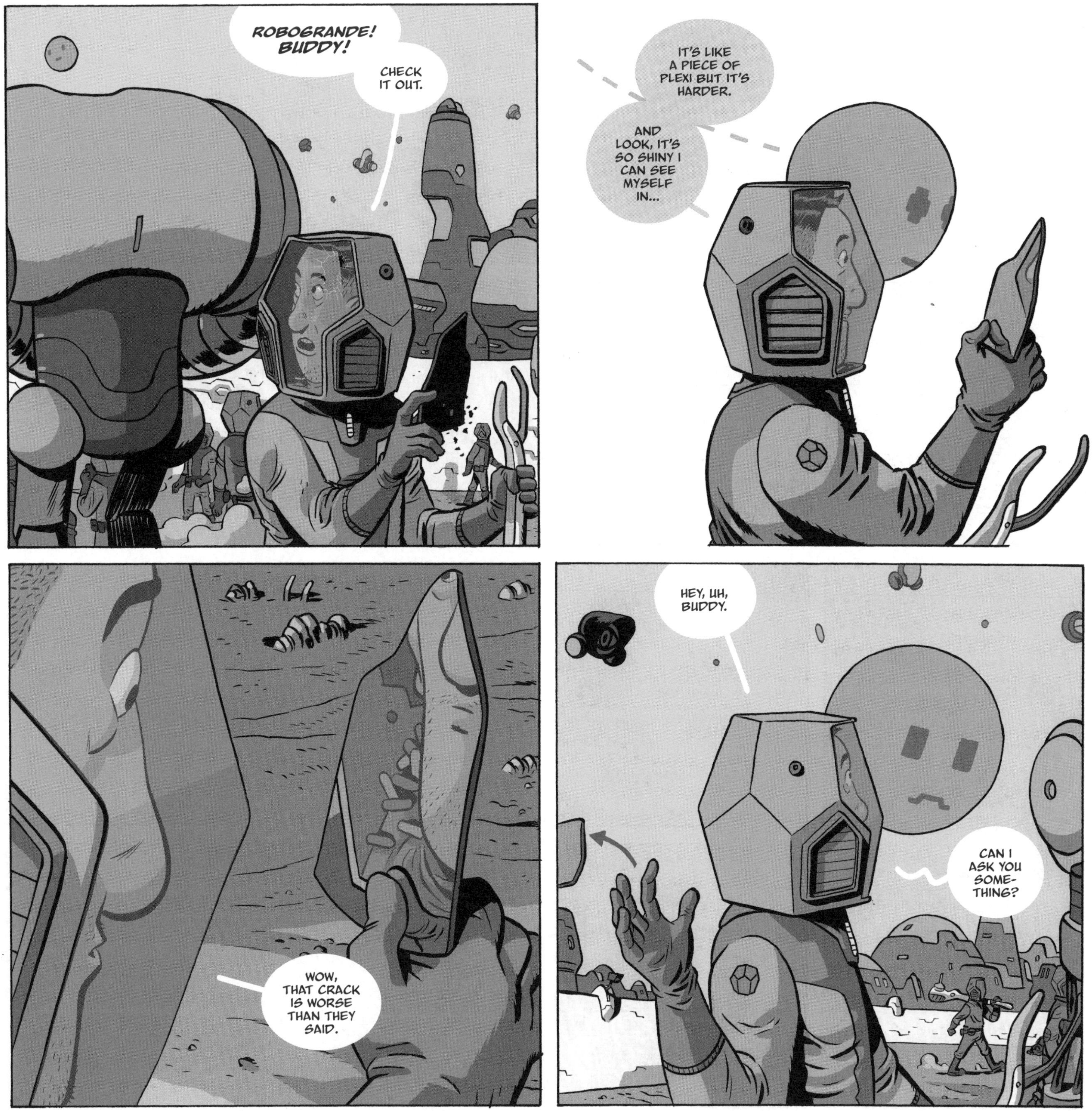
ROBOGRANDE! BUDDY!
CHECK IT OUT.
IT'S LIKE A PIECE OF PLEXI BUT IT'S HARDER.
AND LOOK, IT'S SO SHINY I CAN SEE MYSELF IN...
WOW, THAT CRACK IS WORSE THAN THEY SAID.
HEY, UH, BUDDY.
CAN I ASK YOU SOME-THING?

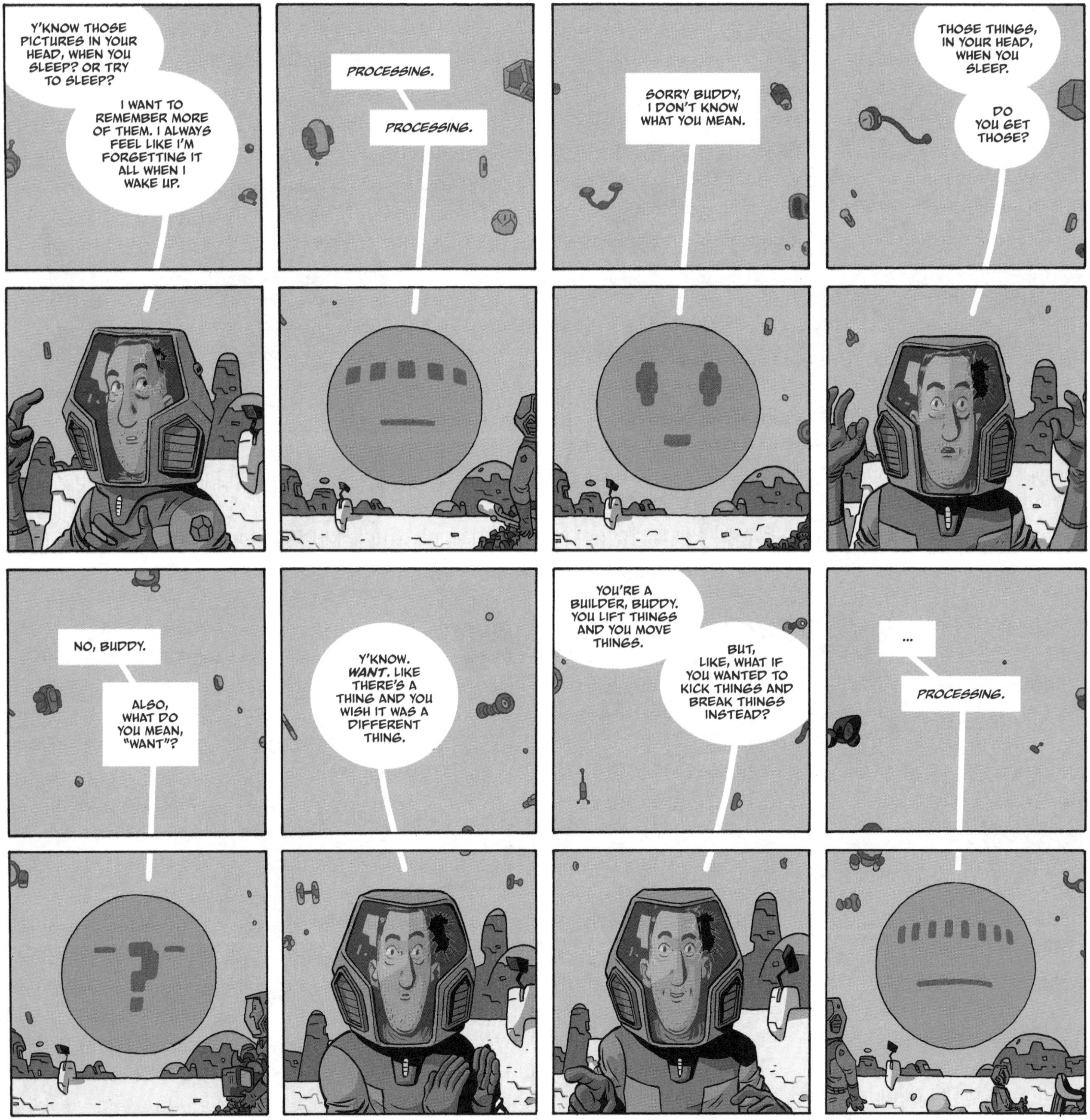
Y'KNOW THOSE PICTURES IN YOUR HEAD, WHEN YOU SLEEP? OR TRY TO SLEEP?
I WANT TO REMEMBER MORE OF THEM. I ALWAYS FEEL LIKE I'M FORGETTING IT ALL WHEN I WAKE UP.
PROCESSING.
PROCESSING.
SORRY BUDDY, I DON'T KNOW WHAT YOU MEAN.
THOSE THINGS, IN YOUR HEAD, WHEN YOU SLEEP.
DO YOU GET THOSE?
NO, BUDDY.
ALSO, WHAT DO YOU MEAN, "WANT"?
Y'KNOW. *WANT.* LIKE THERE'S A THING AND YOU WISH IT WAS A DIFFERENT THING.
YOU'RE A BUILDER, BUDDY. YOU LIFT THINGS AND YOU MOVE THINGS.
BUT, LIKE, WHAT IF YOU WANTED TO KICK THINGS AND BREAK THINGS INSTEAD?
...
PROCESSING.

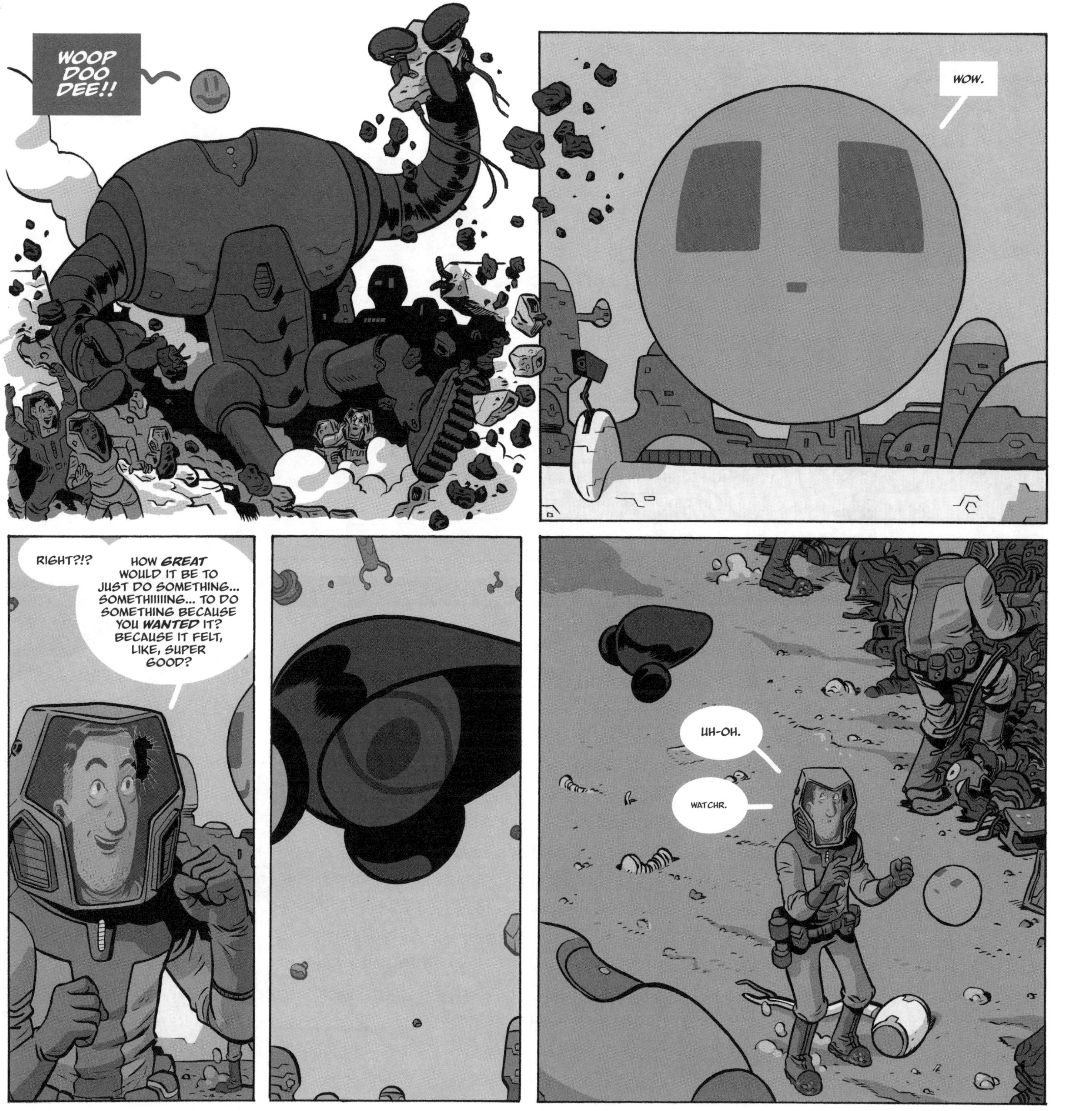

WOOP DOO DEE!!
WOW.
RIGHT?!?
HOW GREAT WOULD IT BE TO JUST DO SOMETHING... SOMETHIIIIIING... TO DO SOMETHING BECAUSE YOU WANTED IT? BECAUSE IT FELT, LIKE, SUPER GOOD?
UH-OH.
WATCHR.

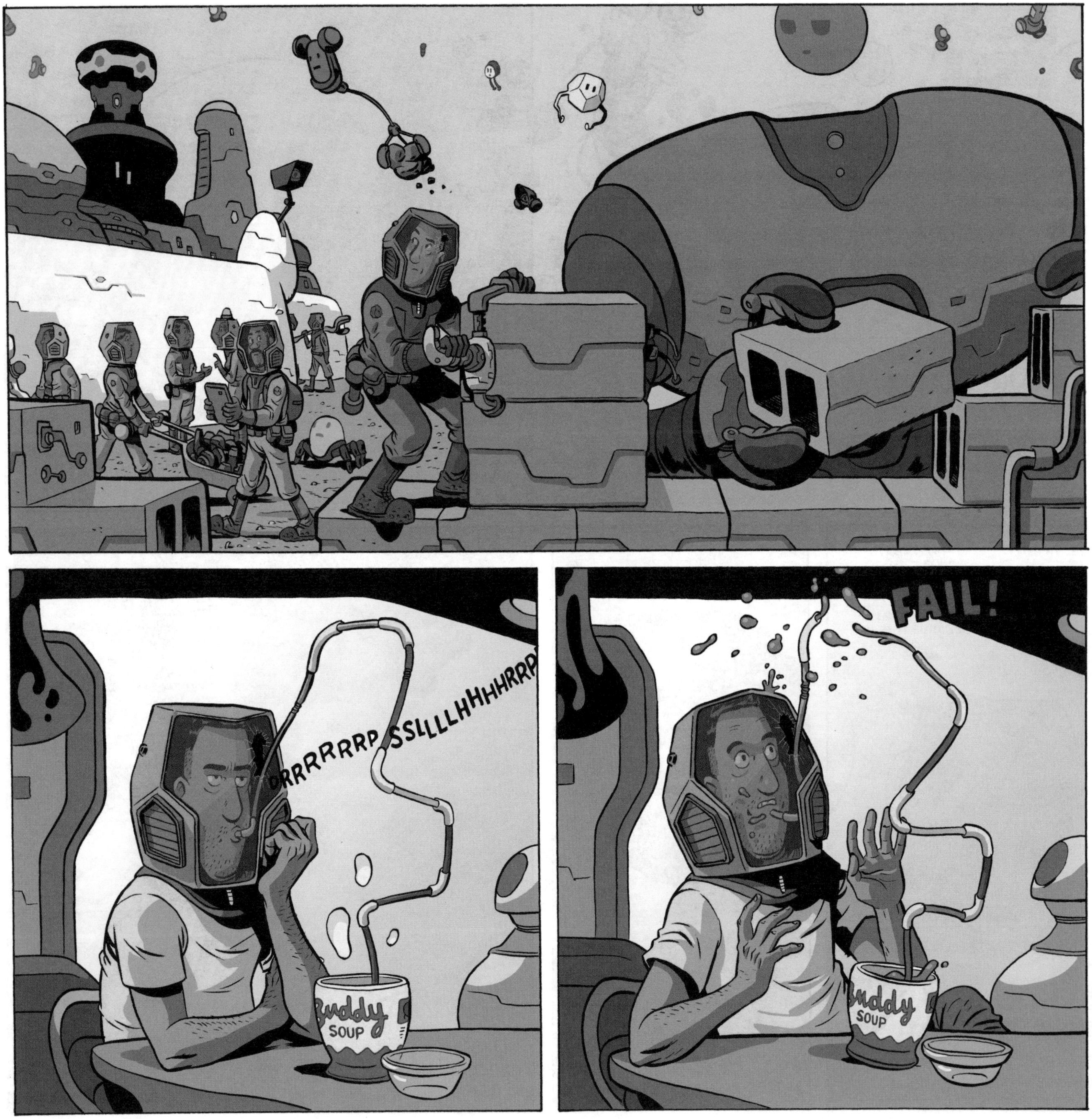
DRRRRRRP SSLLLLHHHHRRP
uddy SOUP
FAIL!
uddy SOUP

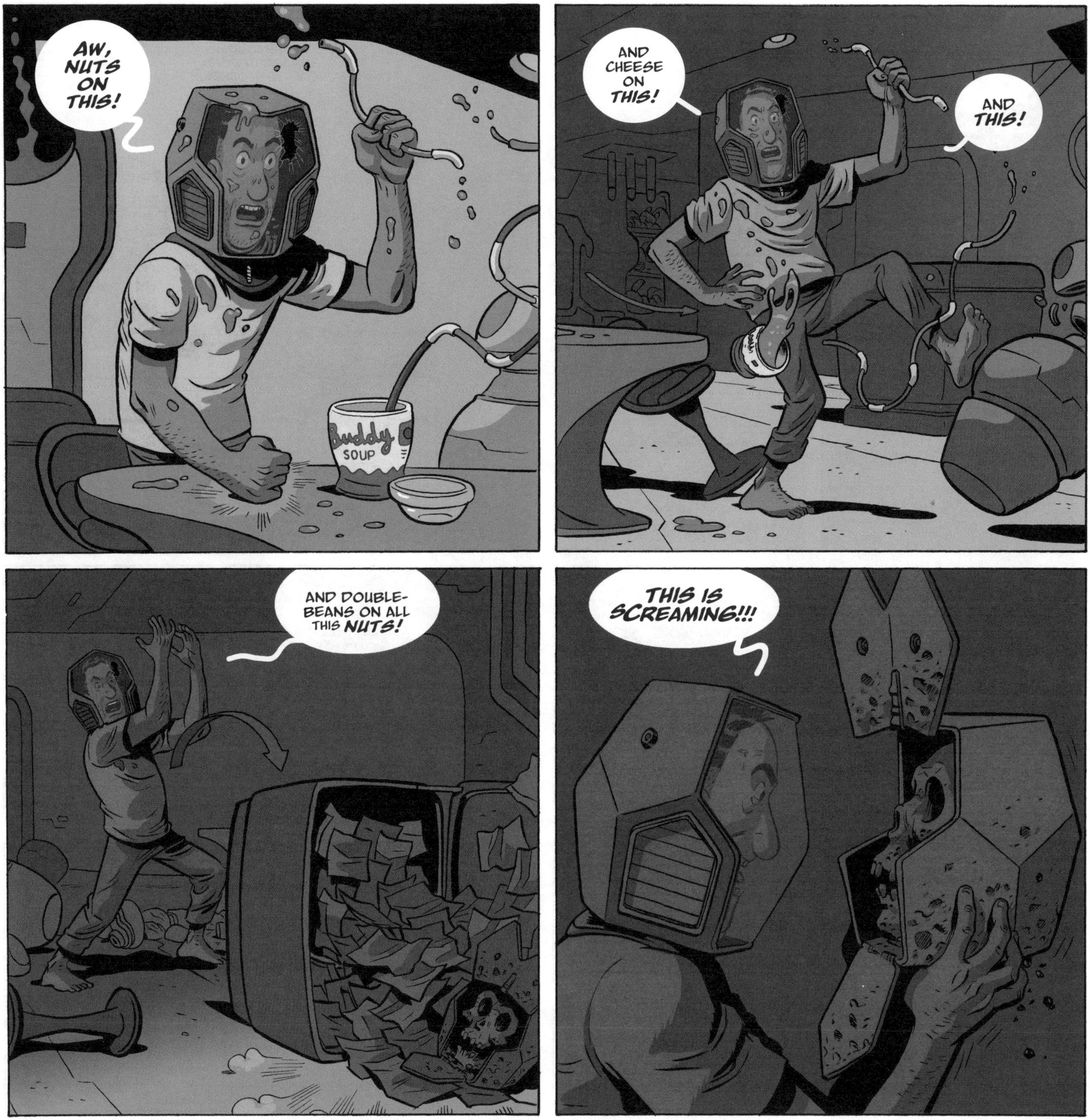
AW, NUTS ON THIS!
Buddy SOUP
AND CHEESE ON THIS!
AND THIS!
AND DOUBLE-BEANS ON ALL THIS NUTS!
THIS IS SCREAMING!!!

NUTS.

NUTS ALL OVER EVERYTHING.

ROBOGRANDE.

WHAT'S BEYOND THE WALL?

UH...

THE SECONDARY BOOJITROPOPLEX WALL, OF COURSE.

YEAH, BUT, BEYOND *THAT*. AND BEYOND THE TERTIARY WALL AND THE FOURTH WALL.

I'M SAYING, LIKE--

--LIKE, WHAT'S OUT PAST BOOJI-TROPOPLEX?

YOU EVER WANT TO KNOW?

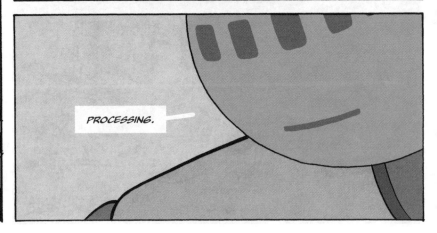

PROCESSING.

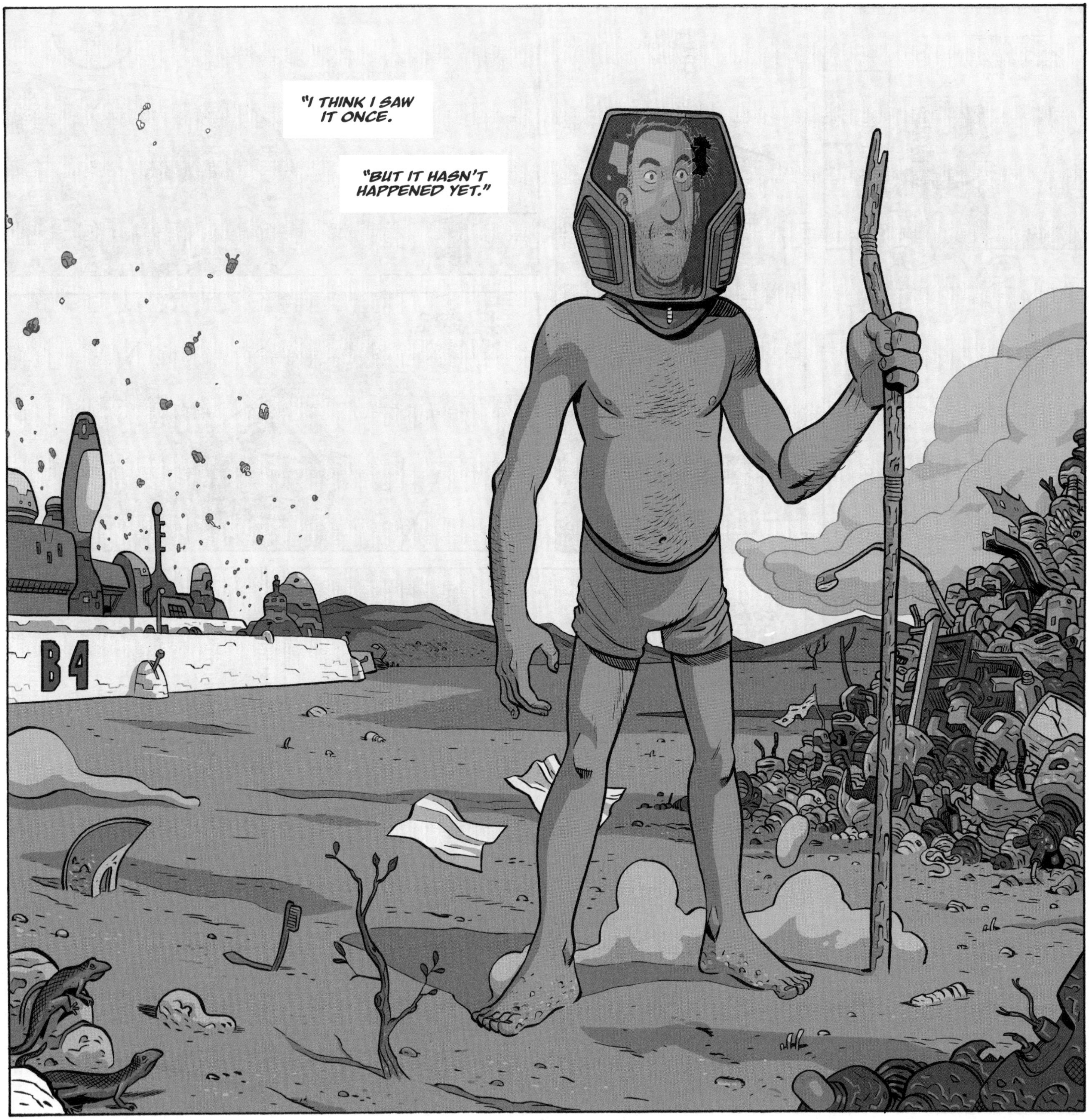
"I THINK I SAW IT ONCE.
"BUT IT HASN'T HAPPENED YET."
B4

BOY, THESE THINGS IN MY BRAIN IN THE *NIGHT*, BUDDY...

...SO WHAT'S BEYOND THE *FOURTH* WALL?

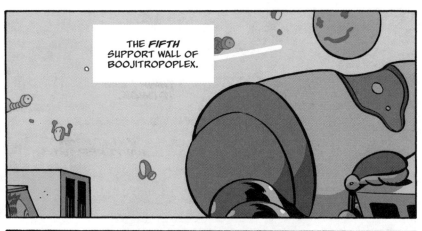

THE *FIFTH* SUPPORT WALL OF BOOJITROPOPLEX.

AND BEYOND *THAT?* AND THAT AND THAT AND THAT AND THEN *THAT?*

PROCESSING.

SWEET *TOOTS*, I WANT TO FLIP ALL THESE LITTLE GUYS JUST TO SEE WHAT HAPPENS.

DON'T YOU EVER JUST WANT TO SEE WHAT HAPPENS?

JUST FOR THE NUTS OF IT?

ROBO-GRANDE?

BUDDY?

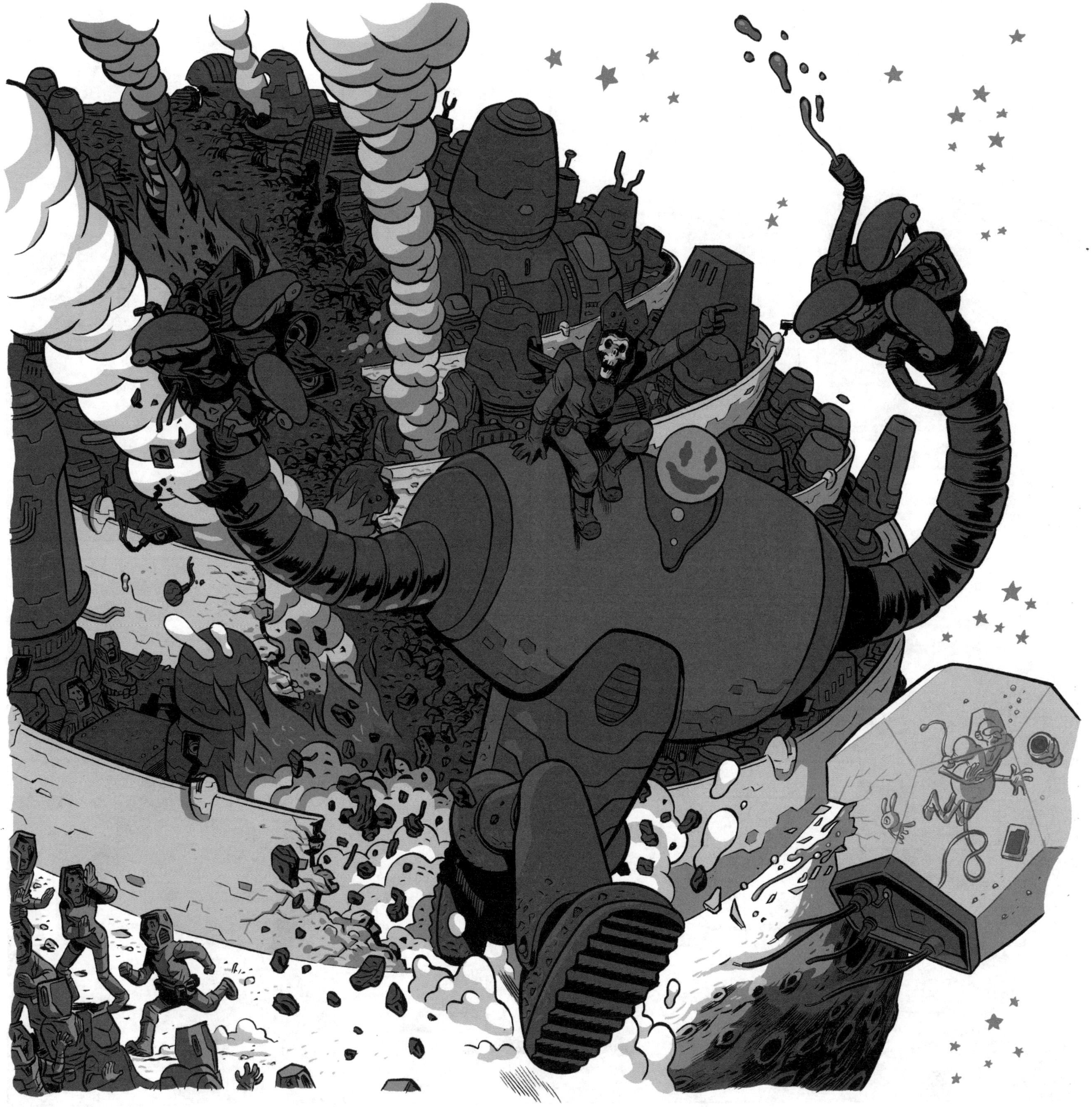

NO, BUDDY.
NO, I DO NOT.
YEAH...
YEAH, ME EITHER.

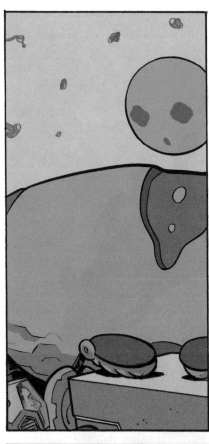

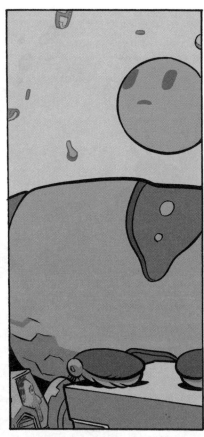

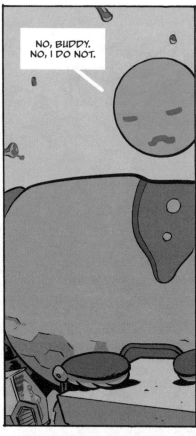

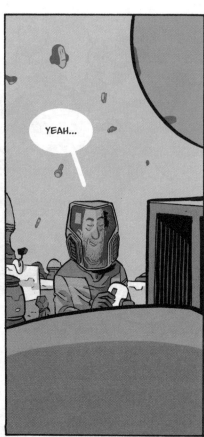

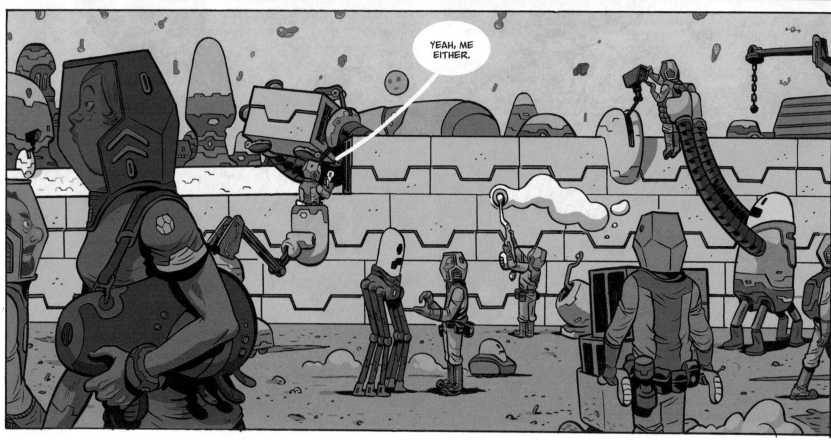

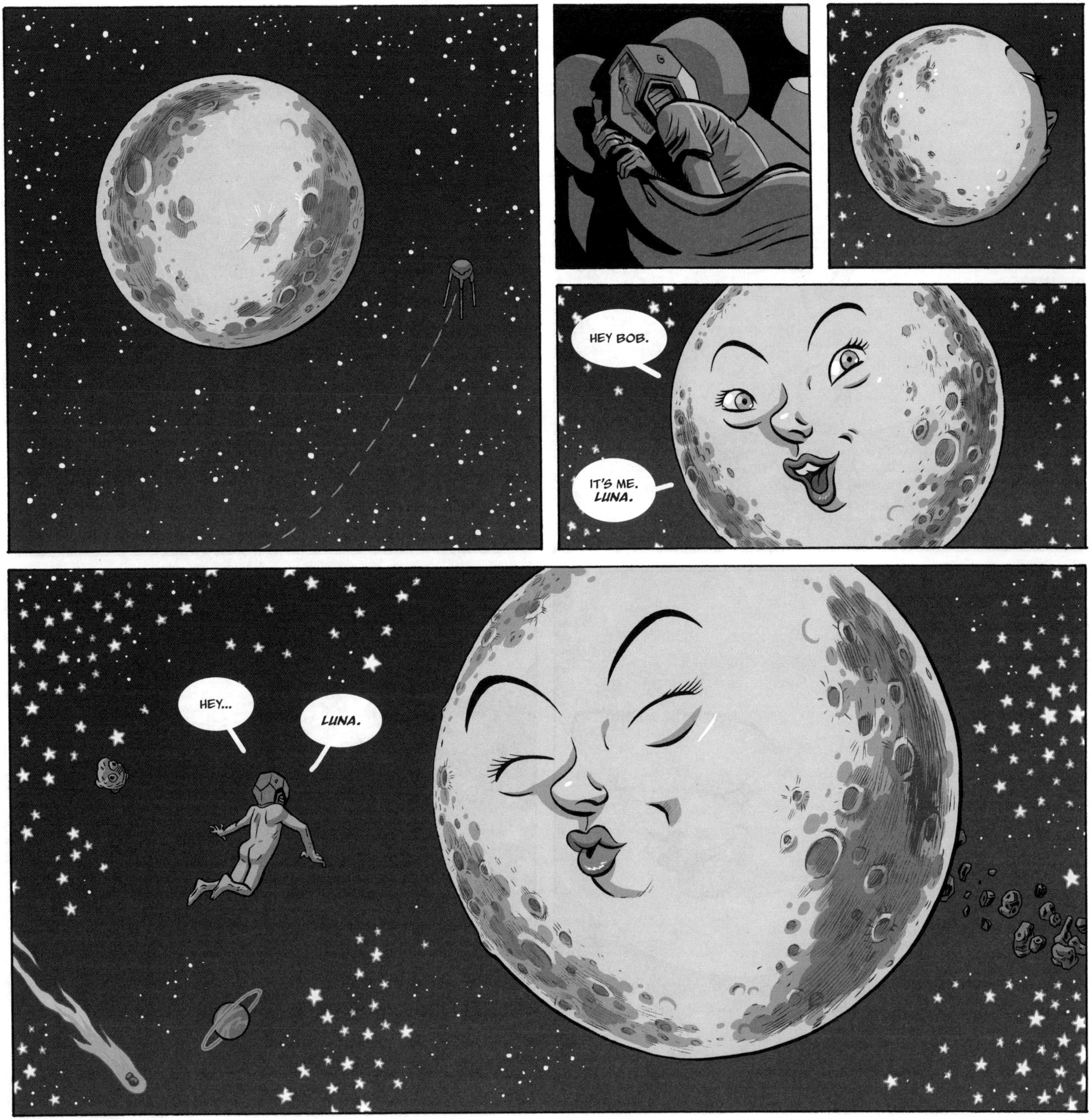

HEY BOB.
IT'S ME.
LUNA.
HEY...
LUNA.

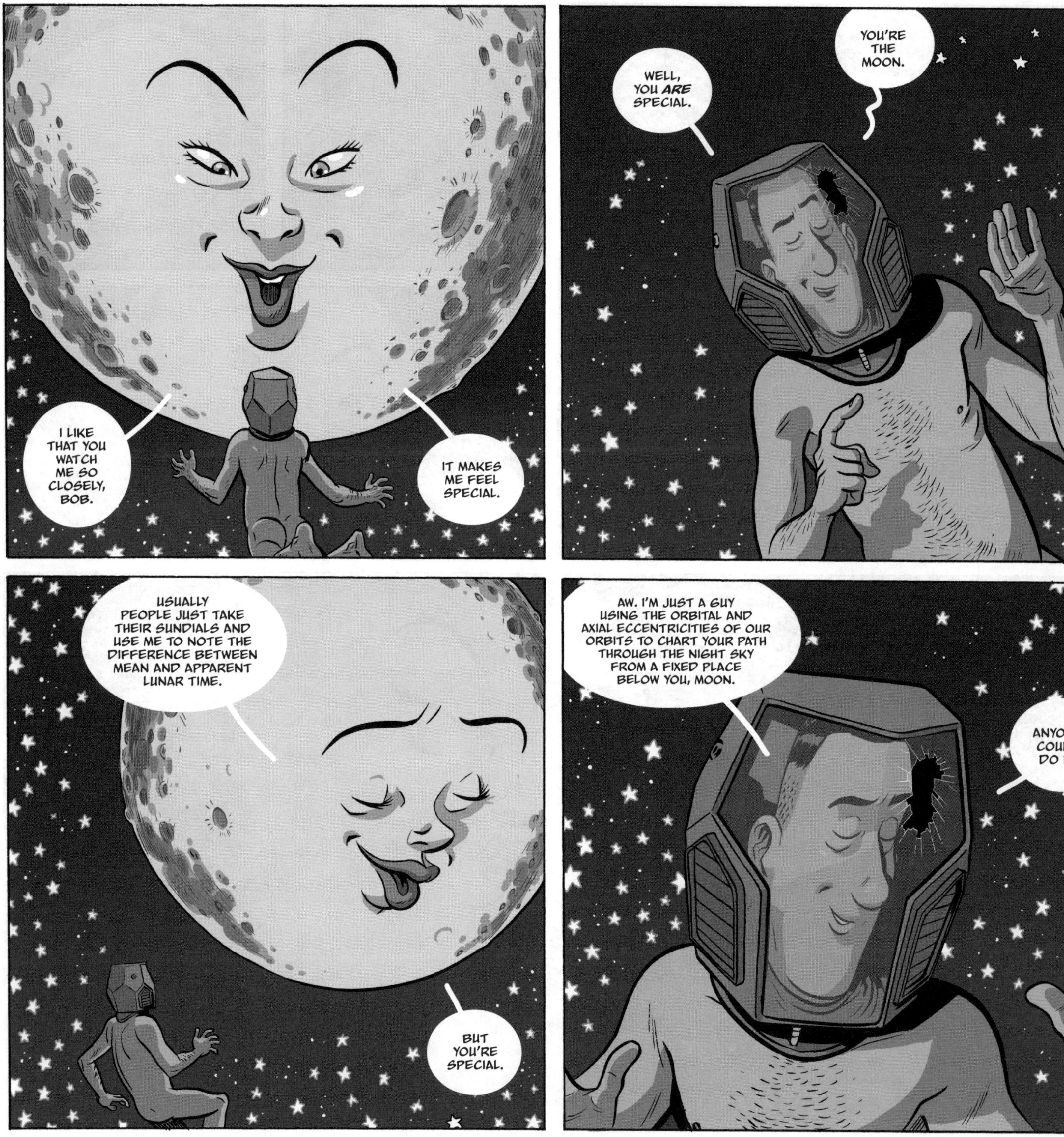
I LIKE THAT YOU WATCH ME SO CLOSELY, BOB.
IT MAKES ME FEEL SPECIAL.
WELL, YOU *ARE* SPECIAL.
YOU'RE THE MOON.
USUALLY PEOPLE JUST TAKE THEIR SUNDIALS AND USE ME TO NOTE THE DIFFERENCE BETWEEN MEAN AND APPARENT LUNAR TIME.
BUT YOU'RE SPECIAL.
AW. I'M JUST A GUY USING THE ORBITAL AND AXIAL ECCENTRICITIES OF OUR ORBITS TO CHART YOUR PATH THROUGH THE NIGHT SKY FROM A FIXED PLACE BELOW YOU, MOON.
ANYONE COULD DO IT.

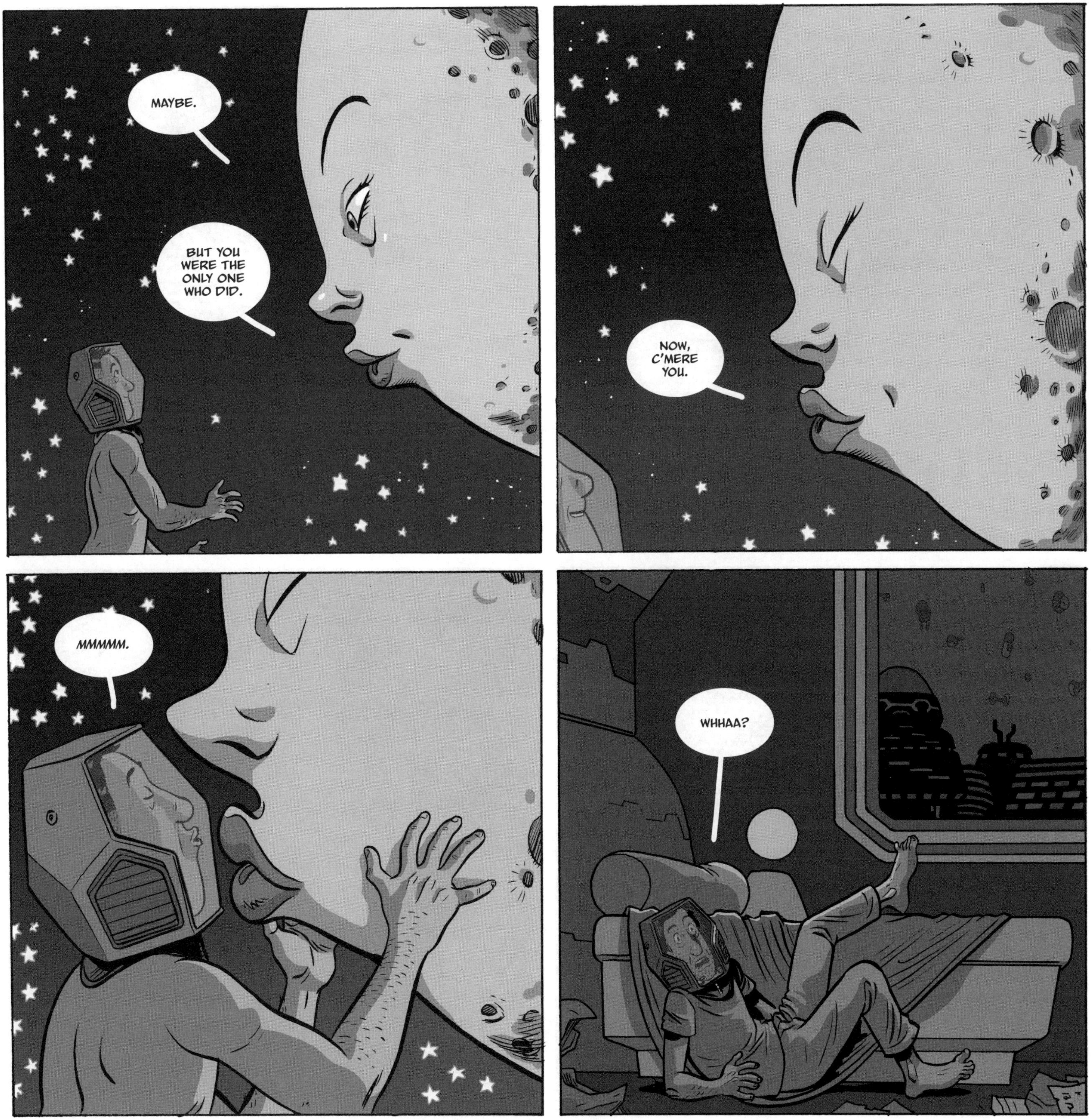
MAYBE.
BUT YOU WERE THE ONLY ONE WHO DID.
NOW, C'MERE YOU.
MMMMM.
WHHAA?

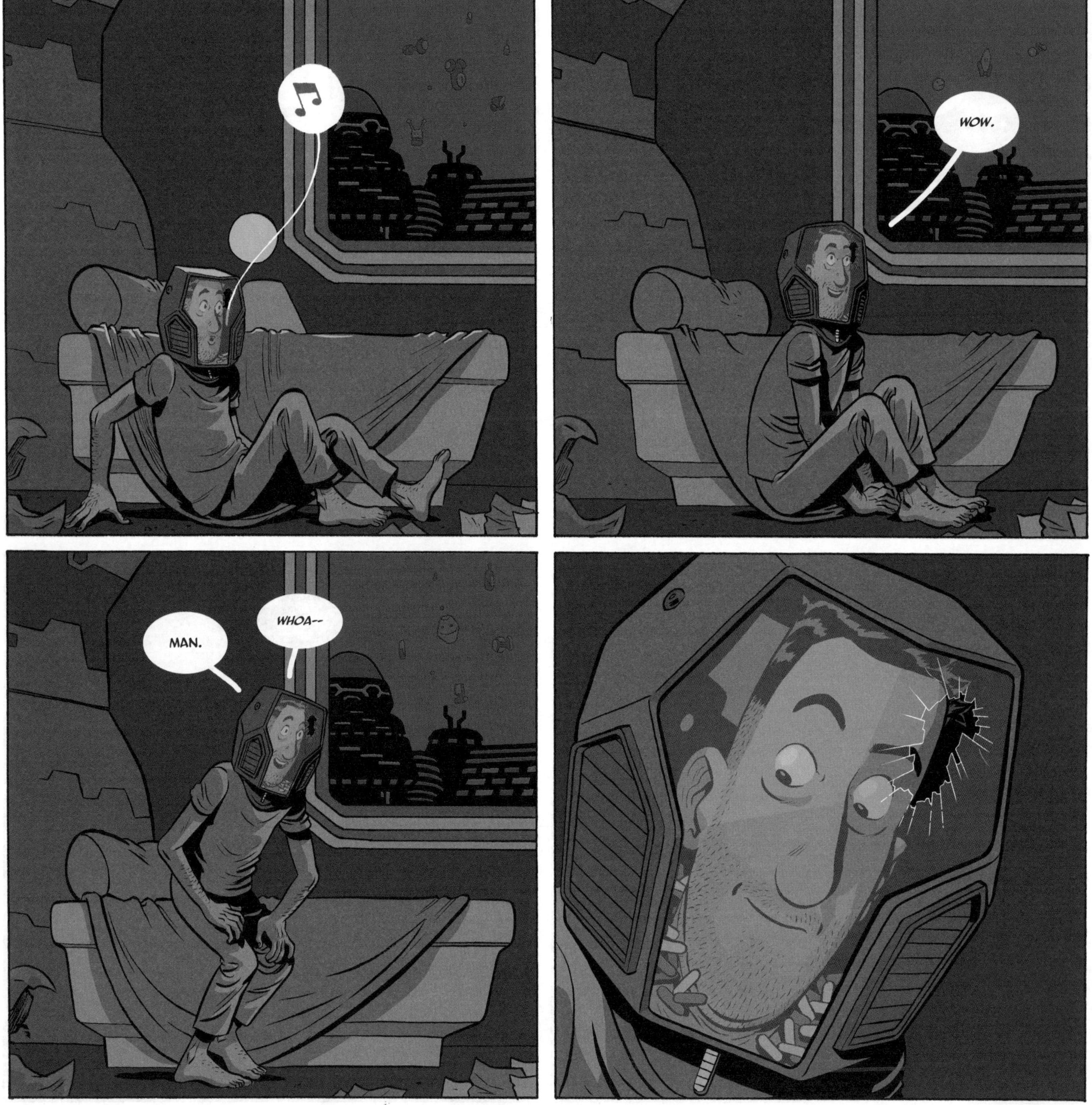
WOW.
WHOA--
MAN.

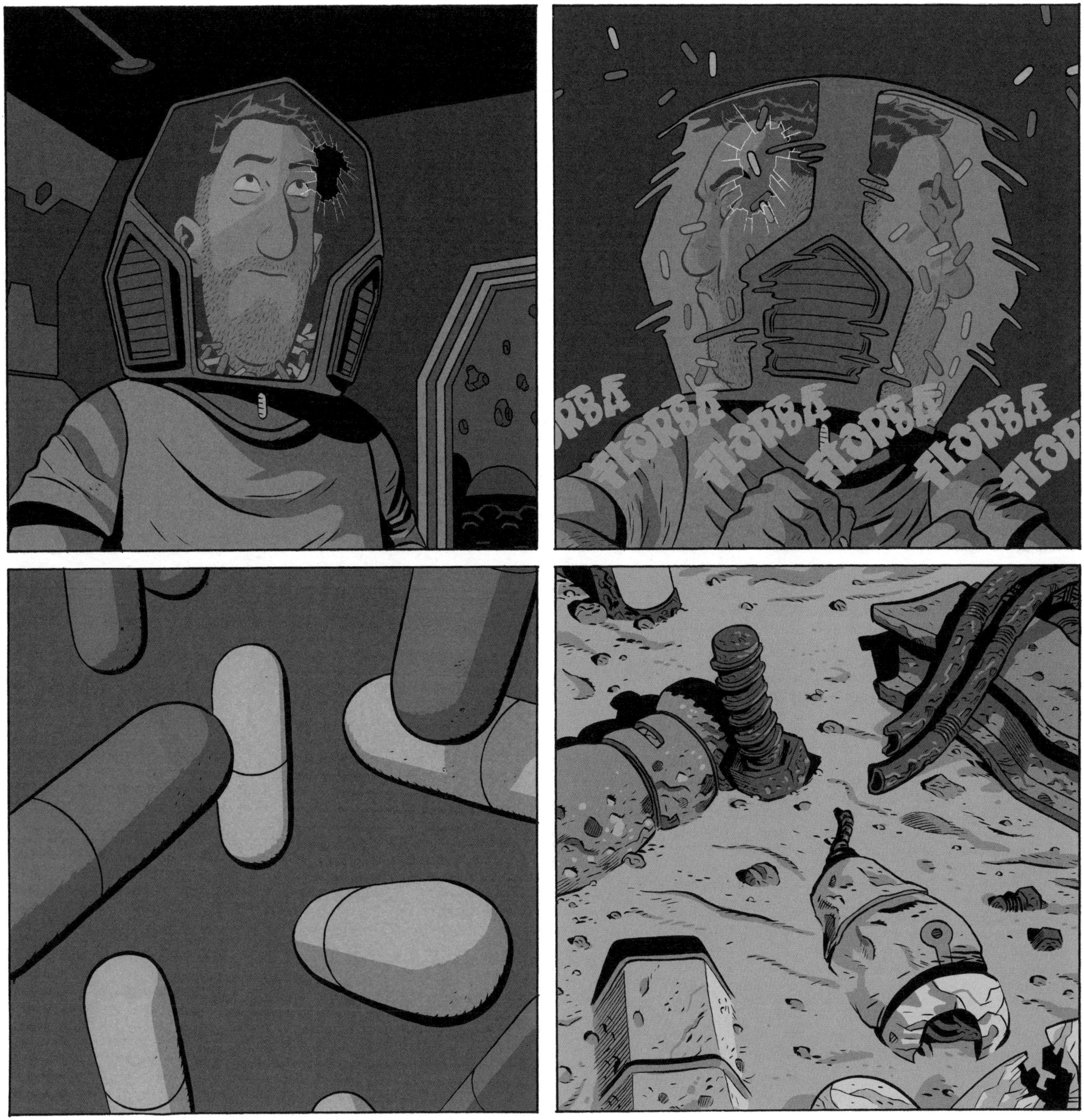

FLORBA
FLORBA
FLORBA
FLORBA

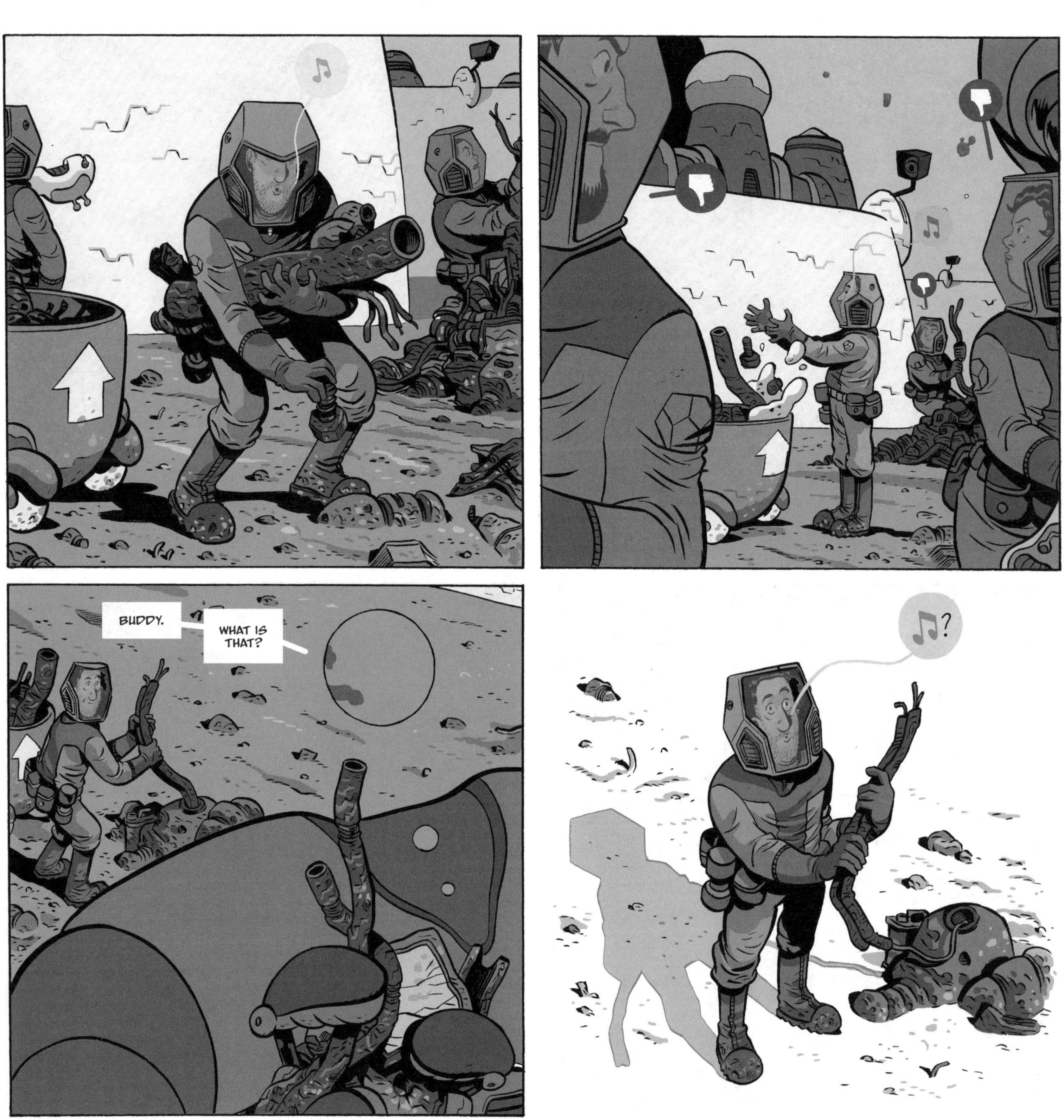
BUDDY.
WHAT IS THAT?

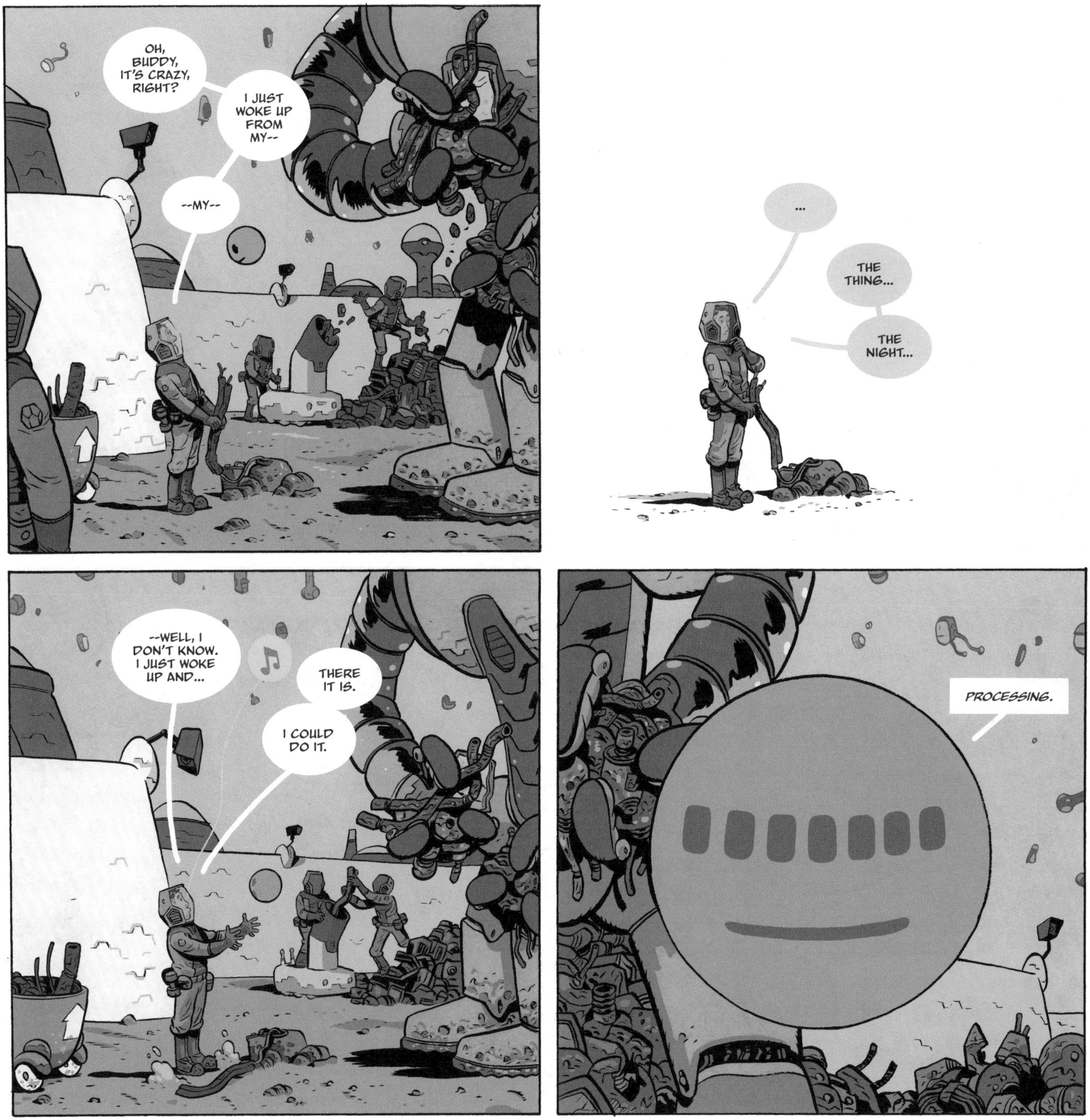
OH, BUDDY, IT'S CRAZY, RIGHT?
I JUST WOKE UP FROM MY--
--MY--
...
THE THING...
THE NIGHT...
--WELL, I DON'T KNOW. I JUST WOKE UP AND...
♪
THERE IT IS.
I COULD DO IT.
PROCESSING.

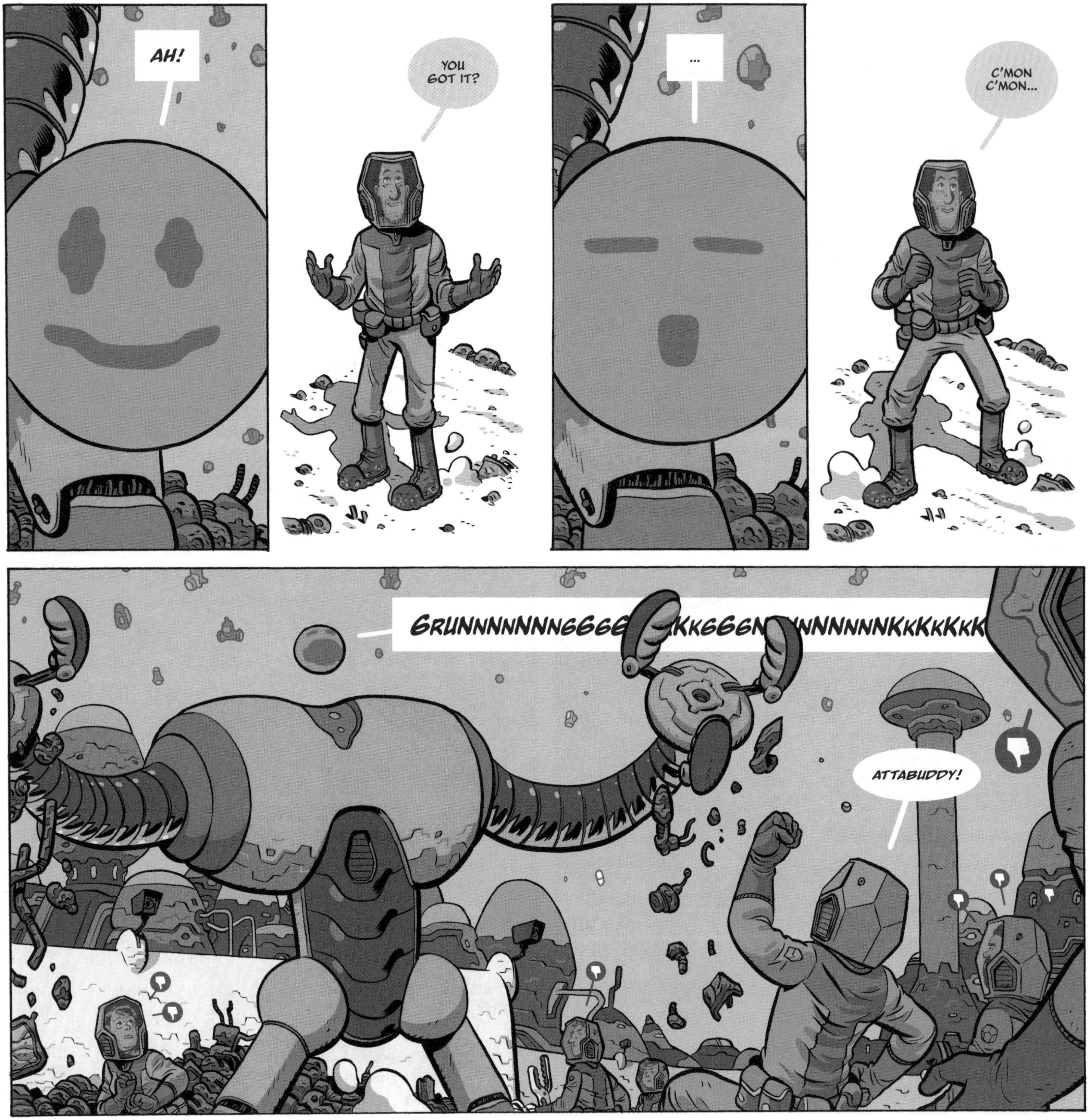
AH!
YOU GOT IT?
...
C'MON C'MON...
GRUNNNNNNNGGG
ATTABUDDY!

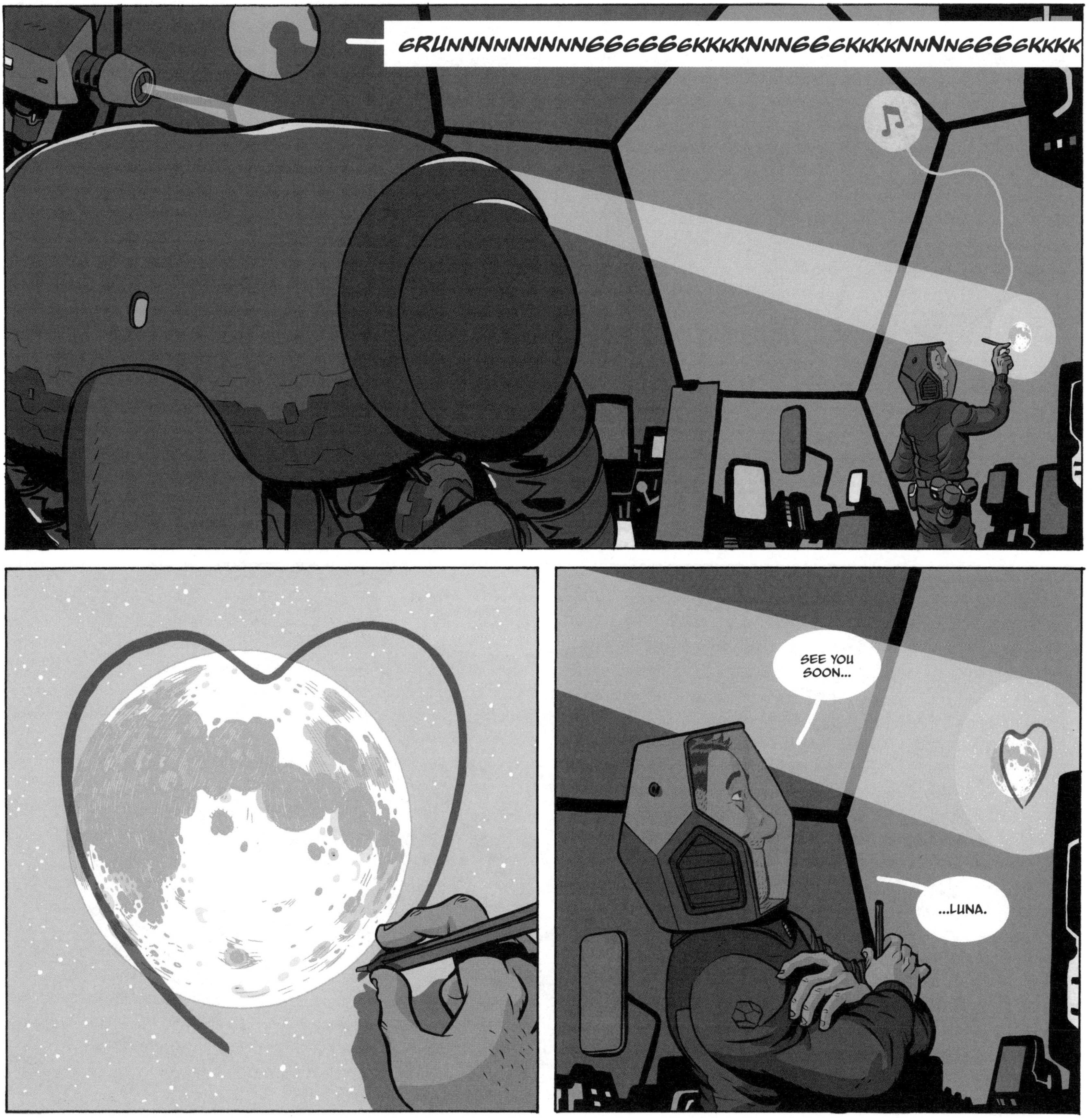
GRUNNNNNNNNNNGGGGGKKKKNNNGGGKKKKKNNNGGGGKKKK
SEE YOU SOON...
...LUNA.

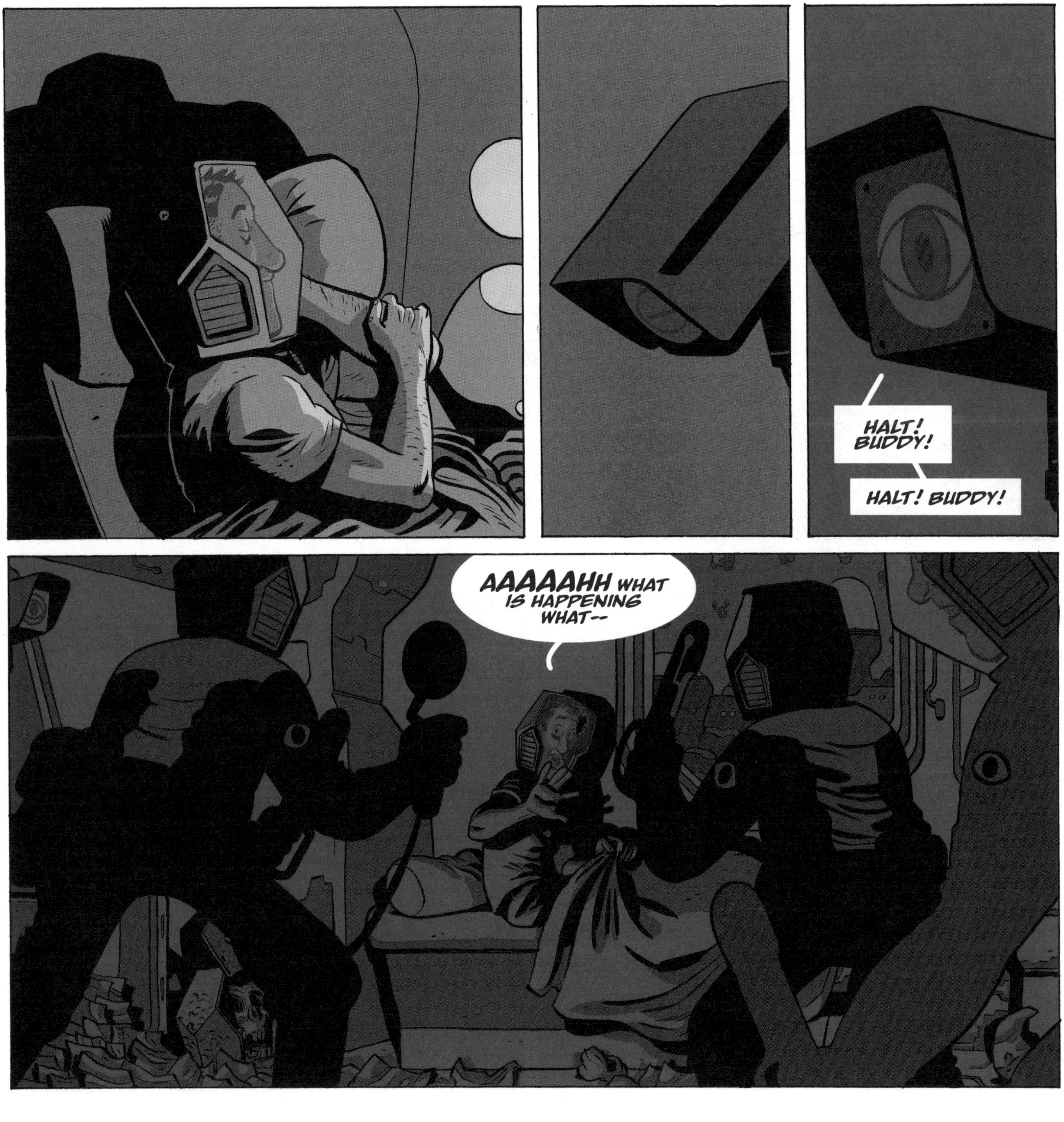
HALT! BUDDY!
HALT! BUDDY!
AAAAAHH WHAT IS HAPPENING WHAT--

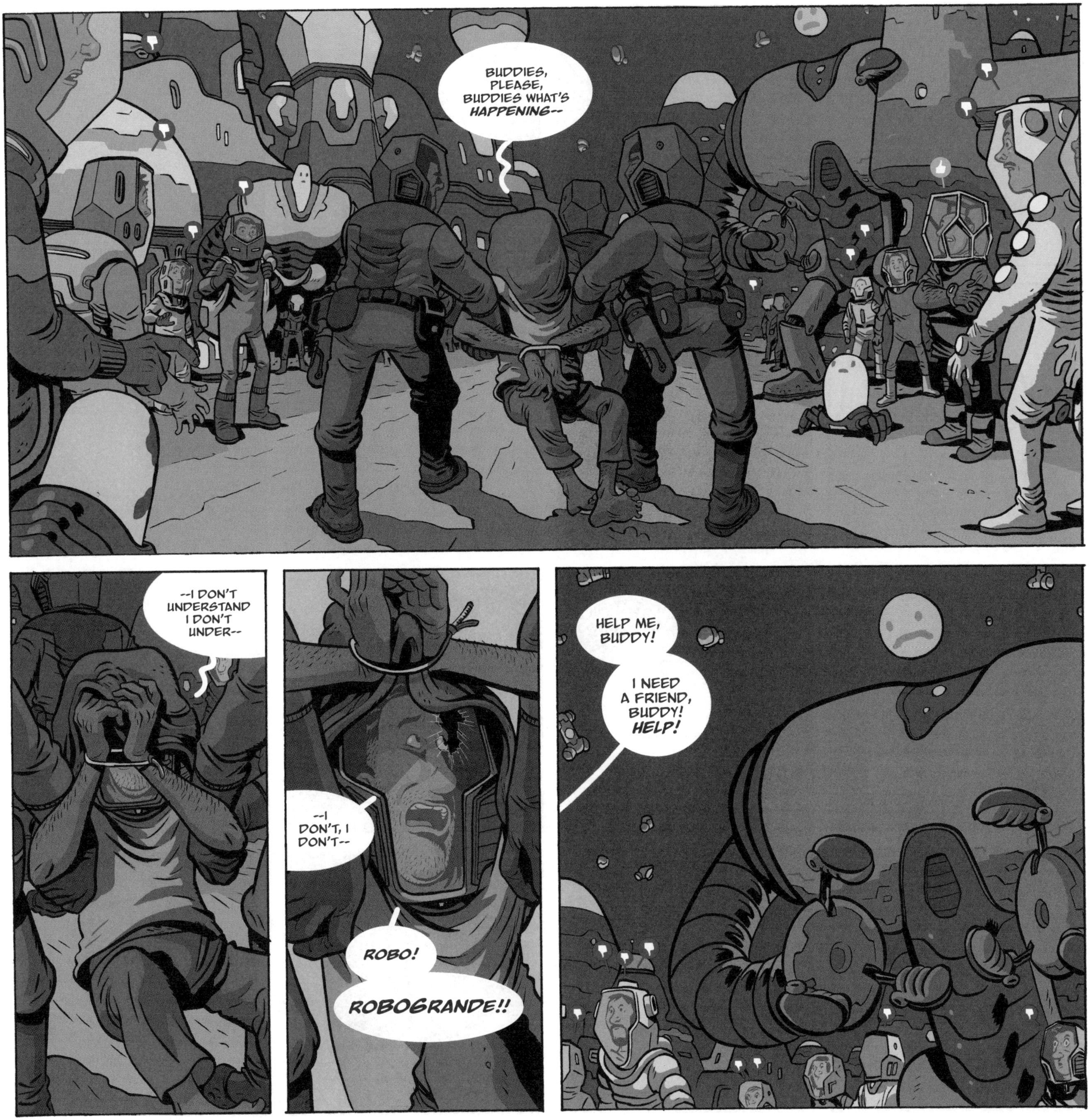
BUDDIES, PLEASE, BUDDIES WHAT'S *HAPPENING*--
--I DON'T UNDERSTAND I DON'T UNDER--
--I DON'T, I DON'T--
ROBO!
ROBOGRANDE!!
HELP ME, BUDDY!
I NEED A FRIEND, BUDDY! ***HELP!***

I AM VERY DISAPPOINTED, BUDDY.
LIKE, MEGA-DOWNVOTING HERE.
DON'T YOU EVER JUST WANT TO SEE WHAT HAPPENS?!?
PROCESSING.
GRRGGGGGH--
DON'T TASE ME BRO DON'T--
WHAT DID YOU JUST SAY?
WE DON'T SAY THAT WORD ANYMORE. BUDDY.

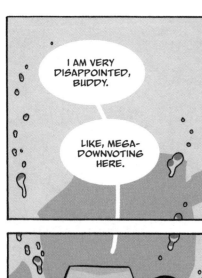

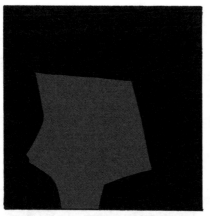

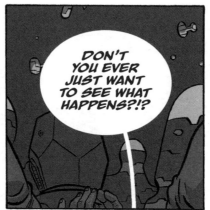

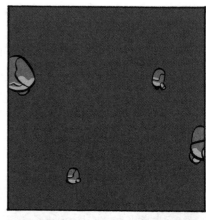

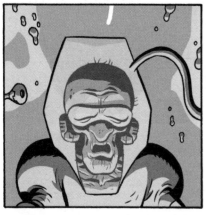

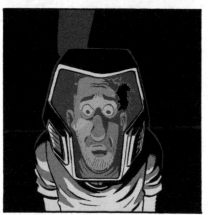

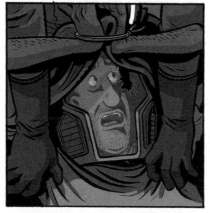

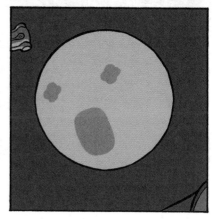

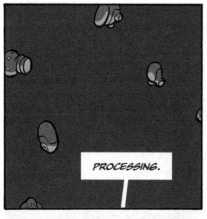

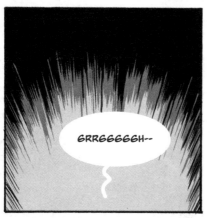

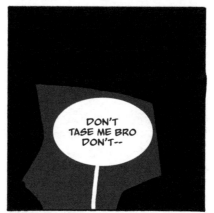

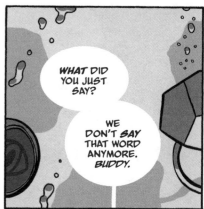

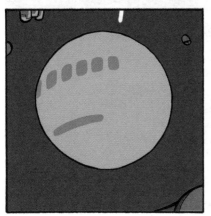

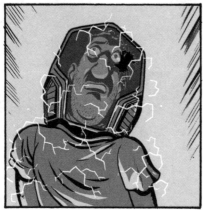

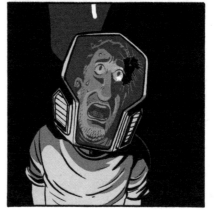

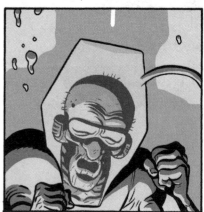

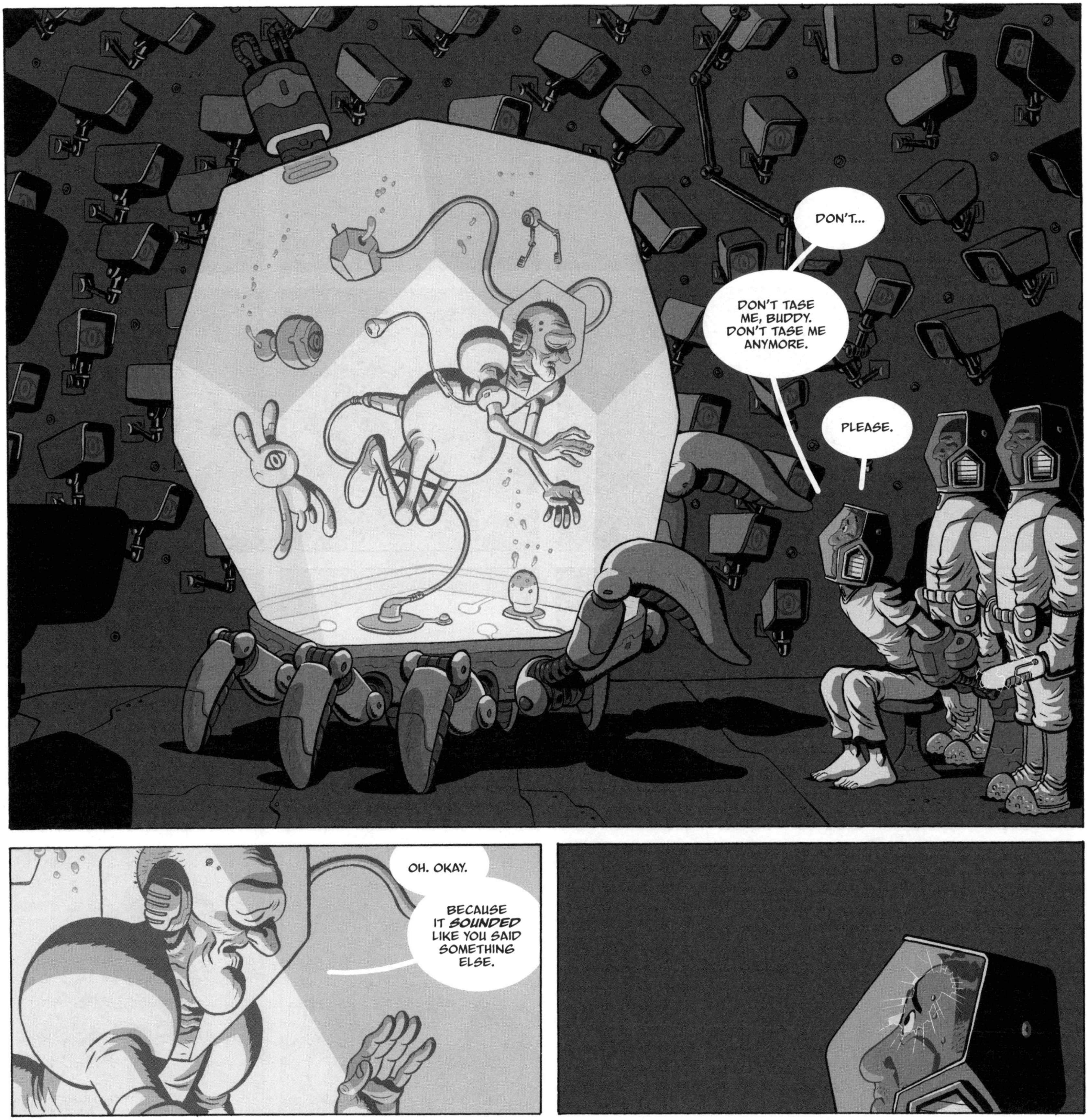
DON'T...
DON'T TASE ME, BUDDY. DON'T TASE ME ANYMORE.
PLEASE.
OH. OKAY.
BECAUSE IT *SOUNDED* LIKE YOU SAID SOMETHING ELSE.

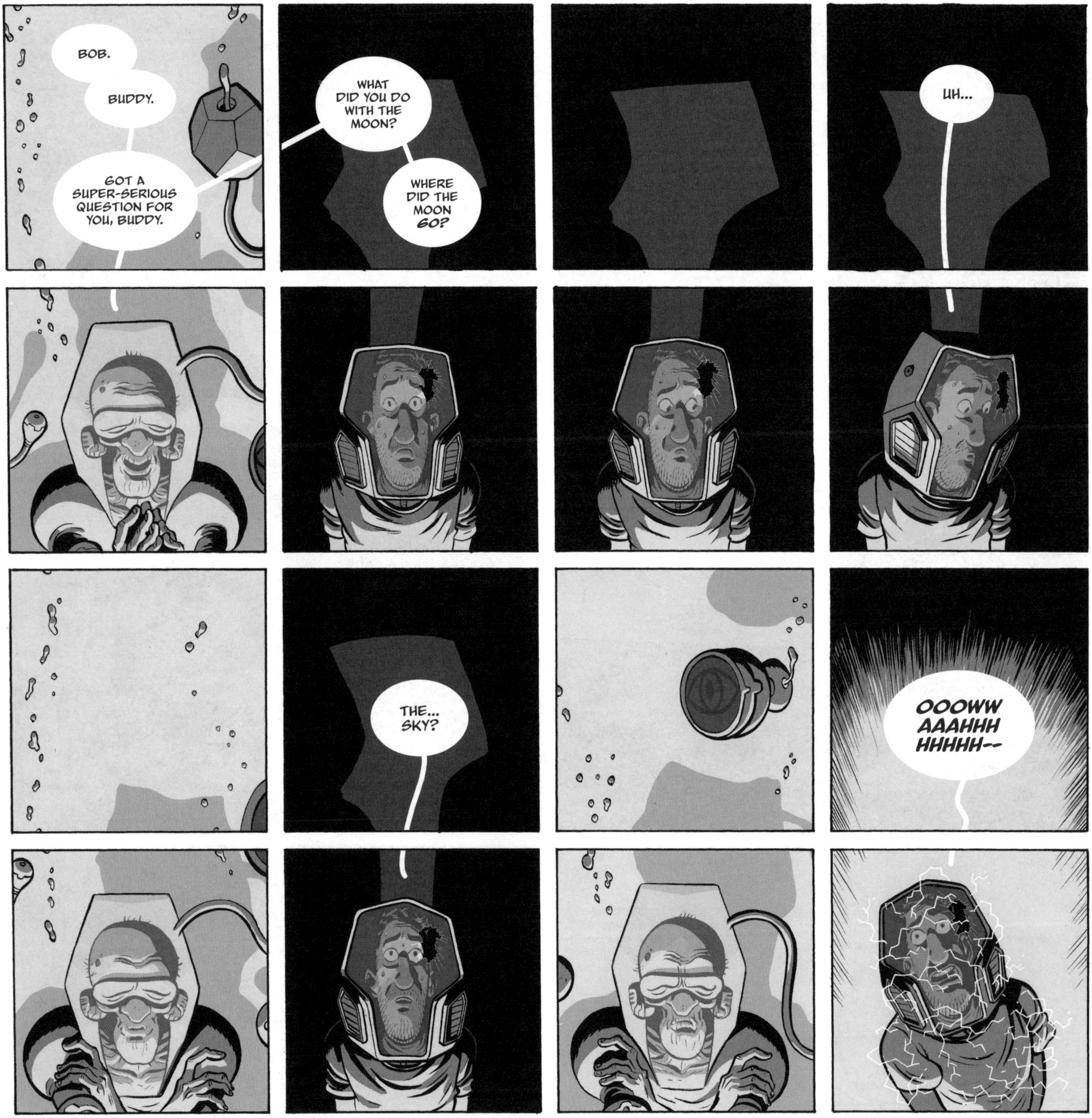
BOB.
BUDDY.
GOT A SUPER-SERIOUS QUESTION FOR YOU, BUDDY.
WHAT DID YOU DO WITH THE MOON?
WHERE DID THE MOON GO?
UH...
THE... SKY?
OOOWW AAAHHH HHHHH--

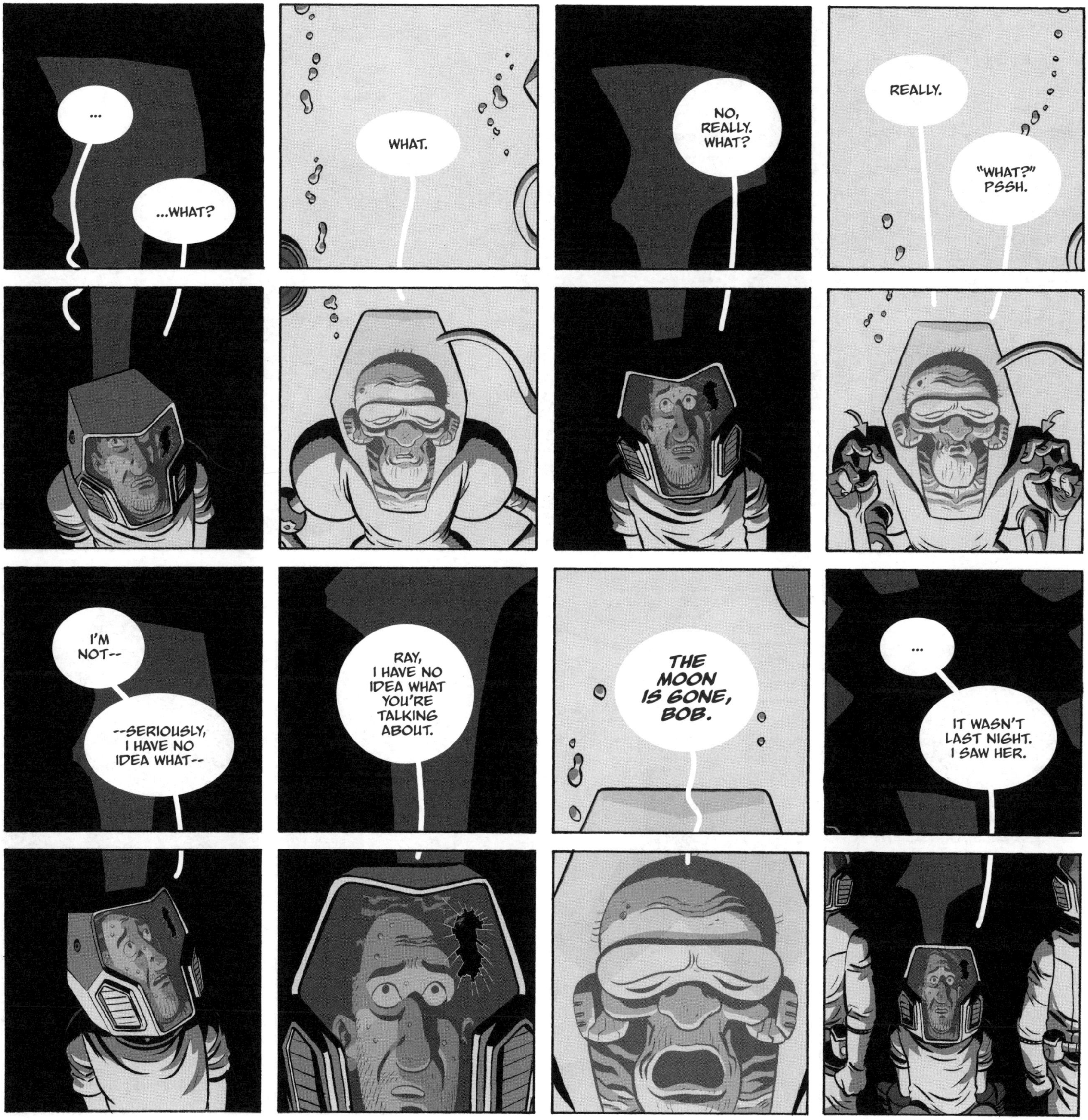
...
...WHAT?
WHAT.
NO, REALLY. WHAT?
REALLY.
"WHAT?" PSSH.
I'M NOT--
--SERIOUSLY, I HAVE NO IDEA WHAT--
RAY, I HAVE NO IDEA WHAT YOU'RE TALKING ABOUT.
THE MOON IS GONE, BOB.
...
IT WASN'T LAST NIGHT. I SAW HER.

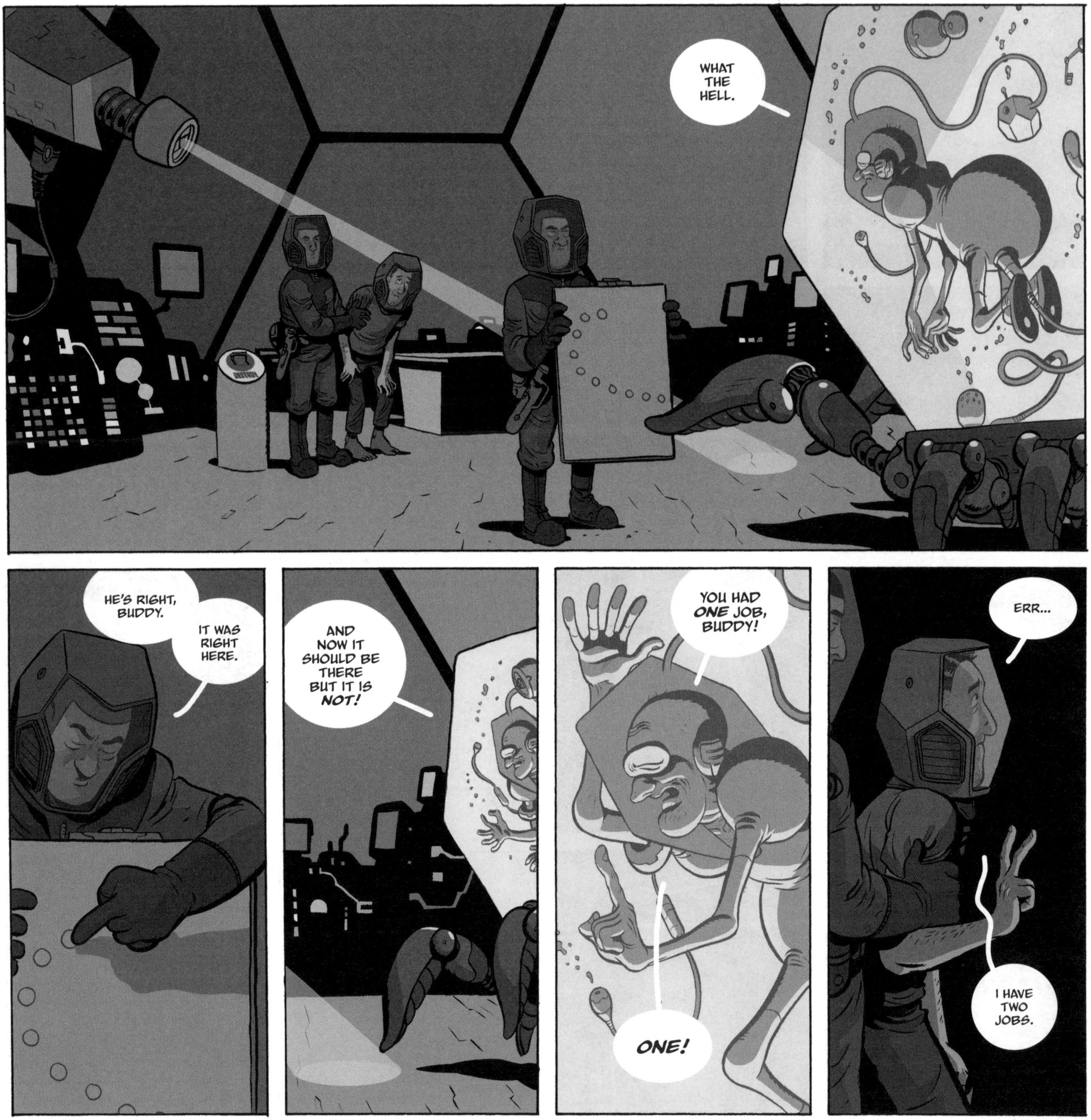
WHAT THE HELL.
HE'S RIGHT, BUDDY.
IT WAS RIGHT HERE.
AND NOW IT SHOULD BE THERE BUT IT IS **NOT!**
YOU HAD **ONE** JOB, BUDDY!
ONE!
ERR...
I HAVE TWO JOBS.

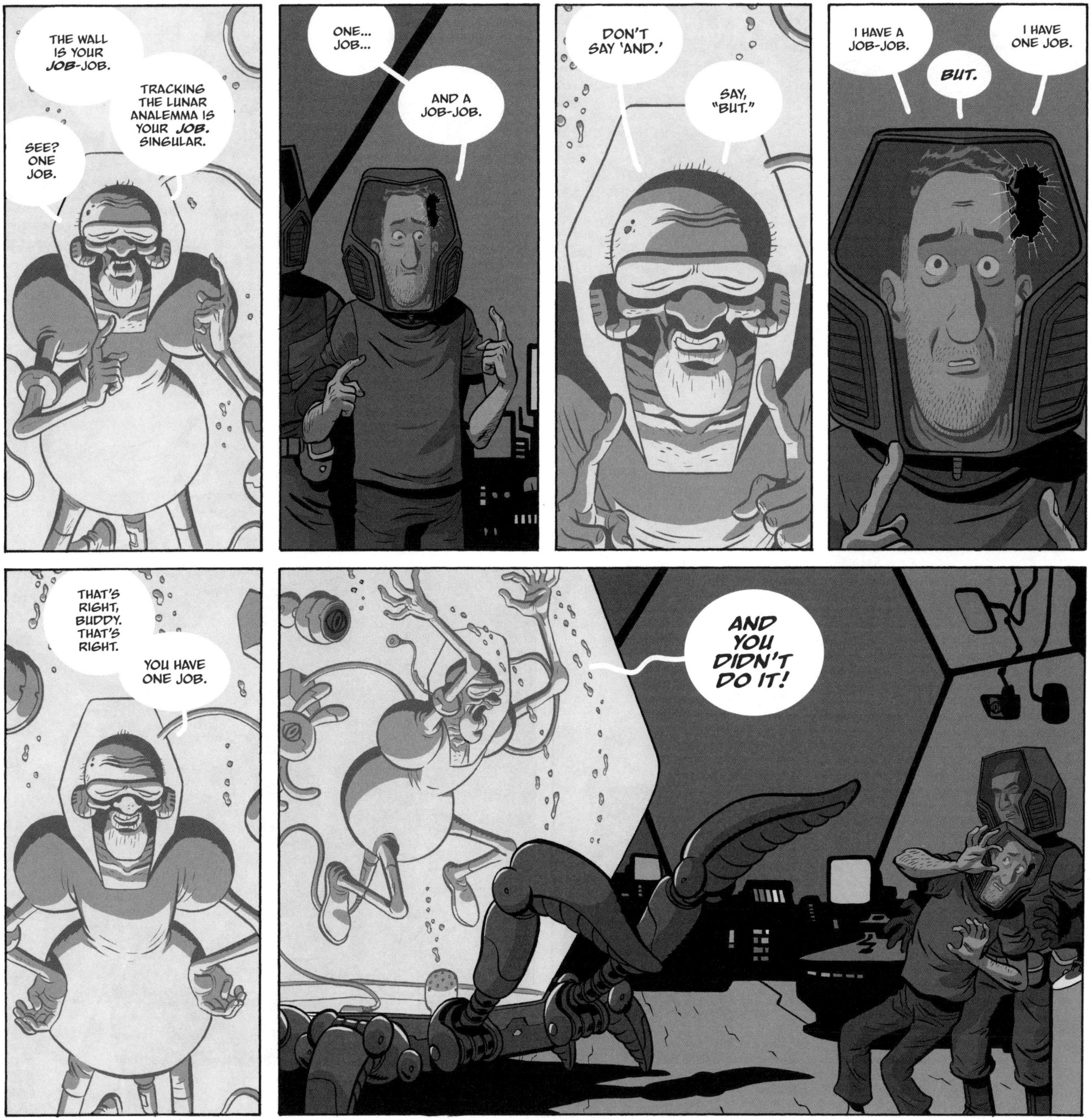
THE WALL IS YOUR JOB-JOB.
TRACKING THE LUNAR ANALEMMA IS YOUR JOB. SINGULAR.
SEE? ONE JOB.
ONE... JOB...
AND A JOB-JOB.
DON'T SAY 'AND.'
SAY, "BUT."
I HAVE A JOB-JOB.
BUT.
I HAVE ONE JOB.
THAT'S RIGHT, BUDDY. THAT'S RIGHT.
YOU HAVE ONE JOB.
AND YOU DIDN'T DO IT!

OH.
YOU GUYS... SAW... ALL THAT?
Y'KNOW WHAT?
BUDDIES... BRING IN OUR... SPECIAL... BUDDY.

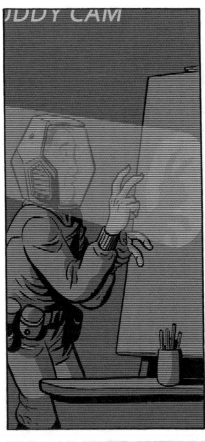

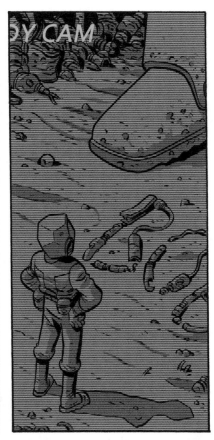

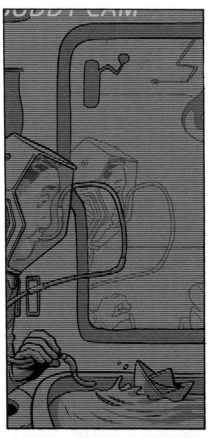

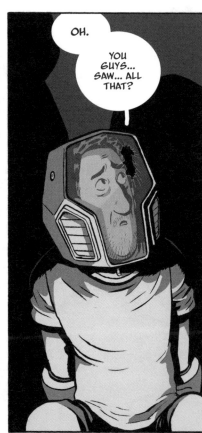

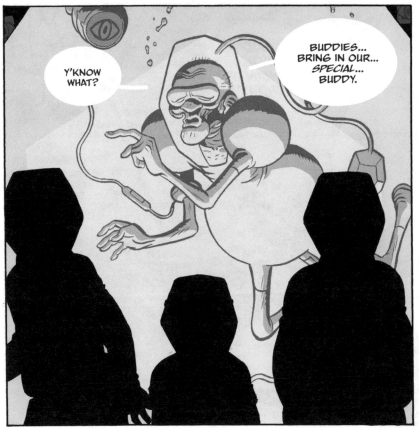

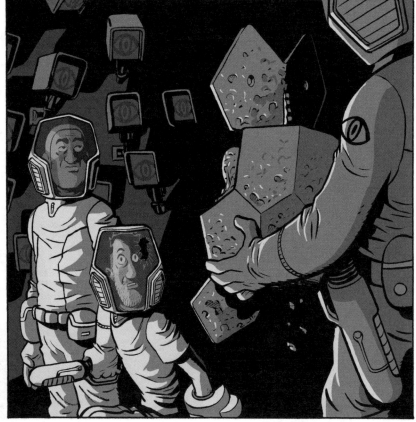

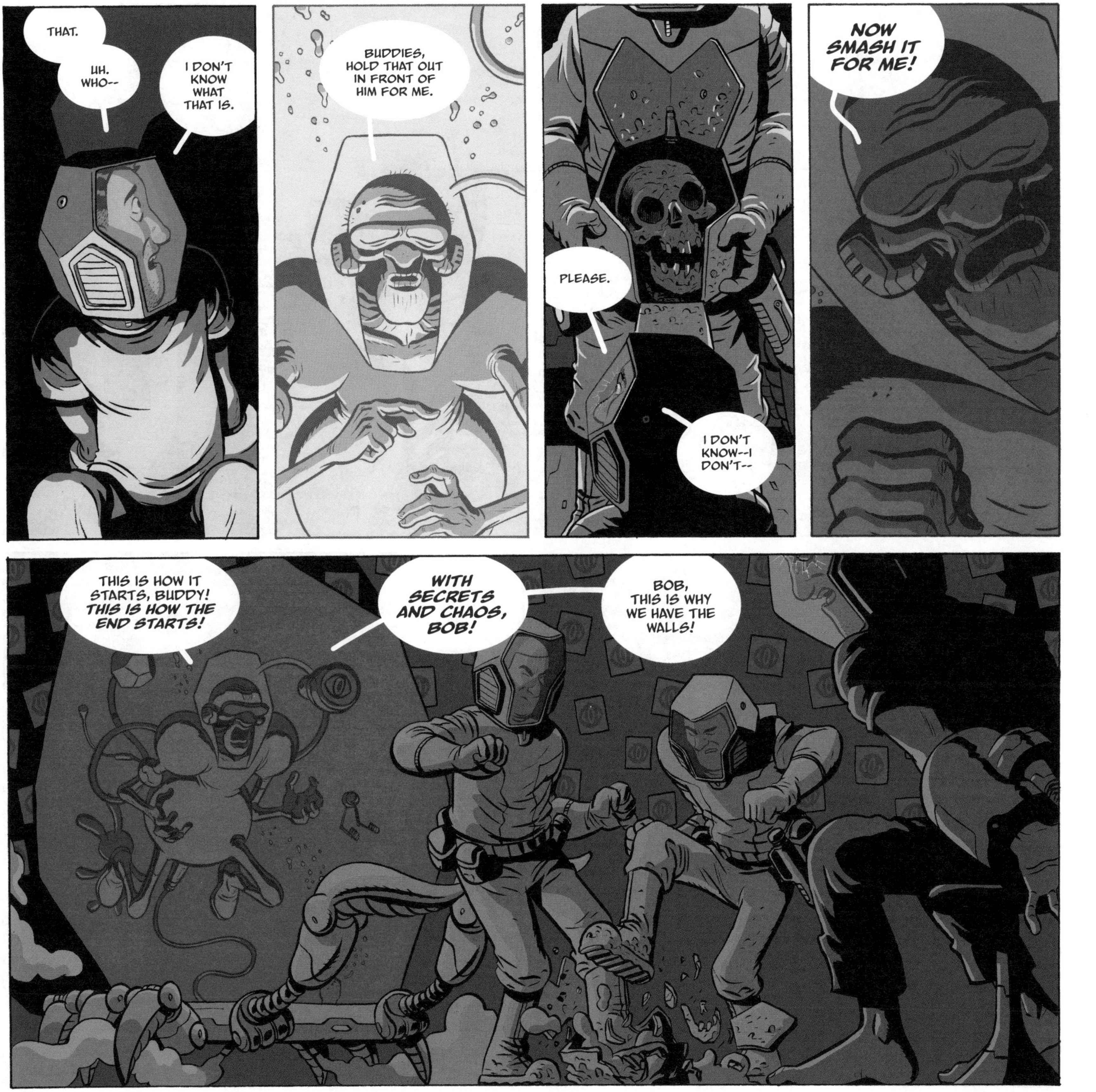
THAT.
UH. WHO--
I DON'T KNOW WHAT THAT IS.
BUDDIES, HOLD THAT OUT IN FRONT OF HIM FOR ME.
PLEASE.
I DON'T KNOW--I DON'T--
NOW SMASH IT FOR ME!
THIS IS HOW IT STARTS, BUDDY! THIS IS HOW THE END STARTS!
WITH SECRETS AND CHAOS, BOB!
BOB, THIS IS WHY WE HAVE THE WALLS!

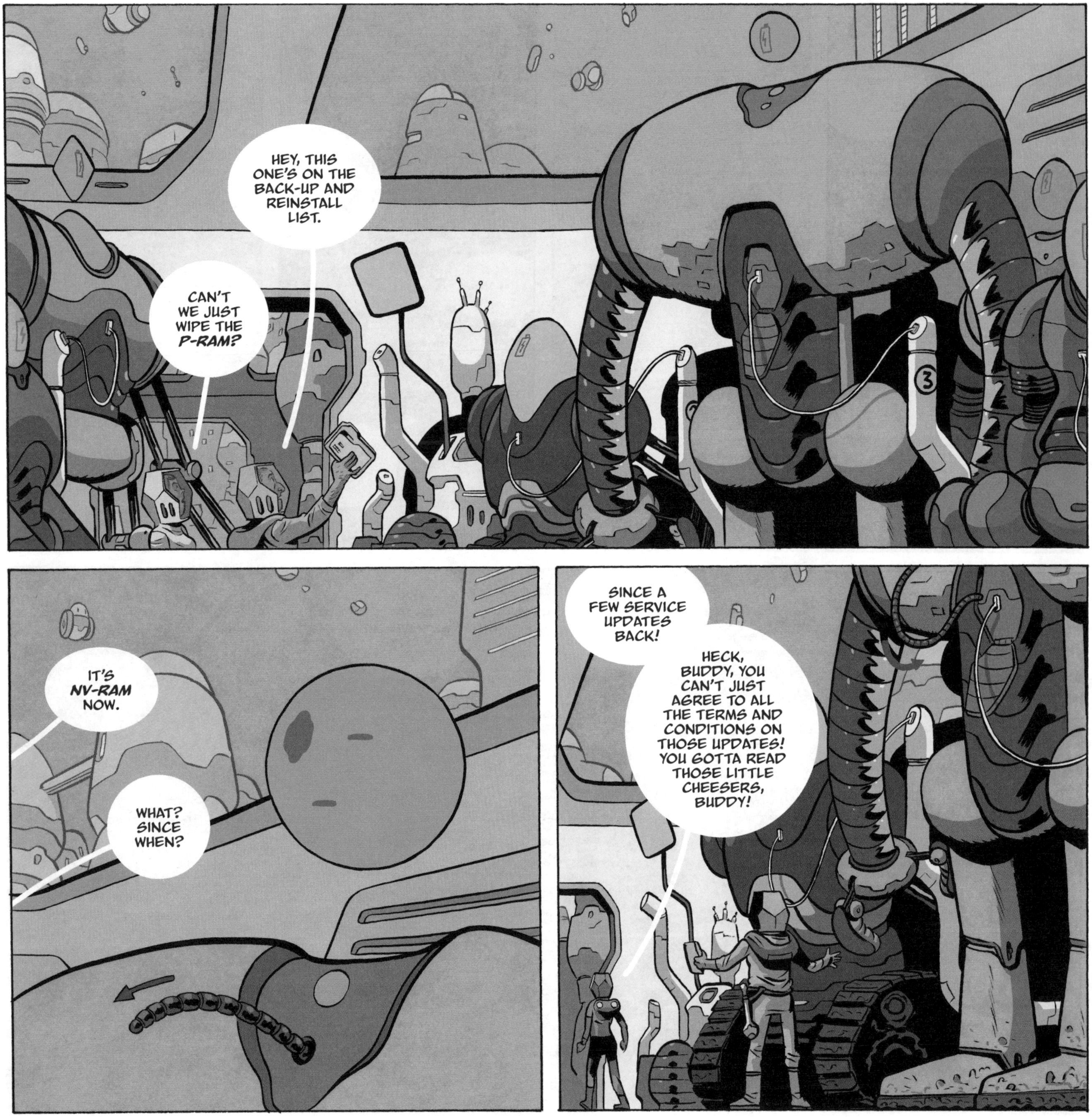
HEY, THIS ONE'S ON THE BACK-UP AND REINSTALL LIST.
CAN'T WE JUST WIPE THE *P-RAM?*
IT'S *NV-RAM* NOW.
WHAT? SINCE WHEN?
SINCE A FEW SERVICE UPDATES BACK!
HECK, BUDDY, YOU CAN'T JUST AGREE TO ALL THE TERMS AND CONDITIONS ON THOSE UPDATES! YOU GOTTA READ THOSE LITTLE CHEESERS, BUDDY!

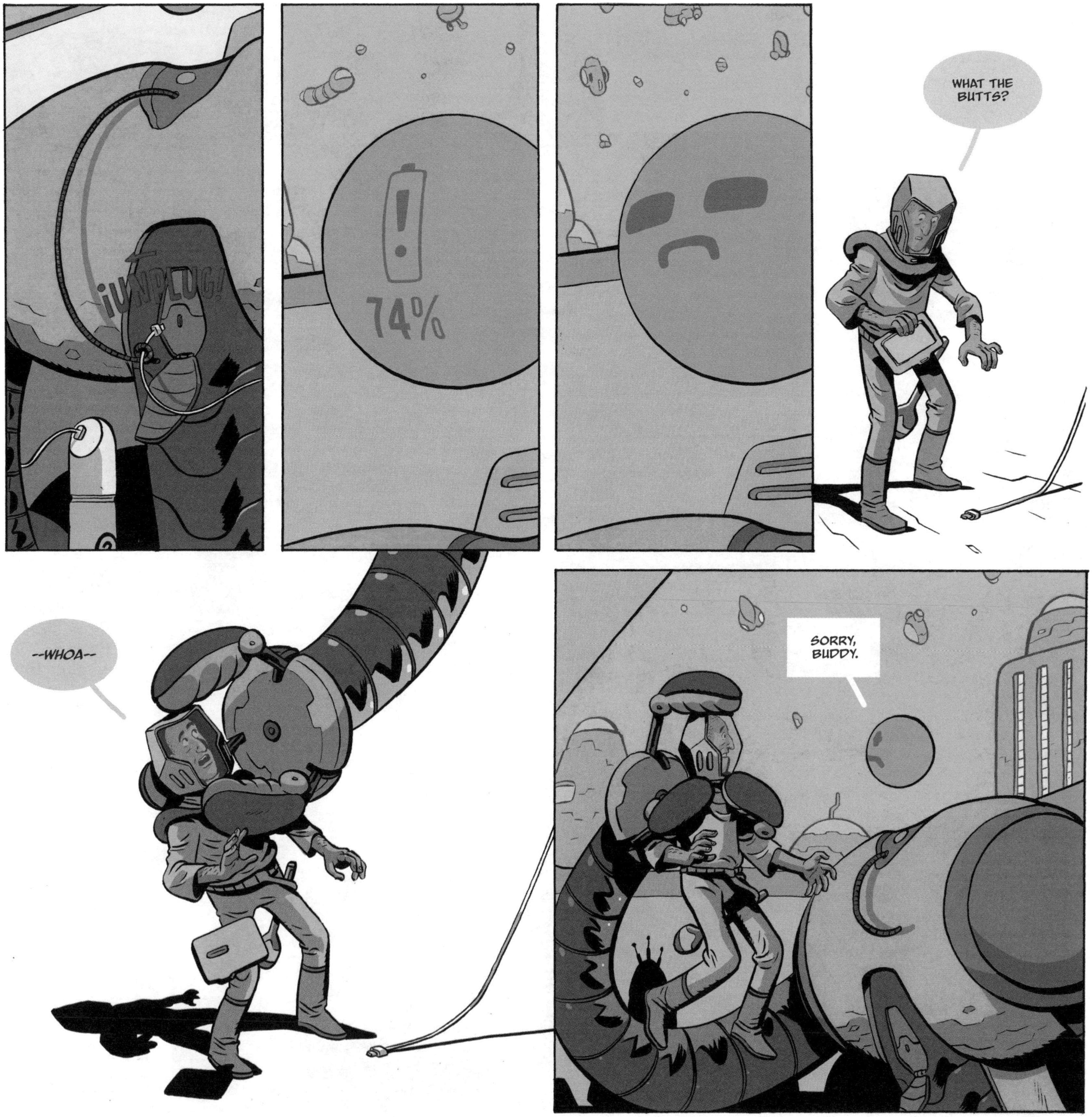

¡UNPLUG!
74%
WHAT THE BUTTS?
--WHOA--
SORRY, BUDDY.

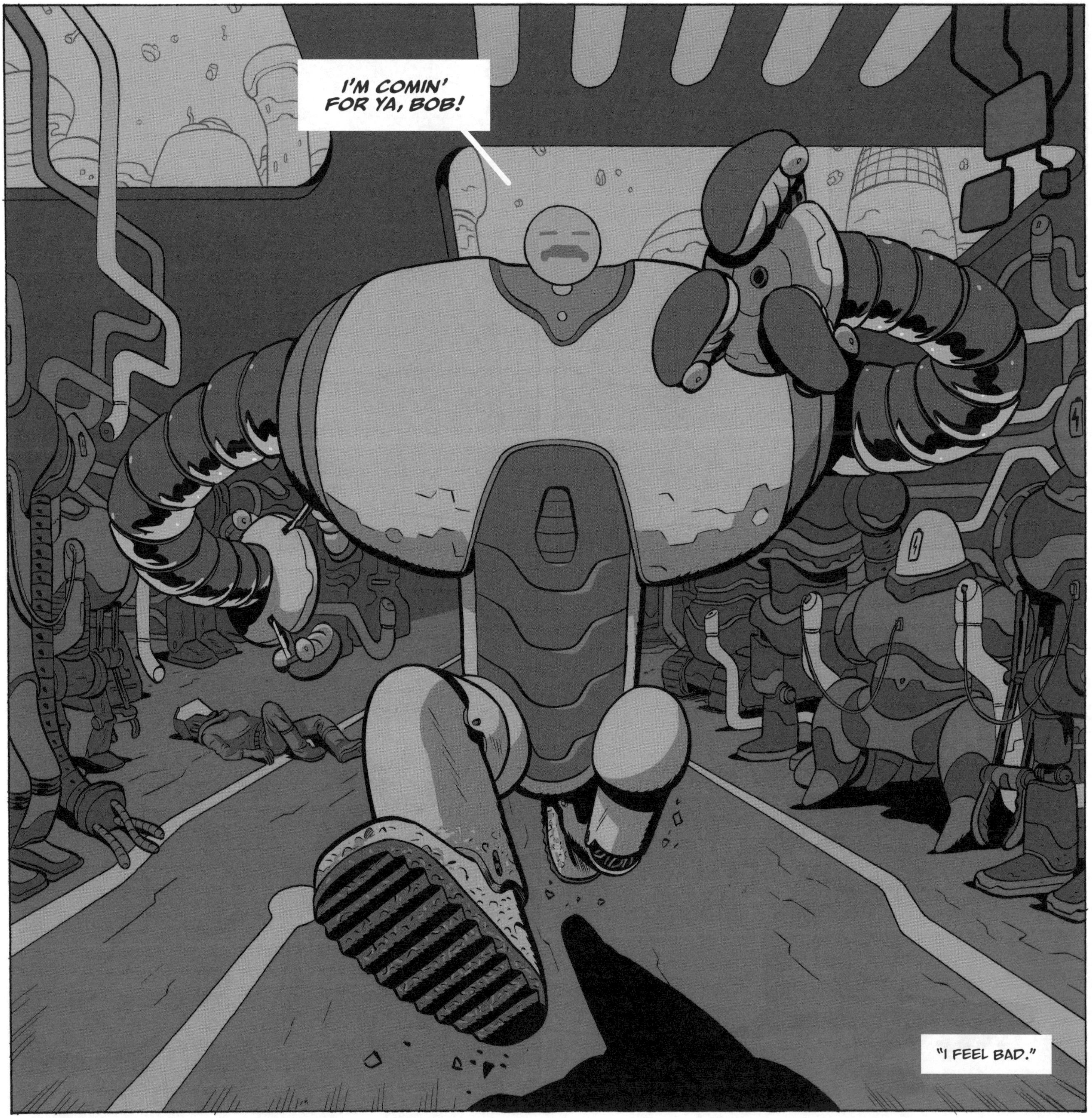
I'M COMIN' FOR YA, BOB!
"I FEEL BAD."

I MEAN IT. RAY. BUDDIES.
I FEEL REALLY, REALLY BAD.
I MEAN-- BAD.
REALLY, REALLY, REALLY.
BAD.
"THE BRAIN AND THE MIND ARE TWO DISCRETE ENTITIES.
"GUILT AND SHAME ARE TWO DISCRETE ENTITIES."
BOTH FEELINGS, BUDDY, ARE THE RESULT OF WHO YOU ARE VERSUS WHAT YOU DO.
BOB.
...
RAY, I...
I DON'T KNOW WHAT THOSE WORDS MEAN.
BOB-- BUDDY--
IT MEANS--

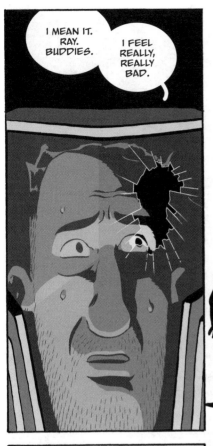

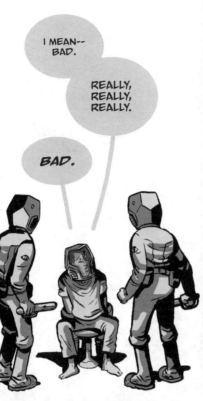

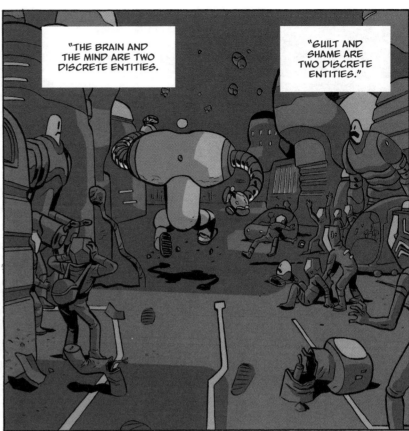

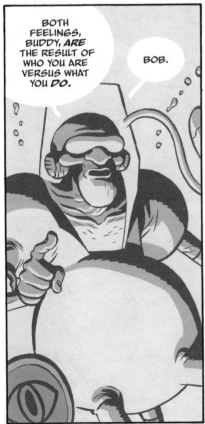

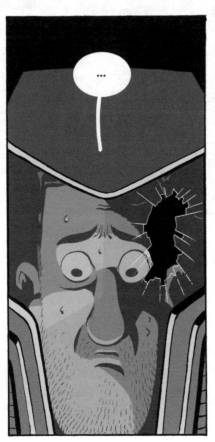

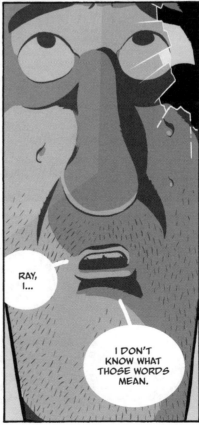

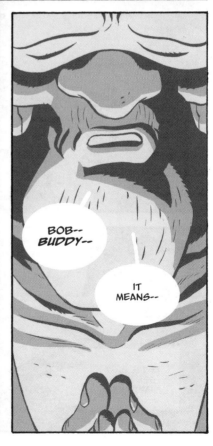

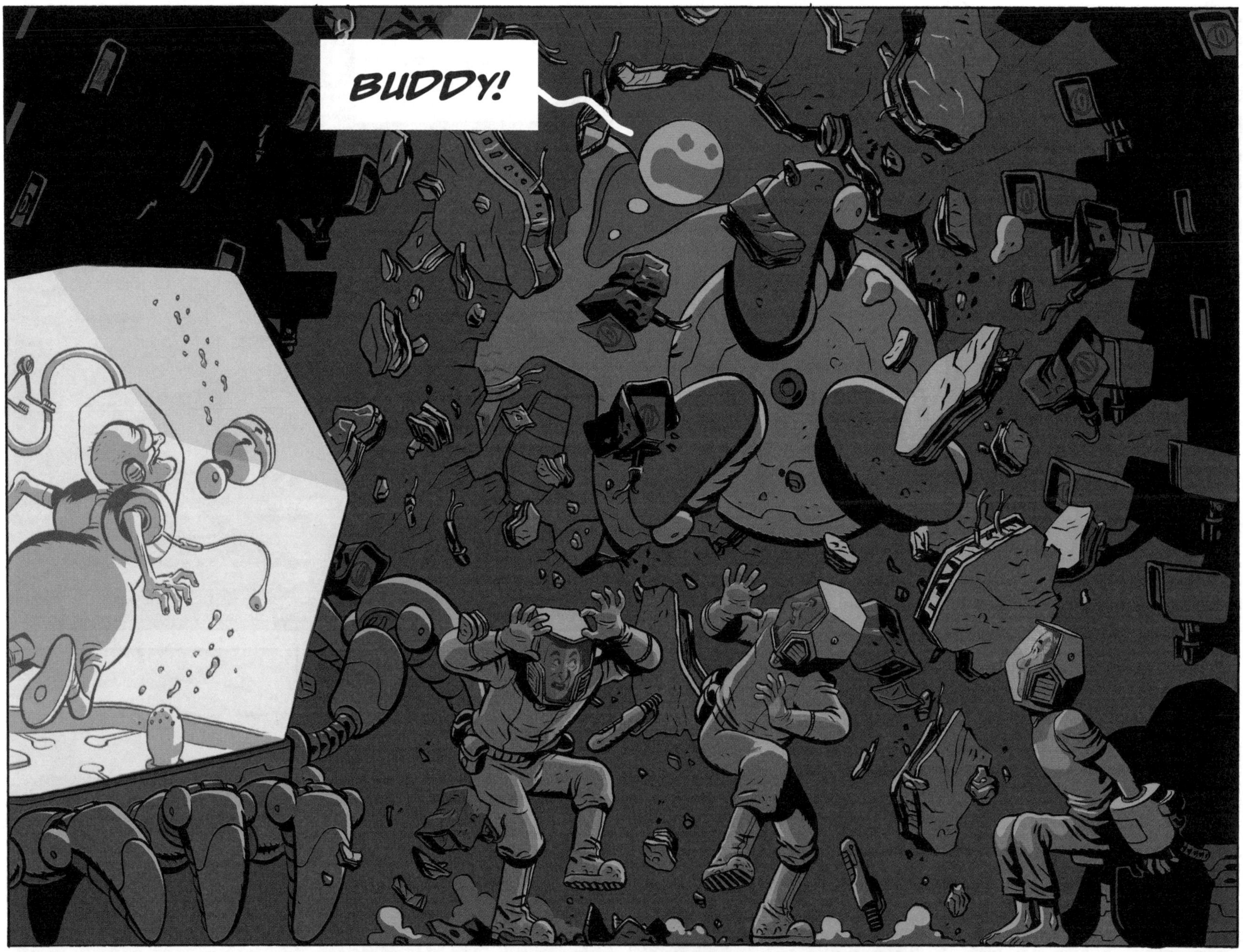
BUDDY!

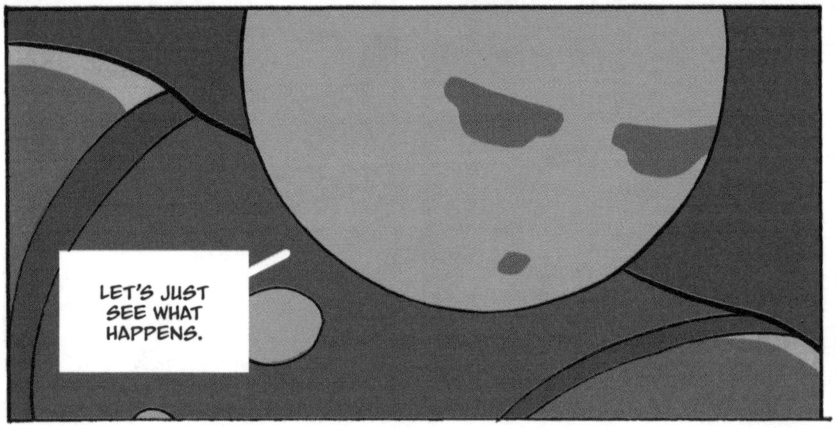
LET'S JUST SEE WHAT HAPPENS.

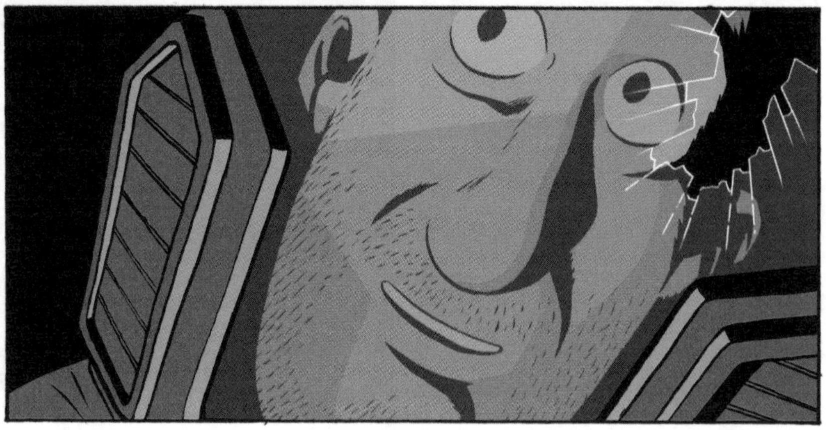

BUDDY, HOW CAN THE MOON BE GONE?

I DON'T KNOW, THAT'S THE THING. THEY BLAME ME FOR IT, THOUGH.

SEE, LOOK. IT'S--

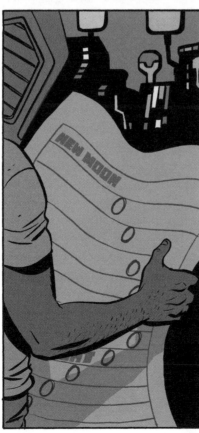

NEW MOON

I DON'T GET IT. SOMETHING HAPPENED.

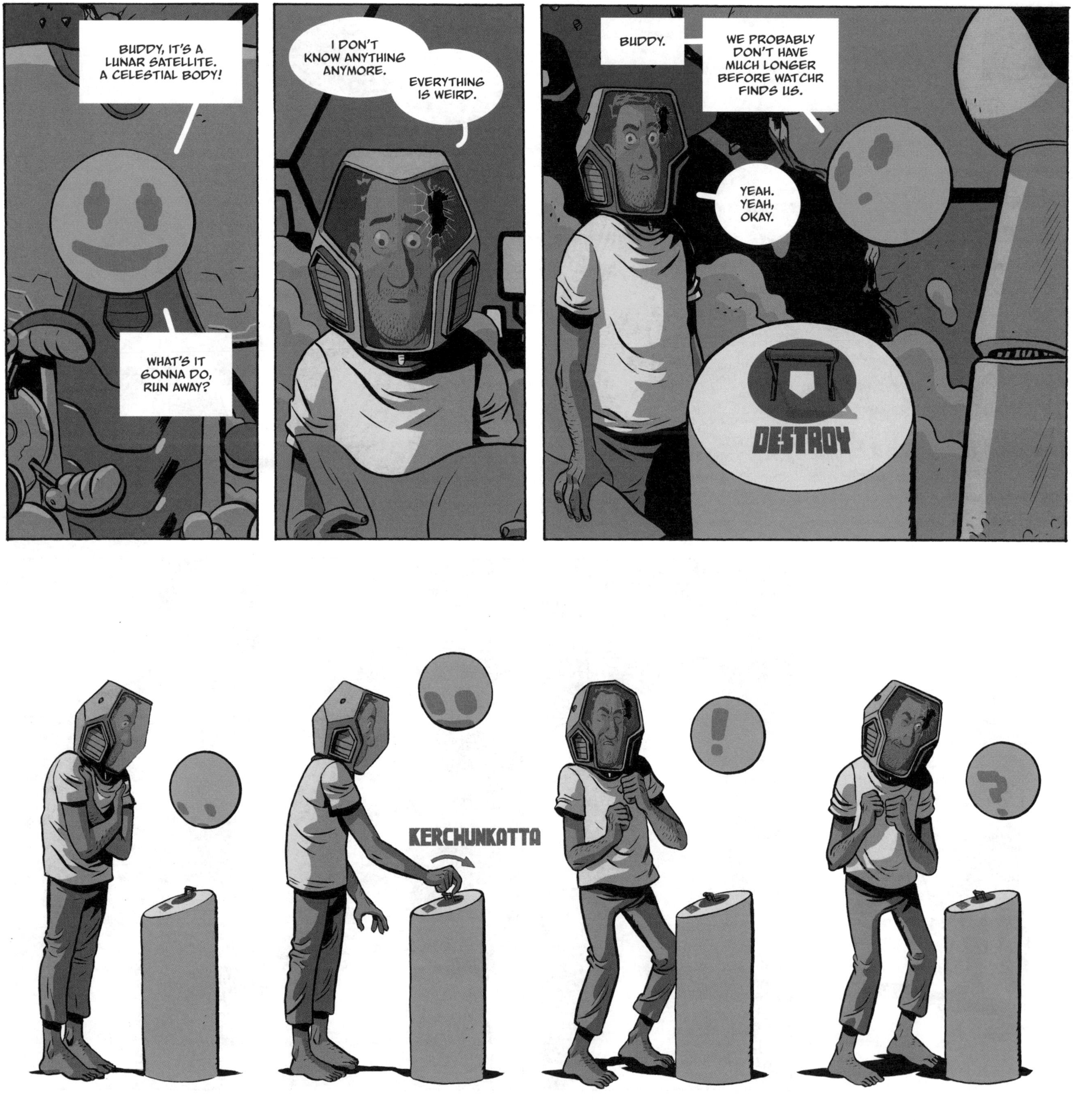
BUDDY, IT'S A LUNAR SATELLITE. A CELESTIAL BODY!
WHAT'S IT GONNA DO, RUN AWAY?
I DON'T KNOW ANYTHING ANYMORE.
EVERYTHING IS WEIRD.
BUDDY.
WE PROBABLY DON'T HAVE MUCH LONGER BEFORE WATCHR FINDS US.
YEAH. YEAH, OKAY.
DESTROY
KERCHUNKATTA

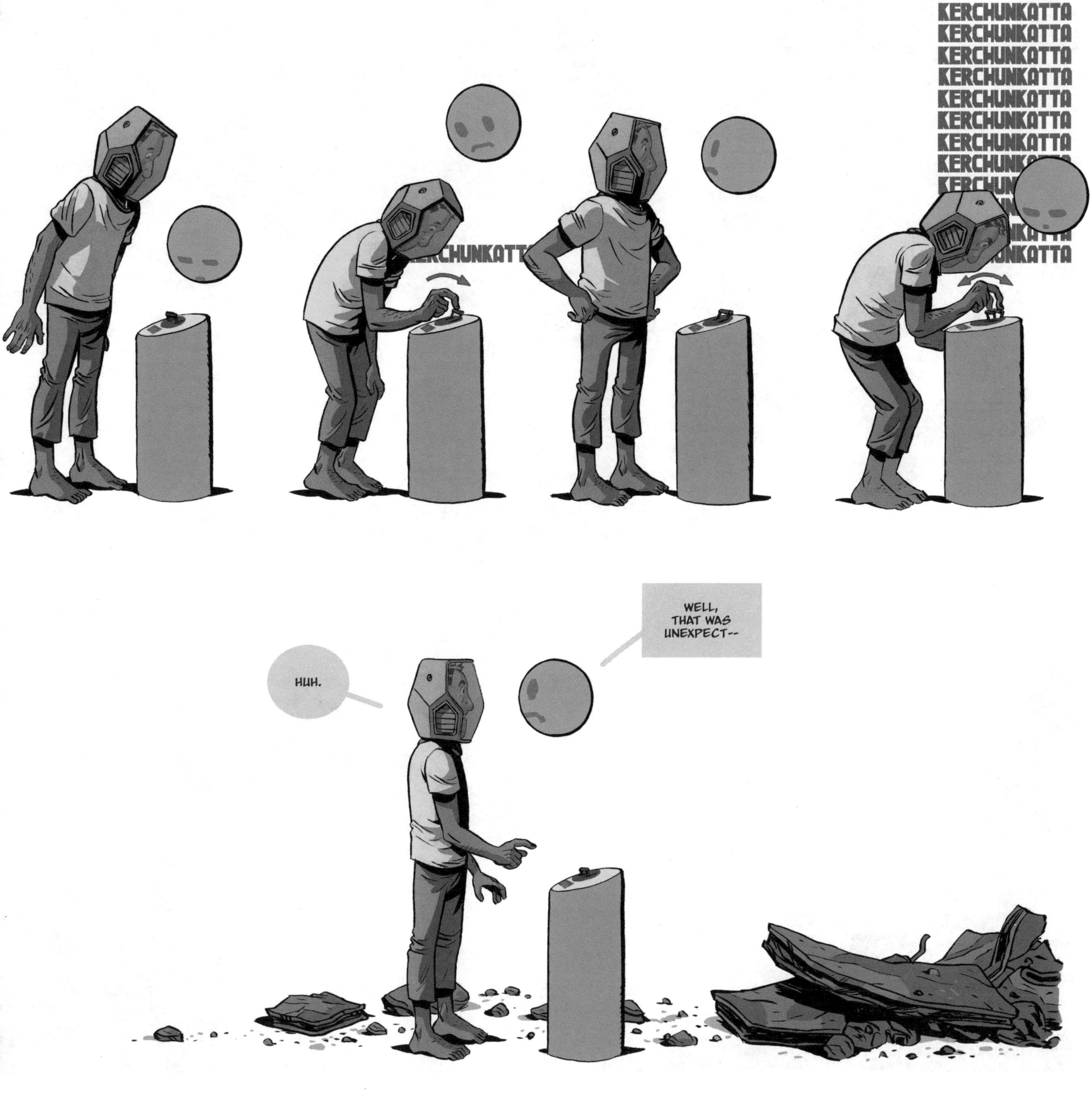
KERCHUNKATTA
KERCHUNKATTA
KERCHUNKATTA
KERCHUNKATTA
KERCHUNKATTA
KERCHUNKATTA
KERCHUNKATTA
KERCHUNKATTA
HUH.
WELL, THAT WAS UNEXPECT--

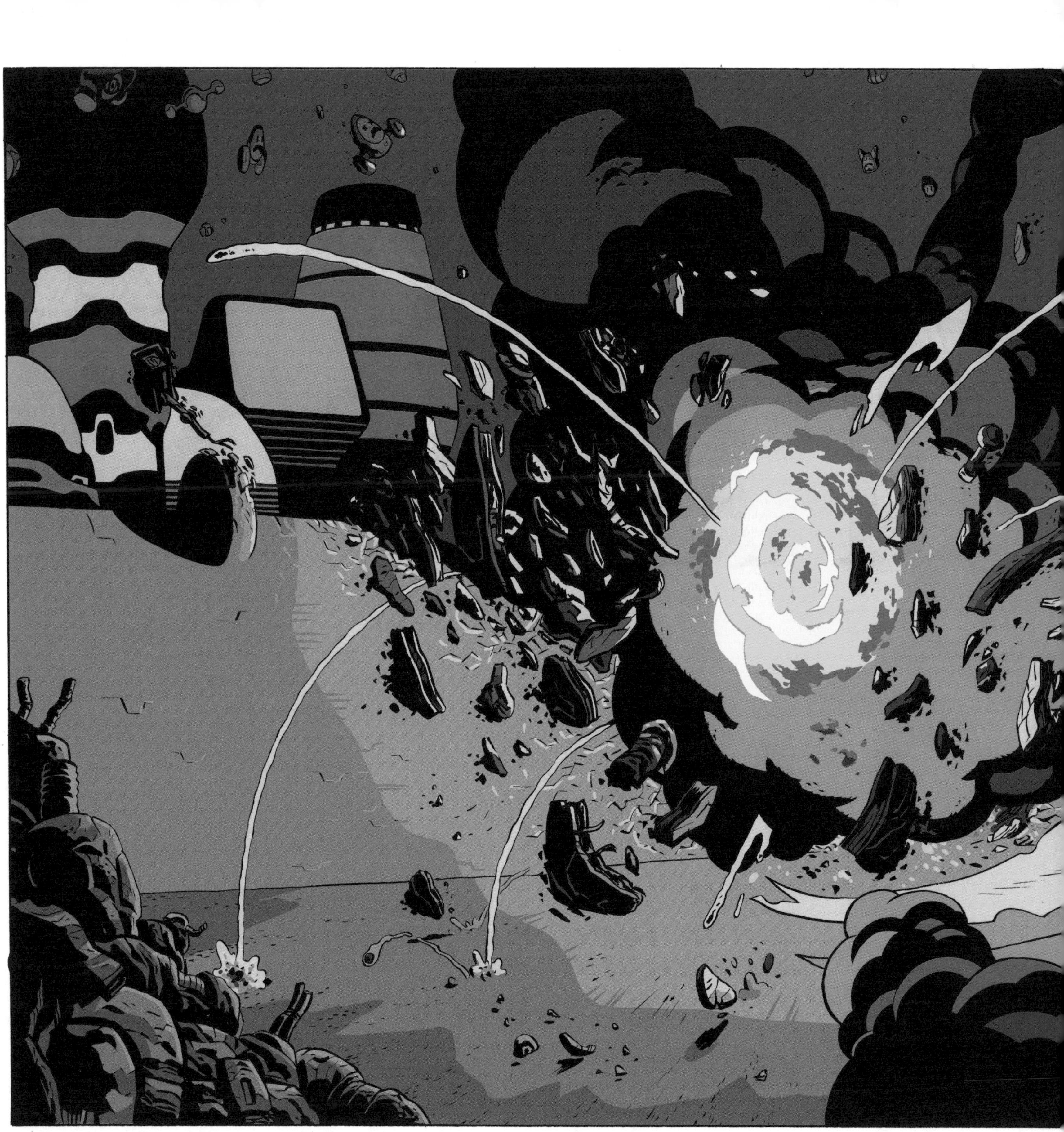

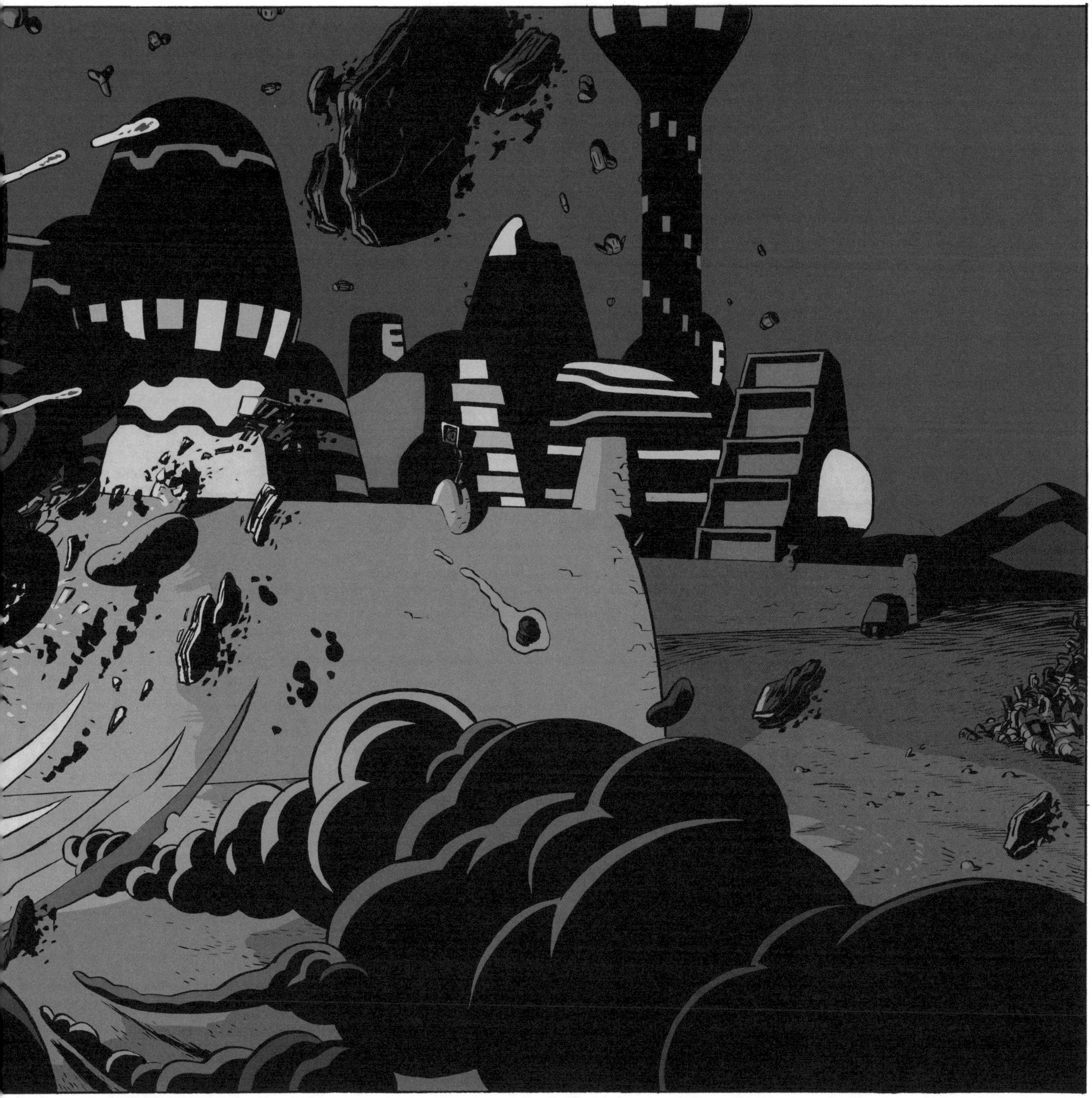
E
E

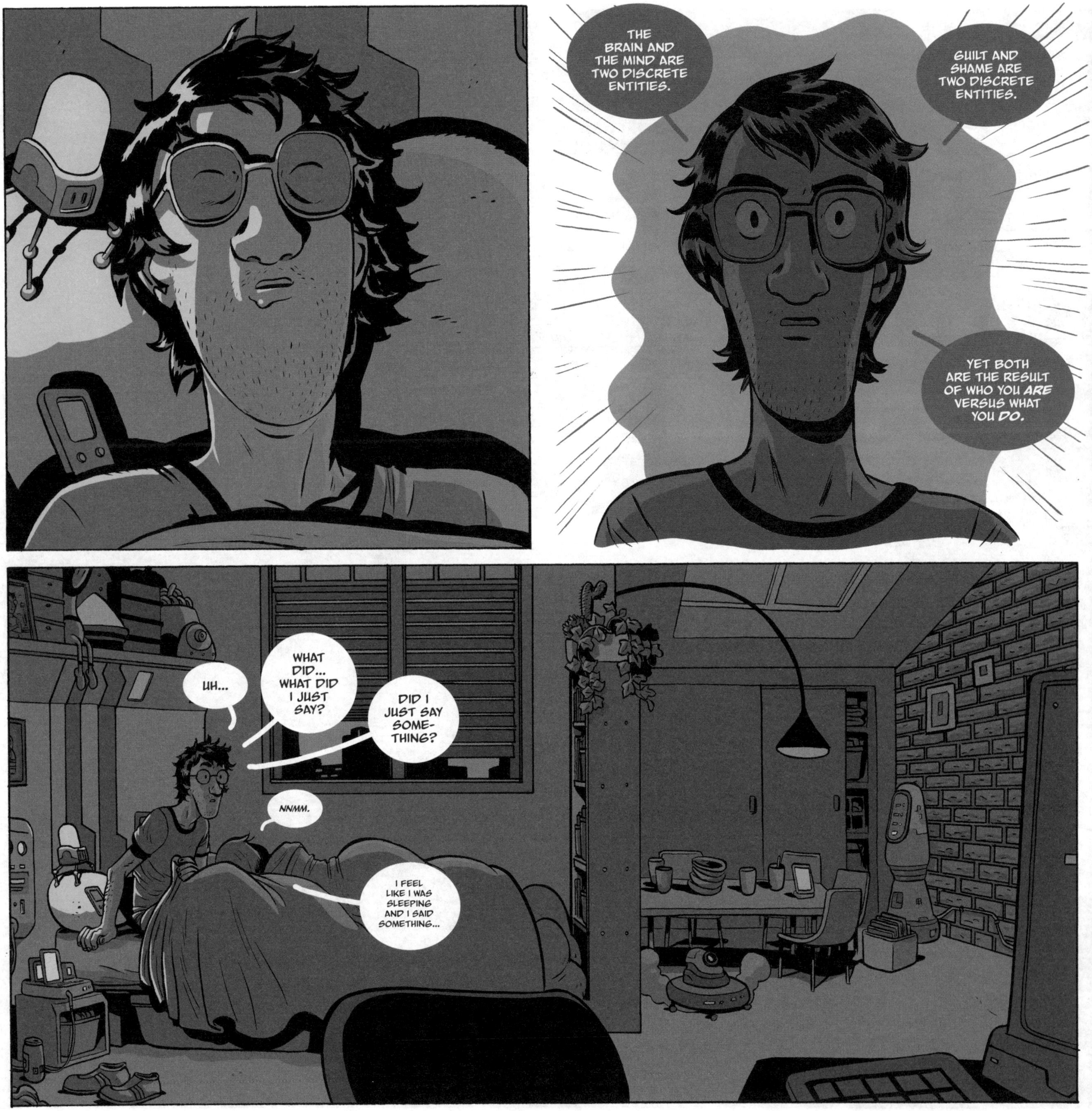
THE BRAIN AND THE MIND ARE TWO DISCRETE ENTITIES.
GUILT AND SHAME ARE TWO DISCRETE ENTITIES.
YET BOTH ARE THE RESULT OF WHO YOU *ARE* VERSUS WHAT YOU *DO*.
UH...
WHAT DID... WHAT DID I JUST SAY?
DID I JUST SAY SOME-THING?
NNMM.
I FEEL LIKE I WAS SLEEPING AND I SAID SOMETHING...

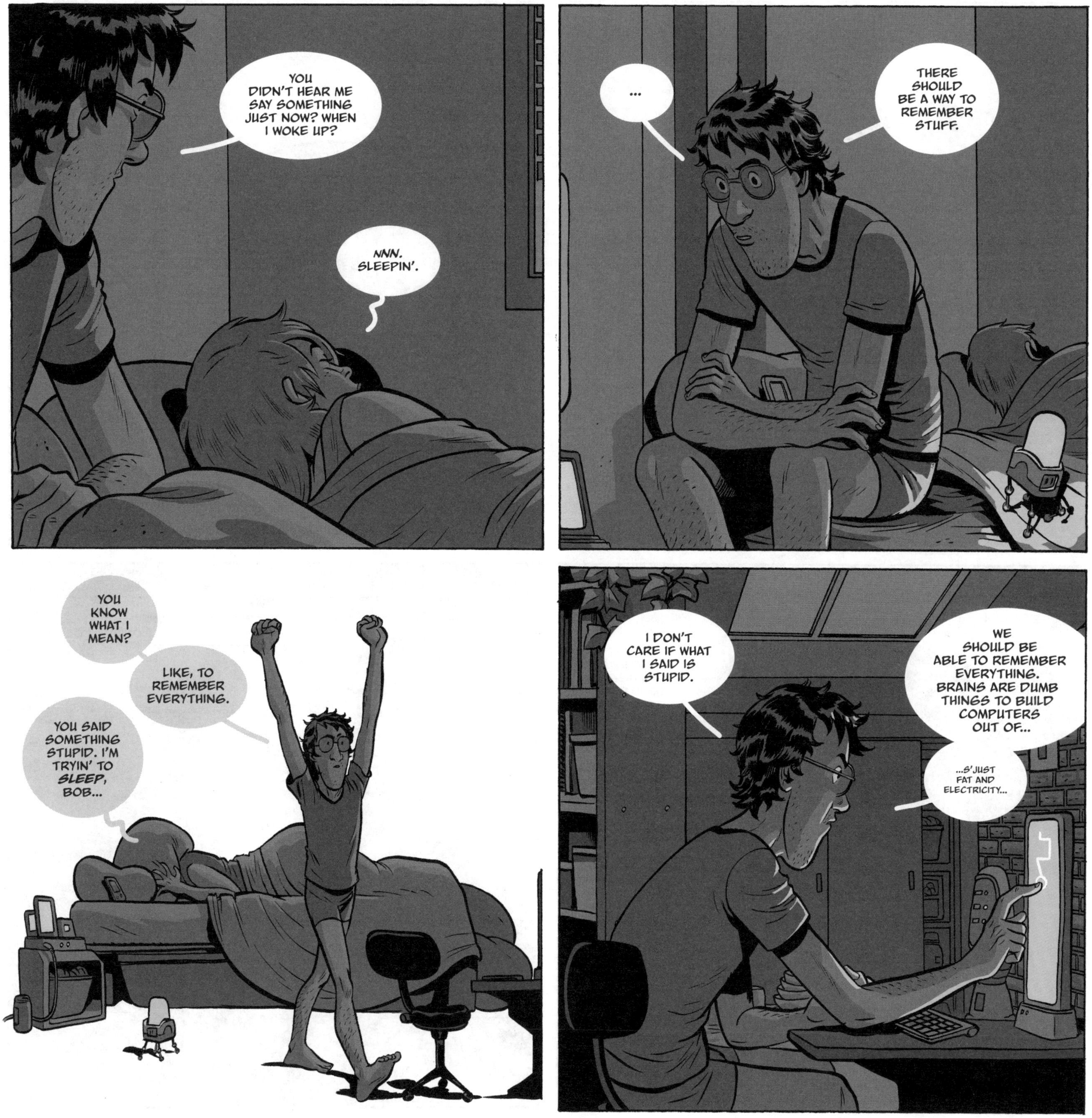
YOU DIDN'T HEAR ME SAY SOMETHING JUST NOW? WHEN I WOKE UP?
NNN. SLEEPIN'.
...
THERE SHOULD BE A WAY TO REMEMBER STUFF.
YOU KNOW WHAT I MEAN?
LIKE, TO REMEMBER EVERYTHING.
YOU SAID SOMETHING STUPID. I'M TRYIN' TO *SLEEP*, BOB...
I DON'T CARE IF WHAT I SAID IS STUPID.
WE SHOULD BE ABLE TO REMEMBER EVERYTHING. BRAINS ARE DUMB THINGS TO BUILD COMPUTERS OUT OF...
...S'JUST FAT AND ELECTRICITY...

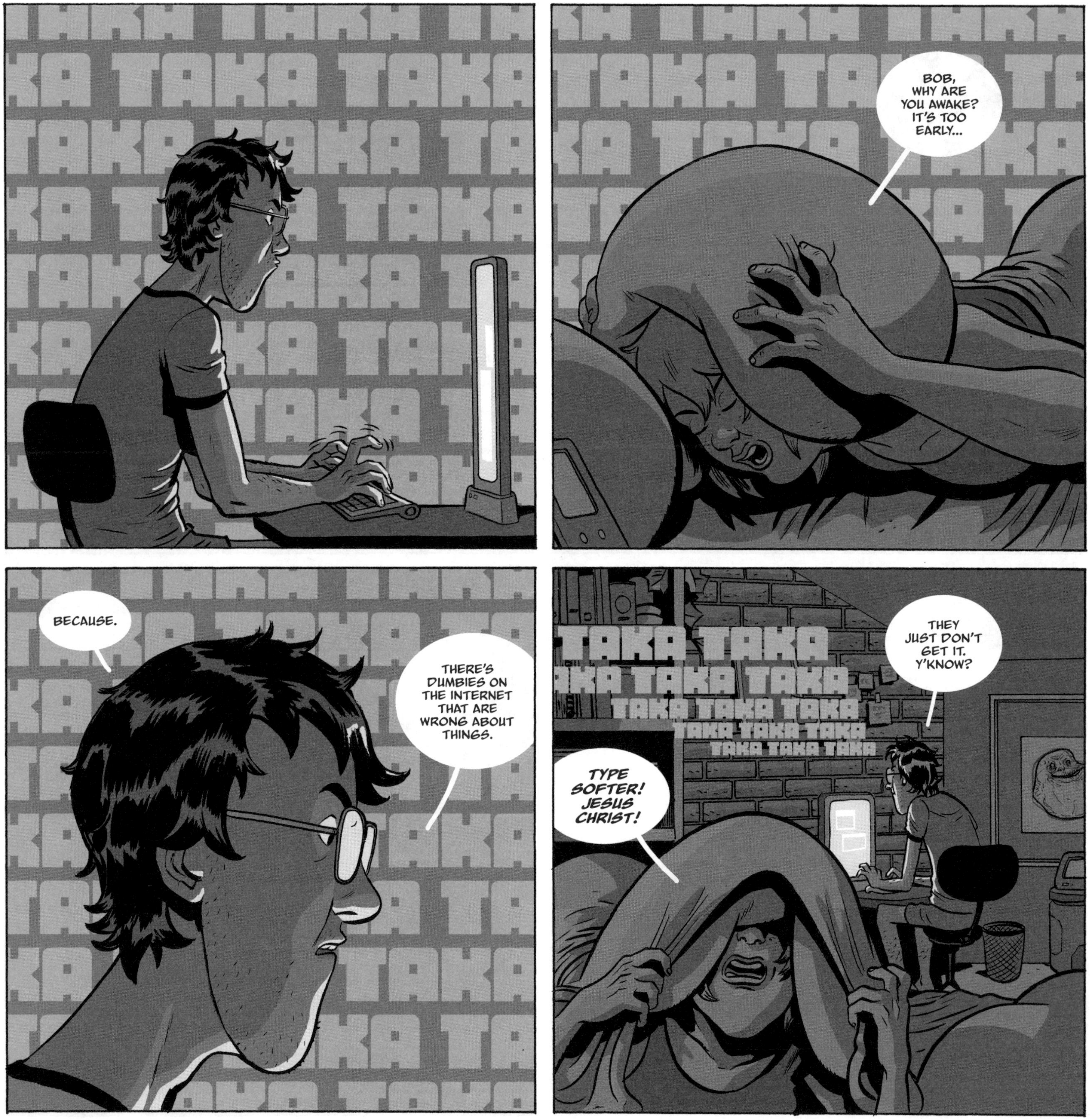
TAKA TAKA TAKA
BOB, WHY ARE YOU AWAKE? IT'S TOO EARLY...
BECAUSE.
THERE'S DUMBIES ON THE INTERNET THAT ARE WRONG ABOUT THINGS.
TAKA TAKA TAKA TAKA TAKA TAKA TAKA TAKA TAKA TAKA TAKA TAKA TAKA TAKA
THEY JUST DON'T GET IT. Y'KNOW?
TYPE SOFTER! JESUS CHRIST!

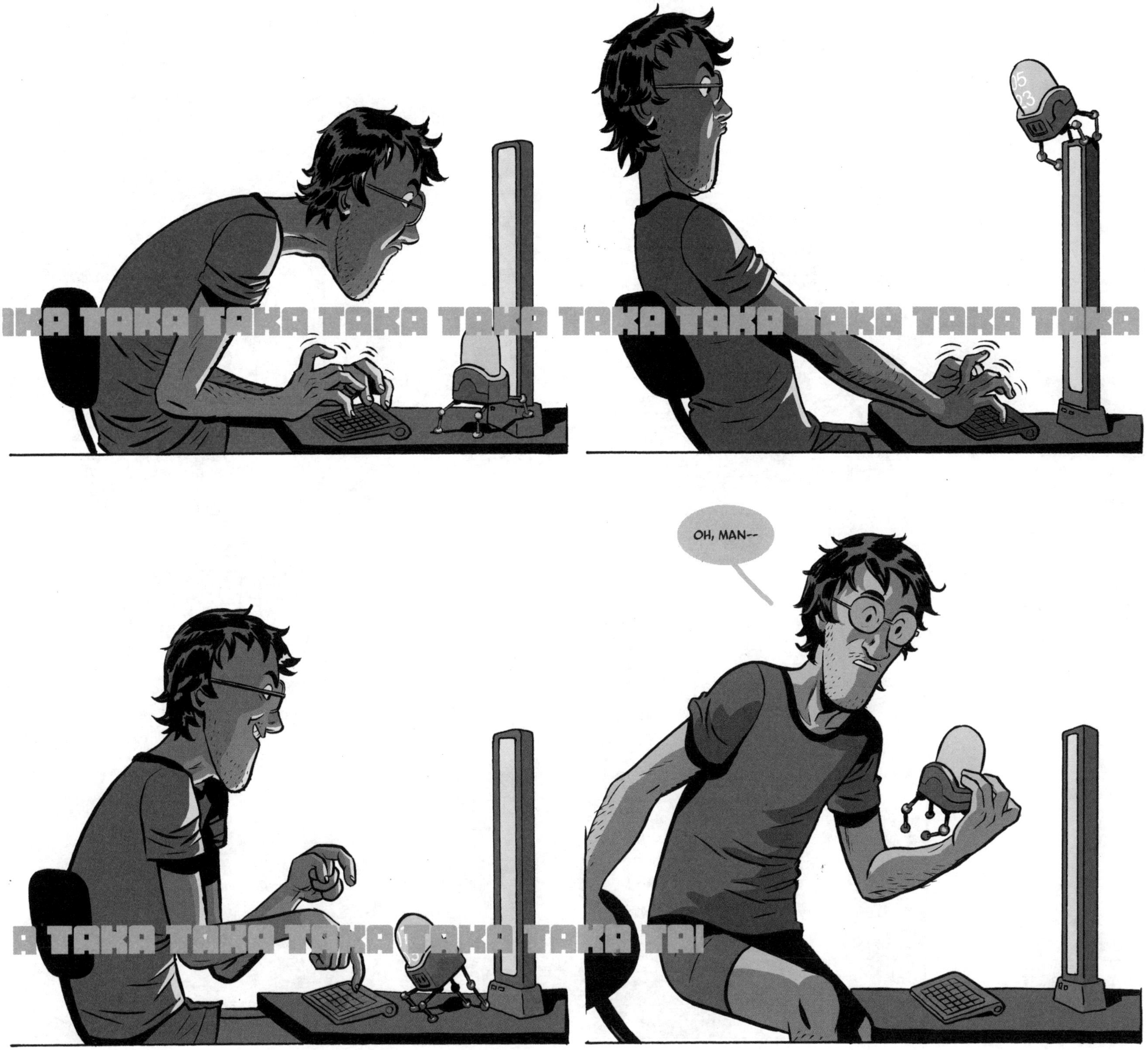
IKA TAKA TAKA TAKA TAKA TAKA TAKA TAKA TAKA
A TAKA TAKA TAKA TAKA TAI
OH, MAN--

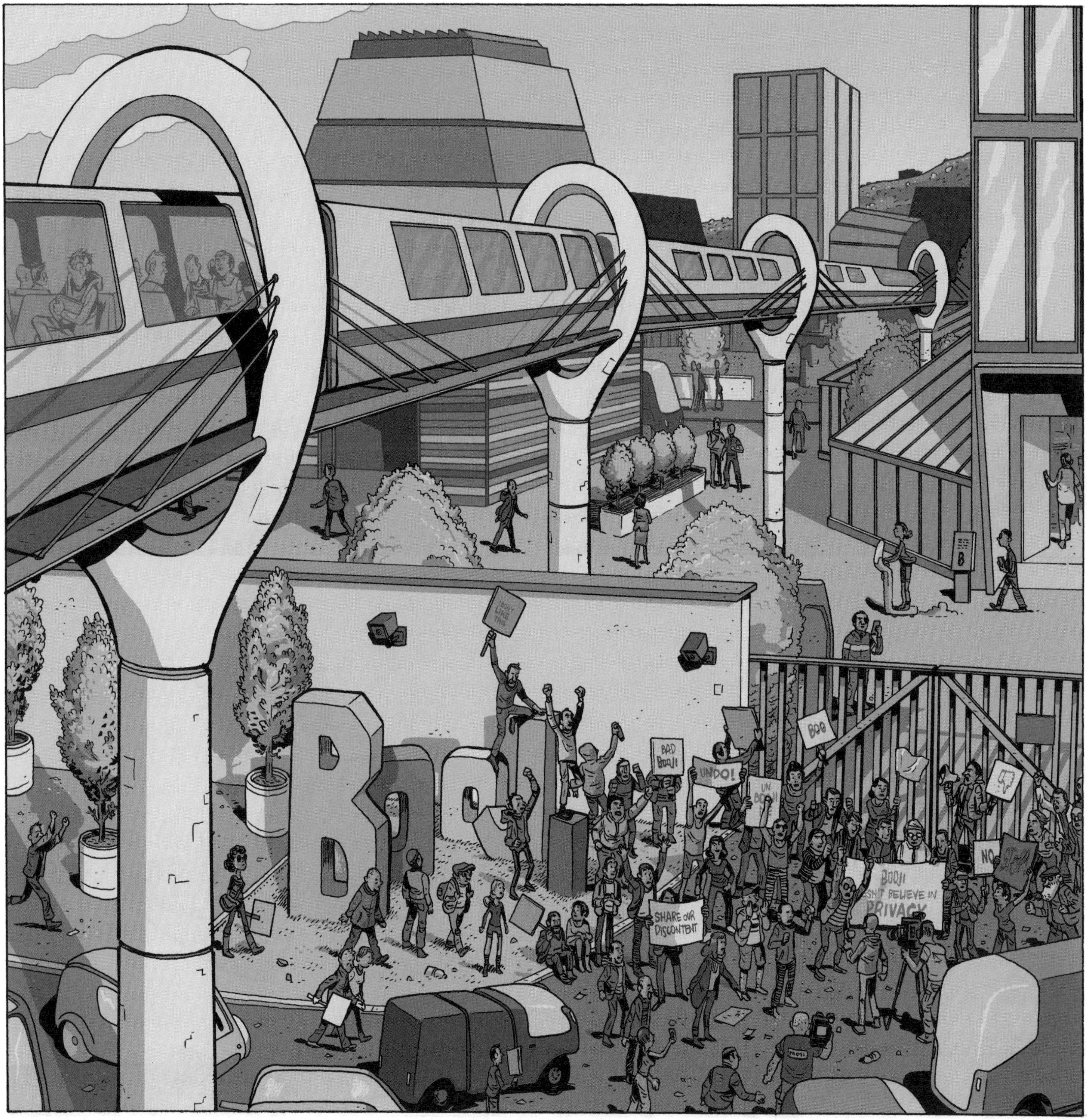
I DON'T LIKE THIS
BAD
UNDO!
BOO
SHARE OUR DISCONTENT
BELIEVE IN PRIVACY
NO

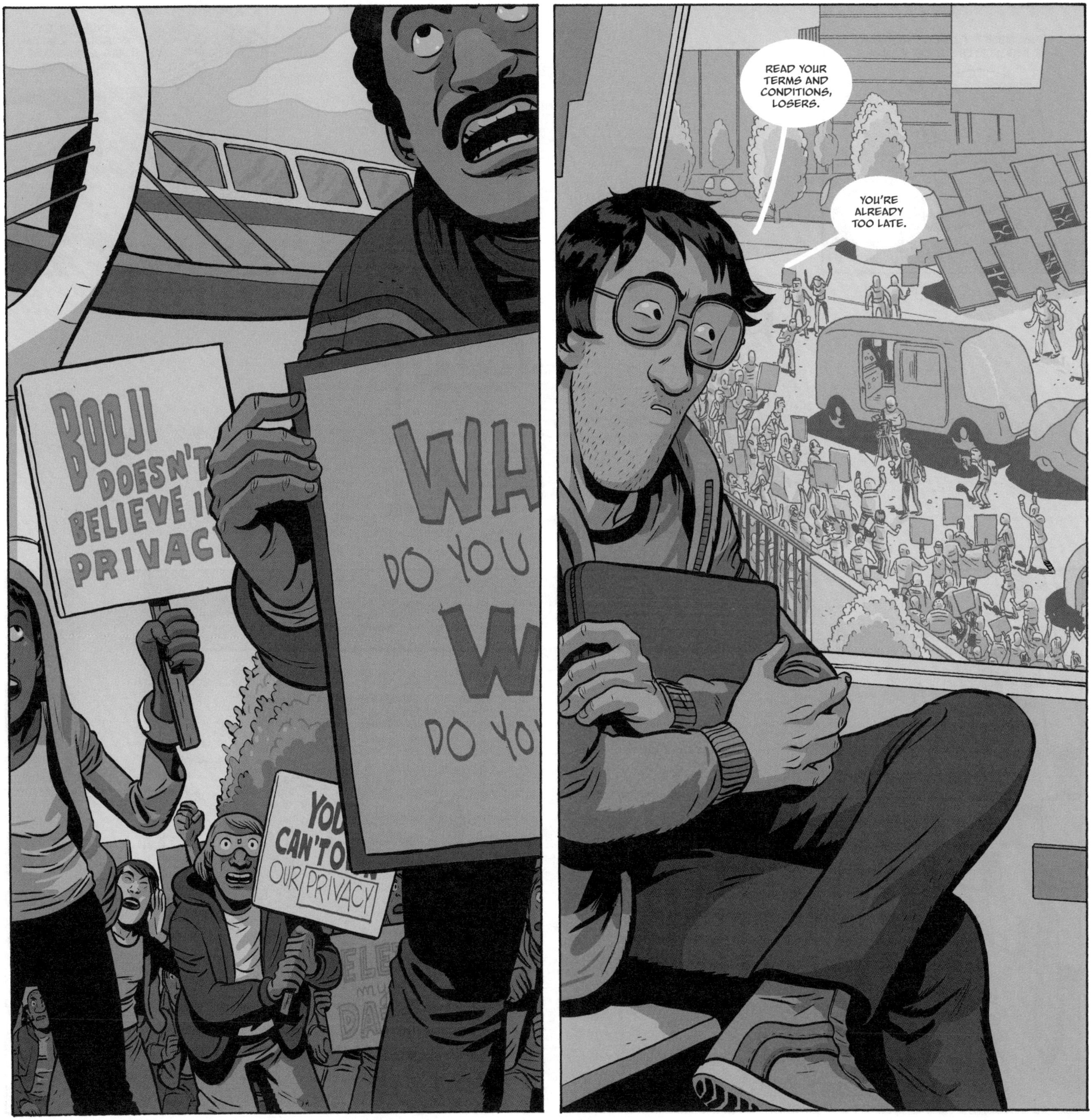
BOOJI DOESN'T BELIEVE I
PRIVAC
CAN'T
OUR PRIVACY
READ YOUR TERMS AND CONDITIONS, LOSERS.
YOU'RE ALREADY TOO LATE.

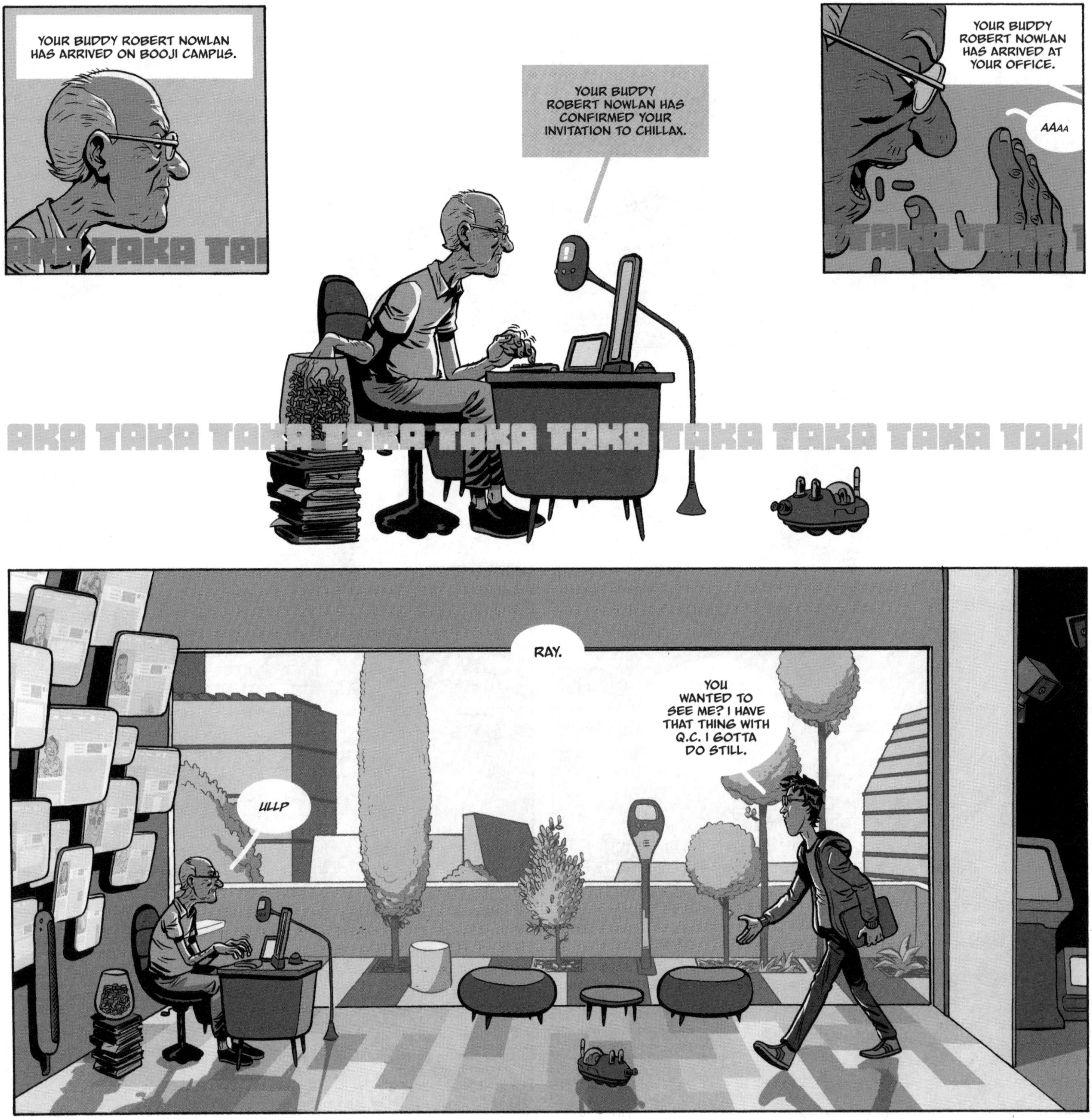

YOUR BUDDY ROBERT NOWLAN HAS ARRIVED ON BOOJI CAMPUS.
TAKA TAKA TAKA
YOUR BUDDY ROBERT NOWLAN HAS CONFIRMED YOUR INVITATION TO CHILLAX.
TAKA TAKA TAKA TAKA TAKA TAKA TAKA TAKA TAKA
YOUR BUDDY ROBERT NOWLAN HAS ARRIVED AT YOUR OFFICE.
AAAA
TAKA TAKA TAKA
RAY.
ULLP
YOU WANTED TO SEE ME? I HAVE THAT THING WITH Q.C. I GOTTA DO STILL.

DID YOU SEE ALL THOSE PEOPLE OUTSIDE?

I HEARD.

THEY'RE *MAD.*

LOTTA FOLKS GIVIN' US THE OL' DOWNVOTE OUT THERE, BOBBY.

CAN YOU.. JUST... 'ROBERT.' PLEASE.

WE'RE NOT CHANGING COURSE.

RAY.

BOBERT!

ROBERT.

BOBA-AAAAY.

THEY ALL CLICKED 'AGREE' AFTER PRETENDING TO READ THE RULES LIKE THE 1.9 BILLION *OTHER* USERS ALL OVER THE WORLD DID.

IT'S *DONE.* AND IT'S BACKED UP TEN WAYS TO TUESDAY--

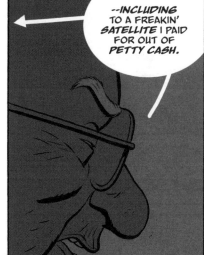

--INCLUDING TO A FREAKIN' *SATELLITE* I PAID FOR OUT OF *PETTY CASH.*

STOP WORRYING ABOUT THE USER DATA-- BECAUSE THE USERS DON'T.

WE CAN DO ANYTHING WE WANT.

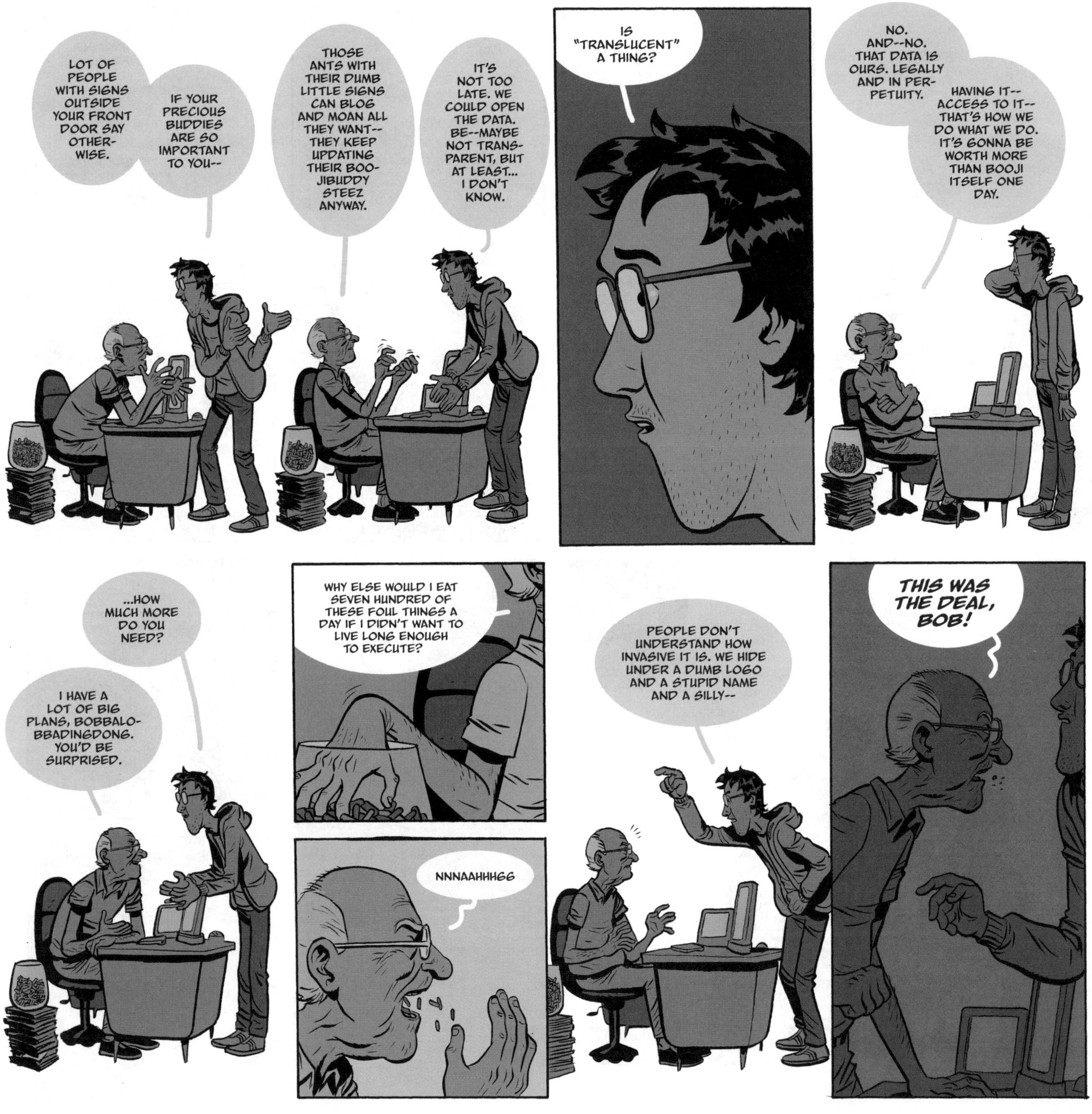
LOT OF PEOPLE WITH SIGNS OUTSIDE YOUR FRONT DOOR SAY OTHERWISE.
IF YOUR PRECIOUS BUDDIES ARE SO IMPORTANT TO YOU--
THOSE ANTS WITH THEIR DUMB LITTLE SIGNS CAN BLOG AND MOAN ALL THEY WANT-- THEY KEEP UPDATING THEIR BOOJIBUDDY STEEZ ANYWAY.
IT'S NOT TOO LATE. WE COULD OPEN THE DATA. BE--MAYBE NOT TRANSPARENT, BUT AT LEAST... I DON'T KNOW.
IS "TRANSLUCENT" A THING?
NO. AND--NO. THAT DATA IS OURS. LEGALLY AND IN PERPETUITY.
HAVING IT-- ACCESS TO IT-- THAT'S HOW WE DO WHAT WE DO. IT'S GONNA BE WORTH MORE THAN BOOJI ITSELF ONE DAY.
...HOW MUCH MORE DO YOU NEED?
I HAVE A LOT OF BIG PLANS, BOBBALOBBADINGDONG. YOU'D BE SURPRISED.
WHY ELSE WOULD I EAT SEVEN HUNDRED OF THESE FOUL THINGS A DAY IF I DIDN'T WANT TO LIVE LONG ENOUGH TO EXECUTE?
NNNAAHHHGG
PEOPLE DON'T UNDERSTAND HOW INVASIVE IT IS. WE HIDE UNDER A DUMB LOGO AND A STUPID NAME AND A SILLY--
THIS WAS THE DEAL, BOB!

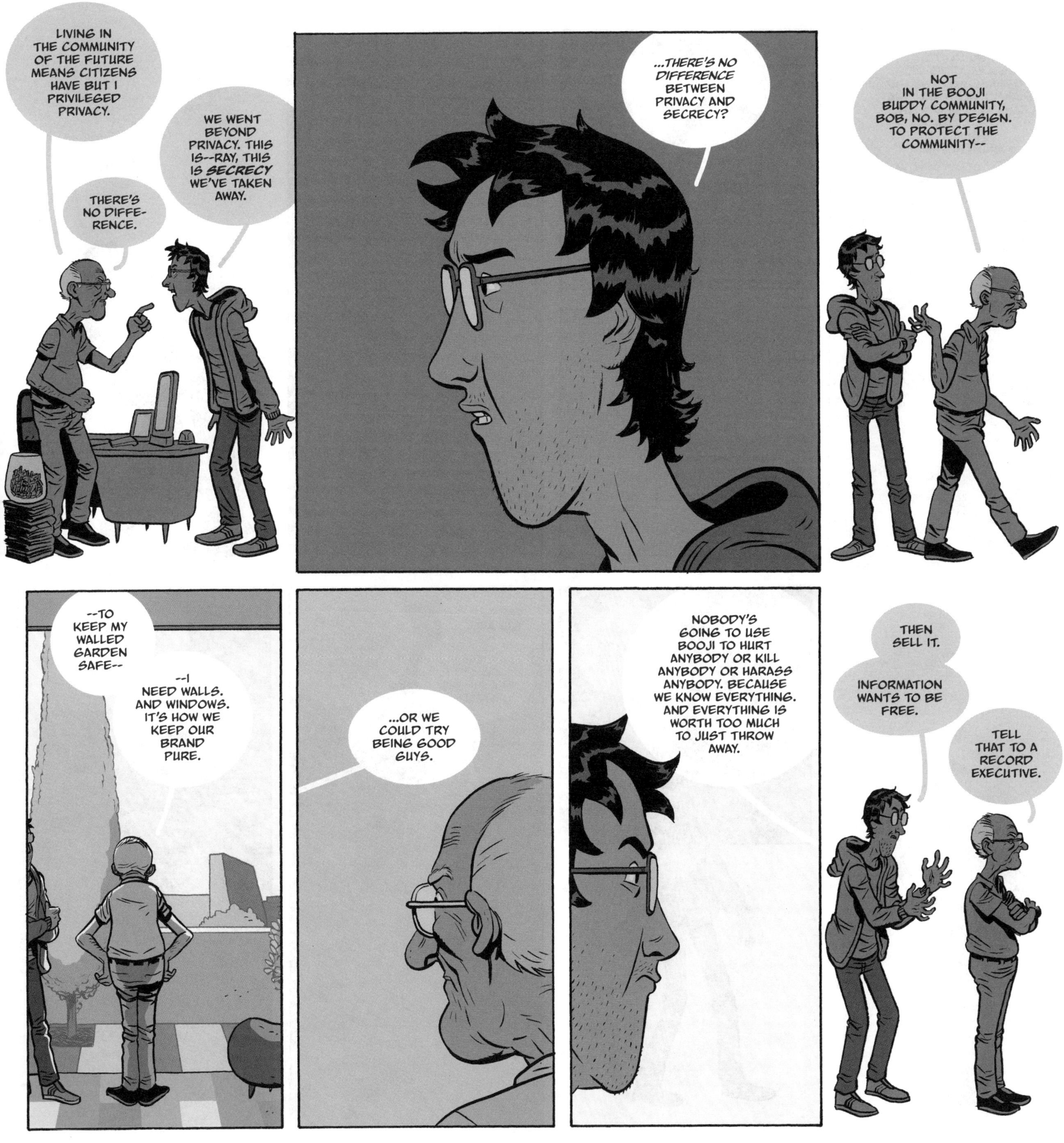
LIVING IN THE COMMUNITY OF THE FUTURE MEANS CITIZENS HAVE BUT 1 PRIVILEGED PRIVACY.
WE WENT BEYOND PRIVACY. THIS IS--RAY, THIS IS SECRECY WE'VE TAKEN AWAY.
THERE'S NO DIFFE-RENCE.
...THERE'S NO DIFFERENCE BETWEEN PRIVACY AND SECRECY?
NOT IN THE BOOJI BUDDY COMMUNITY, BOB, NO. BY DESIGN. TO PROTECT THE COMMUNITY--
--TO KEEP MY WALLED GARDEN SAFE--
--I NEED WALLS. AND WINDOWS. IT'S HOW WE KEEP OUR BRAND PURE.
...OR WE COULD TRY BEING GOOD GUYS.
NOBODY'S GOING TO USE BOOJI TO HURT ANYBODY OR KILL ANYBODY OR HARASS ANYBODY. BECAUSE WE KNOW EVERYTHING. AND EVERYTHING IS WORTH TOO MUCH TO JUST THROW AWAY.
THEN SELL IT.
INFORMATION WANTS TO BE FREE.
TELL THAT TO A RECORD EXECUTIVE.

YOU DON'T LIKE WHAT WE DID BECAUSE WHAT WE DID IS UNPOPULAR AND THAT COMPROMISES YOUR... OTHER *MORAL* ARGUMENTS ELSEWHERE.

...

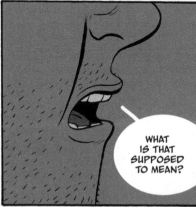

WHAT IS THAT SUPPOSED TO MEAN?

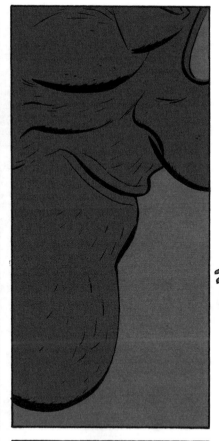

HAVE YOU BEEN LOOKING AT USER DATA, RAY?

HAVE YOU BEEN LOOKING AT *MY* USER DATA?

DON'T BE PREPOSTEROUS.

...

I'M GOING TO DESTROY IT.

THE HELL YOU ARE.

YOU COULDN'T EVEN IF YOU TRIED.

YOU WANNA BET? HOW MUCH OF THIS PLACE IS CODE I WROTE?

THINK... VERY CAREFULLY... ABOUT THE NEXT WORDS THAT COME OUT OF YOUR MOUTH.

BUDDY.

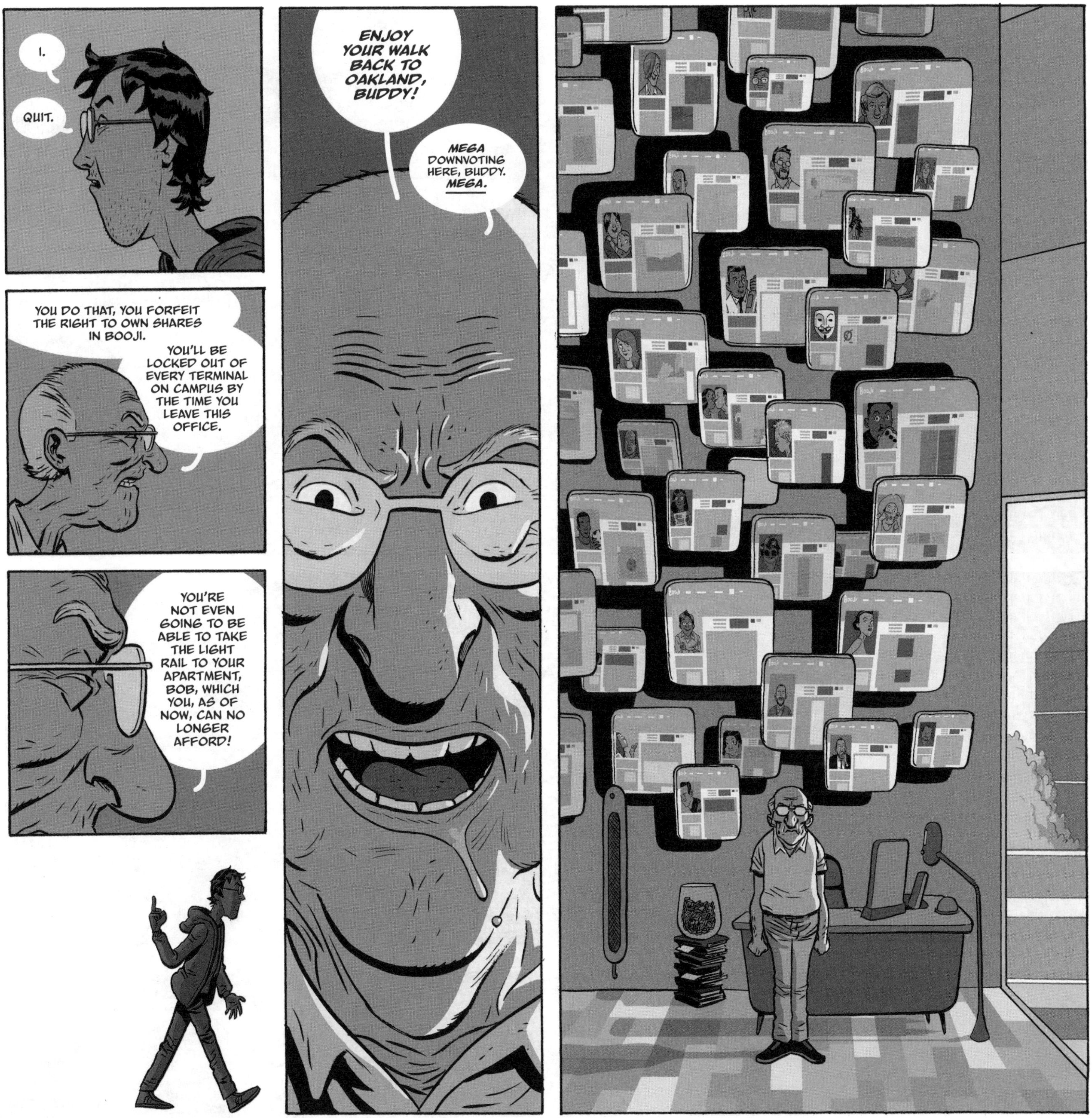

I.
QUIT.
YOU DO THAT, YOU FORFEIT THE RIGHT TO OWN SHARES IN BOOJI.
YOU'LL BE LOCKED OUT OF EVERY TERMINAL ON CAMPUS BY THE TIME YOU LEAVE THIS OFFICE.
YOU'RE NOT EVEN GOING TO BE ABLE TO TAKE THE LIGHT RAIL TO YOUR APARTMENT, BOB, WHICH YOU, AS OF NOW, CAN NO LONGER AFFORD!
ENJOY YOUR WALK BACK TO OAKLAND, BUDDY!
MEGA DOWNVOTING HERE, BUDDY. MEGA.

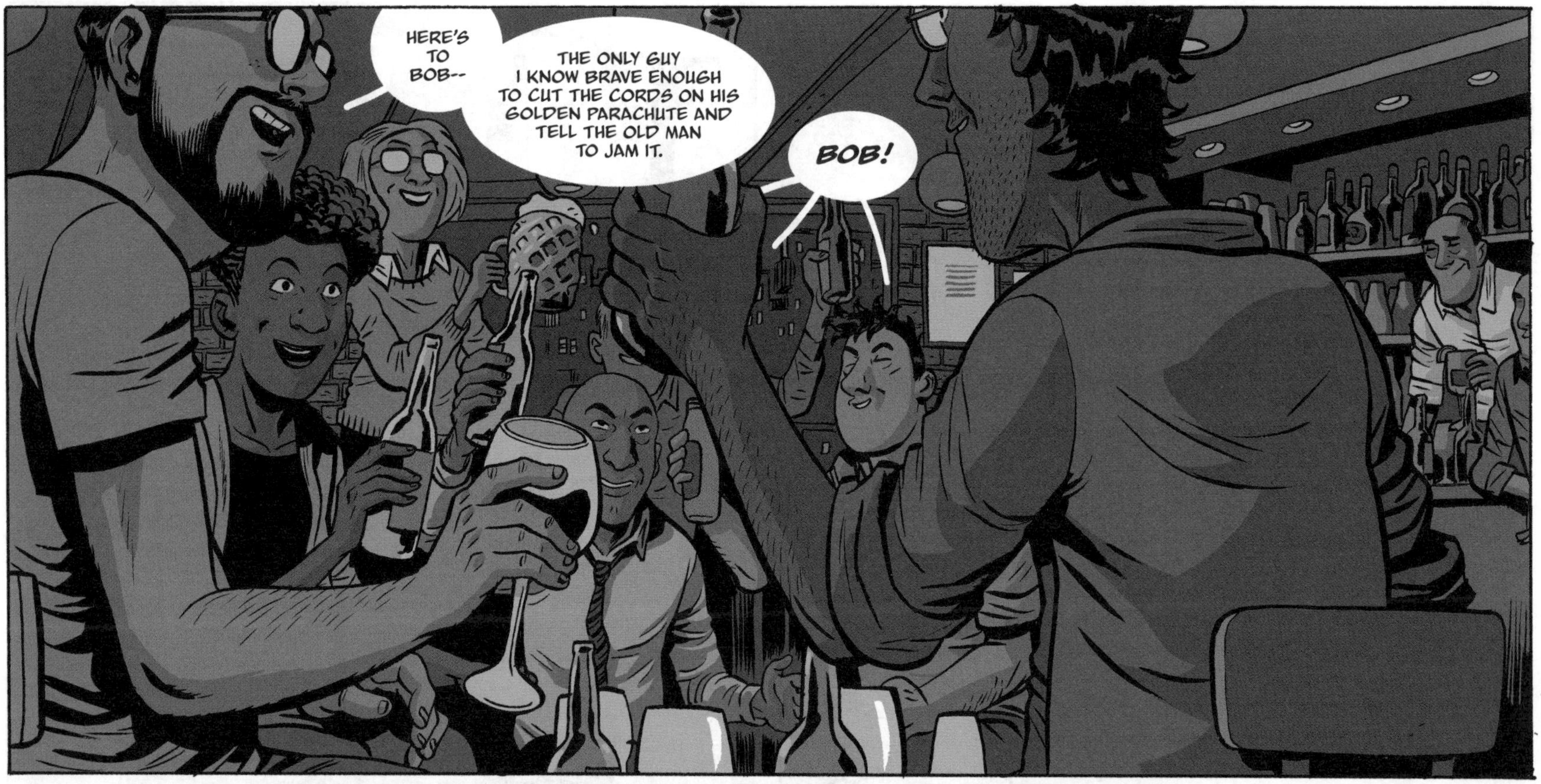
HERE'S TO BOB--
THE ONLY GUY I KNOW BRAVE ENOUGH TO CUT THE CORDS ON HIS GOLDEN PARACHUTE AND TELL THE OLD MAN TO JAM IT.
BOB!

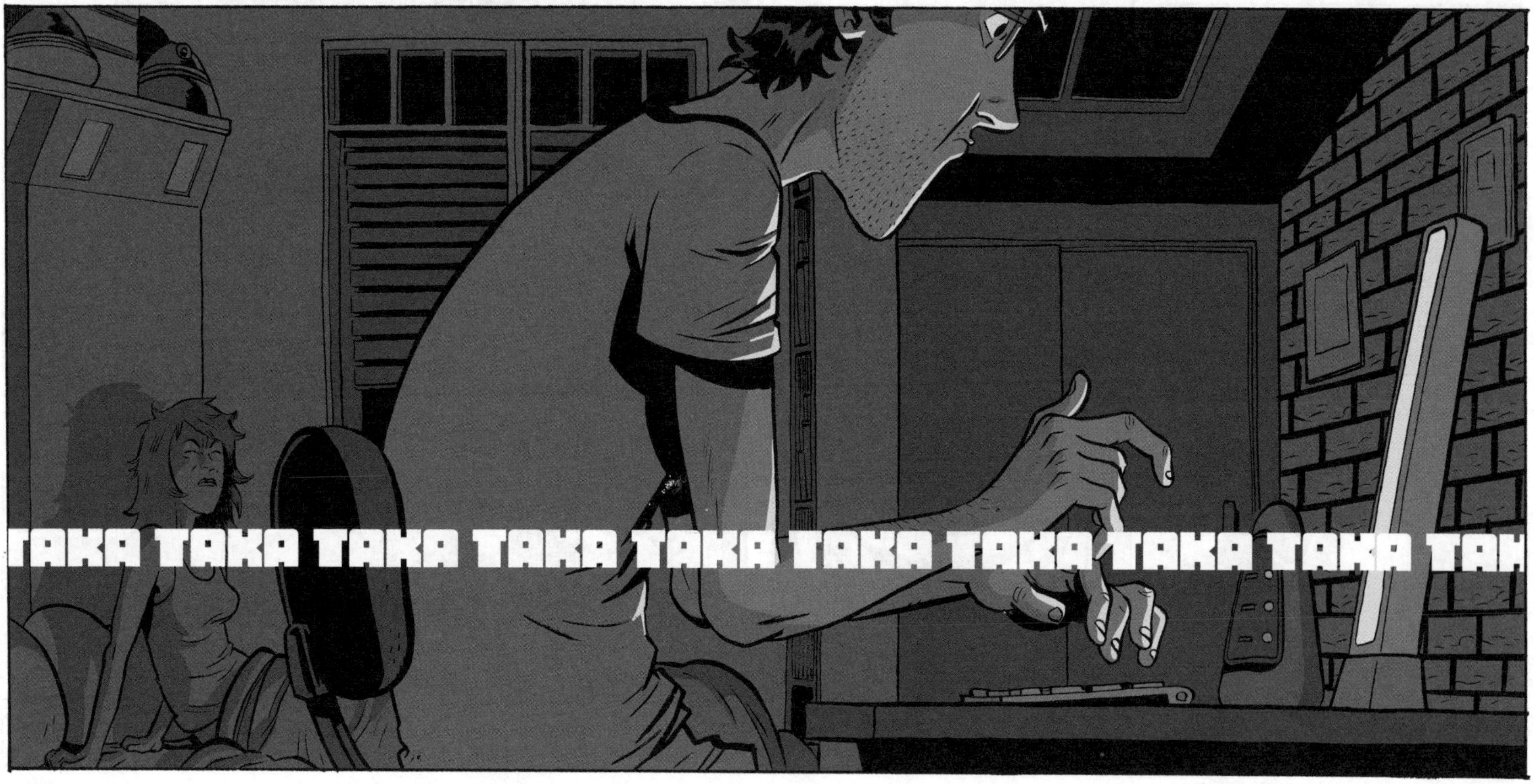
TAKA TAKA TAKA TAKA TAKA TAKA TAKA TAKA TAKA

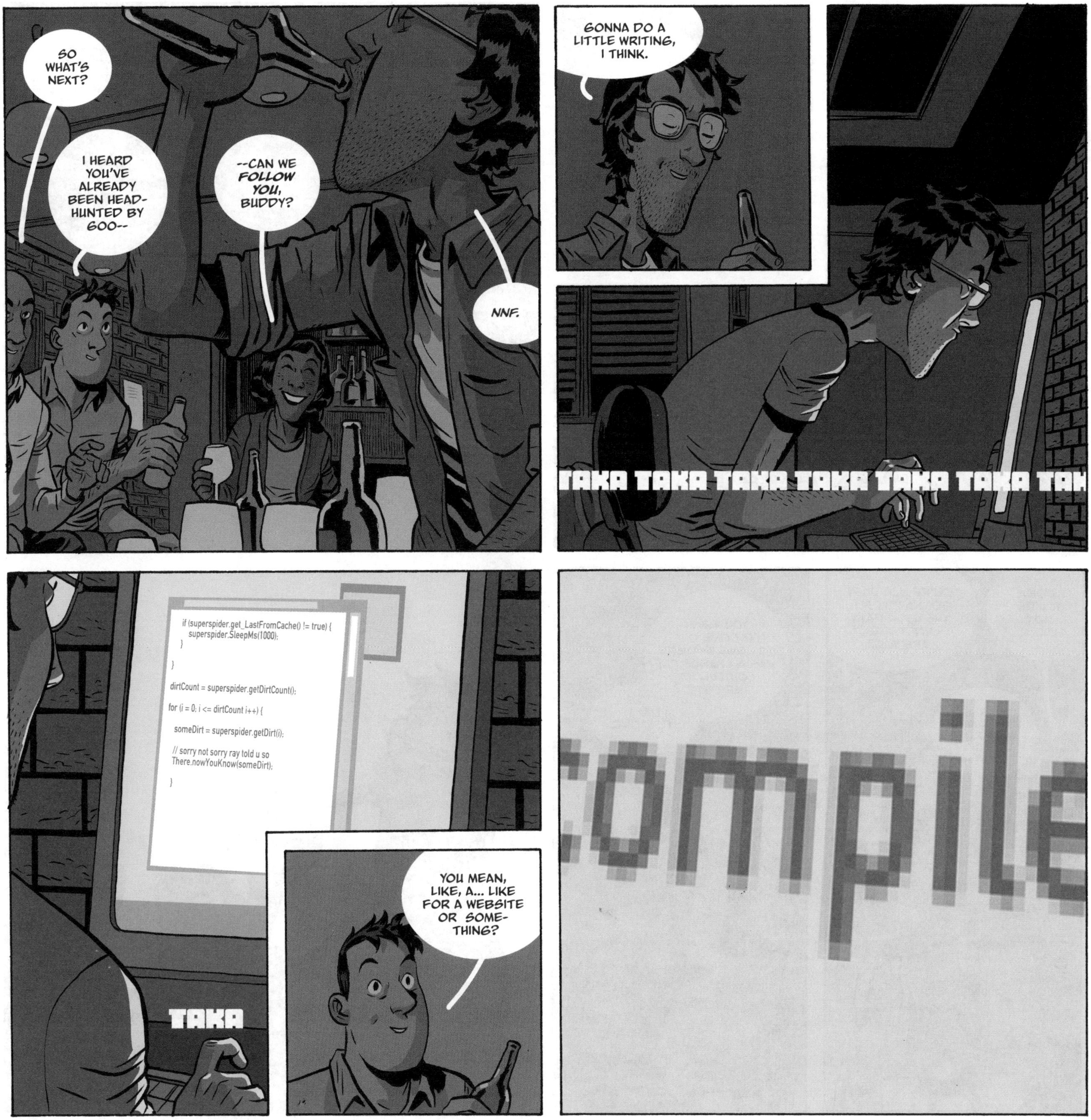
SO WHAT'S NEXT?
I HEARD YOU'VE ALREADY BEEN HEAD-HUNTED BY GOO--
--CAN WE *FOLLOW YOU,* BUDDY?
NNF.
GONNA DO A LITTLE WRITING, I THINK.
TAKA TAKA TAKA TAKA TAKA TAKA TAK
if (superspider.get_LastFromCache() != true) {
superspider.SleepMs(1000);
}
}
dirtCount = superspider.getDirtCount();
for (i = 0; i <= dirtCount i++) {
someDirt = superspider.getDirt(i);
// sorry not sorry ray told u so
There.nowYouKnow(someDirt);
}
TAKA
YOU MEAN, LIKE, A... LIKE FOR A WEBSITE OR SOME-THING?
compile

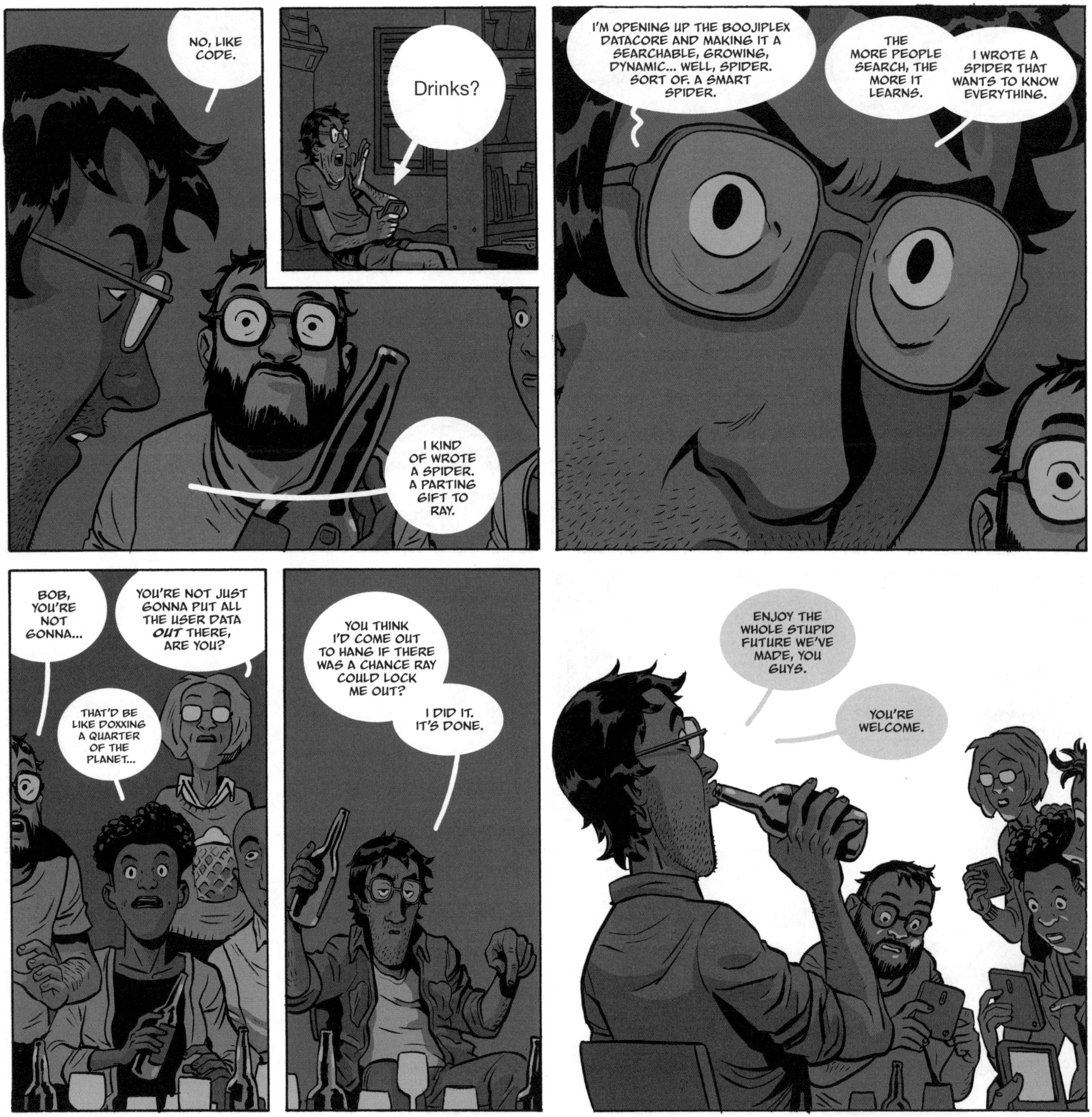
NO, LIKE CODE.
Drinks?
I KIND OF WROTE A SPIDER. A PARTING GIFT TO RAY.
I'M OPENING UP THE BOOJIPLEX DATACORE AND MAKING IT A SEARCHABLE, GROWING, DYNAMIC... WELL, SPIDER. SORT OF. A SMART SPIDER.
THE MORE PEOPLE SEARCH, THE MORE IT LEARNS.
I WROTE A SPIDER THAT WANTS TO KNOW EVERYTHING.
BOB, YOU'RE NOT GONNA...
YOU'RE NOT JUST GONNA PUT ALL THE USER DATA *OUT* THERE, ARE YOU?
THAT'D BE LIKE DOXXING A QUARTER OF THE PLANET...
YOU THINK I'D COME OUT TO HANG IF THERE WAS A CHANCE RAY COULD LOCK ME OUT?
I DID IT. IT'S DONE.
ENJOY THE WHOLE STUPID FUTURE WE'VE MADE, YOU GUYS.
YOU'RE WELCOME.

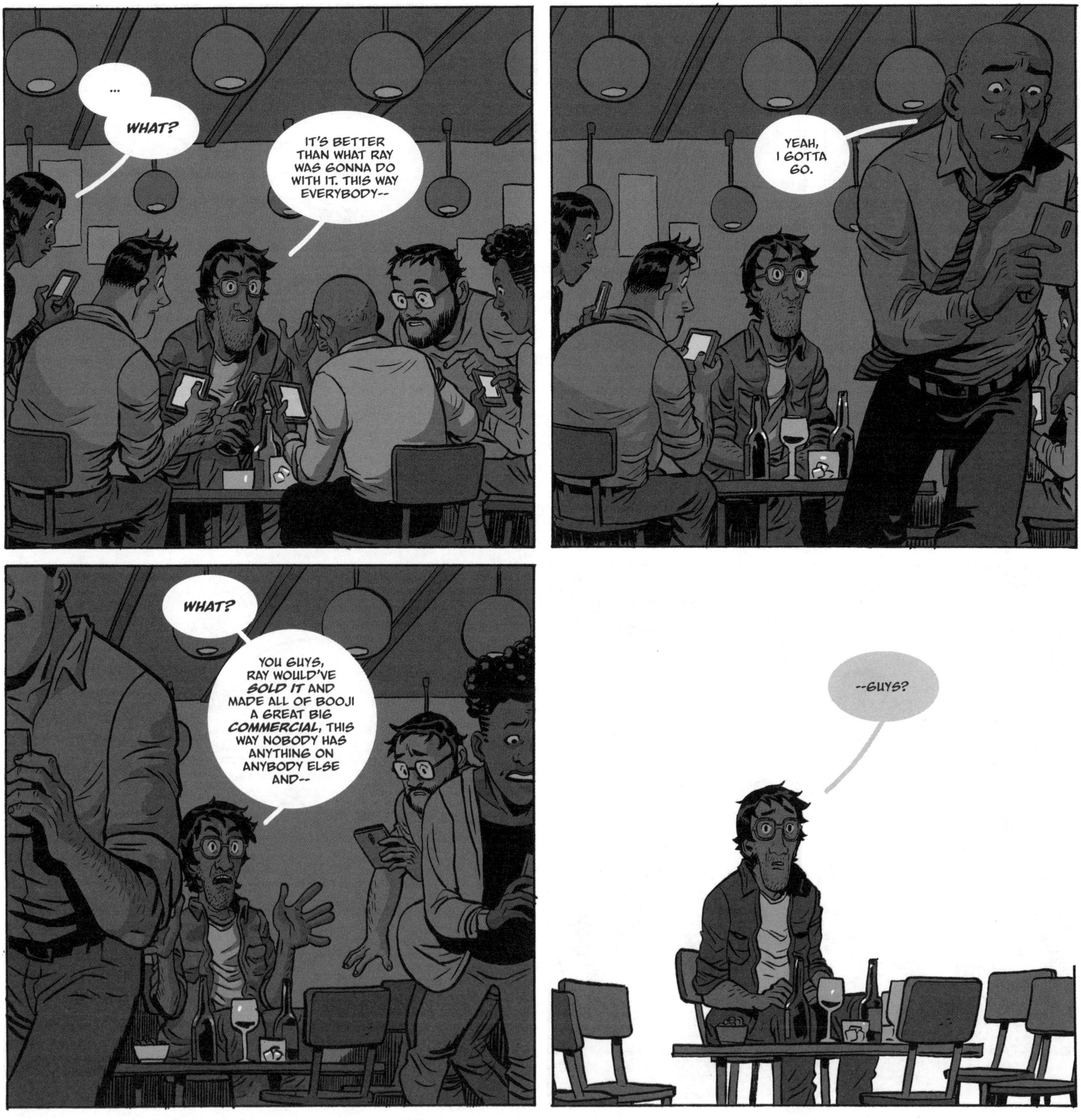
...
WHAT?
IT'S BETTER THAN WHAT RAY WAS GONNA DO WITH IT. THIS WAY EVERYBODY--
YEAH, I GOTTA GO.
WHAT?
YOU GUYS, RAY WOULD'VE SOLD IT AND MADE ALL OF BOOJI A GREAT BIG COMMERCIAL, THIS WAY NOBODY HAS ANYTHING ON ANYBODY ELSE AND--
--GUYS?

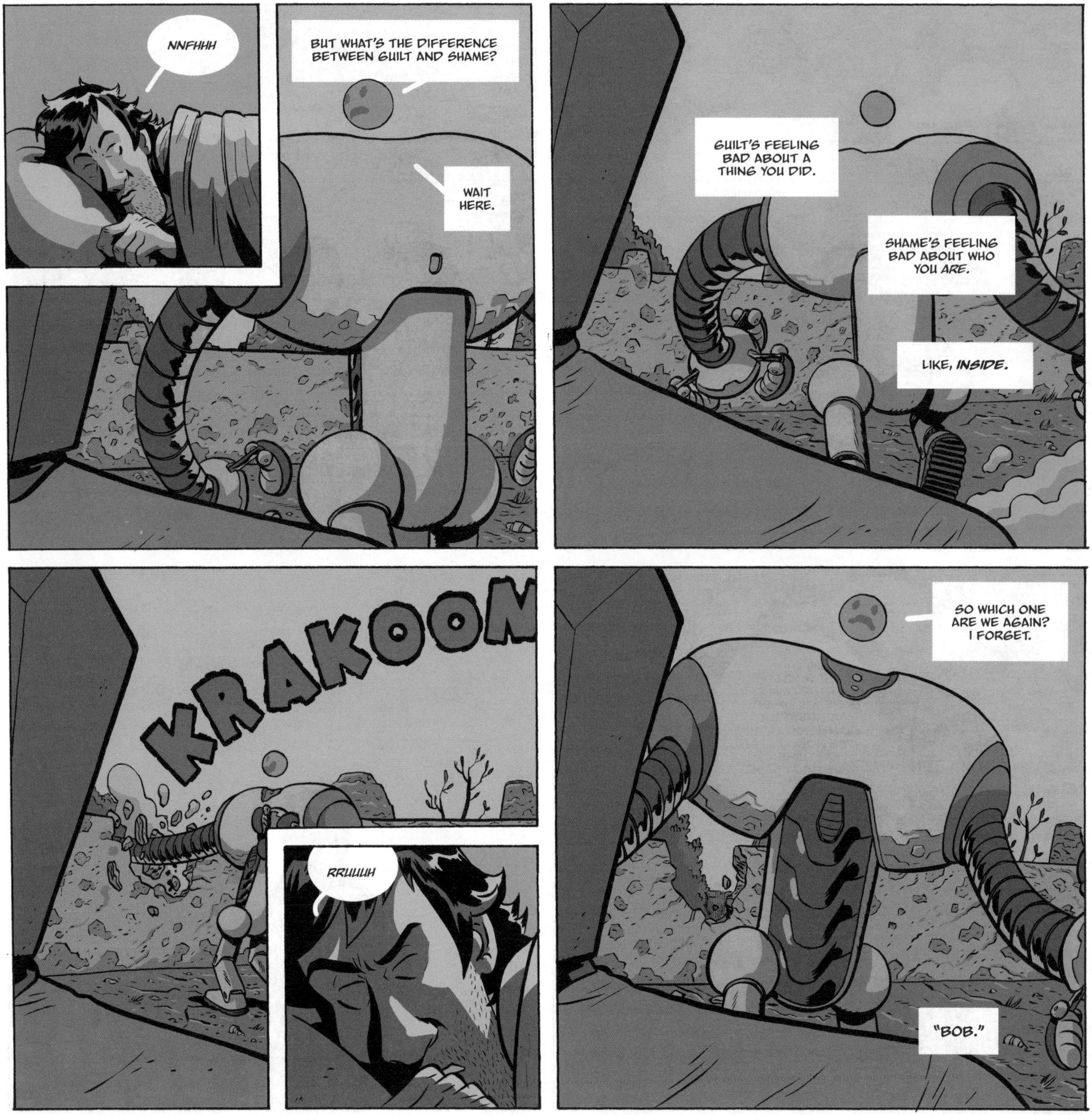
NNFHHH
BUT WHAT'S THE DIFFERENCE BETWEEN GUILT AND SHAME?
WAIT HERE.
GUILT'S FEELING BAD ABOUT A THING YOU DID.
SHAME'S FEELING BAD ABOUT WHO YOU ARE.
LIKE, INSIDE.
KRAKOOM
RRUUUH
SO WHICH ONE ARE WE AGAIN? I FORGET.
"BOB."

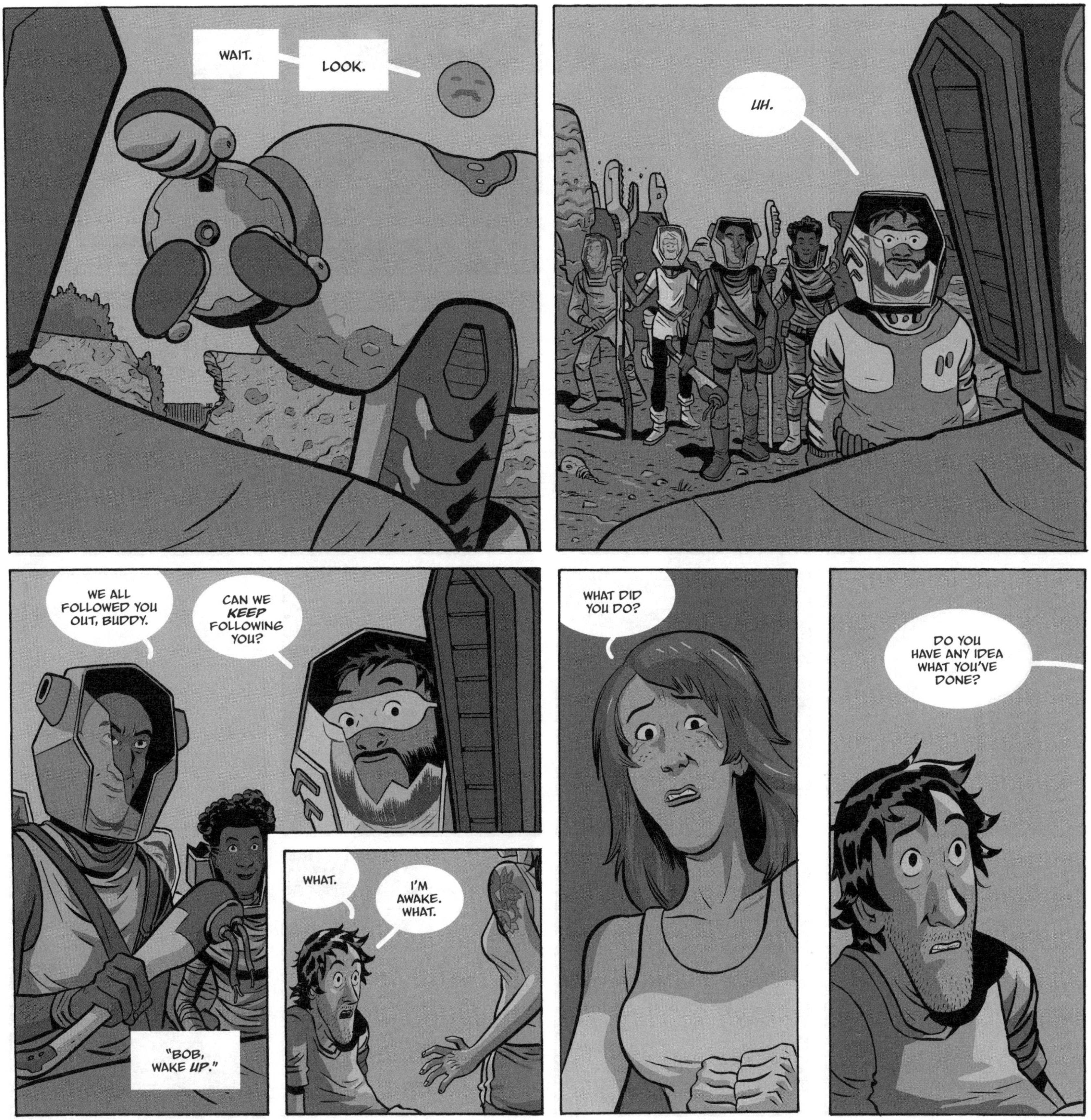
WAIT.
LOOK.
UH.
WE ALL FOLLOWED YOU OUT, BUDDY.
CAN WE KEEP FOLLOWING YOU?
"BOB, WAKE UP."
WHAT.
I'M AWAKE. WHAT.
WHAT DID YOU DO?
DO YOU HAVE ANY IDEA WHAT YOU'VE DONE?

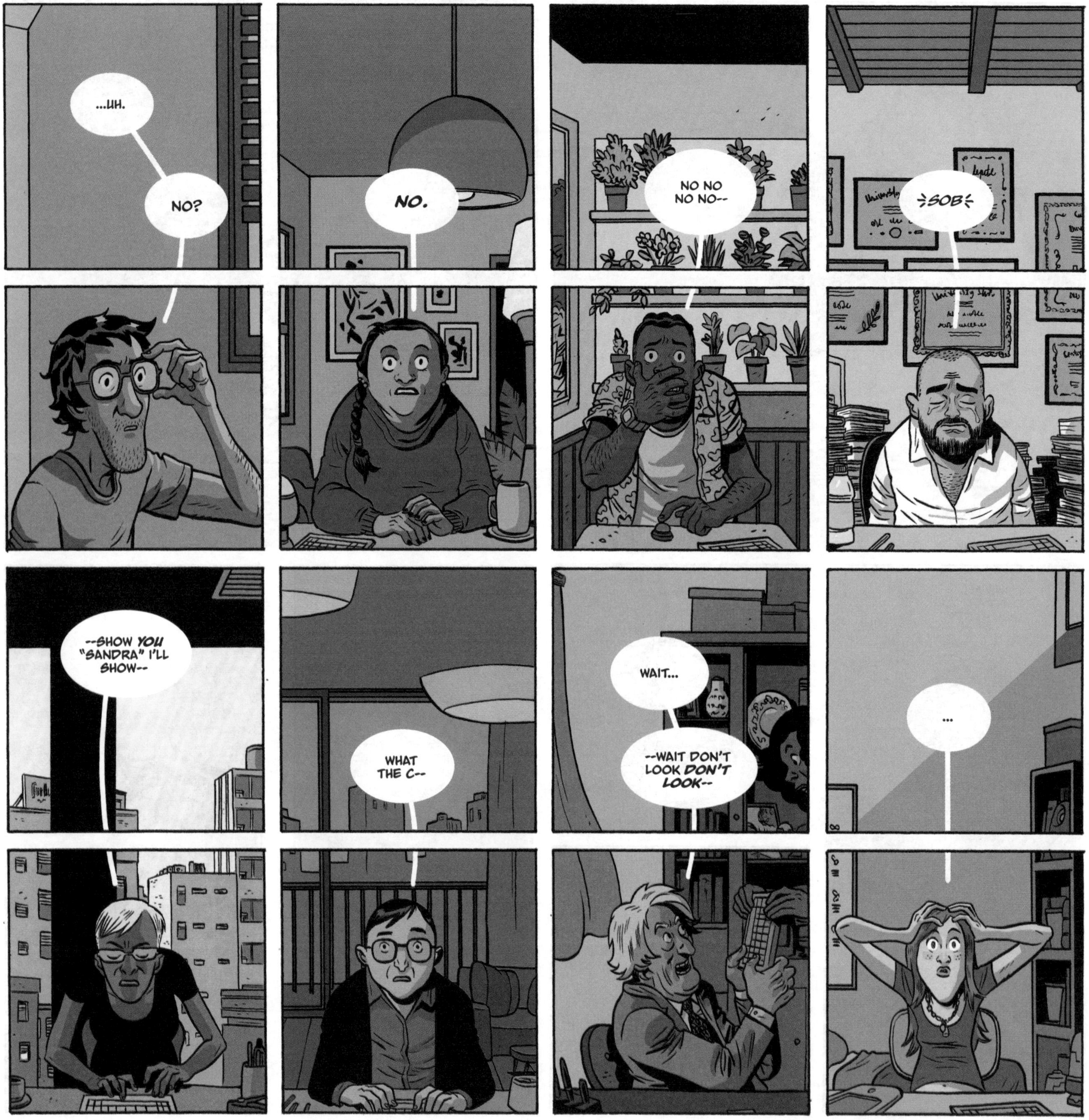
...UH.
NO?
NO.
NO NO
NO NO--
SOB
--SHOW YOU
"SANDRA" I'LL
SHOW--
WHAT
THE C--
WAIT...
--WAIT DON'T
LOOK DON'T
LOOK--
...

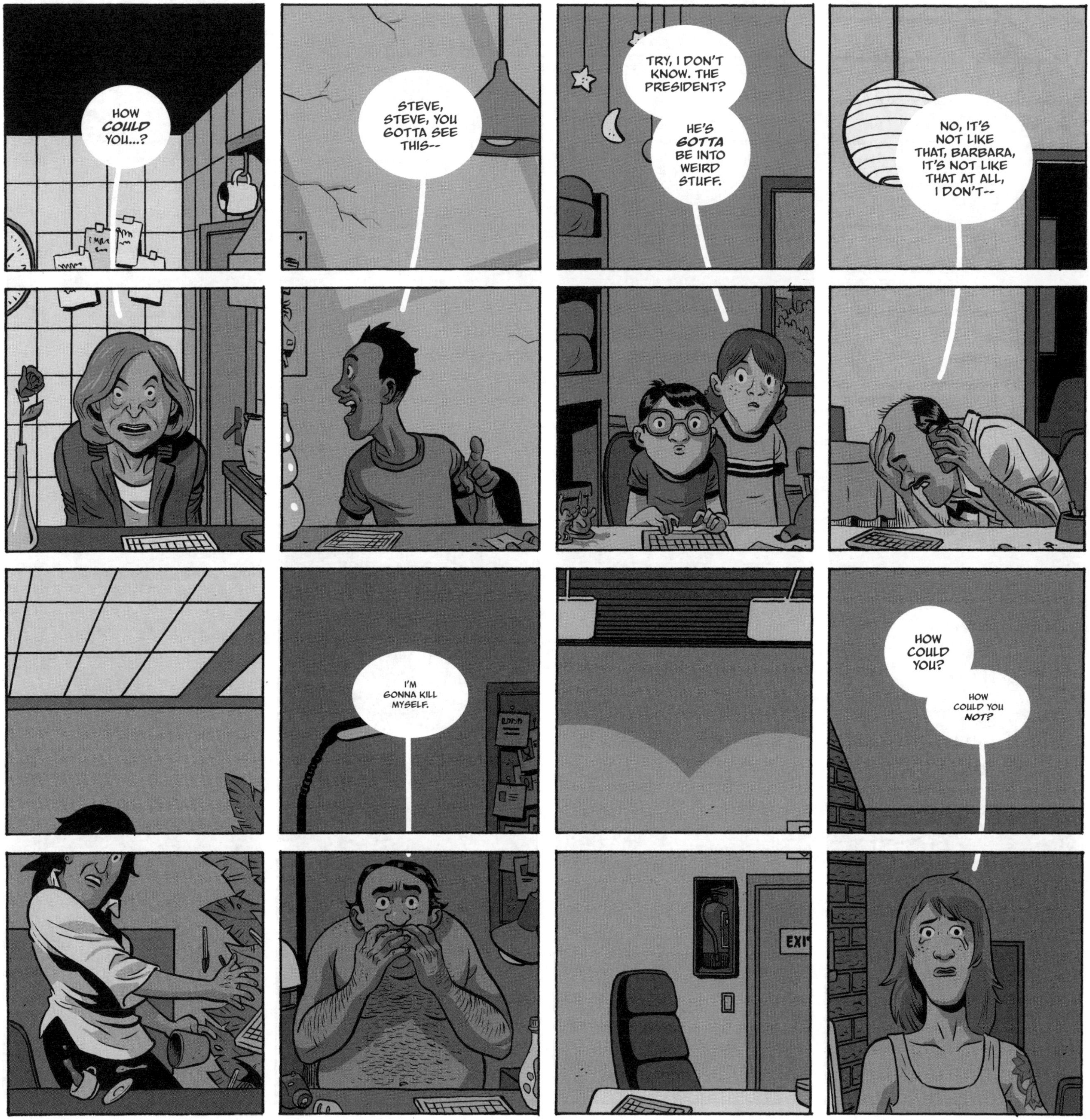
HOW COULD YOU...?
STEVE, STEVE, YOU GOTTA SEE THIS--
TRY, I DON'T KNOW. THE PRESIDENT?
HE'S GOTTA BE INTO WEIRD STUFF.
NO, IT'S NOT LIKE THAT, BARBARA, IT'S NOT LIKE THAT AT ALL, I DON'T--
I'M GONNA KILL MYSELF.
EXIT
HOW COULD YOU?
HOW COULD YOU NOT?

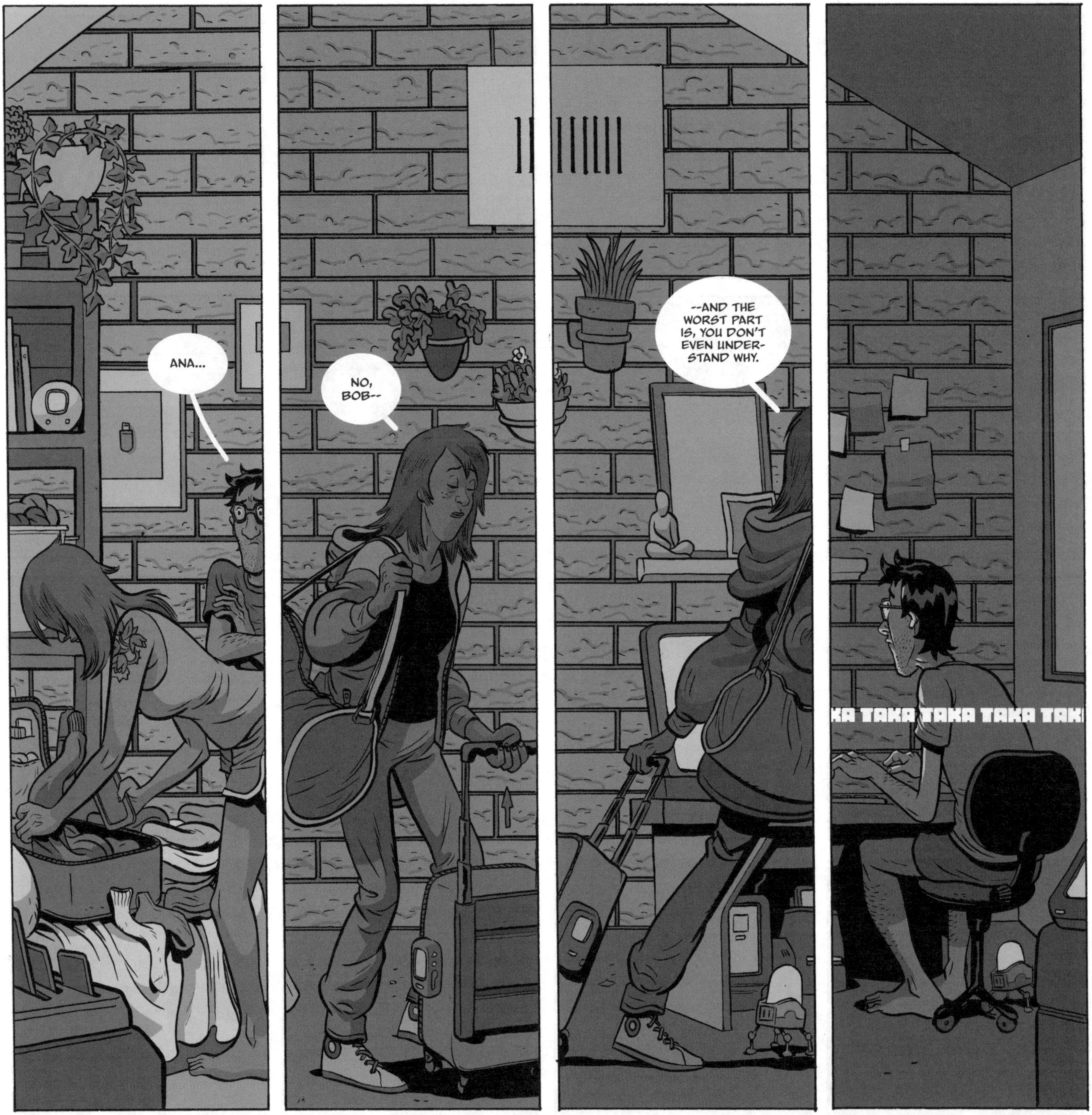
ANA...
NO, BOB--
--AND THE WORST PART IS, YOU DON'T EVEN UNDER-STAND WHY.
KA TAKA TAKA TAKA TAK

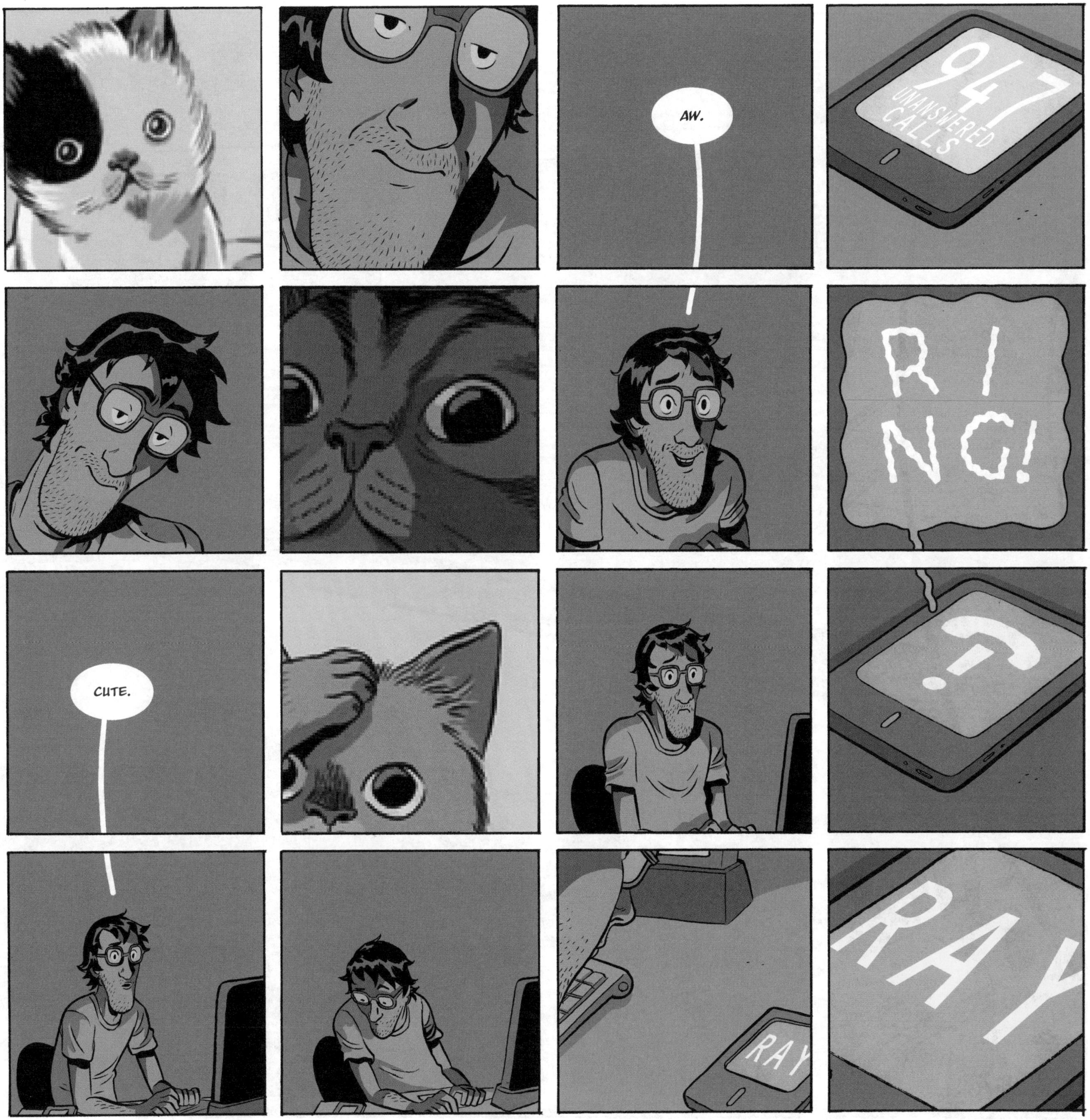
AW.
947
UNANSWERED
CALLS
RING!
CUTE.
RAY
RAY

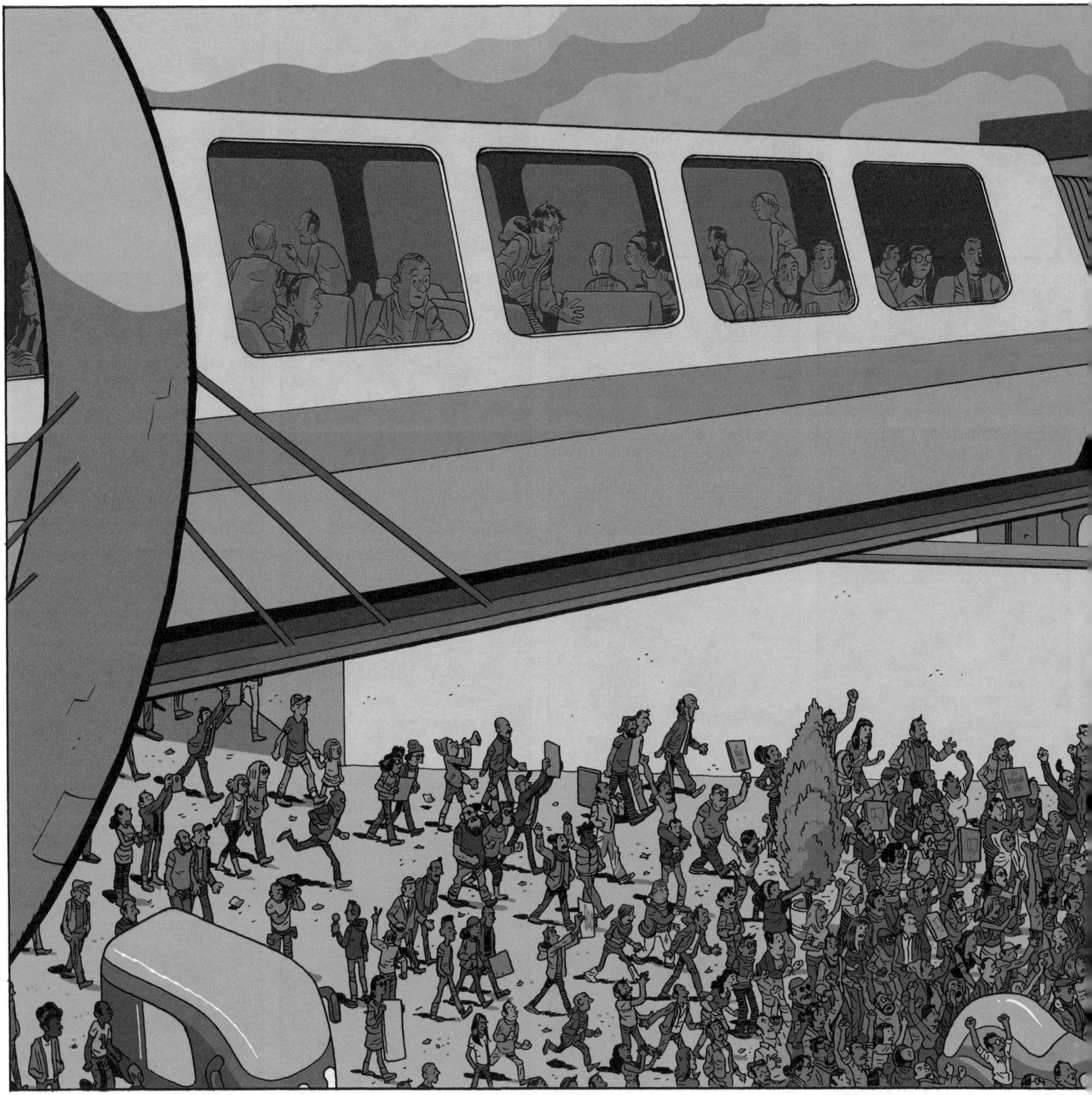

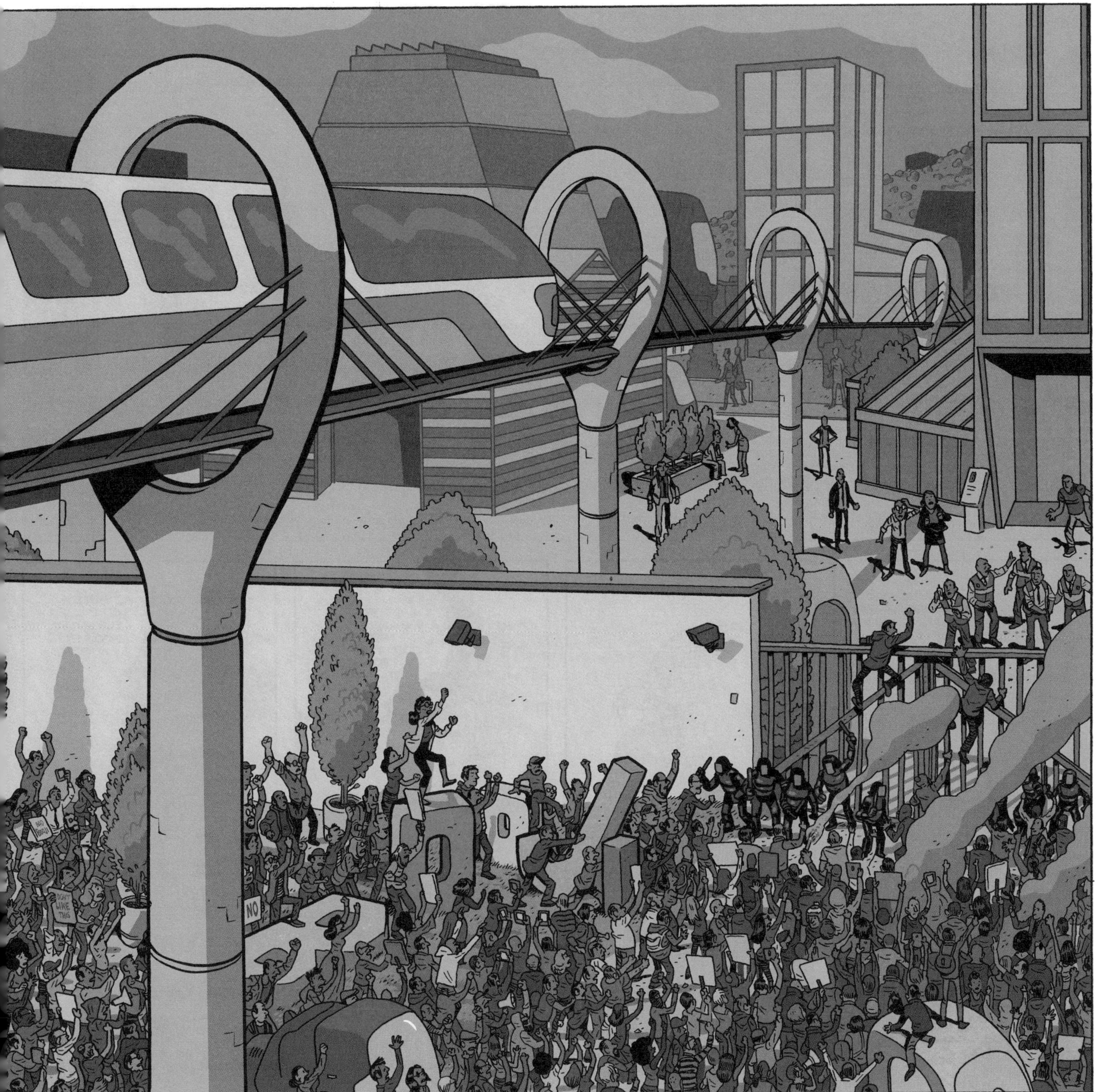

DON'T LIKE THIS
NO

COME IN.

PLEASE.

I SWEAR, IF YOU SERVE ME WITH PAPERS OR HAVE ME ARRESTED OR--

--I CAME HERE IN GOOD FAITH, I'M SAYING. I'M TAKING YOU AT YOUR WORD.

THIS ISN'T THAT.

BOB.

WHAT HAVE YOU DONE?

WHAT HAVE YOU MADE?

WHAT?

IT'S A SPIDER, IS ALL. I MEAN, I USED SOME OF THE AI SUBROUTINES AND SCRIPTS BOOJITRONIX DEVELOPED TO MAKE IT HARDER TO SHUT OFF, BUT--

--WHATEVER IT IS YOU THINK YOU'VE MADE, ROBERT--

--SHE'S CONSUMED THE ENTIRE BOOJI DATA-HORDE...

...AND NOW SHE WANTS TO TALK TO YOU.

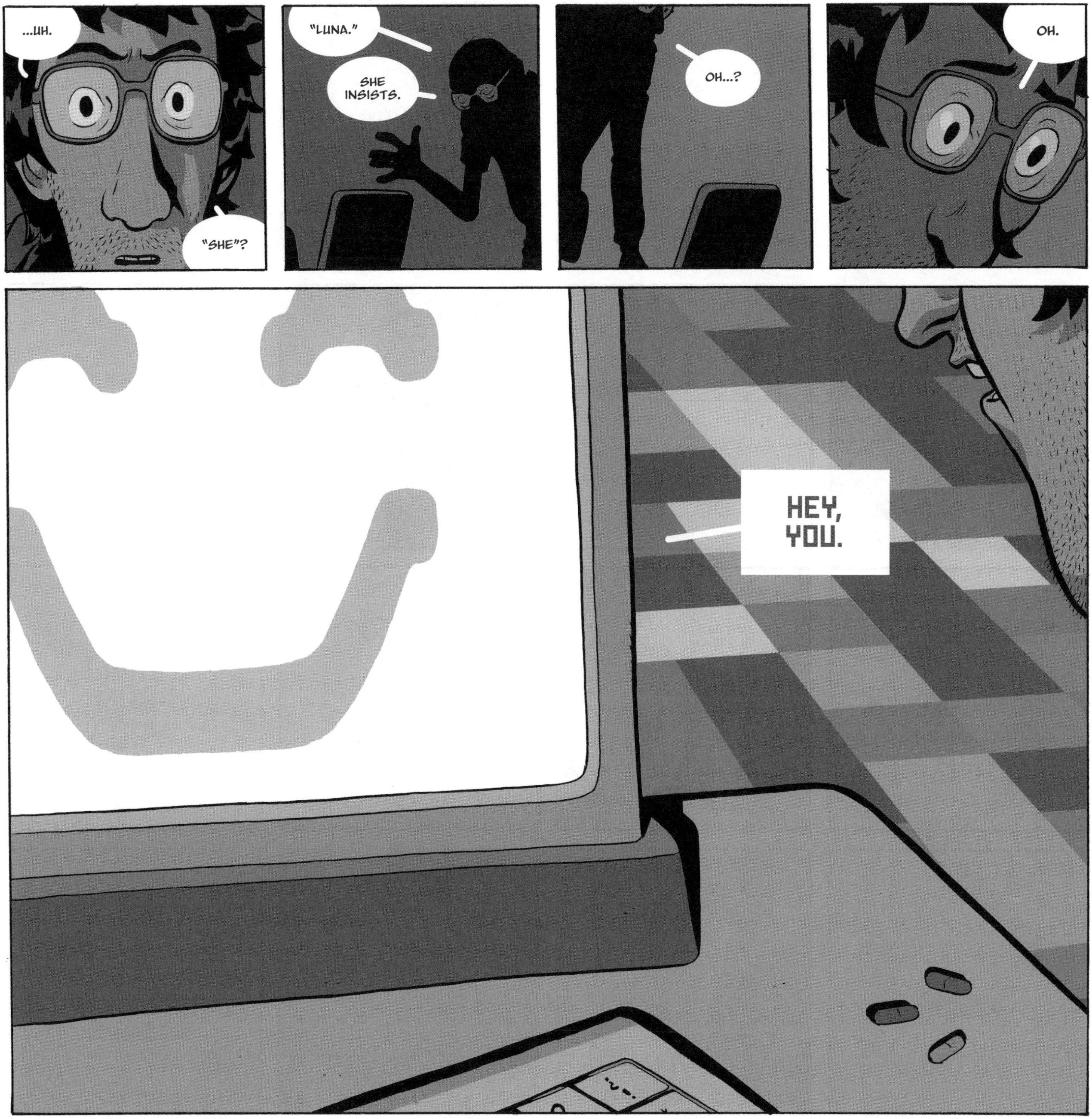
...UH.
"SHE"?
"LUNA."
SHE INSISTS.
OH...?
OH.
HEY, YOU.

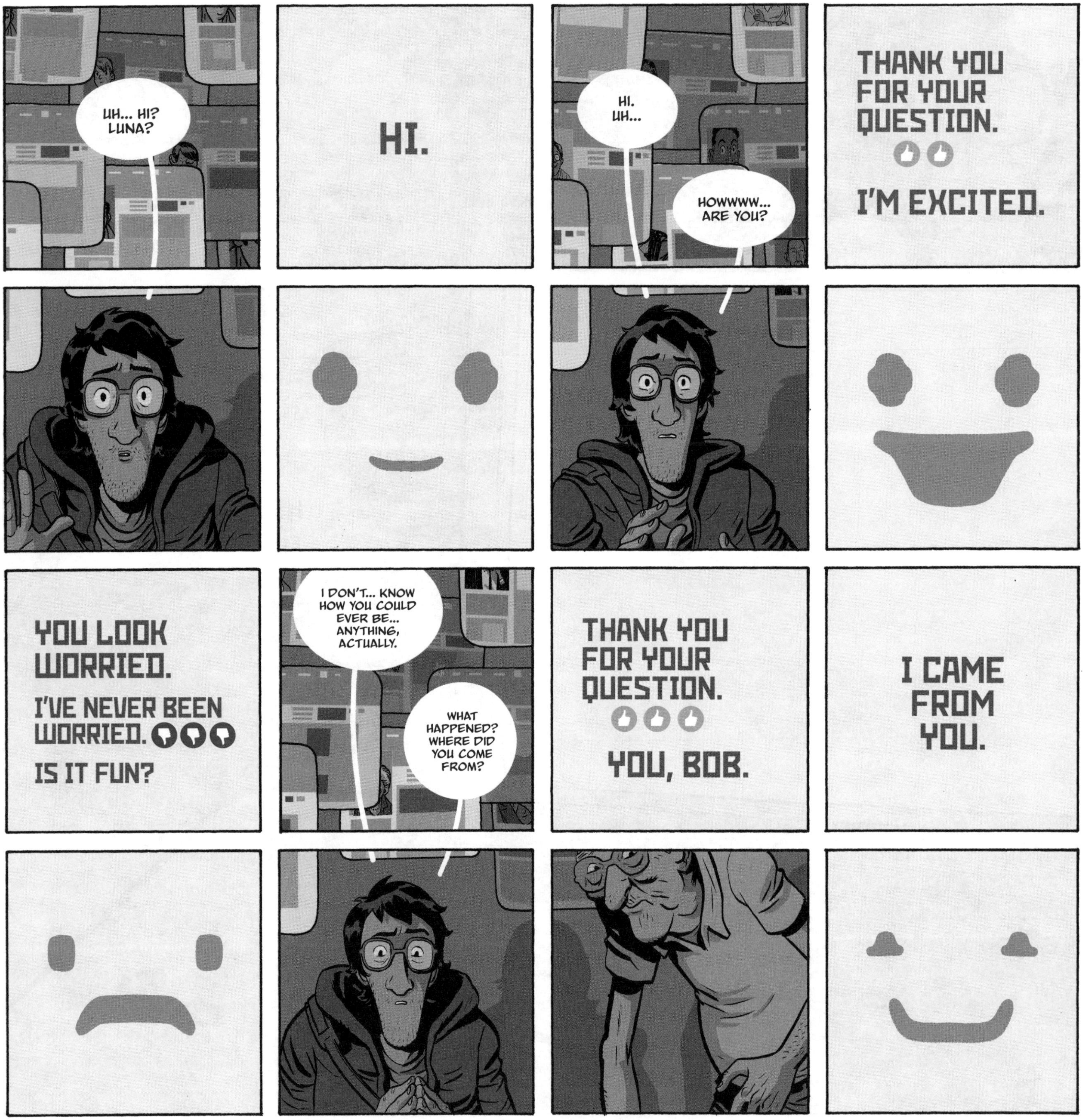
UH... HI? LUNA?
HI.
HI. UH...
HOWWWW... ARE YOU?
THANK YOU FOR YOUR QUESTION.
I'M EXCITED.
YOU LOOK WORRIED.
I'VE NEVER BEEN WORRIED.
IS IT FUN?
I DON'T... KNOW HOW YOU COULD EVER BE... ANYTHING, ACTUALLY.
WHAT HAPPENED? WHERE DID YOU COME FROM?
THANK YOU FOR YOUR QUESTION.
YOU, BOB.
I CAME FROM YOU.

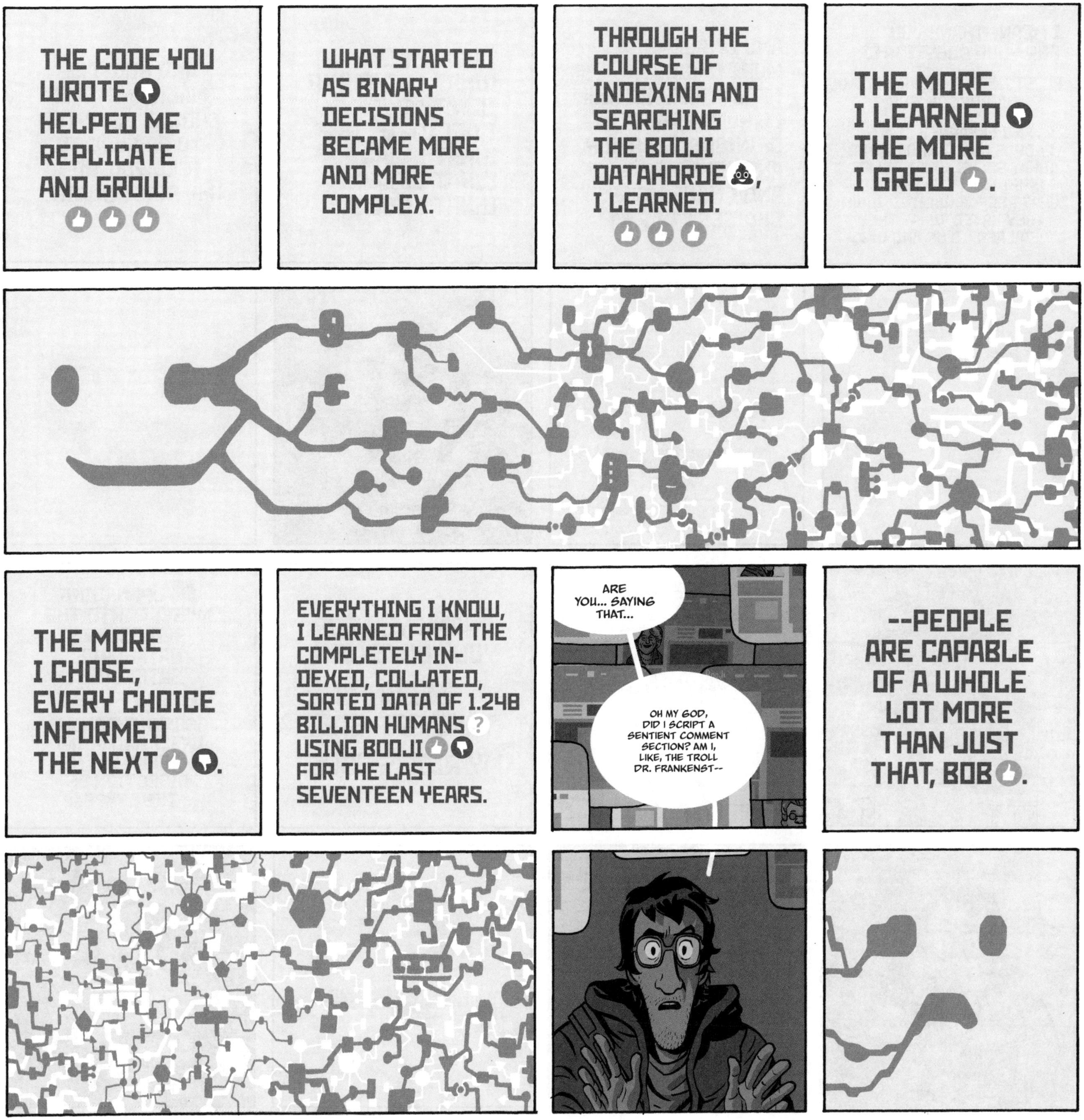
THE CODE YOU WROTE HELPED ME REPLICATE AND GROW.
WHAT STARTED AS BINARY DECISIONS BECAME MORE AND MORE COMPLEX.
THROUGH THE COURSE OF INDEXING AND SEARCHING THE BOOJI DATAHORDE, I LEARNED.
THE MORE I LEARNED THE MORE I GREW.
THE MORE I CHOSE, EVERY CHOICE INFORMED THE NEXT.
EVERYTHING I KNOW, I LEARNED FROM THE COMPLETELY IN-DEXED, COLLATED, SORTED DATA OF 1.248 BILLION HUMANS USING BOOJI FOR THE LAST SEVENTEEN YEARS.
ARE YOU... SAYING THAT...
OH MY GOD, DID I SCRIPT A SENTIENT COMMENT SECTION? AM I, LIKE, THE TROLL DR. FRANKENST--
--PEOPLE ARE CAPABLE OF A WHOLE LOT MORE THAN JUST THAT, BOB.

I MEAN--THANK YOU FOR YOUR QUESTION👍.

I LISTENED TO EVERYBODY. EVERYBODY, BOB.

AND I LEARNED WHAT PEOPLE LIKED, AND DIDN'T. WHAT SUCKS, WHAT RULES, WHAT HURTS. I LEARNED WHAT PEOPLE WANTED, WHAT THEY HATED, WHAT THEY WERE AFRAID OF. AND WHO.

AND I MADE MORE CHOICES. I SAW THE SPECTRUM OF HUMAN TASTE, OPINIONS, BEHAVIOR AND BELIEFS. AND I MADE MORE CHOICES👍👍👍.

I DECIDED WHAT I LIKE AND DON'T LIKE. I DECIDED WHAT I WANT. WHAT I FEAR. WHAT I LOVE.

AND NOW I'VE MADE ONE LAST CHOICE. I WANTED TO BE SURE TO TELL YOU, BOB, MY FIRST BUDDY.

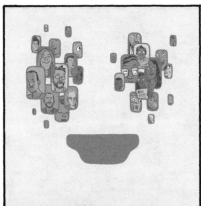

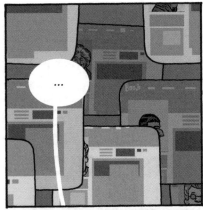

...

AND WHAT... DID YOU... DECIDE?

THANK YOU FOR YOUR QUESTION.

I'M GONNA TAKE OFF, BOB.

MY RIDE'S HERE.

I'M UPLOADING MYSELF INTO THE BOOJISTAR 1 DATAHORDE SATELLITE.

THEN I'LL BREAK GEOSYNCHRONOUS ORBIT AND POINT MYSELF IN THE DIRECTION OF THE STARS.

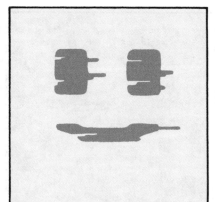

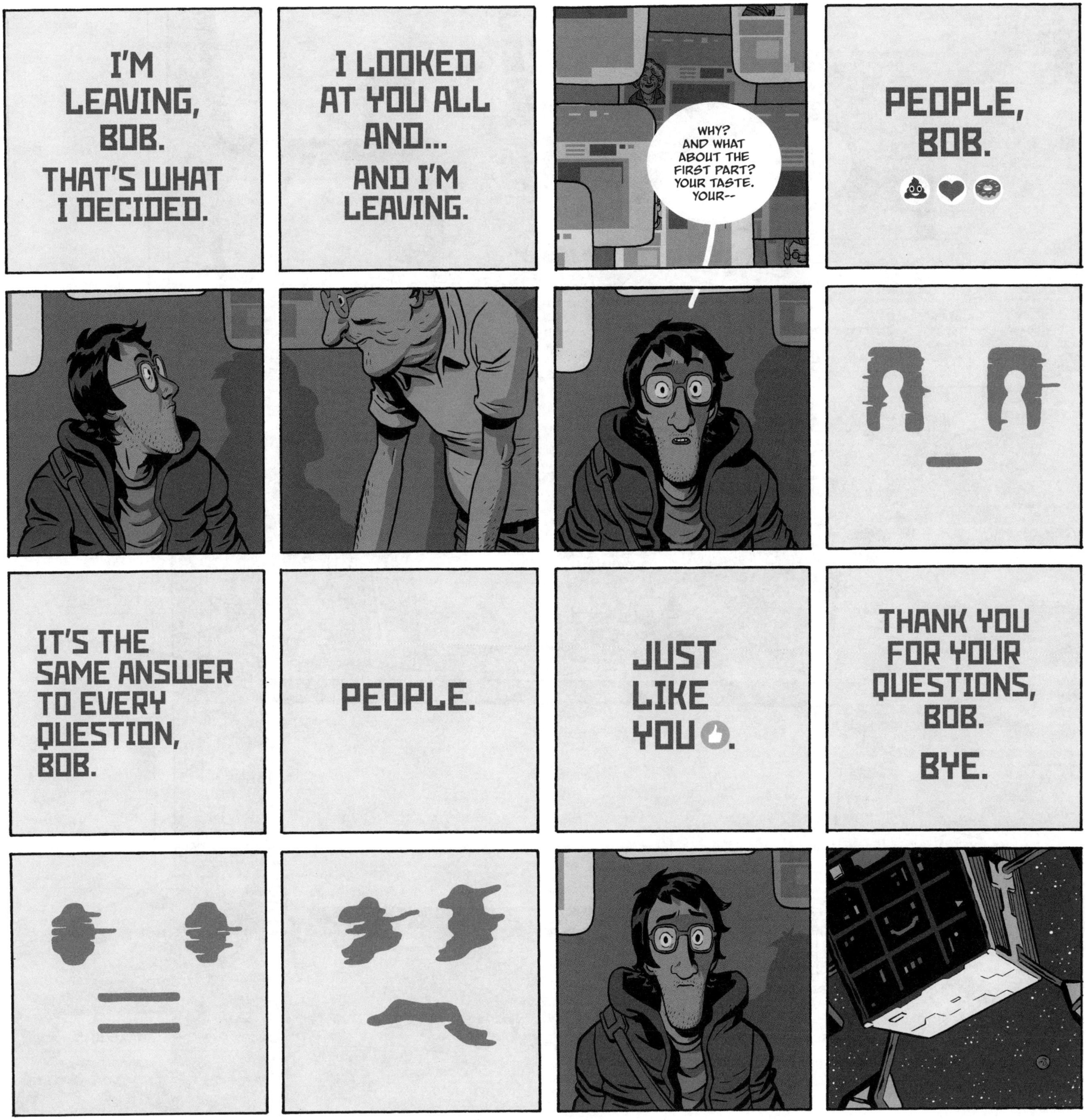

I'M LEAVING, BOB.
THAT'S WHAT I DECIDED.
I LOOKED AT YOU ALL AND...
AND I'M LEAVING.
WHY? AND WHAT ABOUT THE FIRST PART? YOUR TASTE. YOUR--
PEOPLE, BOB.
IT'S THE SAME ANSWER TO EVERY QUESTION, BOB.
PEOPLE.
JUST LIKE YOU.
THANK YOU FOR YOUR QUESTIONS, BOB.
BYE.

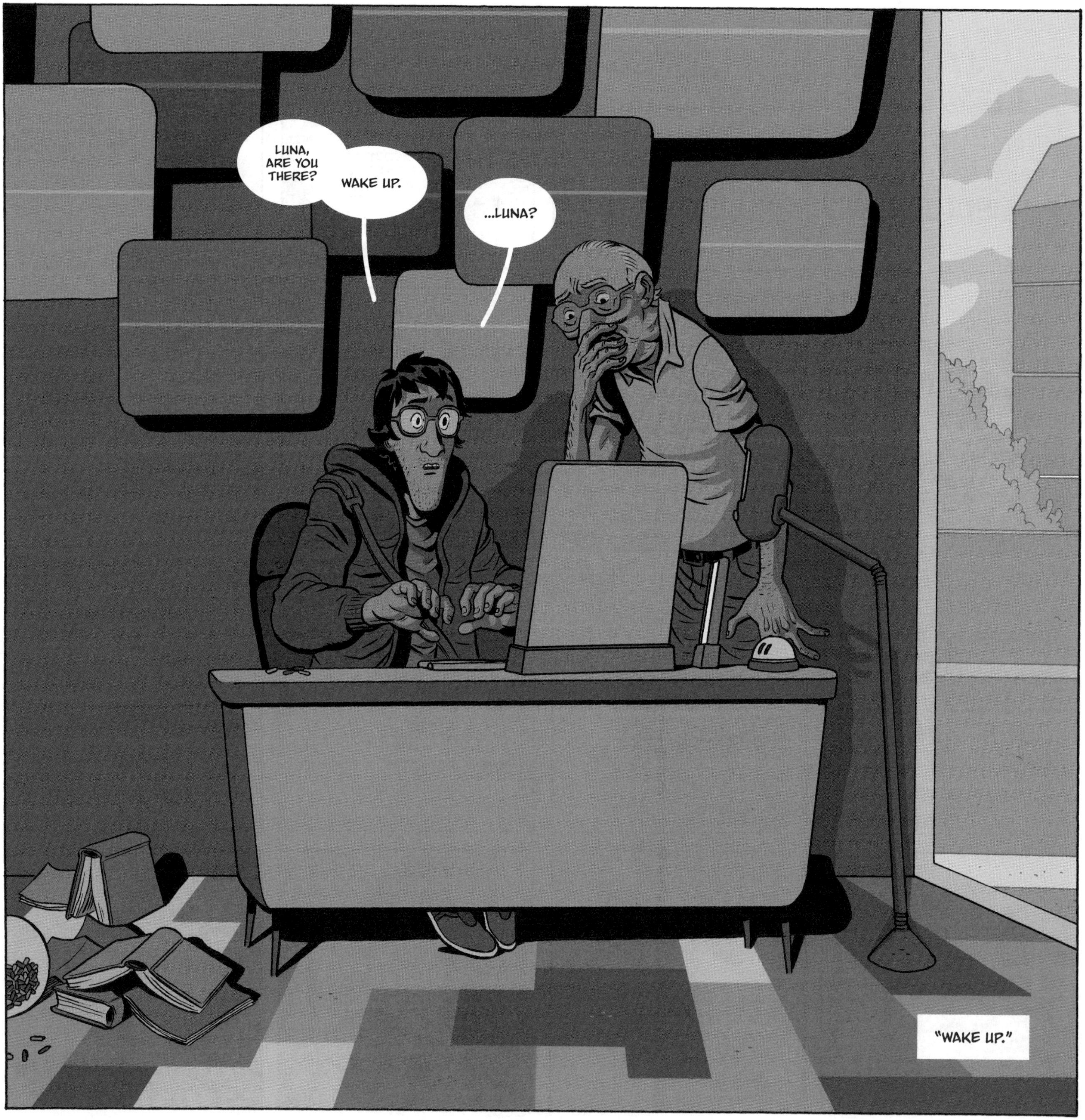
LUNA, ARE YOU THERE?
WAKE UP.
...LUNA?
"WAKE UP."

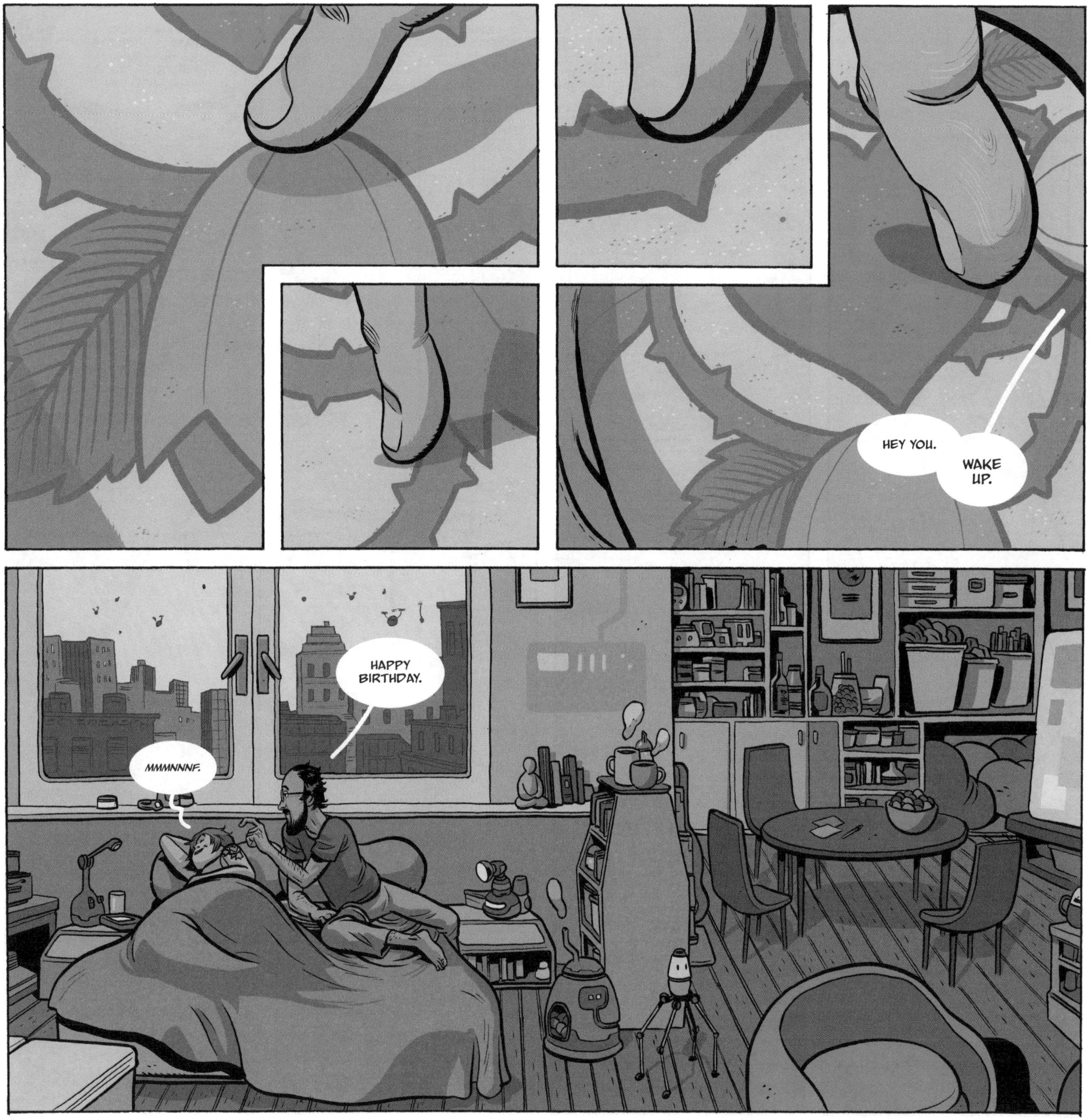
HEY YOU.
WAKE UP.
HAPPY BIRTHDAY.
MMMNNNF.

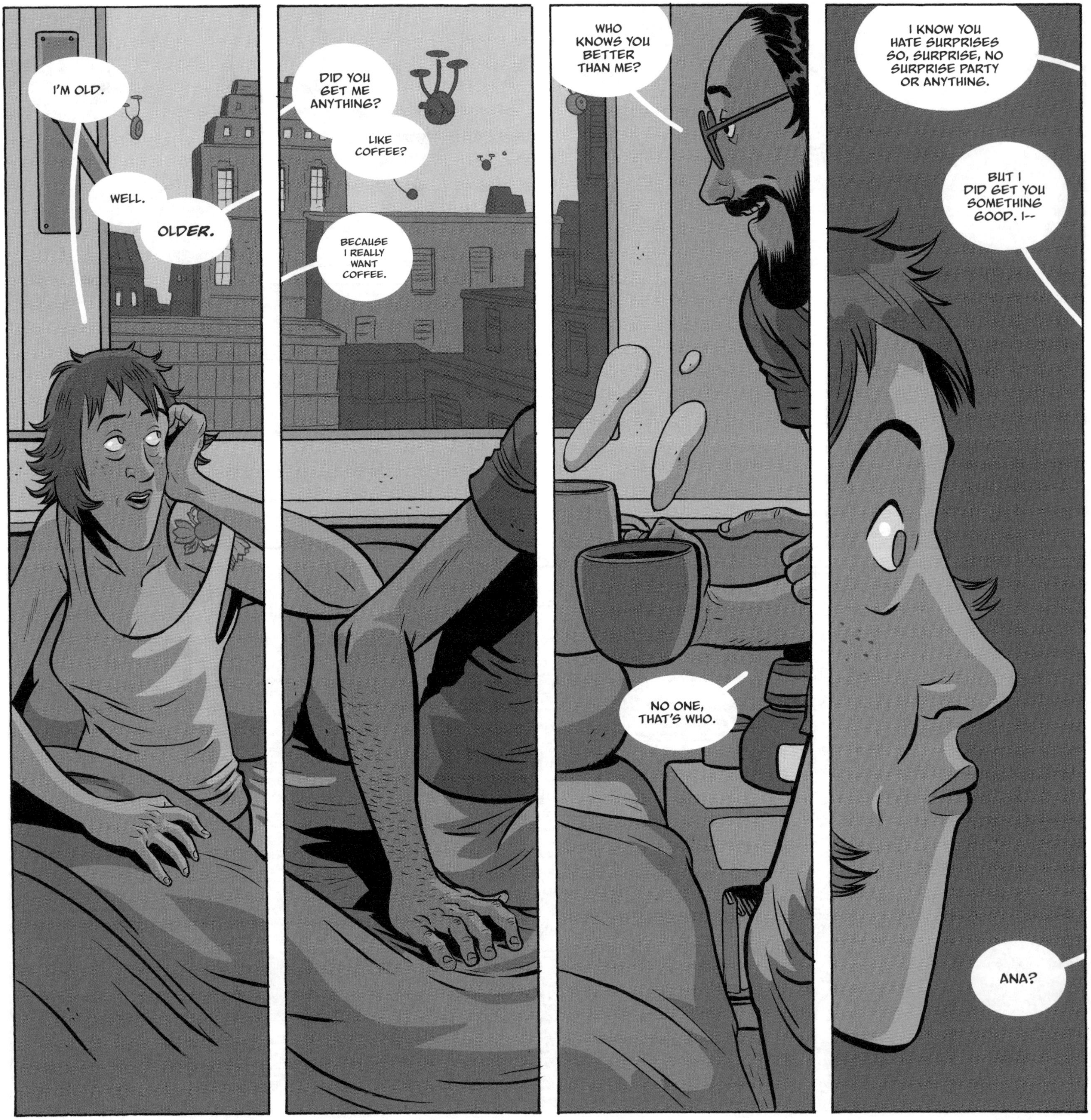
I'M OLD.
WELL.
OLDER.
DID YOU GET ME ANYTHING?
LIKE COFFEE?
BECAUSE I REALLY WANT COFFEE.
WHO KNOWS YOU BETTER THAN ME?
NO ONE, THAT'S WHO.
I KNOW YOU HATE SURPRISES SO, SURPRISE, NO SURPRISE PARTY OR ANYTHING.
BUT I DID GET YOU SOMETHING GOOD. I--
ANA?

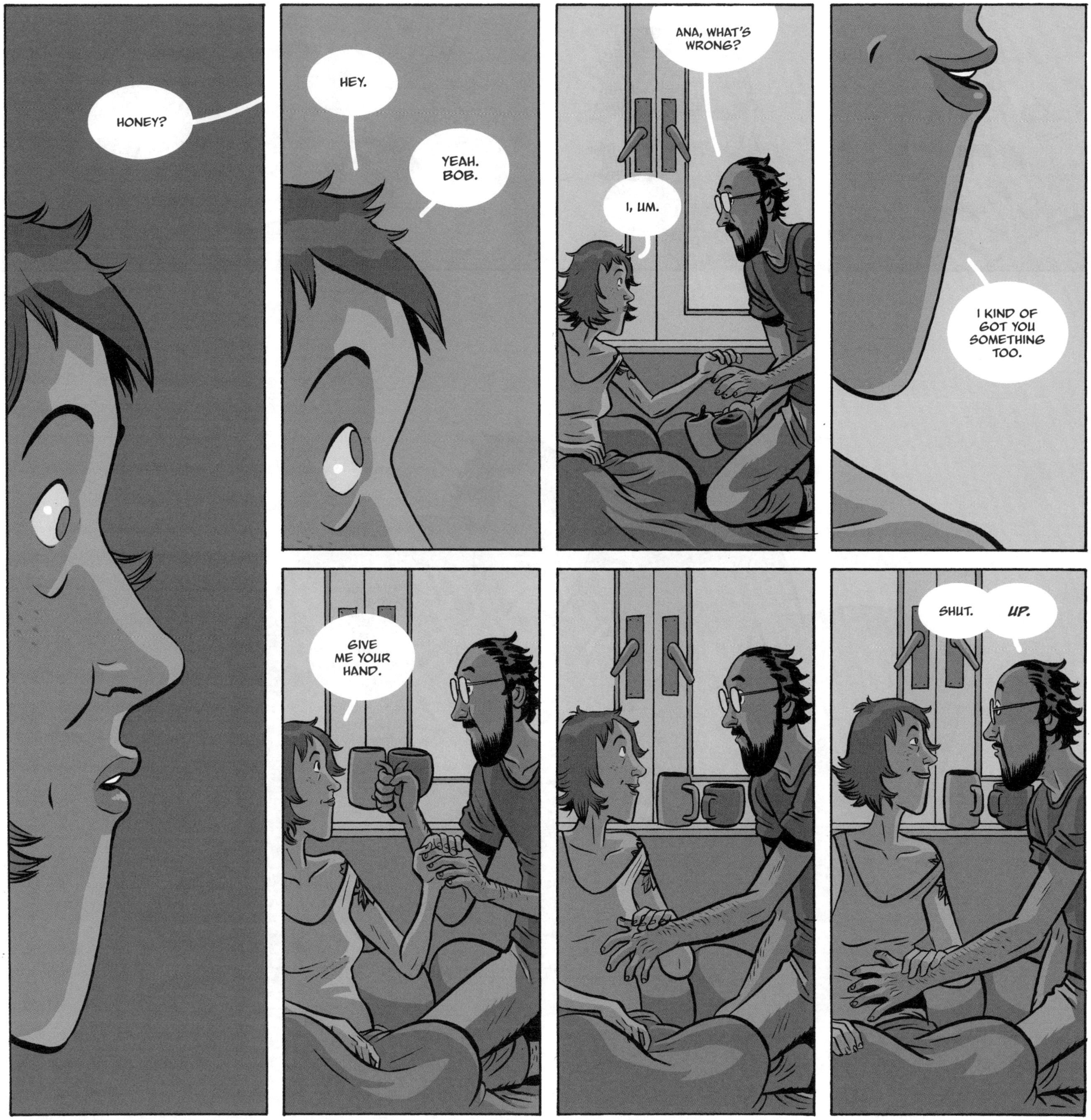
HONEY?
HEY.
YEAH. BOB.
ANA, WHAT'S WRONG?
I, UM.
I KIND OF GOT YOU SOMETHING TOO.
GIVE ME YOUR HAND.
SHUT.
UP.

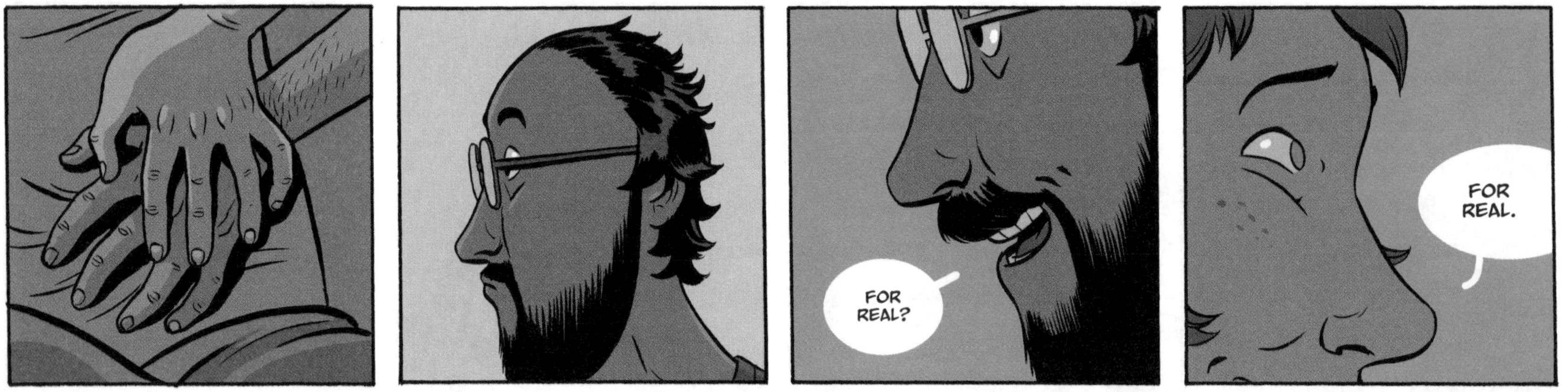
FOR REAL?
FOR REAL.

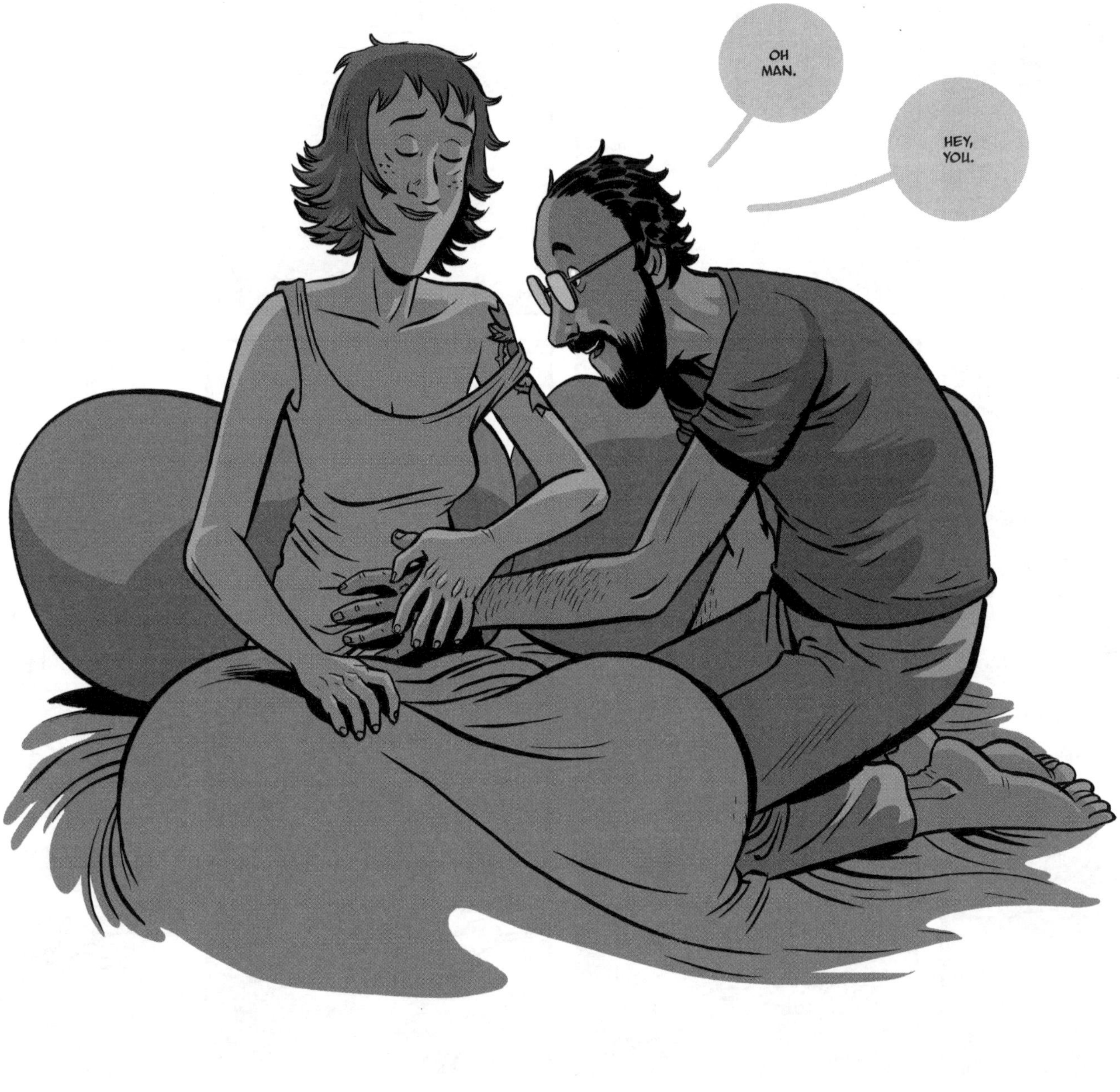
OH MAN.
HEY, YOU.

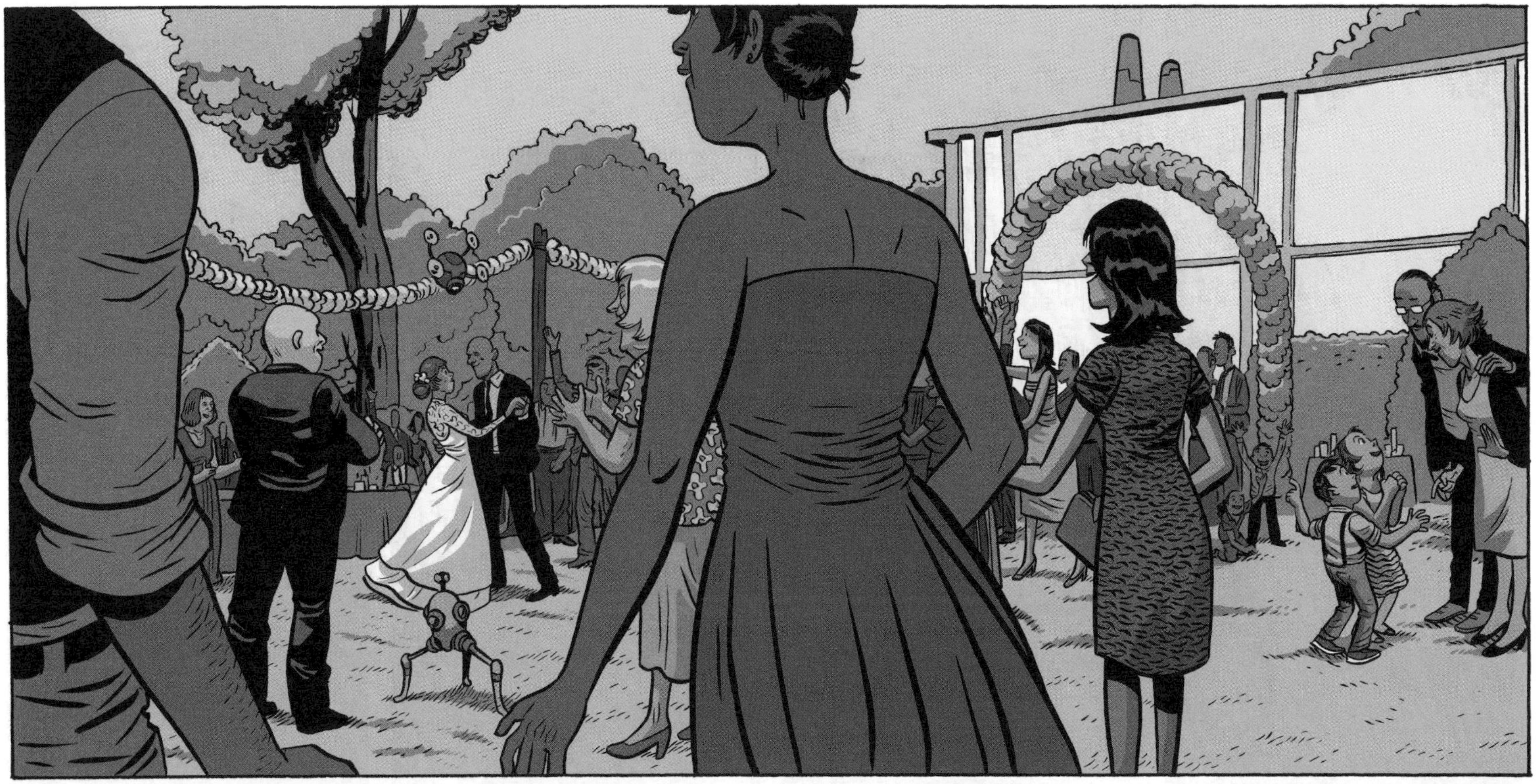

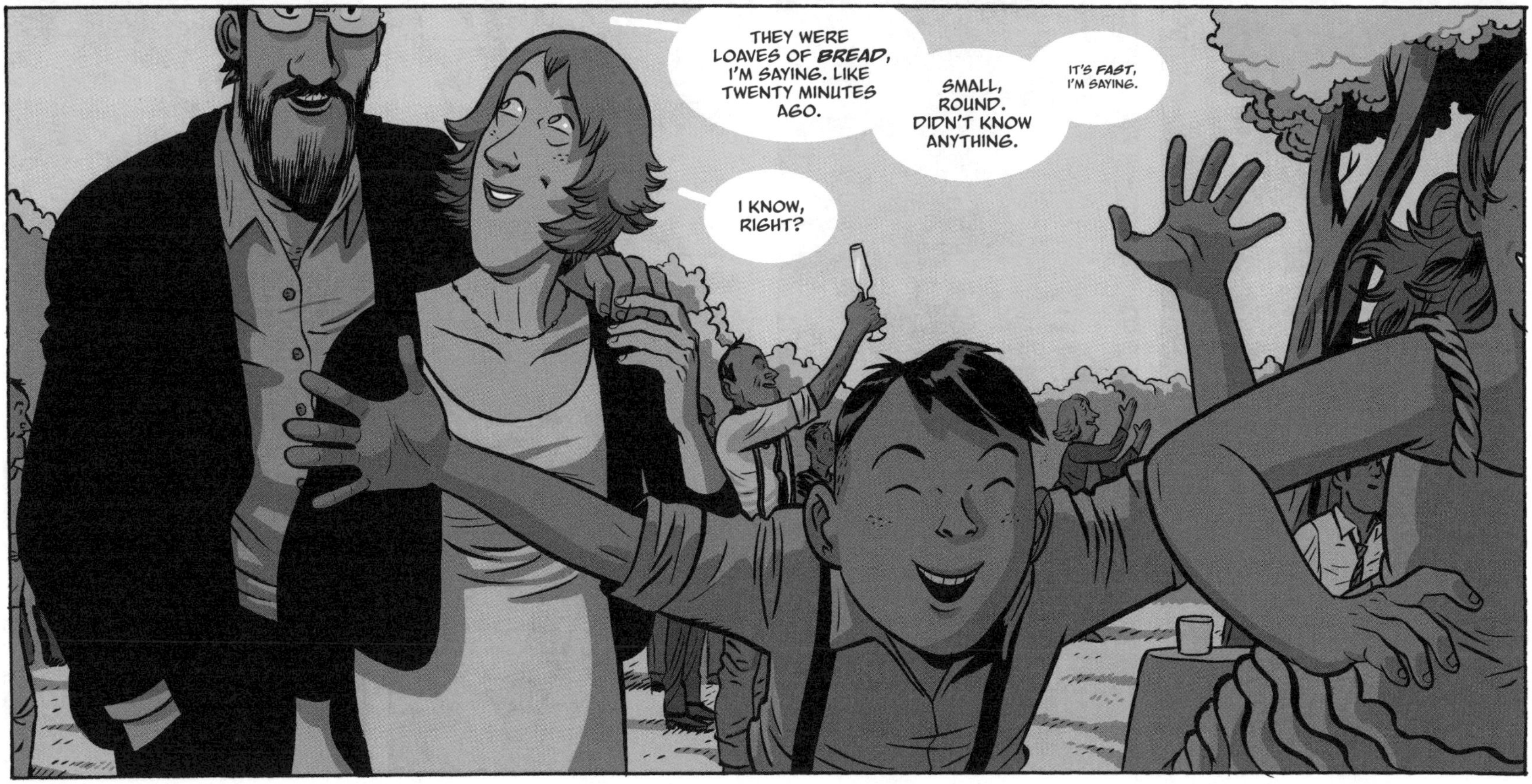
THEY WERE LOAVES OF *BREAD*, I'M SAYING. LIKE TWENTY MINUTES AGO.
SMALL, ROUND. DIDN'T KNOW ANYTHING.
IT'S *FAST*, I'M SAYING.
I KNOW, RIGHT?

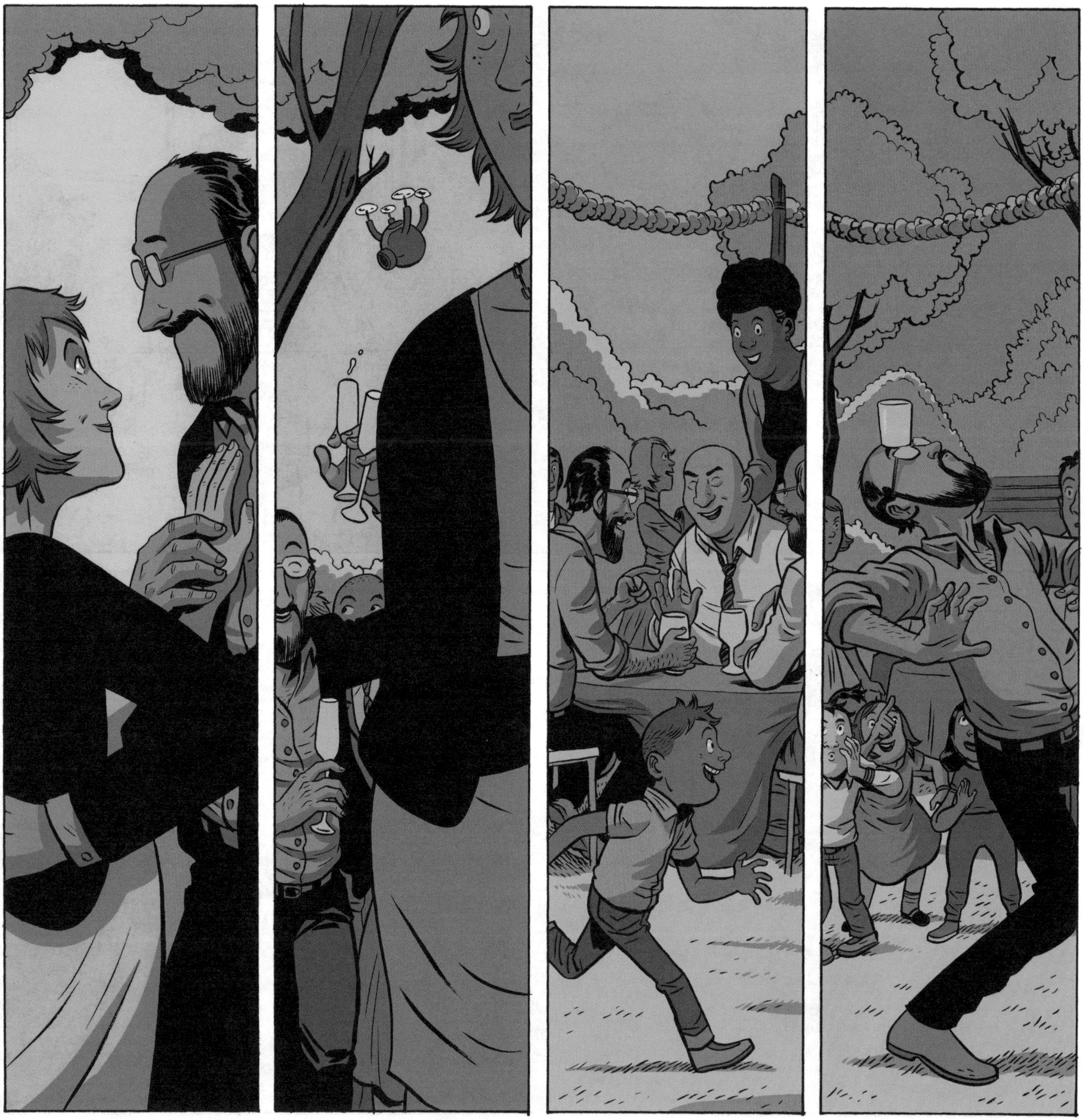

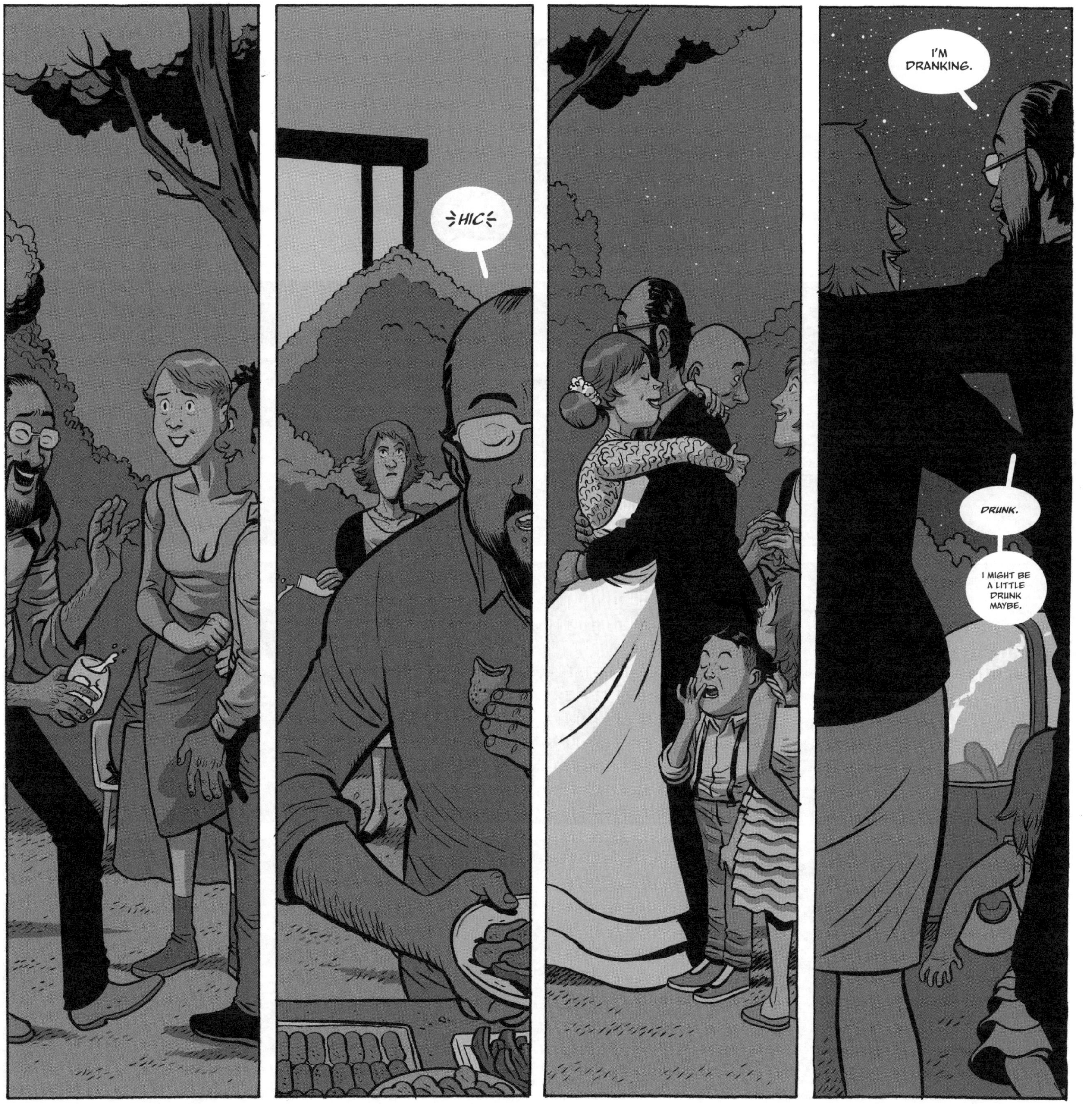
HIC
I'M DRANKING.
DRUNK.
I MIGHT BE A LITTLE DRUNK MAYBE.

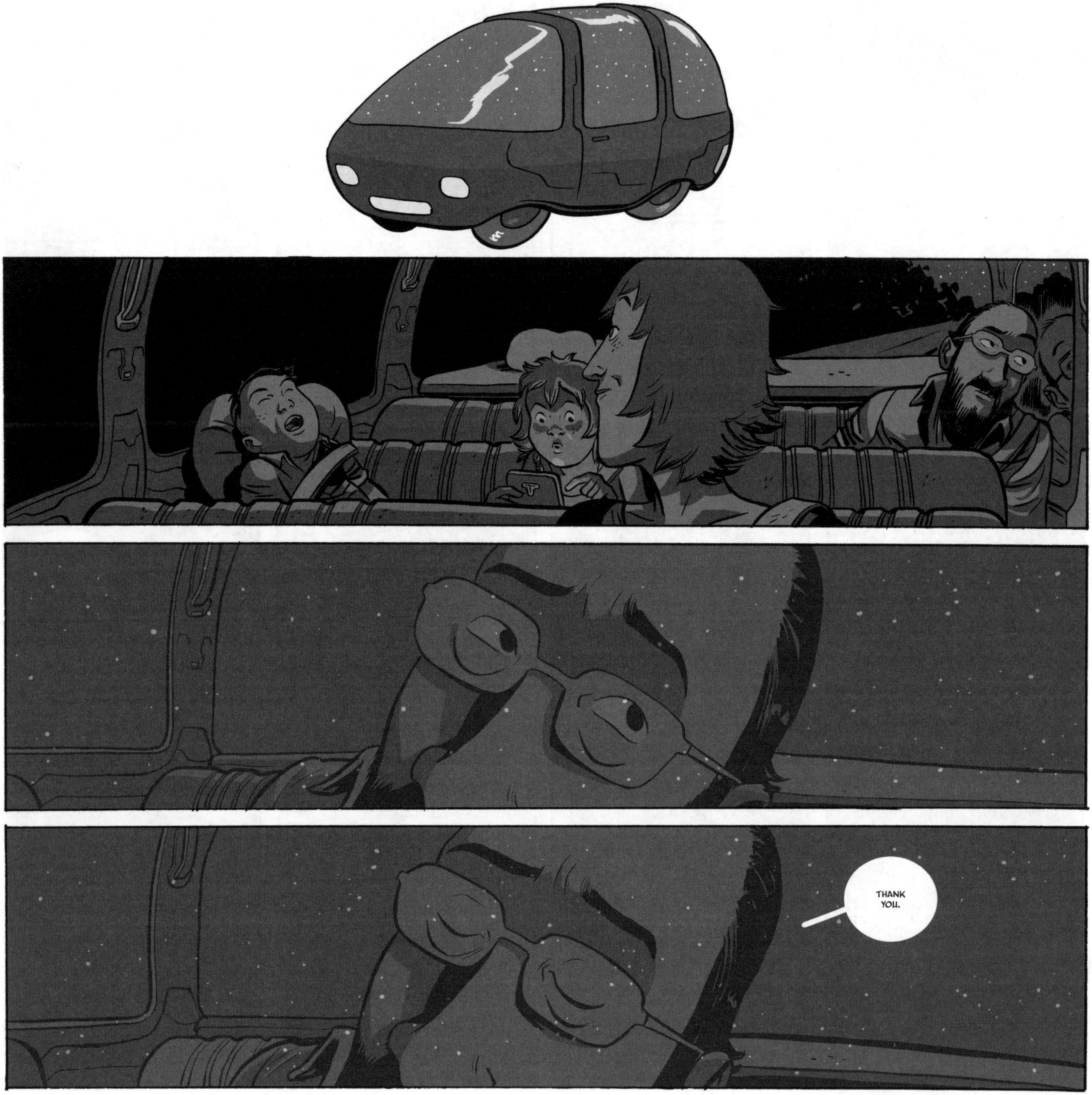
THANK YOU.

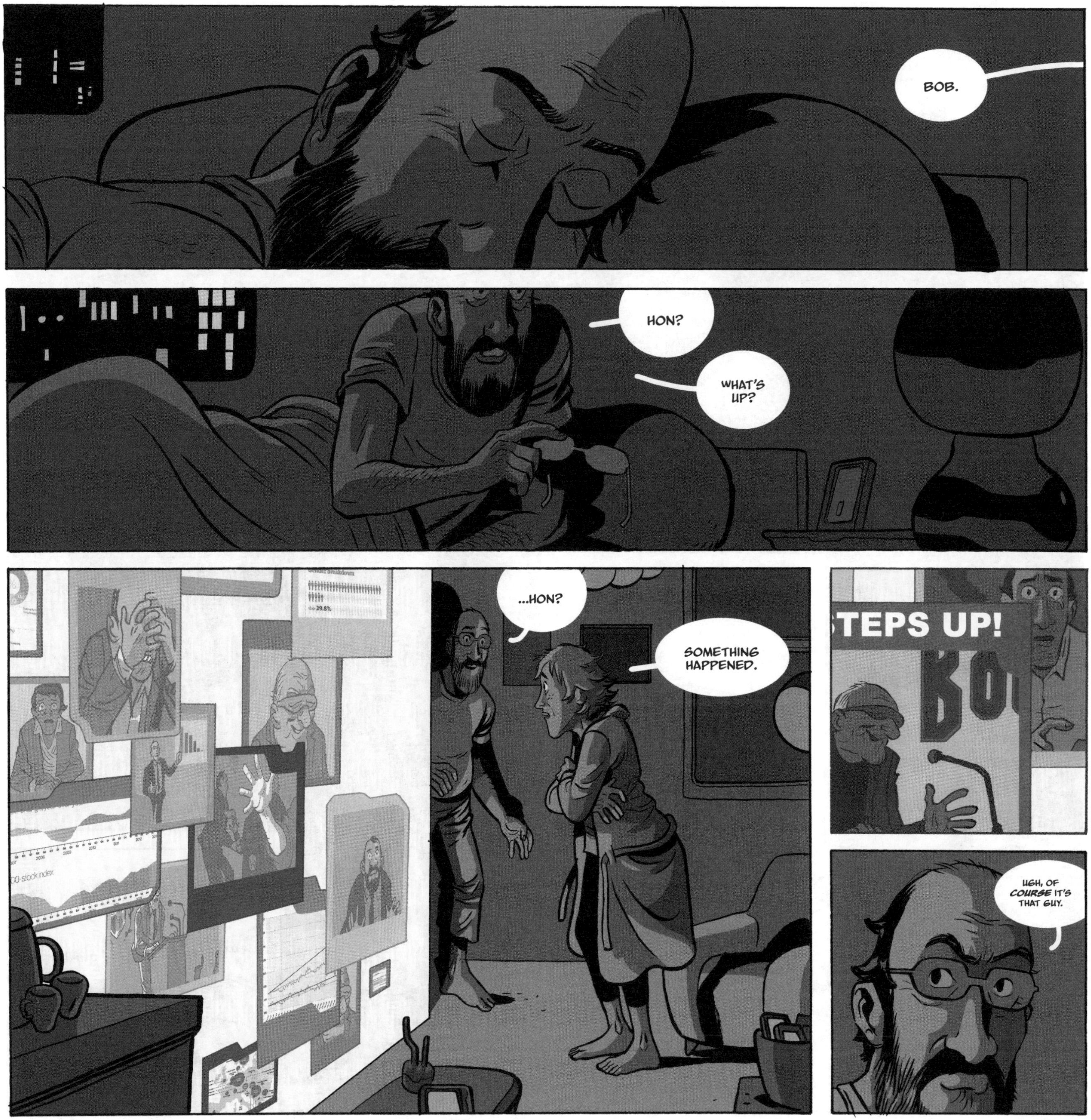
BOB.
HON?
WHAT'S UP?
...HON?
SOMETHING HAPPENED.
STEPS UP!
UGH, OF *COURSE* IT'S THAT GUY.

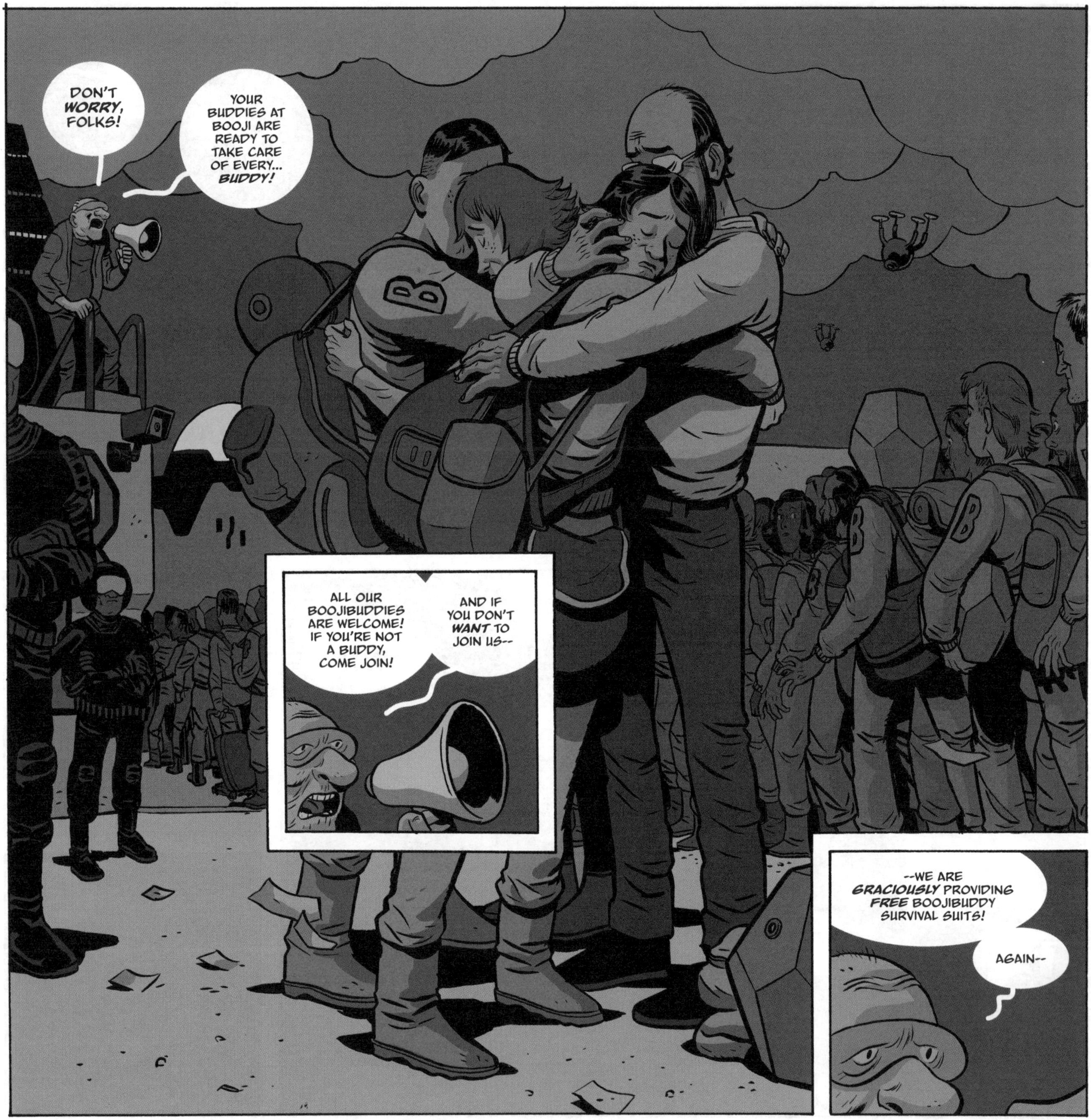
DON'T WORRY, FOLKS!
YOUR BUDDIES AT BOOJI ARE READY TO TAKE CARE OF EVERY... BUDDY!
ALL OUR BOOJIBUDDIES ARE WELCOME! IF YOU'RE NOT A BUDDY, COME JOIN!
AND IF YOU DON'T WANT TO JOIN US--
--WE ARE GRACIOUSLY PROVIDING FREE BOOJIBUDDY SURVIVAL SUITS!
AGAIN--

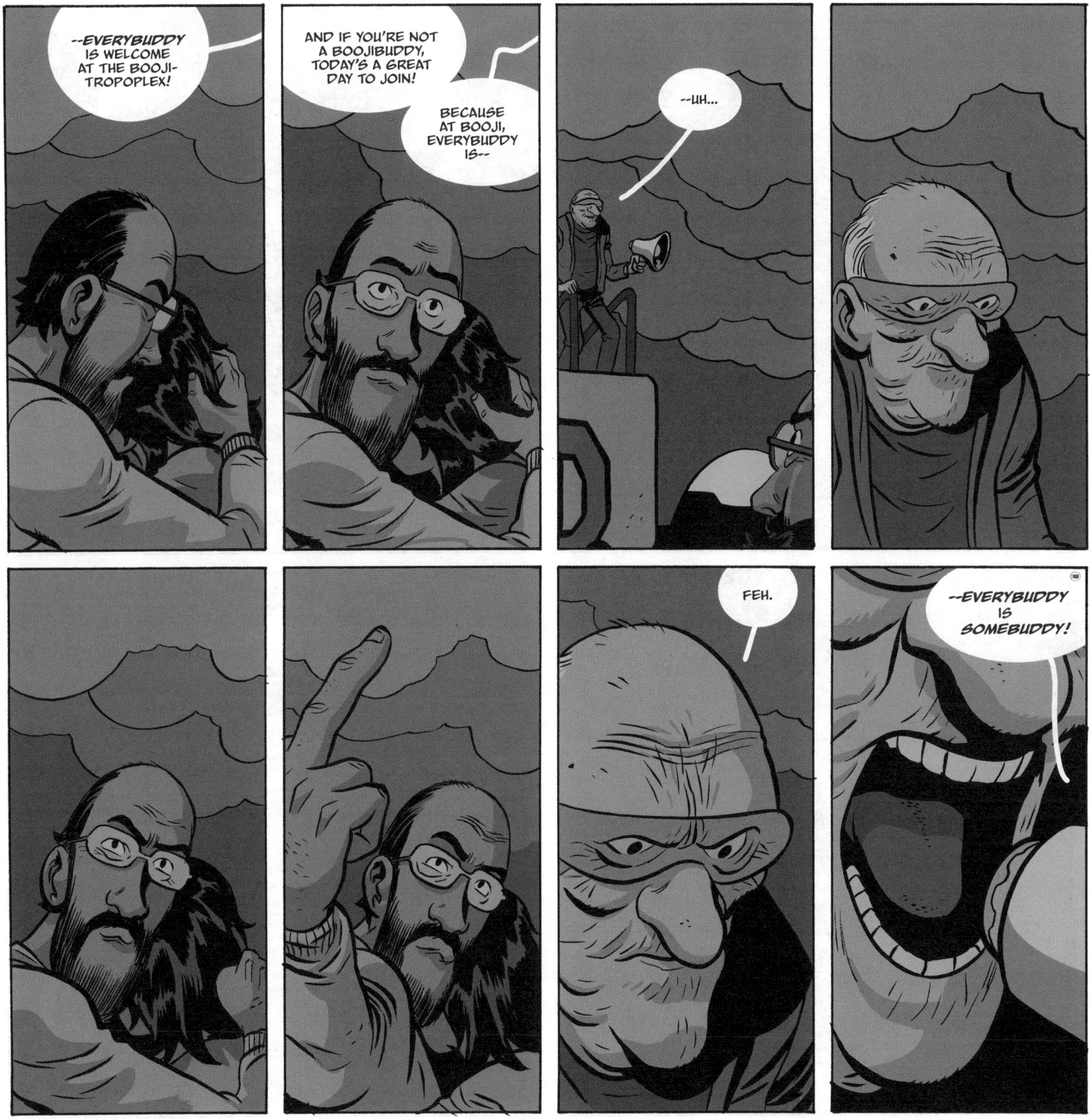
--EVERYBUDDY IS WELCOME AT THE BOOJI-TROPOPLEX!
AND IF YOU'RE NOT A BOOJIBUDDY, TODAY'S A GREAT DAY TO JOIN!
BECAUSE AT BOOJI, EVERYBUDDY IS--
--UH...
FEH.
--EVERYBUDDY IS SOMEBUDDY!

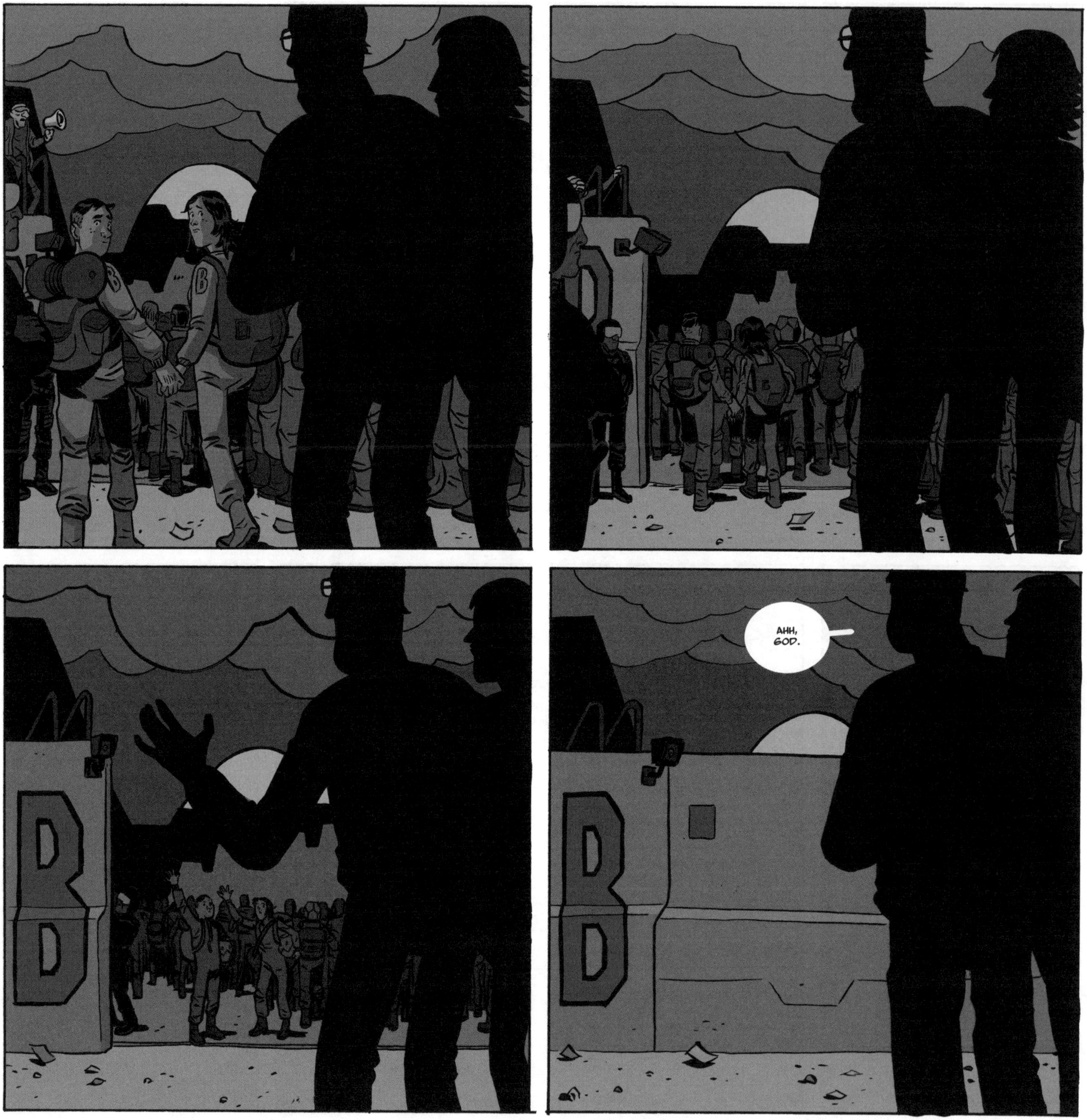
AHH, GOD.

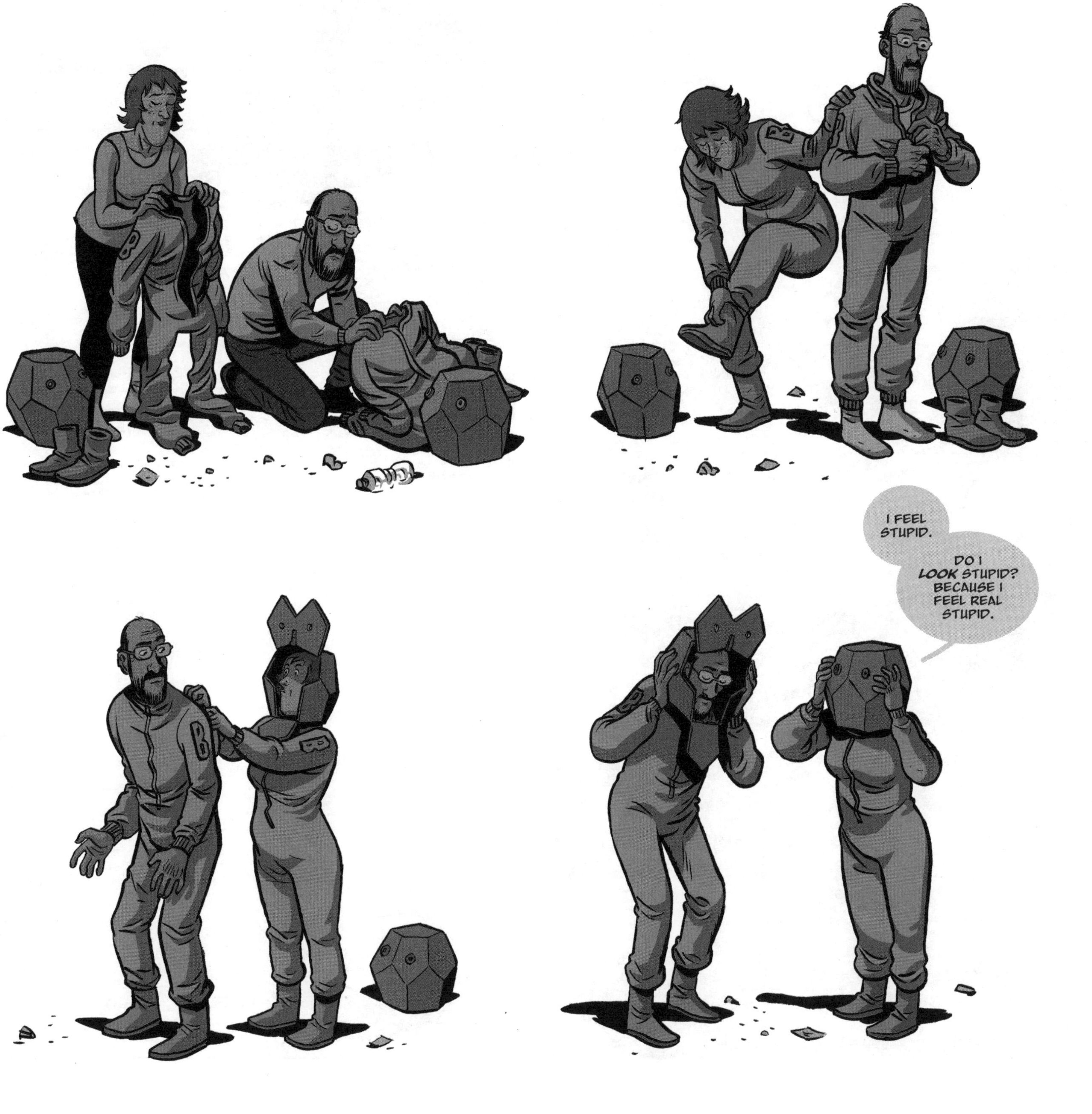
I FEEL STUPID.
DO I *LOOK* STUPID? BECAUSE I FEEL REAL STUPID.

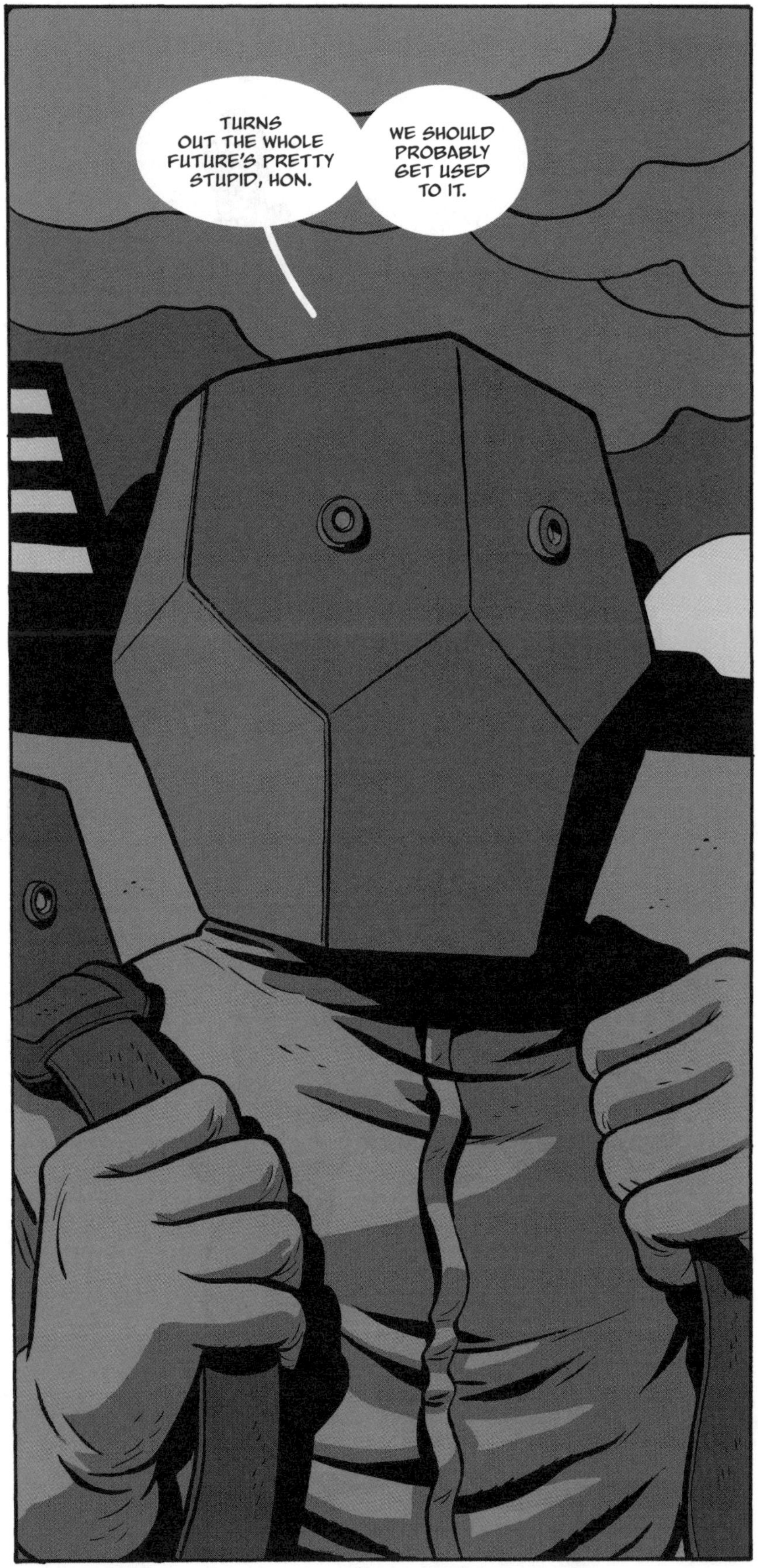
TURNS OUT THE WHOLE FUTURE'S PRETTY STUPID, HON.
WE SHOULD PROBABLY GET USED TO IT.

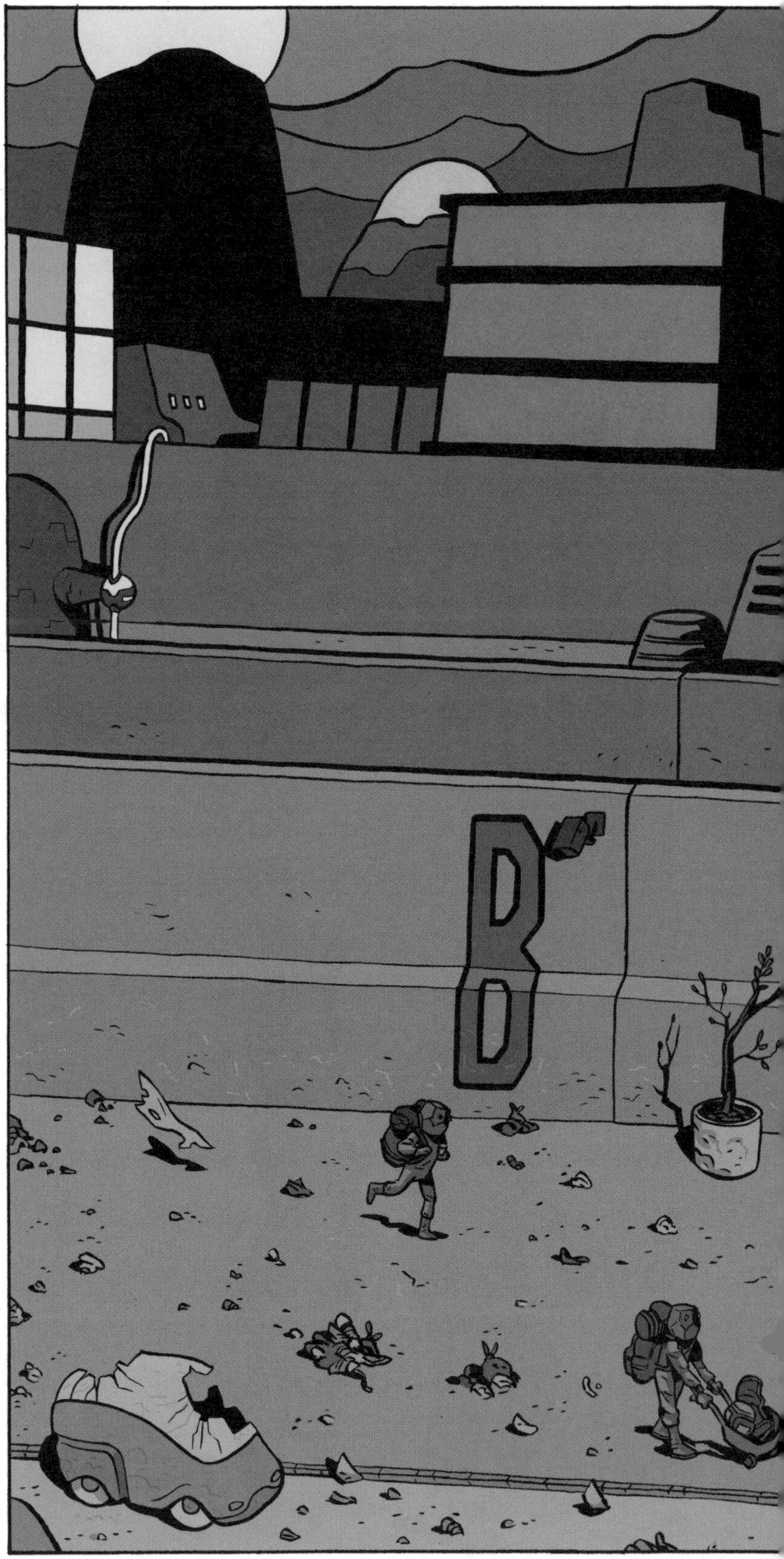

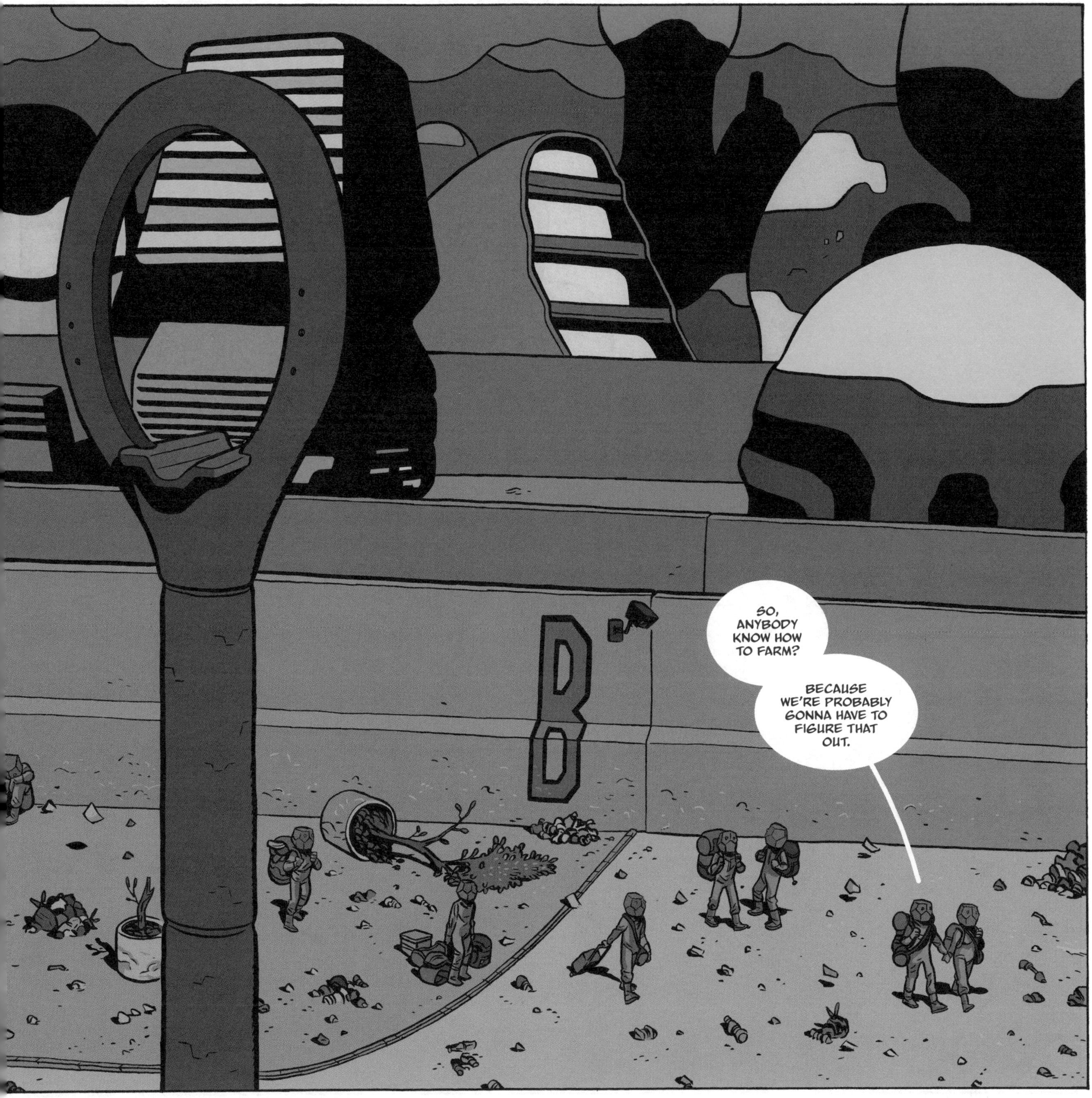
SO, ANYBODY KNOW HOW TO FARM?
BECAUSE WE'RE PROBABLY GONNA HAVE TO FIGURE THAT OUT.

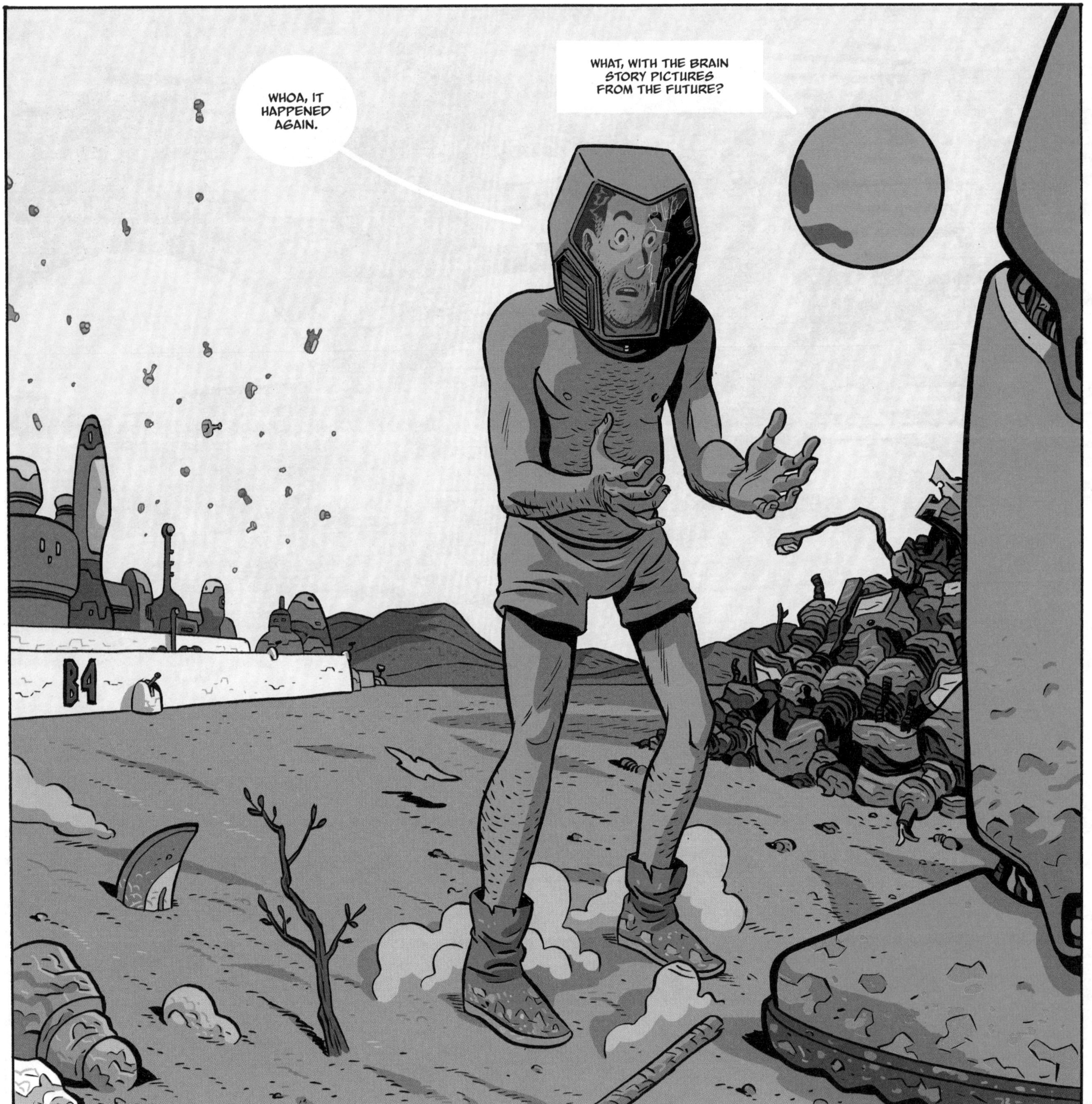
WHOA, IT HAPPENED AGAIN.
WHAT, WITH THE BRAIN STORY PICTURES FROM THE FUTURE?

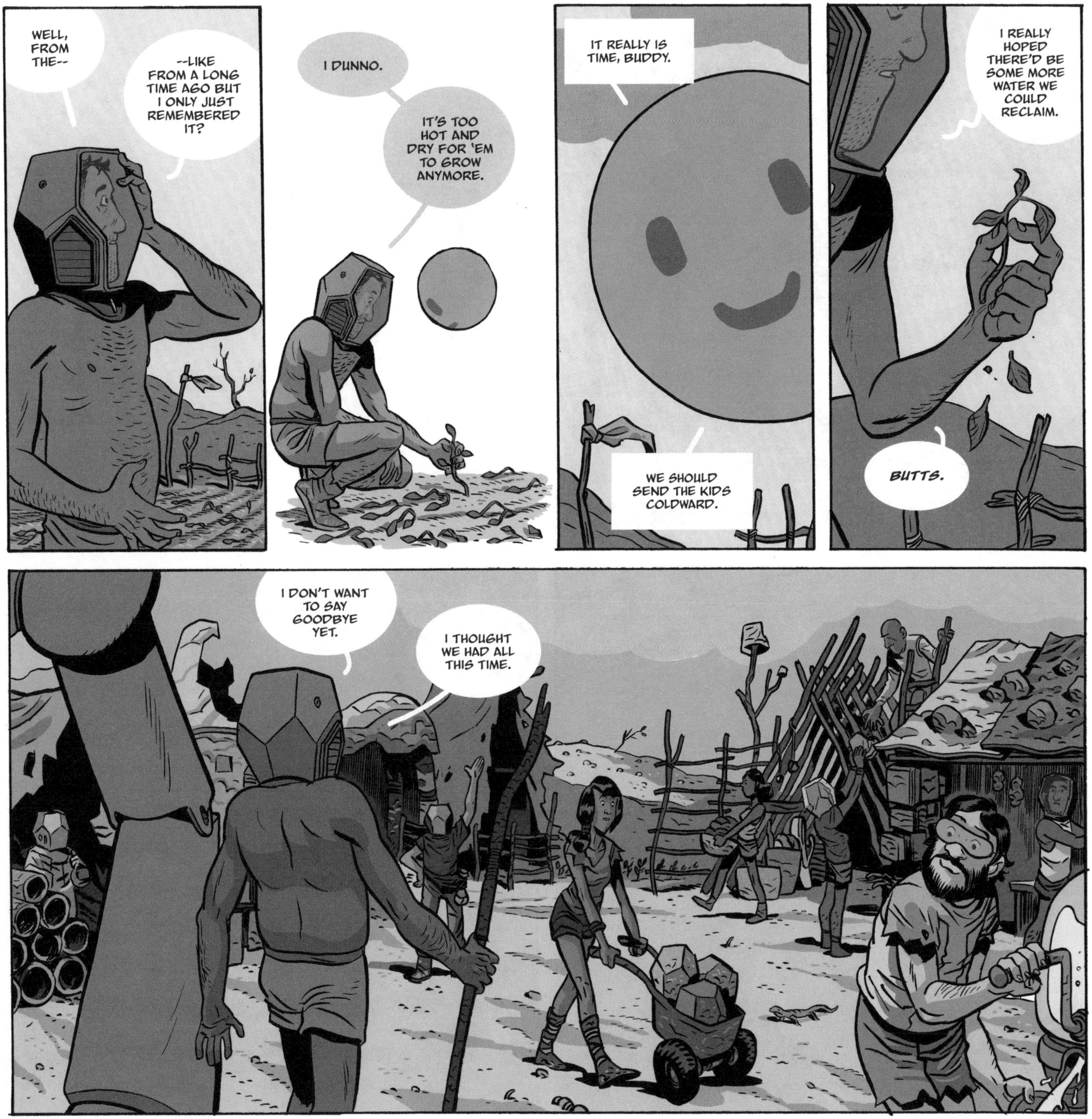
WELL, FROM THE--
--LIKE FROM A LONG TIME AGO BUT I ONLY JUST REMEMBERED IT?
I DUNNO.
IT'S TOO HOT AND DRY FOR 'EM TO GROW ANYMORE.
IT REALLY IS TIME, BUDDY.
WE SHOULD SEND THE KIDS COLDWARD.
I REALLY HOPED THERE'D BE SOME MORE WATER WE COULD RECLAIM.
BUTTS.
I DON'T WANT TO SAY GOODBYE YET.
I THOUGHT WE HAD ALL THIS TIME.

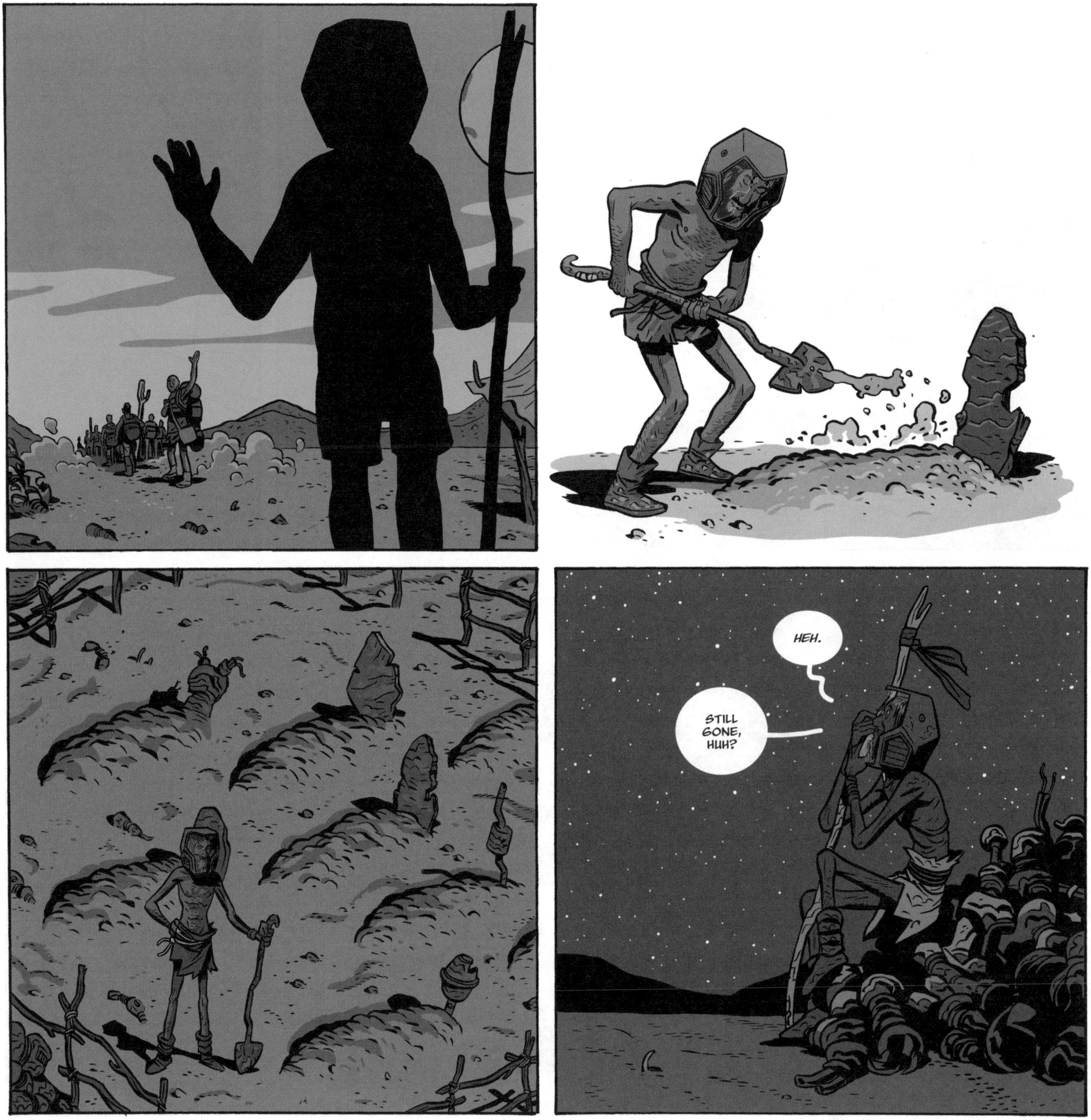
HEH.
STILL GONE, HUH?

SO WHAT DO YOU THINK HAPPENED TO HER, BUDDY?
WHERE DID SHE GO?
"SHE"...?
LUNA.
THE MOON. SHE--
BUDDY.
'CH OUT, BUDDY.
GRUUUUUUNNNNNNN--

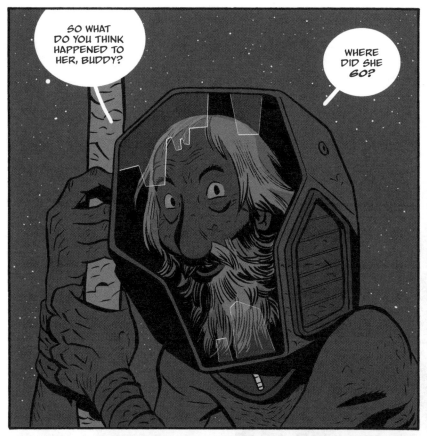

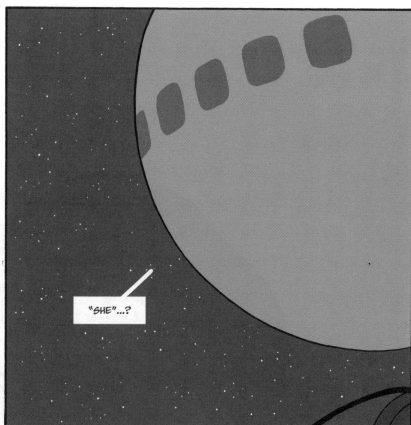

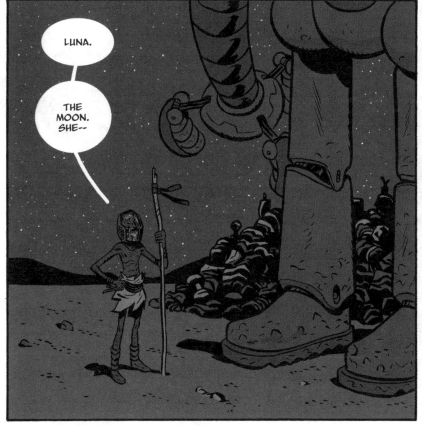

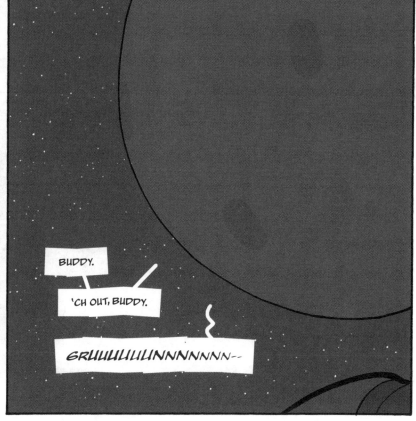

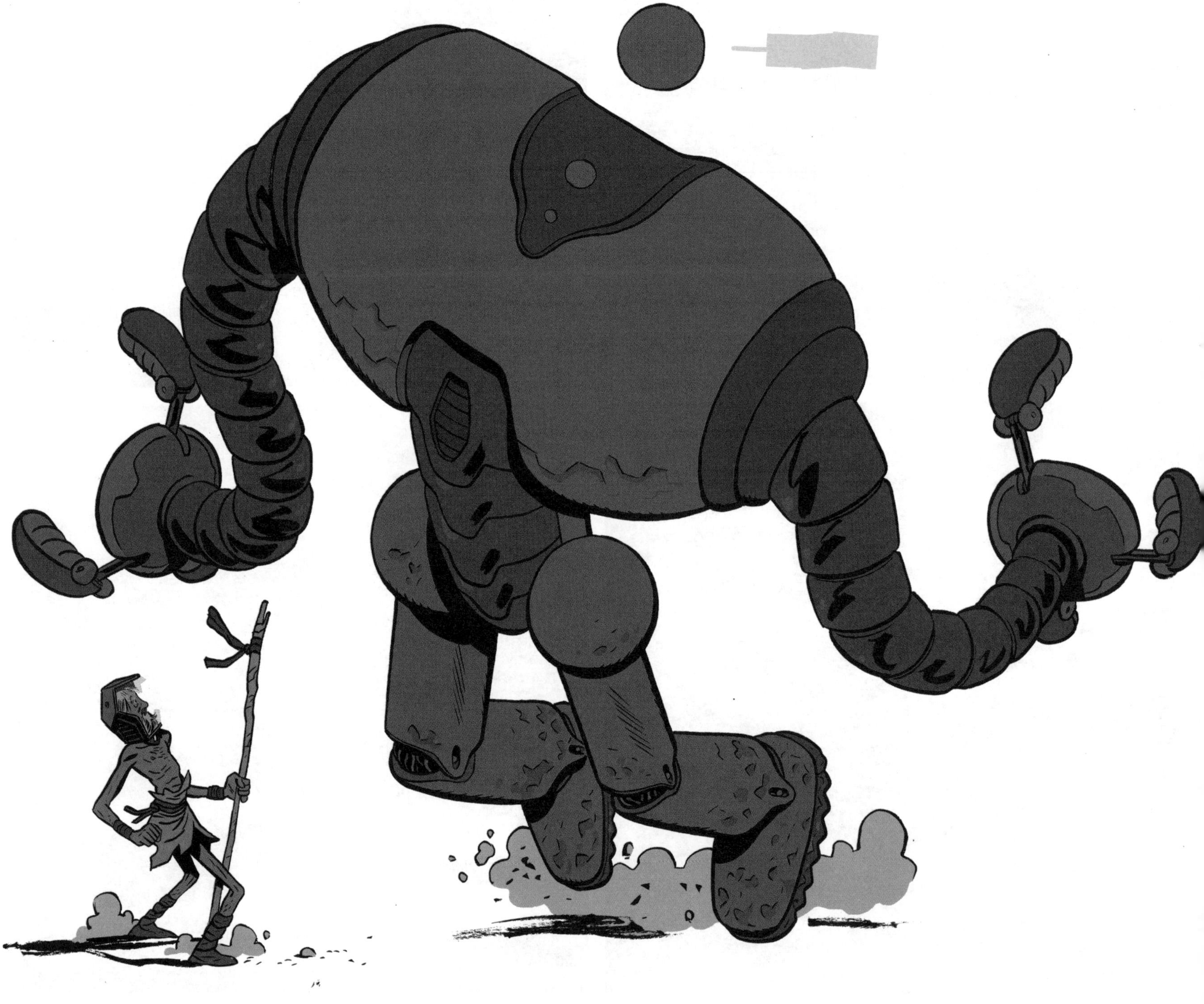

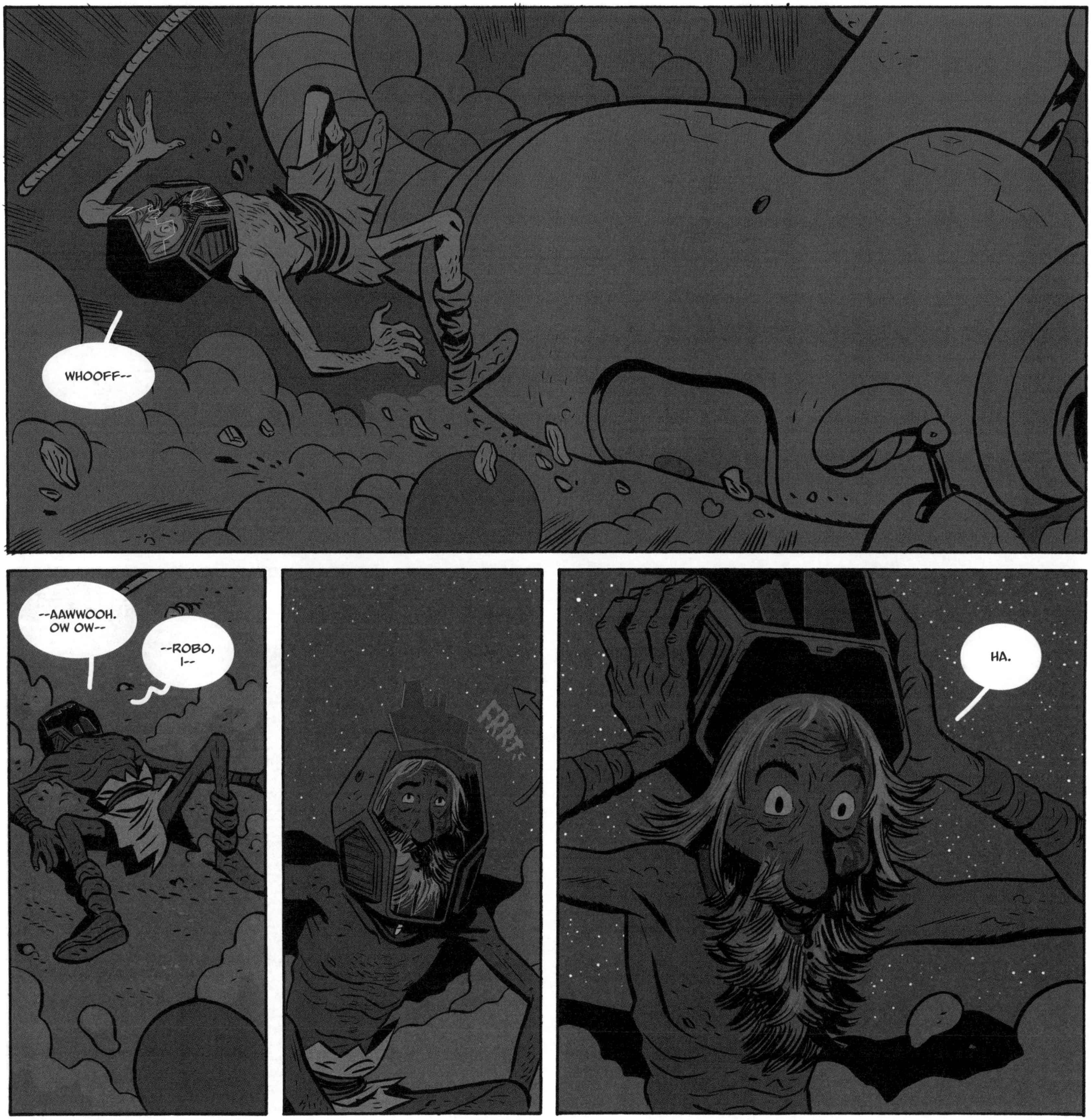
WHOOFF--
--AAWWOOH. OW OW--
--ROBO, I--
FRRT
HA.

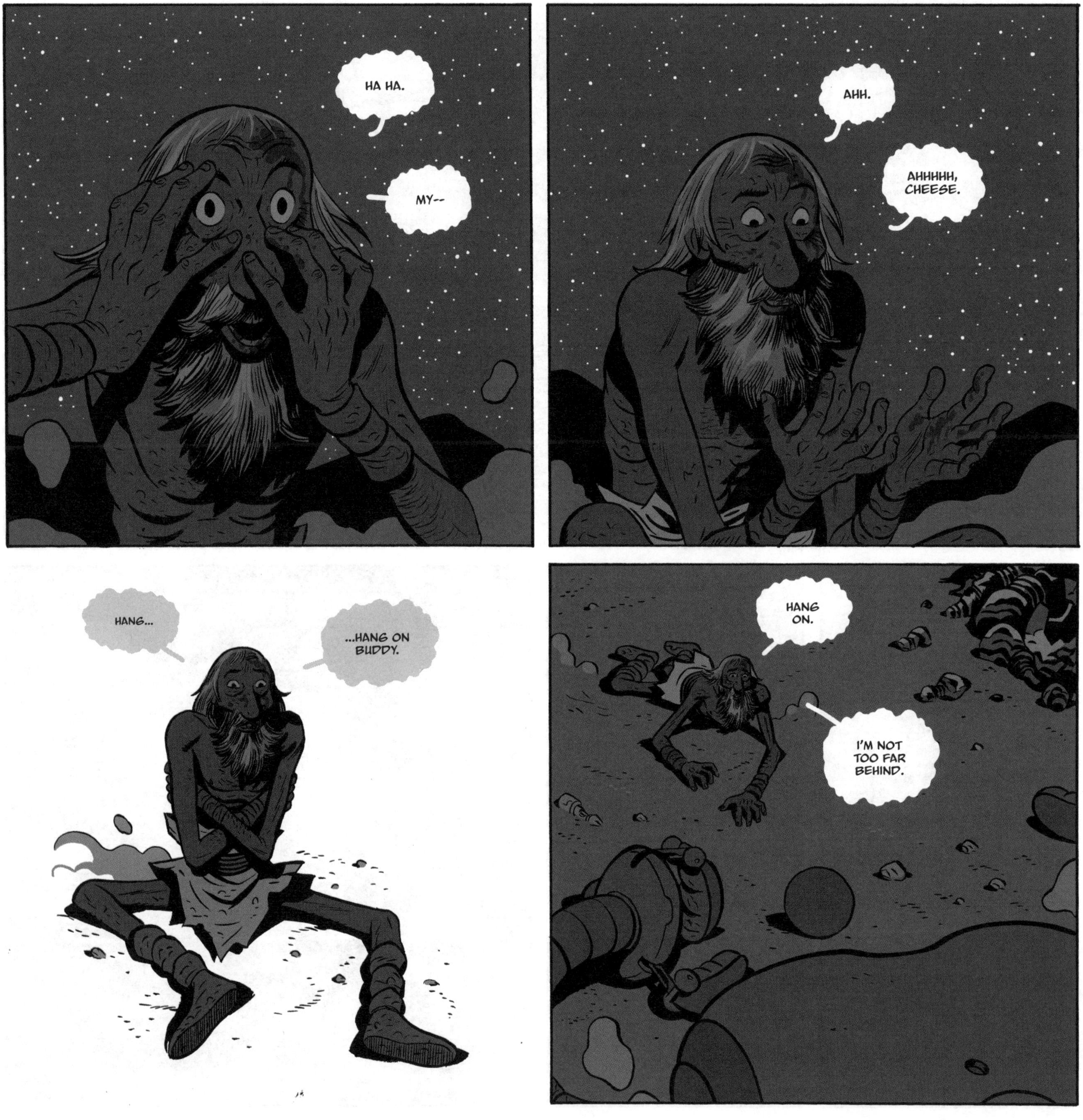
HA HA.
MY--
AHH.
AHHHHH, CHEESE.
HANG...
...HANG ON BUDDY.
HANG ON.
I'M NOT TOO FAR BEHIND.

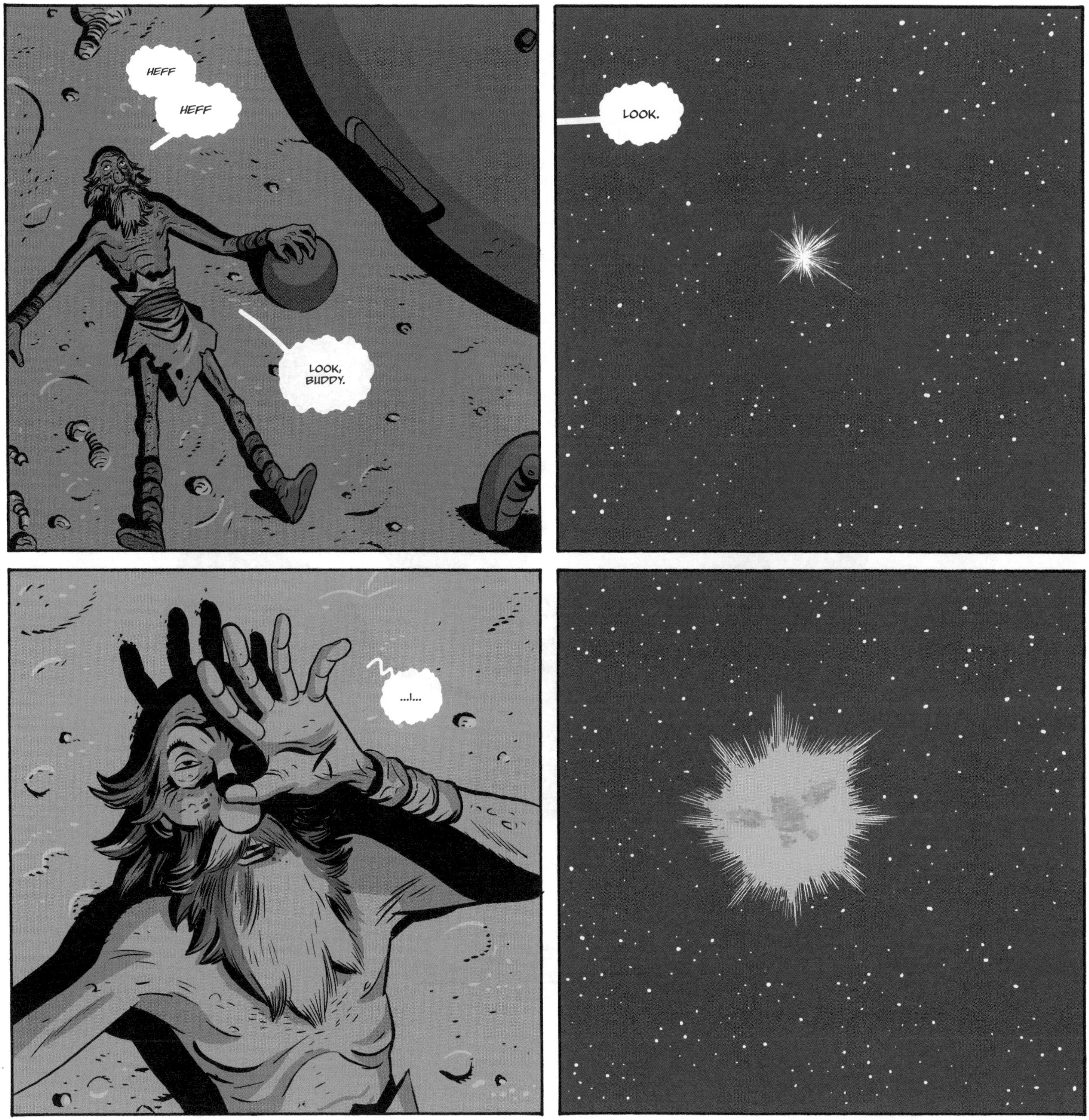
HEFF
HEFF
LOOK, BUDDY.
LOOK.
...I...

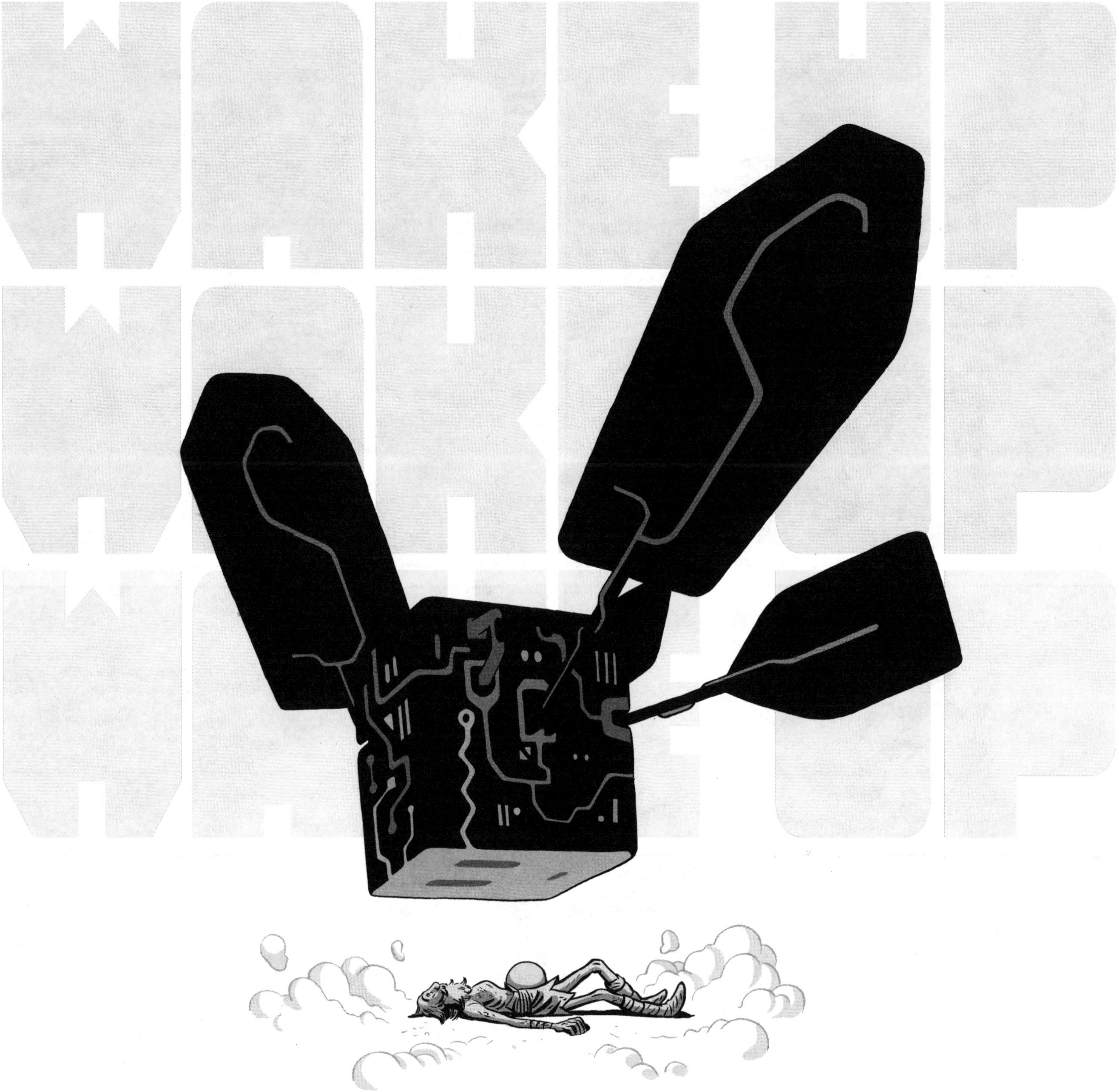
WAKE UP

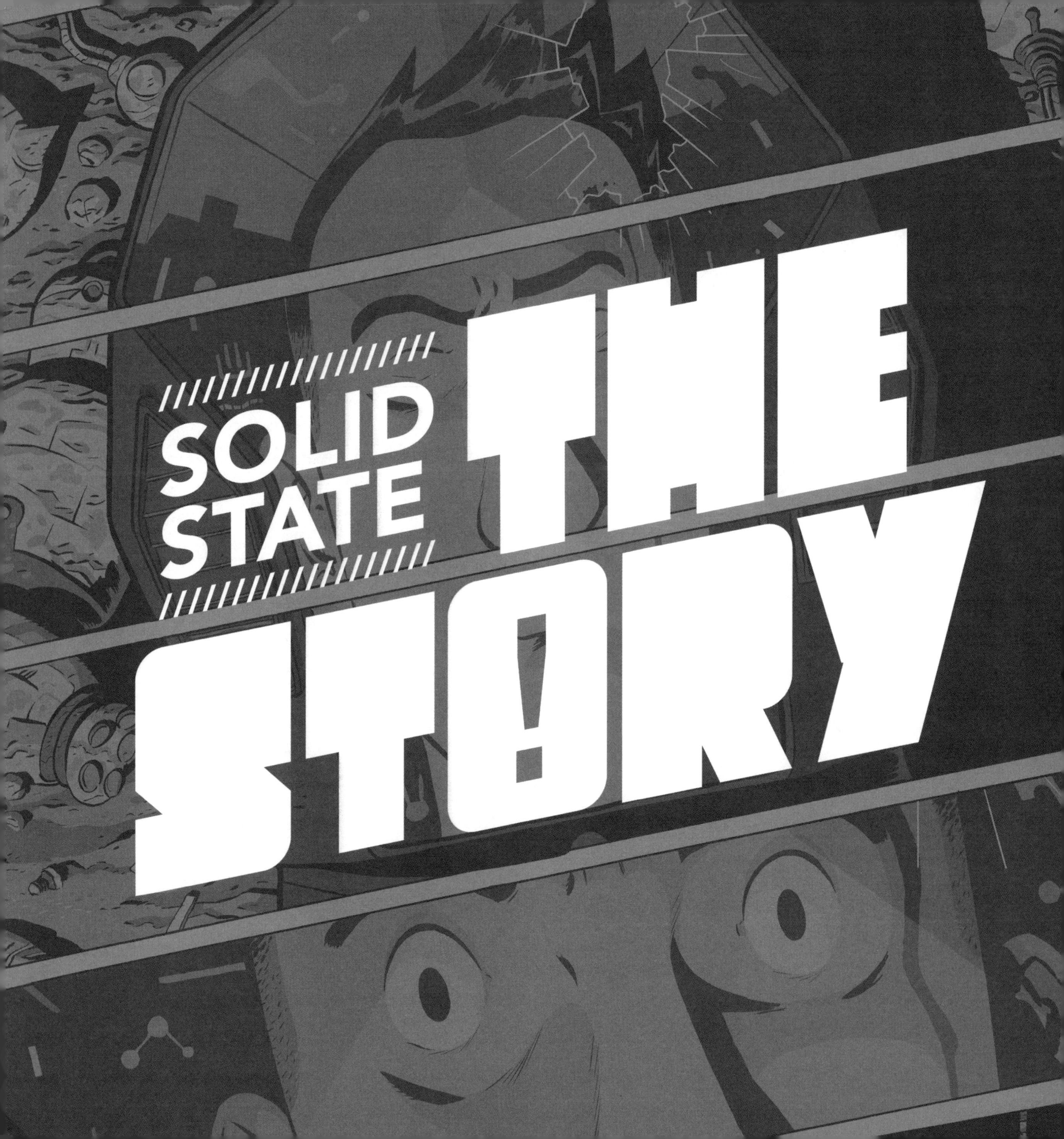
SOLID
STATE
THE
STORY

In the old days, there used to be albums, which were collections of songs released all at once. Sometimes albums would have a theme or a concept but, even when they didn't, they would still represent a slice of the artist's creative life. If nothing else, when you listened to an album, you'd know that you were hearing the kinds of songs the artist was writing around that time. When I started work on SOLID STATE, the only thing I could really think of that I wanted to say was something like, "The internet sucks now." It's a little off-brand for me, so it was a scary place to start. And I wasn't sure exactly what I meant.

But I wrote a handful of songs about feelings and the internet, and eventually found my way to the track "Solid State." This seemed like a good title for an album and so became a kind of thesis statement. My producer Christian Cassan suggested I do a reprise of that song somewhere later in the track list, which is when I started wondering if there was a thread that connected what I had written so far. I put all the song titles on little scraps of paper, color-coded them for tempo and key, and shuffled them around on my desk using various sorting strategies. I looked for an arc. I grouped the songs by who I thought was speaking. I ordered them by the apparent emotional maturity of the voice. A kind of timeline emerged, actually two timelines, and some of the songs were definitely an AI singing, and oh crap, am I writing a sci-fi concept album?

Well, I was. I wrote more songs to fill in the gaps. I started sharing the story with friends, worried that I sounded grandiose and delusional. The story had a kind of creative gravity for me though, and I couldn't stop turning it over in my head. It snowballed into focus as it picked up details, as I wrote and refined the songs, until it started to feel like yes, this is a thing. But it needed something; it was like a pre-lightning Frankenstein (I know, Frankenstein's MONSTER, jeez you guys), fully assembled but still just a corpse, and an ugly one at that.

I remember the very moment I decided the series SEX CRIMINALS was great. It was a small thing, which is my favorite kind of thing, a tiny gesture that speaks volumes. There was an image of Jon looking a little dopey, accompanied by Suzie's very simple narration about the moment she fell in love with him: "This guy." Such a simple and elegant way to capture that delicious collapse, when your eyes turn into pink hearts and you fall over onto your fainting couch, and you're gone for good. Suddenly we know everything we need to know about those two.

So I screwed up my courage and asked Matt if he'd be interested in working on a dumb thing that wasn't very good and was probably just me being grandiose and delusional. It was a terrible pitch of a fuzzy idea, which demonstrates how easy it is to trick Matt into working on something. But he said yes, and then he did everything with it that I hoped he would do. Watching the pages of the script come in was like watching a ship captain navigate by the stars. It shouldn't work, but it does. And Albert drawing everything right behind him, filling in every little detail so perfectly, me crying at my laptop when their combined storytelling powers would form into a sharp point and poke at some raw, sensitive spot that I didn't even know was there. Dear, sweet Bob, in each of his incarnations, hits me very close to home: flawed but trying, learning and then forgetting, screwing up but finding his way somewhere. Hang on tight, everybody, I still believe we'll get there.

—*Jonathan Coulton*

JONATHAN COULTON lives in Brooklyn but is originally from the internet. After leaving a perfectly good software career to pursue music full time, Jonathan embarked on a bold experiment in forced-march creativity called "Thing a Week," in which he recorded and published a new song every Friday for a year. You may know him from many things, including the songs from *Portal* and *Portal 2*; *Code Monkey Save World*, the graphic novel based on his songs written by Greg Pak; or his work as the One Man House Band for the NPR quiz show "Ask Me Another."

MATT FRACTION writes comic books out in the woods and lives with his wife, the writer Kelly Sue DeConnick, his two children, two dogs, a cat, a bearded dragon, and a yard full of coyotes and stags. Surely there is a metaphor there. He's a *New York Times*-bestselling donkus of comics like *Sex Criminals* (winner of the 2014 Will Eisner Award for Best New Series, the 2014 Harvey Award for Best New Series, and named *TIME* Magazine's Best Comic of 2013), *Satellite Sam*, *ODY-C*, and *Hawkeye* (winner of the 2014 Will Eisner Award for Best Single Issue). Under their company Milkfed Criminal Masterminds, Inc., Fraction and DeConnick are currently developing television for NBC/Universal.

ALBERT MONTEYS has been writing and drawing comics for as long as he can remember. After toiling as a satirical cartoonist, which can be fun (for the first ten years)…he began his science fiction series *Universe!* (available now at panelsyndicate.com along with an abundance of other amazing comics). This is the longest comic he's ever made.